# Pawns and Phantoms

## An Everland Mystery

## by Misha Handman

EDGE SCIENCE FICTION AND FANTASY PUBLISHING
An Imprint of HADES PUBLICATIONS, INC.
CALGARY

# Pawns and Phantoms
## An Everland Mystery

### Copyright © 2022 by Misha Handman

EDGE SCIENCE FICTION AND FANTASY PUBLISHING
An Imprint of HADES PUBLICATIONS, INC.
P.O. Box 1414, Calgary, Alberta, T2P 2L7, Canada

The EDGE Team:
Producer: Brian Hades
Edited by: Kathryn Shalley
Cover Design: 100 Covers
Book Design: Mark Steele

ISBN: 978-1-77053-210-6

EDGE Science Fiction and Fantasy Publishing and Hades Publications,
Inc. acknowledges the ongoing support of the Alberta Foundation for the
Arts and the Canada Council for the Arts for our publishing programme.

  Canada Council   Conseil des arts
for the Arts     du Canada

Title: Pawns and phantoms : an Everland mystery / by Misha Handman.

Names: Handman, Misha, author.
Description: First edition.
Identifiers: Canadiana (print) 20220270651 | Canadiana (ebook) 20220270686 | ISBN 9781770532106
(softcover) | ISBN 9781770532090 (HTML)
Classification: LCC PS8615.A552855 P39 2022 | DDC C813/.6—dc23

FIRST EDITION
(20220711)
Printed in USA
www.edgewebsite.com

# Publisher's Note:

*Thank you for purchasing this book. It began as an idea, was shaped by the creativity of its talented author, and was subsequently molded into the book you have before you by a team of editors and designers.*

*Like all EDGE books, this book is the result of the creative talents of a dedicated team of individuals who all believe that books (whether in print or pixels) have the magical ability to take you on an adventure to new and wondrous places powered by the author's imagination.*

*As EDGE's publisher, I hope that you enjoy this book. It is a part of our ongoing quest to discover talented authors and to make their creative writing available to you.*

*We also hope that you will share your discovery and enjoyment of this novel on social media through Facebook, Twitter, Goodreads, Pinterest, etc., and by posting your opinions and/or reviews on Amazon and other review sites and blogs. By doing so, others will be able to share your discovery and passion for this book.*

*Brian Hades, publisher*

# Thursday, August 16th, 1953

**Thursday is usually** harbor day, when ships come in from the Sea of Dreams. My plan was to meet up with some friends, grab an iced tea, enjoy the sun, and make jokes about the tourists. But last night had been a long one — back-to-back afternoon and night shifts at different bars, a few more fights than usual, and I'd stuck around to help clean up after some mobster threw up all over the bathroom, then had his guys carry him out of there like it was no problem. Long story short, I oversleep and wake up in a panic that I'm going to miss the whole thing.

I freshen up, race out the door, and hop a tram down to Coast Street. When I get there, the tram that runs along the shore isn't anywhere to be seen, so I start hoofing it down the boardwalk. Some folks see me coming and cross the street. I'm kind of used to that, though; I'm one of the biggest guys I know, and I basically fight for a living, so I've got a few bruises, a few lumps, and a whole lot of muscle. A buddy once said to me, "Todd, you got a face that could crack a mirror," and he wasn't wrong.

So yeah, I look like a furious thug out to catch the guy who broke a bottle over his head. I don't blame people for getting nervous.

I come around a bend in the road and head towards a stretch of path that runs alongside a rocky section of the bay. That's when I hear a heck of a lot of splashing, plus some curses, coming from the other side of the outcrop. I'm in a rush, but when there's a scuffle, sometimes someone needs a bailout, so I go over to the edge of the rocks to investigate.

There's a man up to his waist in the water past the rocks. He's trying to pull a briefcase out of a mermaid's hands while she laughs and pulls back. As I come over the edge of the rocks, I spot a second mermaid slipping up behind him, presumably to knock him on his back; based on the water dripping off his close-cropped hair, I assume this has happened at least once already.

"Okay, folks, knock it off," I say as I clamber down to the small stretch of beach. Mermaids aren't generally bad sorts. They just like to goof around. The thing is, they're not great at boundaries. Or hints. Or near-death experiences.

The mermaid holding the briefcase drops it as she spins to look at me. The man immediately overbalances and falls backwards into the second mermaid.

"Go away, longlegs!" the first mermaid giggles. "We're playing."

"Yeah, I can tell. Come on, the poor guy has played enough."

The second mermaid wraps her tail around the man with the briefcase and tugs his feet out from under him.

"Don't you know the boats are coming in?" I ask.

"Boats," the first mermaid says with a musical lilt, "are for walkers. We don't care about them." She playfully shoves the sputtering man. "We prefer games."

I cross the beach. "Look, I dunno what this guy did, but I think he's had enough. You're going to hurt him if you keep going." I step into the water to try to pull him to shore, trusting that mermaids don't generally like fights.

This time, I trusted wrong.

A third mermaid, who's been laying low in the surf, pushes off the bottom of the sand and reaches her hands around my waist. "If you want to play, too—"

Which is when I punch her in the face.

I'm not proud of it. But when someone grabs me by surprise, especially when I'm keyed up, I fight back.

From the look of things, no one was really expecting me to do it. The mermaid who had been pulling at me shoves herself backward into the water at top speed. The other two, eyes wide, follow her as fast as they can swim, leaving their victim to flop in the waves. Once they're far enough out to be swimming comfortably, two of the three flip their tails into the air and dive; I know just enough mermaid to know that means something pretty rude. The third one — the one I punched — pauses long enough to put two fingers up to her eyes, point at me, and smile menacingly. Then she flips off and is gone, too.

I shake my head and reach over to help the other guy to his feet. "You okay?"

"I'm good. I'm fine." The guy shakes water off his briefcase, stumbles as the next wave hits it mid-shake, and then lets me take his arm to get him out of the water and onto the rocks; it's not hard to do — I've got a solid seven inches and a hundred pounds on him. He's a thin fellow, maybe thirty or forty years old, and he can't be more than five-eight.

"Thanks for the help. Might have taken me a while to get rid of them, otherwise." He sits down on one of the higher rocks, pulls off a shoe, and starts shaking water out of it.

"Why were you tussling with a bunch of mermaids anyway?" I sit down next to him. My shoes could use a shake, too.

"Following a lead, my boy, following a lead. Those mermaids were witnesses to a clever crime, but unfortunately they rather took offense to my line of questioning." The guy turns a smile on me that probably works a lot better when it isn't part of a general drowned-rat look. I give him a closer look. Short blonde hair, thin mustache dripping onto a suit that looks like it doesn't get rumpled that often, but isn't nice enough to recover from this one. Nice chin, too.

"You don't look like a cop."

"I'm not." The man steps a bit closer. "My card." He reaches into his breast pocket and hands me a soggy business card with a flourish. It reads: 'VANCE CARSON — PRIVATE INVESTIGATOR — DISCRETE. DELIBERATE. DEDICATED."

"Oh, you're that other detective," I say before I have a chance to shut my damn mouth.

Vance's face falls. The thing is, Everland feels like a big city to me, but it's not a big city by mainland standards. Maybe eighty thousand people live here, and half that many live in a handful of small towns and camps around the island. If you work for the big companies, like Hawthorne or

Second Star, you've got investigators on staff to help you out. If you work for the mob, you've got crooks to help you out. If you work for City Hall, you've got crooks to help you out.

For everybody else, there are two private detectives on the island, and I think just about everyone calls Vance Carson 'that other one.'

"I mean, uh…" I start.

Vance waves it off. "I'm a private detective, yes. And you are?"

"Todd. Todd Malcolm." I hold out my hand, and Vance gives it a pretty firm shake, all things considered.

"Well, like I said, Todd, thank you for lending me a hand. Those mermaids didn't know what hit them!"

I'm not sure whether to smile or be mortified. My face sort of flickers between the two, which probably makes me look angry more than anything else. "They were probably just messing around. You know how mermaids can get."

Vance puts his shoes back on and stands up, looking me up and down. "Don't sell yourself short. You know, if you're ever looking for a bit of extra work, I might be able to throw some your way. Nothing illegal, of course, but my investigations sometimes carry me into troublesome situations." He reaches up to pat me on the shoulder. "If you have the time."

"You going somewhere dangerous?" I ask.

"Stop by my office — let's say Saturday morning? I'll fill you in, and you can decide if you're interested." And with that, he's strolling away, cool as a cucumber, as if he's not dripping water with every step. "And again," he calls over his shoulder, "thanks for the assist."

I stare after him for a moment, then go on my way. If I don't get to the docks soon, I'm going to miss the boats.

———— ‹‹›› ————

It's a warm day, so by the time I finally get to the docks I'm dried off. Summer in Everland is pretty nice. Really, every season in Everland is pretty nice. A side effect of living on an island that's maybe made of dreams, alone in a mysterious ocean, is that the weather doesn't make any sense. Sure, we get the usual cold snaps and storms, but in general we get some light snow in the winter, warm rains in the spring, and the sort of long summer days that I've been told are mainly just stories everywhere else.

I spot my friends crowded around a table as I walk up. Holly has got herself set up under the umbrella's shade, sharing gossip about life in Piccadilly Cross. She's got her hair cut short for the summer. Marta's on her right, with a chair chosen for the best sightline to the boats, leaning forward and brushing black curls out of her eyes. And on her left, grinning from ear to ear, is Emeka.

Emeka has a dancer's grace, his hair is cut almost down to the scalp, and he's picked out a beautiful green shirt that perfectly complements his rich brown skin. He looks over at me and smiles, and I can't help but smile back.

Their conversation pauses as I come up. Emeka waves me over to an empty chair next to him. "Todd, you made it! Come on, the boat's already on its way in."

"Thanks, Emeka." I nod to the others. "Looking good, Marta."

"Excuse you. I'm looking great." Marta grins and smooths down her sundress. "Got to show our best faces for the tourists."

Holly smiles and passes me a glass of iced tea as I sit down. "Sorry, the ice is a little melted. What kept you?"

"Oh, you know." I shrug.

"You look like you got in a fight," Marta says.

I snort. "Barely. Just broke up a little tussle."

"Ooh, you've got to dish now." Emeka leans in, nudging me in the ribs. This close, I can smell his cologne; it's an orangey scent that I would recognize anywhere and he's the only guy I know who wears it. "Who was your lucky damsel today?"

"It was just a few mermaids having a laugh at someone."

"Well, that sounds like your good deed for the day." Emeka reaches for an empty glass next to him, tries to take a gulp, and realizes there's nothing left. "Here, give me a sip, huh?" Before I can react, he's grabbed my tea, taken a long draw from it, and pressed it back into my hand. "Only you, Todd Malcolm, could get into a fight with a gang of mermaids — in the surf, no less, from the look of your legs — and then try to tell us it was nothing."

"Mermaids don't come down to the harbor much anymore," Holly says thoughtfully. "Wonder why they were in the area."

"Probably just goofing around," Marta says. "I've been on the receiving end of that a time or two."

"Mermaids don't just goof around. There's always an angle, or at least a game involved." Holly frowns and looks out at the harbor. "I should ask around, see what's going on."

"Our genius detective," Emeka laughs. "Is this a part of one of your cases?"

"No cases right now," Holly says with a very brittle smile.

Our crew is made up mostly of musicians or actors, folks who play the small clubs downtown. The musicians do sets together sometimes, but they're not a proper band — they change up who plays where, and who plays with who, and depending on who's busy, we sometimes don't see people for a few weeks at a time. Holly and I are the odd ones out. She's an apprentice detective; her boss is one of the most famous guys in the city — the one people around here actually think of when you say the words 'private detective'. He plays it down, but everyone in Everland can tell you a story they heard thirdhand about the infamous Basil Stark, who stood at the right hand of Captain Hook, fought the Boy Who Flew, got adopted by the Piccadilly Nation, and has lived for almost a hundred years — so far. Heck, the stories are so big some people get wide-eyed when they hear that I work for him from time to time, and I've only been doing that for maybe six months.

But Holly fits in with the crew. They're all dramatic, expressive, good-looking, and easy-going. Life has crapped on most of them more than once, but they don't let it get them down.

And then there's me.

I'm not the sort of guy people tell stories about, unless those stories start with, "That guy looks like trouble." I guess it doesn't hurt to have the bouncer in your corner, but I'm still not really sure why the crew thinks I'm one of them; I don't act, I don't sing, I don't play any instrument, and I don't really have a lot to say when we're all hanging out together. That's okay though. Someone's got to be the quiet one, and I'm alright with it being me.

Emeka glances at Holly, who is still smiling like she has glass in her mouth, and then up at me. I shake my head as little as I can get away with, and he gets the hint. "Well," he says, "more time for us. There's a show we're playing Friday — tomorrow — at the Golden Hind. I think it's going to be pretty special."

"It's going to be awesome," Marta chimes in. "We've got a new lead singer we're showing around, and you've gotta see this one, I'm telling you. She is something else." She and Emeka exchange a grin.

"What time?" I ask. "I've got work Saturday, but it's not until the afternoon."

"Ten o'clock. Love to have you there." Emeka smiles at me, and then looks to Holly. "Both of you, of course."

"Enough chatting about gigs, the boat is unloading!" Marta interrupts.

If it weren't so expensive and hard to reach Everland, summer would probably find us absolutely overrun with tourists. The thing is, getting here isn't as simple as chartering a flight, and without a real rangefinder compass you'll never survive the trip. Even with one, ships go missing about twice as often as they do out in the regular world, and with fewer survivors. In the old days, people found their way here by mistake; children abducted from their own dreams, sailors capsizing on the Sea of Dreams, and so on. When Darling and Hale worked together to open the routes, it took a lot of hard work and a lot of people who had visited and then escaped to make the first trips — plus stealing the island's fallen stars to build into compasses.

We do get tourists, of course. Everland is the only place I know of where magic is provably real, even if it is a lot weaker than in the bad old days, and everyone wants to see that. But the excitement from the early decades of settlement is gone. We're a curiosity, a backwater that's literally in the middle of nowhere, and aside from fancy-goods shipping companies taking advantage of the island's magical waters to transfer cargo, the loggers and miners searching out lumber and rare minerals, and the various foreign governments still doling out money to Second Star in the hopes of getting some breakthrough, we're pretty much left alone.

The boats that do come in do it on a very strict schedule; it takes three days and three nights to get here, no matter how fast your boat or plane, or how inclement the weather, so you can set your watch by the harbor. Whenever a group of passenger ships is due, a lot of the locals hang out at the docks to watch. You can see the newest fashions, play at guessing why people are in town, and get the first shot at new books or magazines being offloaded.

Of course, it's not all fun and games. Crooks take advantage of the newcomers; con artists are always on the docks trying to sell shining rocks, 'authentic' mermaid crafts, and whatever garbage they can get together before anyone is around long enough to know what they're worth. But hey, that's half the fun.

"Okay, guys," Marta says, "drinking game! Every time someone steps off the boat and starts staring in the sky for fairies, take a drink. Every time someone buys one of those 'mystical Piccadilly talismans,' take a drink. And if someone stops for the three-card Monte, finish your glass."

I raise an eyebrow. "Drinking games for iced tea?"

"Hey, some of us thought ahead, buddy." Marta raises her glass and taps it. "Added a little something to mine. Got some for you if you want."

Emeka laughs. "I can't. Mine's empty. I'll just have to watch you all."

"I'm not drinking right now," Holly says. "Sorry."

"Oh my God, you are all such buzzkills." Marta crosses her arms and turns to look at the boat. The gangplank has been dropped, and the first tourists are stepping off. "Fine. No drinking games. Guess the visit?"

"Now that, I can do." Emeka stares at the first guy to step off the gangway. He's stocky, wearing a full suit and hat in the heat, and staring ahead. "That one's government. American, I'd bet. The Brits do their ties up better."

"Of course he's American, it's an American boat," Holly points out. "I doubt they'd send a British official Stateside just to reroute him here."

"I bet he's got a bunch of meetings with Second Star over defense contracts, or weaponizing bears." Marta taps the table as she thinks. "He looks like he doesn't want to be here, so it's probably punishment detail. What do you think, he didn't work enough late nights at the office?"

"Or one too many, with the wrong person," Holly says. "Now he's running from a jealous lover. How about those two?"

There's a young couple stepping off the boat — a white man and a black woman, both looking tired but joyful as they stare around. They've got a handcart with three giant suitcases and a couple of hat boxes perched precariously on it. The man's unfolding a map and turning it around, and the woman's pulling him out of the way of the other passengers.

"Honeymooners," Holly says after a moment.

"Not just a romantic vacation?" Marta asks. "They don't seem very honey-mooney."

Emeka is watching them thoughtfully. "Holly's right," he says after a moment. "Look. Every time they touch, they pull away a bit."

I blink. "That makes them honeymooners?"

"They're not used to being allowed," Emeka says flatly.

The table goes silent. I feel myself go red and I can't figure out what to say next. I was barely more than a baby when I moved here. Holly and Marta were born on the island. Of all of us, Emeka's the only one who was already an adult when he left the States, and he doesn't talk about it much.

Holly breaks the silence. "So, not tourists, then," she says cheerfully and deliberately. "A couple of lovebirds starting a new life. That's nice."

"It is." Emeka smiles, runs a hand over his close-cropped hair, and then looks past the couple. "Oh, now, that one is trouble."

There's a man walking towards the boat, reaching out his hand to shake with the first man who got off. He's tall, almost as tall as me, but he's real skinny. Black suit, black tie, slicked-back hair and square glasses, and already lighting up a smoke. "Definitely government," Holly says, looking him up and down. "Walking like he owns the place."

"He's not one of the passengers," Marta objects. "No points."

"He doesn't look like a local, either," Holly shoots back. "And he's meeting a passenger. Probably his contact or something."

As the two men walk past the honeymooning couple, the tall man's face wrinkles a bit. Then he looks past them at us. He looks at me, then at Holly for a long moment, and then smiles thinly and adjusts his glasses as his gaze moves on to Emeka.

"I think someone doesn't like being watched," Emeka laughs and deliberately makes eye contact with the man. "Should we put on a show for the tourist?" He reaches over and takes my hand just as I'm reaching for my glass. Heat rushes up my arm, and I know that I've gone beet-red. I turn and find that Emeka's face is turned just a bit towards me and is a lot closer than it was a moment ago.

I cough. "Uhh..." Across the way, the man stares at us for another long moment, and then turns away.

Emeka laughs, letting go and patting my hand. "Sorry. Silly of me." He scratches the back of his head. "Guys like that just grind my gears, you know. Didn't mean to drag you into it."

"Nah, it's okay. It's fine. No problem." I quickly grab my iced tea and down half of it in one go, which is not making me feel less entirely embarrassed, but at least I can focus on the cold of the glass and not on the heat from his hand.

When I glance back at him, Emeka is already focused on the next person clambering off the ship. I let myself slip into the background while we pass the next hour chatting about new arrivals and their possible goals on the island. Eventually, though, folks have to get going for work, so we all agree to meet up later.

As he and Marta head down the street to their next practice, Emeka turns to call to us. "Don't forget! Tomorrow, ten o'clock, the Golden Hind. You'd better be there!"

I grin, and wave back. Holly and I have a meeting up at Mr. Stark's office, so it's just the two of us walking to the tram stop. As we get safely away from the others, Holly looks up at me with an impish grin. "So, big night tomorrow, huh? Should I duck out, let you see it alone?"

I rub my forehead. Holly is sweet; I like hanging out with her. But one thing she's inherited from her parents is a real fondness for meddling. "Emeka's trying to show off the band. It's not a thing."

Holly sighs heavily. "Oh my god, it's Uncle Basil all over again."

I can feel my face turn red this time. "I wasn't... I didn't..."

"You did! You are exactly like him, and his romance-meter broke about fifty years ago. Remember the whole thing with Adelaide last winter? It was embarrassing. Don't be embarrassing, Todd."

"I'm not embarrassing," I mutter.

"Not yet. But if you keep tiptoeing around and pretending to be the big bouncer guy who isn't adorably into a cute musician, you are going to be."

"Holly—"

Holly turns and pokes me in the chest. "Go to this thing with Emeka."

"I will! But it's not a thing. It's just friends seeing friends on stage."

"Now you're even starting to sound like Uncle Basil. Next thing you know, you'll be telling me things are too dangerous right now and I shouldn't go out at night."

"The blackmail case?"

"I don't see why he's making such a big deal of it! I've gotten involved in all sorts of dangerous things working for him. We got attacked by mobsters that time. A living shadow jumped us in the office. And remember when that one guy tried to get me eaten by wolves?"

"I don't. When was that?"

Holly pauses and counts on her fingers. "Oh. It was before we met, never mind."

"Eaten by wolves?"

"It wasn't that big a deal. The wolves apologized for the guy and escorted me back to Piccadilly territory. They don't eat people. But the guy who tried to kill me didn't know that!" Holly shakes her head. "The point is: this is just a blackmail case. I don't see why he won't let me help."

"If it makes you feel any better, the only thing he's asked me to do this week is take Glimmer out for exercise and snacks a few times."

"That does actually make me feel better," Holly admits. "As long as he's being patronizing to both of us."

"We could always go work for Vance Carson."

Holly laughs. "Oh, yeah, that would work out great."

I fish out the soggy business card I got earlier, and wave it at her. The ink has run a bit, but it's still legible. "I mean, he did ask me."

"Oh my God. When did you meet Carson?" Holly snatches the card. "Wait, was he the guy you rescued? Did *Vance Carson* offer you a job? Uncle Basil would absolutely flip!"

I blink. "He's not that bad, is he? I haven't heard Mr. Stark talk about him much."

"Define 'that bad.' I think Uncle Basil just doesn't like him because he's not a very good detective, and because he's not a very perceptive person, and also because he mostly does cases for the rich folk who don't have time for people like us. Plus maybe a bit of jealousy about the fact that Vance is still the one who gets invited to all the nice parties." Holly looks at the card thoughtfully. "He really gave you this?"

"Yeah. He seemed nice enough."

"Well, you did just save him from mermaids. Maybe he's smitten."

"I'm stopping by his office tomorrow, just to see what's up," I say, mainly because Holly will keep teasing me if I get annoyed. "You could tag along. Bet he'd be twice as happy to have the real Holly Blossom working a case as he would some random tough."

"No, don't tempt me. You do jobs for Uncle Basil, but I'm actually on the payroll. I can't work for the competition just to make my uncle mad." Holly thinks about it for a moment.

"Well … no. No, I can't. But I definitely want to hear all about it." She thinks about it again. "I definitely want to hear all about anything non-confidential."

"You think I should tell Mr. Stark?"

"Better he hears it from you than from Vance bragging or something. If you do end up taking work, that's not going to stay quiet."

"Unless I just don't go."

"No, definitely go. This could be cool, Todd! I've tossed a few cases Carson's way before. We're sort of competition, but we're not actually rivals or anything. Island's too small for that kind of friction. Just wait, I bet that Uncle Basil will be delighted to hear you got the job."

———— «» ————

"He was … hah!" Basil Stark, Everland's premiere detective and renowned former pirate, generally considered one of the five most dangerous people on the island, is laughing too hard to get a straight sentence out. "—Mermaids!"

"It was kind of serious," I say. "I mean, they were probably just playing with him, but I thought they might actually drown him."

"No, you're quite right, mermaids are very serious," Basil says in between chuckles. "They're very violent, and they know just enough about human behavior to mask it well. I just can't help but imagine Carson walking directly into the surf and serving himself up like a prize catch, presumably in the process of throwing a half-dozen inane questions their way. I suppose someone on the Hill flushed a valuable necklace down the toilet and is hoping that Carson can dig it up."

"He, uh, he kinda gave me his card and offered me some work."

Basil's laugh dies away, and he considers me. We're in his office, and by 'we' I mean all four of us. Basil is sitting by Holly's desk, since his own desk is in another room — it's close enough he can see just about everything in the main room, but he likes to spend time with everyone else. Holly is there, too, on the other side, flipping through Basil's hand-scrawled investigation notes and trying to type them into something like a readable report — Basil never learned to type right; he says that kind of fancy new technology isn't really his thing. I'm sitting in the chair Basil bought for me a couple of months back, when he said I hung around enough I might as well have my own. And Glimmer, a six-inch tall fairy in a sleek green dress, is sitting on my shoulder, nibbling on a piece of popcorn the size of her head.

Glimmer used to live with a friend of mine, so I've known her most of her life. Basil sort of adopted her around the same time I started working for him. My fairy-speech is still a bit wobbly, so I only really know what she's saying when she slows down, but she's a sweetheart and she seems to like me. Or maybe she likes being able to look down at everyone else. Either way, she sits on my shoulder a lot when I'm in the office.

Right now, though, she's stopped chewing and is glaring at me. She says something that doesn't sound too nice and flares her wings.

"Glimmer!" Holly says, proving my guess right. "It is not! Vance Carson isn't a bad guy."

Basil is rubbing his jaw thoughtfully. "No, he isn't. And you're a discreet young man, Todd. If you want to do a few odd jobs for Carson, I won't mind. Heavens knows he could use someone who's actually able to spot a clue hanging around."

Glimmer is settling back down, but I keep an eye on her as I respond. Fairies only process one emotion at a time, and the last time she got mad I ended up with a piece of popcorn shoved up my ear. "Is he really that bad a detective, Mr. Stark?"

"He's an embarrassment," Basil says, shaking his head. "The fact that he makes a living at this is a mark against humanity as a whole. He gets by on a flashy smile, a bit of luck, and knowing all of the high society types who would consider a janitor to be the criminal element." He snorts and reaches for his tea. "But, and this is definitely worth considering, his clients are wealthy, and he is not shy about passing that money on to his contractors. He'll probably pay you more than I can."

"You might be able to pay us more if you got arrested less," Holly suggests.

"I might be able to pay you more if I had Captain Hook's buried treasure," Basil retorts. "Why deal in fantasies?"

"Speaking of fantasies," Holly says, pointedly setting down the case notes, "how's your case going?"

"It's complicated."

"Are you going to need me for anything today, or is this another 'sit at the office and do crosswords' sort of afternoon?"

"Holly, we've been over this. The case that I am working on right now is both sensitive and dangerous, and the client wants to keep things as quiet as possible."

Holly narrows her eyes, but her voice stays sweet. "I can be quiet."

Basil groans. "That's not the point."

"No, the point is that you're treating us like children!"

"You are not taking part, and that is final!" Basil slams his hand down on the desk. "And I would like to remind you, Holly, that you are my assistant, not my partner. I do not owe you involvement in every case, and in fact, deciding which cases you will be involved in is one of my responsibilities as your employer. And this is a case that you will have no part in." He stands, gathers his notes, and walks to his office.

The door doesn't quite slam shut behind him, but there's definitely some force in its closing.

Holly takes a deep breath and clenches her fists. "Sorry, Todd, I don't think there's anything for you to do today."

"Ah, that's okay." I rub my chin. "You want me to take Glimmer out for a walk around the block?"

Holly glances over to Glimmer, who shakes her head and says she'd rather stay in for the moment, if I don't mind.

"Yeah, no problem." I stand up. "Listen, if it were up to me…"

"I know, Todd. Have a good day."

"Thanks." I don't like leaving the office like that, but there's not much I can do, so I give Glimmer one last piece of popcorn, let her fly over to sit by Holly, and head out.

# Friday, August 17<sup>th</sup>

**I look like** a chump.

The Golden Hind isn't a ritzy place, but it's not a dive, either. I did my best to fit in with the folks coming by, which meant my nicest jacket, a white shirt, and my best slacks. I'm not wearing a hat, because I've never found one that fits my head, and I'm not wearing a tie because ties make me look like a monkey. I tried to slick my hair back a bit, but I'm pretty sure that just makes my eyebrows stand out. Compared to the folks strolling in and out of this place, I look like the help.

Nothing for it. I shove my hands in my pockets, take a deep breath, and step through the doors. At least there's no line. The bouncer gives me a quick up and down, decides I'm okay, and turns his attention back to the rest of the crowd.

Inside, things are done up in the latest pirate chic. The walls are covered in fake-wood paneling, with a massive world map on one side covered in markers of major pirate events. There are old chandeliers, wired up with lightbulbs, and fake crossed bones over the bar, below which bartenders wear colorful pirate clothing. Waitresses dressed up with long coats and short skirts wind their way around the tables. It's gaudy, but it kind of works.

I get a beer and find an empty seat off to the side. There's no sign of Holly or any of our other friends, and I have a sinking feeling that I'm the only one of the crew here. It's still a few minutes before the show's supposed to start, but I don't think there's much chance of getting backstage, so I just sit and wait for the music to start.

When the lights go down to half, the chatter dies out and people look over at the stage. The building's drummer comes out, followed by Emeka and Marta — both wearing dark red tuxedos lined in black — who take their spots on sax and piano. From my spot in the corner, I see all the waiters pause to watch the stage. Something's up. The drummer starts the beat, Marta picks up the melody, and Emeka steps up to the mic. "Folks, we are Hkuri and the Steppers. Thank you." He lowers the mic, steps back to his spot, and starts playing. A moment later, the lead singer prowls onto the stage, and anyone who was still talking stops.

The only thing I can think is that Holly is going to be kicking herself to have missed this; Hkuri, Emeka's new lead singer, is a tiger.

She's gorgeous. Glittering green eyes, sleek fur with orange so deep it's almost red and black stripes that shimmer under the stage lights. She's wearing thick gold bands on all four legs, and her tail is wrapped in white ribbons that catch the light with each flick. She pads up to the mic, flicks out one talon, and taps it twice. She looks out into the silent crowd.

And then she starts to sing, and I have to admit that Emeka was right about this, too. It's classic jazz, a rich contralto, and we're all rapt. The others are doing good, too, but they could be playing pots and pans and it wouldn't matter.

When the set ends, the audience erupts into applause. They drag the crew back on stage for an encore, which I've never actually seen at the Hind, and the room is buzzing when the band is finally allowed to leave.

Emeka and the tiger, Hkuri, come out from backstage as the next band starts warming up. They're met by a lady who gives Hkuri a friendly pat on the back and hugs Emeka, then leads them to a table set up in the corner with a few chairs and a large cushion around it. Emeka spots me and waves me over; I grab a round of drinks and head over to join them.

"That was a hell of a set," I say as I sit down between Emeka and the lady I don't know. I slide Emeka his beer and put Marta's whiskey in front of an empty seat, then I look over to the tiger. "Sorry, I didn't know what you were having."

Hkuri gives a purring snicker. "Not many tiger drinks on the menu," she says. "I have something coming from backstage. But Michelle might like something." The tiger looks over to the lady.

"I always start with a Jack Rose," Michelle replies. She gives a lazy wave, and a waitress appears at the table with a chilled glass of red liquor, complete with a little wooden sword, a low bowl with something green in it that is placed in front of Hkuri, and another mug of beer. "I didn't realize you'd made other arrangements, Eme."

Emeka looks between us and smiles. "It's no problem," he says. "Wasn't planning on only having one drink, after all. Todd, this is Hkuri, our new lead singer, and her manager Michelle Arsenault. Hkuri, Michelle, this is our friend, Todd." He looks past me. "No Holly tonight?"

I shrug.

"That's a shame. I was looking forward to meeting the mysterious Holly Blossom." Michelle stirs her drink. "I've heard so very much about her. I suppose she's off solving crimes?"

"Could be," I say. "I think it might just be family stuff, though."

Michelle makes a dissatisfied noise.

"She is the Piccadilly girl, yes? The one who lives with the pirate?" Hkuri asks.

"Ex-pirate," I say automatically, and then bite my lip. "Sorry. He gets kind of sore about it."

Hkuri nods seriously. "That is fair. It is a proud thing to have escaped. I misspoke."

This is about when Marta arrives, with some kind of mixed drink that she's already swigging. "You all started without me?" she asks, dropping into the empty seat and sliding it a bit closer to the rest of us. "Oh, Todd, you shouldn't have." She grabs the whiskey with her free hand and sets it next to the drink she already has.

"We were just getting through introductions," Michelle says. "So, Todd, how did you meet Eme?"

"Uh, through work, actually. I'm a bouncer."

"You don't say."

"Yeah. One of the places I work is a club these two play at pretty often. The Poplars, maybe you've been."

"I don't think I've had the pleasure yet."

"Well, we sort of made friends over a few drinks after work, and, here we are." I don't know why, but I feel like I should be adding more. There just isn't any more to add, so I move on. "And how about you? How did you hook up with Emeka?"

It's a bad choice of words. Emeka chokes on his beer. Michelle gives me a broad, lazy smile. "Well, it's the funniest story. We met on the ship that brought us both over. That was, oh, six years ago, wasn't it, Eme? He was coming to seek his fortune and I'd just gotten a job offer. Bonded over an old Biederbeck record we found in the galley." She puts a hand on Emeka's arm. "We were quite close those first couple years. But we drifted apart. Different careers, I suppose."

"Different paths," Emeka agrees, gently pulling his arm free to grab his beer. "Anyway, Hkuri's been looking to get on stage, but there've been some…"

"Logistical problems," Michelle says dryly. Hkuri snorts.

"Yeah," Emeka says. "But Michelle's done business in tiger lands, so Hkuri got in touch with her, and Michelle got in touch with us." He looks over at Marta, who gives him a grin back and raises her glass in a mock-toast. "And after we heard Hkuri sing, how could we say no?"

Hkuri's nose wrinkles and she lets out another snicker. "Easily, and yet you did not, to my good fortune."

"And it's been so nice to catch up," Michelle says. "I've been working so hard the last few years, I just entirely dropped out of touch. But I've been building up leave time and HR started getting on my case to spend it. You know how it is."

I've never worked anywhere that gave paid days off, but there's no sense saying that. "So, you're using your vacation to work?"

"Well, is helping a performer find their place in the world really work? I think of it as spiritual fulfillment. And Eme has just been an absolute doll, looping us into the band. Couldn't have done it without him."

"Michelle works down at Hawthorne," Hkuri explains. "She controls their markets."

Michelle laughs lightly, looking pleased as punch, and rustles Hkuri's fur. "Oh, I think that's overstating things a bit." She looks back to us. "Kuri means that I'm in charge of several marketing accounts. Well, I'm not quite in charge, but I have done quite well."

"Huh, didn't know that a big logging company like Hawthorne needed much marketing," I say. I mean it as a conversation starter, but I see Michelle's eyes narrow and her smile falters as she turns to look at me. Behind her, Marta gives me an exasperated look, and Hkuri tilts her head slightly.

"I would say it's especially important for a large resource company," Michelle's bright smile is back in place as if the moment hadn't happened. Maybe I imagined it. "Logging and mining in Everland are expensive. We have treaties to uphold with the Piccadilly, the mermaids, the wolves, bears, and tigers..." she pauses to smile at Hkuri. "Those come with high regulatory costs, and delicate relationships. Our job is convincing overseas buyers that our goods are worth enough for them to buy in anyway. It's not like advertising a beer or a car, mind you. I meet with high-end clients from across the world."

"Wow," I say. "Yeah, that makes sense."

"Of course it does."

"You must have met some really interesting people," Marta says. Michelle nods and launches into a story about meeting with the former King of Egypt and his luxurious parties. From there, she shifts over to a story about trying to arrange a meeting between a visiting Australian millionaire and a team of very unimpressed bears, and we spend the next little while having a couple of drinks and listening to stories. Emeka and Marta chime in from time to time, but it's mostly the three of us listening to Michelle. I have to admit, her stories are something else.

"Oh, but Todd could tell some stories, too, eh, Todd?" Marta says at one point. She's about five drinks in and slurring a bit, but she's still pretty focused. "You almost got eaten by a shadow last winter."

"Oh, I wasn't really that involved," I say.

Michelle has straightened a bit. "Eaten by a shadow?" she echoes.

"Todd works for Basil Stark," Marta says. "Helps him solve cases and everything."

"Oh, really."

I rub the back of my neck. "I mean, I lend a hand. I don't think I actually do that much."

"No, that must be fascinating," Michelle says. "Any juicy cases going on right now?"

"Not really. Nothing like what you've got. Mostly I just hang around and make sure no one gets in a fight."

Michelle's eyebrows are raised to the roof. "Basil Stark needs someone to protect him?"

"Aww, heck no." I laugh. "I mean, I even tangled with him once myself, and he just about wiped the floor with me. You should see him. Thing is, though, he wins fights. I just stop them. People look at me, they think maybe it's not a good time to throw a punch."

Hkuri nods. "Ah, you help others choose wisely." She looks over to a silent bouncer a few feet away. "As Chuck does. A good role. It is good to know when to roar, and when to pounce."

I grin. "Are there many bars on tiger lands?"

"No. There is music, of course. All feeling beings have music. But we do not build as bears do, or bring in humans to build for us as the wolves might." She bares her teeth slightly. "It is just as well. Few humans would come to us, even if we asked."

"But you're here."

"Yes. I am … interested in your musical styles. There is an excitement to them. And there are stories to tell of this strange city. I do not know if I will perform here for a long while, but it is something new, and something interesting. Your Emeka and my Michelle have been very good, showing me the many sides of this city." Hkuri licks her chops. "It is a fascinating experience. If it goes well, maybe I will convince others to follow my lead. It has not been so long since all the humans on this island were our enemies. Many of my fellows imagine it is only a matter of time before they are again. I think more visits would do well for us both."

"Yeah, I'd think so. I've lived here my whole life, and I've seen maybe three or four tigers. It'd be nice to meet more of you."

"That is very kind of you, Todd. May I call you Todd?" Hkuri struggles a bit with the 'T' sound, but not any more than I'm working on the 'H' when I answer her.

"Of course, Hkuri. Should I call you that, or is there something more polite?"

She shakes her head. "One name is enough for me. You humans have too many. I hope that is not rude to say." She laps at her drink. "It is because there are so many of you, I think. You need new ways to show who you are."

I grin. "Never thought of it that way. Well, I'm happy to just be Todd around you."

"Good." Hkuri hesitates, and then nods. It's not quite a casual gesture. "I think that I am growing tired. Michelle, we will leave now?"

Michelle smiles and finishes her drink. "Of course, dear." She turns to us. "You don't mind if we leave a little bit early, do you, Eme?"

"No, of course not. Have a good night, both of you." Emeka waves.

Marta downs the rest of her latest drink. "I'll come with, if it's okay. I'm in that direction."

"You are welcome with us," Hkuri assures her. "Emeka, I will see you soon. Todd, it was a pleasure to meet with you. I hope that we will meet again soon, as well."

"I'll see what I can do," I say.

The crowd parts to let Hkuri and the others go by, then closes behind them. And suddenly it's just me and Emeka at the table. He's leaning back in his chair, stirring his latest cocktail, and he gives me a lopsided smile as he catches me looking at it. "How's the drink?" I ask.

"Too expensive," Emeka says. "They call it a 'Buried Treasure', but I think the only thing getting buried is my wallet."

I chuckle. "Why d'you think I've been sticking to beer? I'm just about tapped out."

"You always stick to beer."

"Well, I'm always just about tapped out."

Emeka laughs. "Okay, then, big guy. Why don't we blow this joint and hit up somewhere a little more wallet-friendly. My treat."

It's after midnight, but that's not so late. Plenty of time to have a couple more drinks and still get a full night's rest before my double shift. Anyway, afternoon shifts are slow. I can do them in my sleep. "What about your sax?"

"I'm playing again tomorrow. It's locked up backstage. Come on." Emeka drops some cash on the table and pulls on my arm. I let him lead the way out of the bar. A few people turn to watch us, or say something nice to Emeka about the set, but most folks stopped paying attention when Hkuri left.

As we step outside, I look over at him. "Eme, huh?"

Emeka groans. "I hate that nickname. But Michelle won't quit with it." He shakes his head. "Thinks it's cute."

"I don't think she likes me much."

"Can I tell you a secret, Todd?" Emeka leans in close. "Michelle doesn't like anybody much. I'm surprised she's helping manage Hkuri. Probably got volunteered by someone in the top brass when they found out she knew musicians." He shakes his head. "You're probably right, though. That whole 'how did you meet' routine? She knows about you. I've told her about you. She was trying to take control, keep you off-balance. She's not a bad person, but I don't know if she knows how to talk to people without treating it like a corporate negotiation anymore."

"Huh. She seemed a lot friendlier than that."

"Yeah, that's something else she's always been good at. Seeming." Emeka sighs. "We used to date. I think she wants to start up again. But that door is closed."

"Huh." It makes sense. They'd be a real flashy couple. Probably tore up the dance floor together. "So, when she said 'quite close', she meant..."

"It was a long time ago, Todd. And it wasn't all bad, but it's over now. Anyway, I think Marta's got an interest."

Marta has a thing for unobtainable women. "Think it'll work?"

"It'd take a miracle."

"So, why are you working with her? Just the chance to work with Hkuri?"

"Pretty much. I hadn't spoken to her in more than three years. Then there she is, out of nowhere. Musical opportunities, big promises. Almost told her to take a hike, but she was right. It's too big a chance to pass up." The night's getting colder as we walk along, and Emeka shivers a bit and steps closer to me. "Should have thought ahead," he says. "No jacket."

"You want to borrow mine for a bit?"

"I'd probably get lost in it," Emeka says with a laugh, but then he shrugs. "You know what, sure. If you're sure you'll be okay."

I pull it off and pass it to him. "Been out in colder than this wearing less."

"Really? You'll have to tell me that story." Emeka wraps my jacket around himself like a cape.

"Not much of a story, really. Just late nights at the bar, sometimes the weather turns."

"Yeah," Emeka says. "Had a few nights like that myself."

We walk quietly for a while after that. It's a nice night for a walk. There aren't many people out; it's too late for the evening partiers, and too early for the all-night crowd. Eventually we turn a corner and there's a blue neon sign flickering against the night, proclaiming 'The Rust Bucket' is open for business.

"Doesn't look like much, but they've got some decent booze dirt cheap, and I know one of the bartenders." Emeka grins, one hand dipping into his pocket as we approach the door; he pulls an envelope halfway free as if to check it's still there, and then shakes his head and tucks it back when he sees me looking. "Checking my funds," he says. "Anyway, I know my pal is on shift tonight because he couldn't come out to the show, so we might be able to get some pretty stiff shots if you want."

"Not too stiff. I'm working tomorrow."

Emeka chuckles. "Working stiff," he says, poking me in the ribs.

I'm about to joke back when I see something weird down the side alley: a guy kneeling by an open door. I think I see a spark. He stands up.

Then the front windows blow out and there's fire everywhere.

The next couple of minutes are a blur. I get to the doors and help pull people out and get them to the side so more folks can make a run for it. Once the doors are clear, I can see inside; the whole back of the bar is on fire, and there are people still inside, on the ground or crouching in a panic by the bar. The bouncer pushes some scrawny teenager into my arms and goes back for someone else. The kid is covered in soot, bleeding from a dozen cuts. He looks up at me wide-eyed, and tries to say something, but he's coughing too hard. He collapses, and I heft him up and carry him towards the street.

Emeka shouts directions for people to clear space for the ones who are hurt. When he sees me, he passes me my coat to spread on the ground; we set the kid down on my picnic blanket of a jacket, and I loosen his collar. The kid's eyes have rolled back, and he's clutching my hand. He's not coughing anymore.

"It's gonna be okay. You're gonna be okay!"

The kid meets my eyes. I think maybe he tries to smile. But then he's gone.

I stand up. I don't know what I'm thinking. Maybe I'm going to run back in and try to get anyone else out. Maybe I'm just going to scream. But before I can do whatever I was going to do, I see someone coming out of the alley. A middle-aged guy in a nice overcoat, his hands tinged with soot. The guy I saw kneeling, starting the fire.

People scatter as I charge him. He looks over too late, and my first punch drops him like a sack of bricks. I drop with him, grabbing him so he can't run away, and then three people are pulling me off him, and someone clocks me on the head, so I turn and clock them right back, only they're a cop.

Next thing I know, I'm being bundled into the back of a police car, and the last thing I see on my way out is Emeka, still kneeling by the dead kid and trying to bring him back, and I know I've messed it all up again.

# Saturday, August 18<sup>th</sup>

**I've never been** arrested in the West Precinct before. Usually, when I get arrested it's because I got into a fight downtown, so they haul me straight into the First Precinct. The First Precinct is real fancy — it was built right at the start, when they thought Everland was going to be a big deal, and a lot of money got spent on it. It's got a big open-front area, a carved mural of the last battle against the Pan, glass-faced offices, wide corridors, the works. Even the cells are nice. They're roomy, they get some light, and you don't usually have to share.

West Precinct was built about five years ago, when they realized a lot of poor folks were still moving in and they needed somewhere to leave them. It got put together on the cheap, and it looks it — grey bricks, low ceilings, small windows, those new fluorescent lights that make your eyes hurt. I don't get to compare the cells right away, because as soon as I arrive they dump me in an interrogation room, and I stay there for the next few hours cooling my heels while they decide what they're going to charge me with. Then a couple of bored-looking cops come in to take down my version of events, there is a lot of eye-rolling and smirks but no actual attempts to beat a confession out of me. Once they've got the details, they leave.

The next guy who strides in looks familiar, but I can't quite figure out why. He's tall, almost as tall as me, but a lot skinnier. He's dressed like a high-priced lawyer — black suit and tie, a pair of square glasses that he adjusts as he drops the manila file folders he's holding on the table and looks me over. His hair is slicked-back smooth, and he's got a bit of a smirk. I already hate him. "Well, well, well. Todd Malcolm, our would-be arsonist."

I grunt and clench my teeth. "You've got it wrong," I say. "The other guy is the arsonist. I just jumped him to keep him from getting away."

"The 'other guy' is a respected member of Second Star's scientific staff," the man says, sitting down across from me and flipping open his files. "Respected, intelligent, pillar of the community. Whereas you have quite the file." He glances down at his pile of papers. "Todd Malcolm, born in nineteen-twenty-six, moved to Everland in nineteen-twenty-eight. Son of James and Ginny Malcolm. Father was a millworker, signed up for the draft in thirty-nine, killed in action nineteen-forty-three. Mother still works in the Holland Factory uptown." He flips through the pages. "Your arrest record is ample. Drunk and disorderlies, mostly, but a few for assault and battery, one for petty theft, three for drug use, some trespassing." He shakes his head. "Tell me something, Mr. Malcolm. Which of the two people I've described sounds like someone who would set fire to a low-rent club in the bad part of town?"

I frown. "You're the guy from the docks."

The man raises an eyebrow. "Excuse me?"

"You were down at the docks yesterday, meeting some American government guy. That's where I know you from. You were glaring at me then, too."

To my surprise, the man smiles a bit. He reaches into his jacket and pulls out a cigarette, lighting it up. "You're smarter than you look, Mr. Malcolm. I suppose you'd have to be to work at a detective agency, even if you're mainly hired muscle."

"So, who the heck are you?" I ask. "You don't look like the local cops I know."

The man takes a drag on his cigarette. "I am, in fact, a member of law enforcement, if not one of your local beat cops. Agent Harper, FBI. I've been called in to handle a complicated situation. Yesterday, I was meeting a few of my men who came over to assist. And then, just as my team is assembled, we have a break in the case. How coincidental."

"You're investigating arsons?"

"What I am investigating, Mr. Malcolm, is less important than your presence in my investigations. You've moved up in the world recently, haven't you? One of your friends was murdered last winter, and somehow you came out of it working for a local legend. How very lucky for you."

I'm halfway out of my chair before I can stop myself. The man tenses, but he smiles again when I force my fists open and sit back down. "You don't know what you're talking about," I growl.

"How did you know that bar was going to burn down?"

"What?"

Harper gives me a long look. "Don't take me for a fool, Malcolm. The Rust Bucket used to pay protection to Quentin Lark, a local mob boss. Perhaps you remember him. He also died last winter, in mysterious circumstances, just after a series of public confrontations with your employer. Is Stark giving up on his neutrality and moving back into the mob game? Is that why he's started hiring toughs?"

"Buddy, you are so far off course you're at sea." I'm too surprised to stay mad. "Mr. Stark's no mobster. If that place was a mob joint, maybe that's why it got burned."

"By the respectable researcher you assaulted."

I don't have an easy answer for that one, so I look down at the table. Harper laughs, finishes his cigarette, and grinds it out on the table's edge. "So why don't you tell me why you were at The Rust Bucket."

"We'd just wrapped up at the Golden Hind. It was close, and the drinks are cheap."

"If that's the way you want to play it," Harper says. He stands up, leaving the cigarette butt behind, and gathers his folders. "I'll be back once the investigator's initial report is complete. Maybe by then you'll have a different answer." He walks out of the room, and a couple of officers come in to take me away.

The cells are about as grimy and dark as I expected based on the rest of the building, and I spend the whole day alone in them. Someone comes by to give me a stringy beef sandwich at one point, and a few hours later I get some lukewarm soup, and then I'm pretty much left to try and figure out where things went wrong. They won't even let me call my boss to let him know I won't make my shift.

The sun is getting low by the time Agent Harper gets back, with a couple of cops in tow. He gestures, and they unlock the door. "You're free to go, for now, Malcolm," Harper says to me. "But you're still a person of interest in this case. Don't leave town."

I snort. "Where would I go?"

"You have Piccadilly friends."

That catches me. I didn't think about Holly's place as being somewhere you couldn't get arrested, but I don't actually know what would happen if a bunch of police tried forcing their way in. I just shrug and nod. "Sure. Nice meeting you guys."

Harper puts a hand on my shoulder as I turn to follow the cops. I'm still keyed up and feel the urge to throw a punch, but I keep my fists from curling and turn back to him. "Yeah?"

"One more thing." Harper leans in close, like he doesn't want anyone to hear. "You tell Stark to stay the hell out of this. It's a federal case."

I'm too angry to be baffled. "You think a message like that'd *stop* Basil Stark, you really don't know Everland." I push his hand away. "Maybe you should look up the last guy who told him to butt out of a case." Out of the corner of my eye, I see one of the cops reach his hand down by his waist. It's the side with a club, not the side with a gun, but I take the hint and raise my hands, palms open. "Just having a chat, guys. Nothing happening."

"It had better not be," Harper says, his eyes drilling into me. He adjusts his glasses, turns on one heel, and strides away.

"Damn feds," one of the cops mutters. The other one quickly nudges him, and he turns the anger on to me. "Come on, you. Get the hell out of our precinct before you start something else."

"Yessir, officer." I almost salute sarcastically. Instead I let the cops march me to the front desk like big shots pushing the tough around. If they really thought they were letting a crook go, I figure I'd have a detour to get a few bruises knocked into me. Either they like Harper even less than that, or they think I'm just a drunk who messed up. Again.

Basil and Holly are at the front desk, chatting with the desk sergeant. They break off as I come up. "You must be Todd Malcolm," the sergeant says. "Got your wallet and jacket. Sign for 'em."

I take his pen and sign the papers, not looking up at the other two. "Thanks. What do I owe ya?"

The sergeant snorts. "You're spending too much time with this guy." He thumbs at Basil. "Just be glad you're walking out of here. You got the weirdest alibi ever."

I look up. "Huh?"

"Not many folks get to use one possible felony as an alibi for another one. The guy you jumped said you came roaring out of the crowd, but the fire was set in the basement. If you'd been the arsonist, you'd have had to have come from behind him." The sergeant shrugs. "So, unless that guy decides to press charges for decking him, you're good." He takes his pen back from me. "You'd better hope he doesn't."

"Yessir," I say.

"Come on, Todd. Let's get out of here. Thank you for the heads-up, Daniel." Basil waves lazily and leads the way out of the station, gathering us on the sidewalk before we say anything else. "You alright?"

"Yeah. Mr. Stark, I—"

"Why am I not surprised to find the usual suspects gathered around?"

We all turn to see Commissioner Steven Darling step out of a car. His bushy eyebrows draw tight as he looks us over, and his thick mustache quivers. "One month, Stark. Could you go one month without causing an international incident?"

"With due respect, Commissioner, I wasn't even the one brought in for questioning this time." Mr. Stark smiles broadly.

Darling gives Stark a sour look. "I would warn you about causing trouble if I thought for even a second that you would listen. But you won't, and I have places to be, so I'm going to ignore you."

"Is that all it takes? Blessed be, I should have gotten you 'places to be' years ago."

Darling grits his teeth, and he turns to look at me and Holly. "You two might not be entirely lost causes. You are aware that this is an American federal investigation?"

I nod. "Yessir. Met the guy in charge."

"That's right, you did. Which I say to point out that the 'guy in charge' is not me on this particular case, which means that my famously lenient attitude towards your employer's many, many misdeeds will not be in evidence."

"You have me arrested on a monthly basis," Mr. Stark says pointedly.

"That's right. I don't have you shot."

"Hrm." Mr. Stark takes a step back to think about that, and Darling turns to me.

"The Americans aren't as laid back as Everland's finest. Whatever Harper's interest in you is, I'd advise that you keep your heads down and stay out of it. Maybe even convince your bullheaded crook of a boss to do the same."

"What is the FBI even doing here, Commissioner?" Mr. Stark asks. "I didn't realize they had jurisdiction in Everland.

"Special request of the mayor's office." Darling's face is screwed up like he's bitten into a lemon. "They don't think we can handle it ourselves."

"It?" Basil prods.

"Some people would say that digging for information is the exact opposite of staying out of it, Stark." Without waiting for an answer, Darling sweeps past us into the building.

"Well, seems like we're back to normal," Holly says.

Basil shakes his head, looking worried. "I wouldn't say so, no. Commissioner Darling is not only the head of the local police, he's also the adopted brother of one of Second Star's CEOs, albeit the one that chooses not to live here. He has tremendous political sway, and, as a former Lost Boy, he has faced death on innumerable occasions."

"I know all of that, Uncle Basil. What's your point?"

"My point is that if he has lost control of this investigation there are indeed some very powerful people involved, and now Todd is on their radar." Stark turns to me. "Darling is a bit of an ass, but he was right about one thing: you shouldn't take lessons in vigilantism from me. My understanding is that you were nearly in a phenomenal amount of trouble today. You still might be. Do you know who you assaulted?"

"Some Second Star guy?"

"You could say that. His name is Dolph Henries. He's a VP of their research division, and he has the personal ear of the mayor." Basil shakes his head. "There were likely worse options, but I'm damned if I can picture one. What were you thinking?"

"I was thinking he was an arsonist," I mumble, feeling like dirt. "The kid was dead, I guess I just…"

"Alright. What did you see?"

I stumble. "Huh?"

"Maybe you were wrong, but maybe you saw something," Basil says. "Don't doubt, just think it through."

I take a deep breath. "Okay. Emeka and me, we were coming down the street towards the club."

"Which street?"

"Smee Way, towards Marooner's. Saw the guy in the alley. At least, I think it was him. There was definitely someone there, kneeling by a door, right before everything blew up."

"That fits what happened. The fire was started in the basement. Lots of high-proof, poorly stored liquor; that was the first blast, and then the fire spread quickly. If someone set it up and tossed a match down the stairs, that would have done it." Basil rubs his chin. "Are you certain it was the same person?"

"No." I grimace. "He looked the same, and I thought he was coming out of the alley, like he hid there until the coast was clear, but I was drunk, there was smoke, and I didn't get a good look at him. I think I must've jumped the wrong guy. Why would a guy like that try to burn down a low-rent mob club?"

"Good question," Basil says. "It could be that he was trying to slip away because he didn't want the bad press of being seen at a place like that. Or it could be that he was committing arson to cover something up." He shakes his head. "Either way, attacking him was likely a mistake."

"Uncle Basil!" Holly snaps. She puts a hand on my arm. "You were trying to help, Todd."

"Yeah, well, maybe I shouldn't have tried so hard," I say. "I hurt some guy who probably didn't deserve it. How bad was it?"

"One dead," Basil says gently. "A young man by the name of Oscar Turnbull. They'll have a cause of death soon, but I heard he was in the back of the room and got stuck in the commotion. Heat, smoke inhalation. I'd say it was too late before you and your musician friend got him to safety. But there are other people who are alive because you were there."

"Doesn't make me feel better. And I missed my shift. My boss is going to go spare."

"He'll understand, right?" Holly looks uncertain. "I mean, we can vouch for you."

I shake my head. "I don't know exactly what he's going to say, but I don't think it's gonna be great."

———— «» ————

"You're fired."

"Aw, come on, Mr. Hendricks. Give me one more chance."

"I gave you one more chance two months ago, after you picked a fight with one of my best customers." Mr. Hendricks pokes me in the chest, leaning over his desk. We're in the back room of the Drowned Mermaid, which is my main gig. It's not much of a bar, but I know the folks, and I've worked here for years.

"That guy hit his girlfriend!" I protest.

"Yeah? And who was it who broke the chair over your head in the middle of the fight, huh?"

"The girlfriend," I mutter, staring down at my knuckles.

"Yeah. Great job, hero. And then you come in here, smelling like stale beer and smoke, your shirt a mess, and you missed the whole day. You were at that bar burned last night, huh?"

"Yeah."

"Let me guess. You were the guy who got arrested for starting another fight." Mr. Hendricks shakes his head. For a moment, he doesn't look mad. Just tired. "Todd. Kiddo, I like you. I've put up with a lot of shit from you because you've got a good heart. But a bouncer is supposed to stop problems, not start 'em. So, you're fired. Get your last pay from Ernie, go home. Get some sleep. Find a job that doesn't involve punching things. You're too good at that."

I go, and Ernie gives me a wave as I walk up to the bar. "You look like crap."

"Thanks."

He hands me an envelope. "Boss already gave me the word. Sorry, man."

And that's it. Three years of my life, over just like that. A couple of waiters give me sympathetic looks on my way out the door, but no one says anything. I don't say anything either.

Holly's hanging around outside, talking quietly with Glimmer. She looks up as I come out. "Oh, hey. You need that vouching?"

"It's fine," I say, walking past.

"So, I'm guessing that he was not reasonable."

"I need a drink."

"You need a bed." Holly grabs my wrist. "Come on. Let's get you home, and you can figure things out in the morning."

"I messed it all up, Holly," I mumble, as she pulls me into her mom's old car. "Don't know what I was thinking."

"You were thinking that someone got hurt, and you saw the guy that did it. You're not really the 'stand back' sort of guy."

"Well, maybe I should be." I fold up into the front seat, knees to my chest, and look out the window as she starts driving. "You know, yesterday things looked pretty good."

"They'll look pretty good again tomorrow."

"Doubt it."

Glimmer hops onto my shoulder, and for a moment I think she's going to punch me in the ear, but then she gives me a hug instead. She turns and whispers something to Holly.

"Stay with...?" I frown. "You want to what?"

"Good idea," Holly says brightly. "Glimmer's going to keep an eye on you for a bit. I would, but if I don't bring the car back by nightfall Mom'll flip, and Dad needs it tomorrow anyway."

"I don't need someone to stay with me."

Holly continues as if I hadn't spoken. "I've got some things to do tomorrow, so you can drop Glimmer back at my place in the evening. Are you going to talk to Carson?"

I don't know if my head is spinning because I'm tired or because of Holly. "Talk to him about what?"

"About work. I mean, I can check with some of the guys about whether there are any logging jobs open, but I'm going to be honest, you're not the outdoorsiest person I know."

"Oh, yeah. Carson." I fish around in my pockets for a moment. Vance Carson's card is still there, wrinkled, a bit stained, smelling like smoke. "I don't know, Holly. It feels weird."

"See, I thought you were going to say that. It's not weird. People work two jobs all the time."

"For competitors?"

"Uncle Basil already said it was okay!" Holly groans. "See, this is why I asked you. You were going to just lose the card, weren't you?"

"I was not!" I think about it, and sigh. "No, you're right. I don't think I would have called him."

"Well, now you need money, and Uncle Basil's busy working his dumb solo act so we don't have much for you. Call him." Holly parks outside my apartment building. "After you get some food in you. And maybe some sleep, I don't know. Glimmer, will you make sure that Todd makes that call?"

Glimmer salutes, and I rub my forehead. "I don't need people living my life for me."

Holly looks over at me. "No, but you have people looking out for you. Come on, Todd. You're good at this. Vance would be lucky to have you."

"Fine, fine, I'll call him." I get out of the car. "Thanks for the ride, Holly."

"No problem. See you tomorrow!"

Usually, having an apartment on the third floor isn't too bad, but today I can barely drag my feet up the stairs, and I fumble my keys twice trying to get the door open. As I close it behind me and stump towards the shower, Glimmer zips past me and into the kitchen. I'm too tired to be worried.

She's got it handled, and she knows where I keep the sugared crackers. It'll keep her distracted while I freshen up. A long, hot shower is what I need. A lukewarm shower is what I get, but it's better than nothing.

I step out of the shower, towel around my waist, to a heck of a surprise. There's a salad sitting on the table next to a jug of orange juice. It's not fancy, just lettuce, carrots, some peppers, and chunks of ham, but it's fresh. Glimmer is sitting next to it, looking smug.

"Where'd you get fresh veggies?" I ask as I sit down.

Glimmer explains that Holly dropped them off while I was in jail.

"Holly stocked the fridge?"

Glimmer nods.

I gape for a moment, and then shake my head and laugh. "You two must be really worried about me. I'm fine."

I get a heck of a look at that. I grin and pick up the salad bowl. "Hungry. But fine."

Glimmer has her own tiny bowl, and she digs in next to me. We're eating in a companionable silence when there's a knock on the door.

I stand up, start to the door, and realize I'm still not wearing much. "Just a second!" I shout, doubling back to grab some clothes.

I step out of the bedroom, my pants unbuckled and my shirt over my head. The door is open and Emeka is standing halfway into my apartment.

"Glimmer!" I snap.

She gives me a big grin and goes to sit on top of my couch.

Emeka is staring. "I, uh, I brought, came to bring back, I, coat. Yours. Your coat." He holds it out in front of him like a shield. "You left your coat at the bar."

I quickly pull my shirt down, button my pants up, and smile. "My coat! Right. Of course. Hah." I reach out, and Emeka shoves it into my hands. The back is all covered in dirt, and it smells like smoke. There's some blood on the inside, more than I thought the kid had left.

"You okay?" Emeka asks.

I startle as he touches me on the back, and quickly step over to the couch, draping my coat across its arm. "Yeah. How'd it go after I got taken away?"

"Pretty much what you'd expect with a body on the scene. Police grabbed most of the bystanders, asked a lot of questions. I told 'em I'd only just shown up with you, and I didn't know the guy we were helping. I think the bouncer backed me up, because I didn't get arrested. How about you?"

"Got kept overnight, and most of the day. No charges yet, but I got fired."

"Oh, Todd, I'm sorry." Emeka puts his hand on my arm, more gently this time.

"Eh, it's a dump anyway."

"Obviously." Emeka grins. "Not having to work for those assholes might be a good thing. Listen, I'll ask around. Maybe someone else is looking. Anyone would be lucky to have you."

"Oh, yeah, I'm just a treat to be around. Maybe I can punch out someone's manager next, really make some waves." Emeka's eyebrows raise, and I can't help but smile. "Sorry."

"Hey, if anyone's got the right to be upset right now, it's you. You want to go get a drink? I mean, to chat about it?"

"A drink sounds real good right now." I glance over to Glimmer, who is watching us intently and quietly. "But I need sleep, I think."

Glimmer's sigh is audible.

Emeka nods seriously. "Makes sense. Cells aren't a great place to pass the time." He looks over my shoulder. "And it looks like you need to finish eating, too."

"You want to sit down for a bit? I think there's extra."

Emeka looks at the food. "I just ate, but I could stay a minute."

He joins me at the table, and I grab him a glass to pour himself some juice. "You handle yourself pretty good in an emergency," I say between bites of salad.

"Do I?"

"Sure. You were cool, collected. Really helped people out."

"Thank you. To be honest, one of the cops said the same thing, but I wasn't sure if he was being serious, or just chatting me up. You weren't half bad yourself, though." Emeka looks into my eyes, and I feel my cheeks starting to grow warm. I quickly turn my attention to my salad.

"I just pulled a couple of people out of a doorway. Didn't even make it inside."

"Didn't hesitate." Out of the corner of my eye, I can see Emeka grinning at me. "Trust me, some of the places I've worked, we'd do just about anything for a bouncer who didn't freeze up when things got rough."

"You ever been anywhere things got that rough?"

"Once," Emeka says. His smile fades. "Back in the States when I was a teen. We were playing a gig in a little place in South Carolina, and a group of angry farmers threw a whole damned bundle of burning hay through the window. We had to run out the back."

"Damn. What was their problem?"

"Us, mostly."

"Damn," I say again for lack of anything better.

"Yeah. But we made it." He shrugs. "There were a lot of better days, too." Emeka launches into a story about a bar in Charleston and some of the old guys that he learned from. I'm too tired to follow all the details, but it's nice to have Emeka here and chatting, so I let the words wash over me while I eat. After a few minutes, the story winds down and Emeka looks me over. "You're half a world away, big guy."

"Sorry. Just thinking about that kid again. Basil said his name was Oscar." The boy's face swims into my mind, that scared attempt at a smile. "Wonder if I should talk to his family."

"It's a sweet thought. What would you say, though? You weren't responsible for the fire, and you weren't responsible for the kid." Emeka reaches across the table and puts his hand gently on top of mine. "You did your best, Todd. You know that, right?"

"Yeah." It doesn't feel like it, but I force a smile.

"You carry the world on your shoulders. It's sweet."

"I just like to look out for people. When I can." I stab my fork into my bowl and discover there's nothing left.

"Well, it's my turn. I'm going to let you sleep. You joining the gang for lunch on Monday?"

"Sure."

"Good. Then I'll see you there, big guy." Emeka glances down, realizes he's still touching my arm and quickly turns it into a friendly pat on the shoulder, then he stands and heads out into the hall. I get up, close the door, and turn around to find Glimmer in midair, arms crossed, glaring at me.

"What?"

She makes a kissing face.

"You did not used to be like this. Holly is rubbing off on you."

I'm not entirely sure what Glimmer says next, but if I'm parsing it right it is absolutely filthy.

"Glimmer!"

She shrugs and returns to finish off her food. I give up and reach for the phone.

I'm lucky — Vance hasn't gone home for the day, yet. "Vance Carson's office, Vance speaking."

"Mr. Carson? This is Todd Malcolm. You'd asked me to drop by this morning."

"Todd? Oh, yes, Todd! Great to hear from you. I was worried that you'd gotten too busy."

"Well, Mr. Carson, if I'm gonna be honest, I got too arrested."

There's a pause on the other end of the line. "You don't do things by half, friend. What for?"

"I punched a guy I thought was an arsonist."

"That fire last night, down on Smee Way?"

"Yeah."

"Well." Another hesitation, and then I hear him chuckle. "Alright, my boy, we can work with that. Are you still interested in work?"

"Yeah. It turns out I need some cash if I'm going to make rent this month."

"Your other job didn't take the news so well?"

"Not so much."

"Well, their loss is my gain." Vance chuckles a second time. I don't know if he's making fun or just happy, but he moves on pretty quick. "But if you're working with me, one rule. No punches unless I say so, alright?"

"Yeah, of course. You're the boss. You're okay with hiring me?"

"It'd be a bit rich for me to get upset that you try to help people, given that's how we met. Besides, we all make mistakes sometimes. Now, I could definitely use extra help on my current case, and I expect to have at least a few days of work. How does twelve dollars a day sound?"

It sounds better than what I made at the bar. "I think I can do that."

"Perfect! Let's see, I have a lunch meeting tomorrow, so why don't you stop by my office at about one o'clock? We'll sign the paperwork and get right to the case! Good night, my boy. I think we'll work well together."

"Yeah, I'm looking forward to—" But he's already hung up. I set down my phone, and look over to Glimmer, who is watching me with a raised eyebrow.

"Yeah," I say. "He's a little much. But he seems like a nice enough guy."

She snorts.

"Come on," I say. "Let's hit the hay. We've got places to be tomorrow."

# Sunday, August 19th

I **wake up** to find Glimmer sitting on the end of my bed, dressed for the day and tapping her foot against the baseboard. When she sees that I'm up, she flies down and nudges me.

"Let me guess," I say. "Breakfast."

Glimmer nods.

"I'll take two eggs."

She smacks me on the ear, and I laugh. "Okay, you're right, you did supper, it's my turn. Gimme a sec."

I fry up a few eggs and some toast, and give Glimmer a share. "I've gotta go into town and see Vance," I tell her once we finish eating. "You want to tag along, or should we stop off at the office?"

Glimmer's eyes go wide, and she giggles and starts chattering at top speed. When she sees I can't keep up, she sighs heavily and slows down, spelling out each word. I follow along as best I can, although it looks like we've drifted off the original subject.

"Yeah, I know I'm not good at this. I'm not good at languages! I know that you know my language, that's because you are good at languages. Yes, you can come if you want to, but no, I don't think Vance will pay you. And yes, we can stop by the office on the way down so that you can change."

Glimmer shrugs, and then goes to wait by the door while I get myself together. I go to grab my suit jacket, and then remember that it still needs to be cleaned. At least I have an extra belt. After a bit of consideration, I grab a plaid button-up shirt and my best remaining pair of pants. It's not fancy, but it's the best I can manage.

I grab my keys and wallet as we head for the door. "You've got your pass, right?"

Glimmer pulls it out of her woven backpack and waves it at me, looking sour. I don't blame her. If I needed a pass to be out in public, I'd be sour, too. Fairy personhood is a nasty issue in Everland right now, and a lot of folks treat them like kids, or animals. Most fairies have to choose between living out in the woods, safe from humans but without much to eat, or coming into town for better food and shelter but risking getting rounded up as potential threats to the public order.

There was a push for full fairy equality a few years back, and it got a lot of support, but the mayor's office and Hawthorne both campaigned real hard against it, arguing that fairies were too unpredictable to be given that kind of representation. Second Star stayed quiet, so a lot of people figured they weren't too keen on the idea either, which leaves us here in the middle of the mess.

Glimmer used to buck the system. She hid out at a friend's place and stayed under the radar. But she got caught trying to help Mr. Stark, and now she's recorded. She can go around because Mr. Stark signed a bunch of papers saying he'd be responsible if she did anything, but that's a mess, too, because it means he could decide she was dangerous and lock her up if he wanted to.

"You can still make rude gestures with it, I just don't want to get arrested twice in two days," I tell her. She laughs, gives me a thumbs-up, and we head out.

Mr. Stark works down on Jane Street, near the edge of downtown. Like half the places down there, the offices started as apartments in the late twenties, back when people thought Everland was going to become one of the biggest cities in the world. Once everyone realized that you can't really make magic industrial, immigration slowed down and a lot of those buildings ended up empty. So, the locals converted them into offices, four to a floor. Mr. Stark's on the second floor of a four-story brownstone. Right now, he's sharing the floor with an accountant who wanders out to grump at him about his hours, a mail-order business of some kind, and someone who's just using their office for storage.

I let myself in, and Glimmer zips off to her nest to change. Being in the office alone makes me a little nervous, even if I know I'm technically allowed. I head over to the kitchen and grab a glass of water. One advantage of the office being converted living space is that it has almost a whole kitchen, although Mr. Stark had the oven pulled out. He said that there were enough ways to kill him in there already, he didn't need fire on top of it.

I'm done my water and am cleaning the glass when Glimmer whistles me over. I come out to see her posing proudly in front of her nest. "Holy heck, Glimmer, where'd you find that getup?"

Somehow, Glimmer has found a black trench coat, with slits in the back for her wings. It goes down to her knees, but she's got it tied loosely so that I can see she's got a white dress on underneath, and she's slipped on a little pillbox hat. She beams and explains slowly that she got a friend to sew it for her.

"You are one fancy detective," I say. "Now I definitely feel underdressed."

Glimmer flies over, pats me on the cheek, and then goes to shoo me out the door.

———— «» ————

Vance Carson's office is a bit smaller than Mr. Stark's, but it's a heck of a lot nicer. It's on the second floor of a walk-up not far from the Hill, and it's obvious that the building isn't just converted housing. I walk past a little deli and an accountant on the main floor, head up to the second floor, and stop at the frosted glass marked 'Carson Investigations.' It looks like something out of a movie set.

I take a deep breath, and knock. I hear a bit of shuffling, and then Vance calls out, "Come on in."

I open the door and step into the waiting room. It's got plush carpet, padded chairs, and a small secretary's desk with a typewriter and a phone. There's a kitchenette in the corner with a half-full coffee pot and a little fridge, and as Vance steps out of his office and closes the door behind him I catch a glimpse of an oak desk and a fancy portrait on the wall. "Oh!" he says with a grin. "Good to see you, Todd. Welcome to the office."

"Glad to be here, Mr. Carson."

"Call me Vance. You got me out of a scrape, after all." Vance walks over and reaches up to pat me on the shoulder. He looks up at me, and then past me to Glimmer, who is sort of crouching behind my shoulders. "And ... you've brought a fairy?"

"Yes. Mr. Carson, this is Glimmer. Glimmer, Vance Carson, private detective."

Glimmer takes a deep breath, stands up, and then hops down onto my arm and holds out her hand for Vance to shake.

"Well. It's a pleasure." Vance collects himself and holds out a finger for Glimmer to shake. "Are you applying for work, too?"

Glimmer laughs, and I translate her explanation when it's clear that Vance has not understood her. "Glimmer just wanted to tag along and see how a cool detective operates."

Glimmer shoots me a look at my editorializing, but Vance seems to have bought it. "Well, that should be alright, then. Any friend of yours is a friend of mine. I drew up some paperwork for you to sign. Nothing too complicated, just to show that we're working together. Step into my office, and I'll walk you through the case so far."

Vance's office is nice, in a quiet sort of way. The portrait I saw turns out to be some family thing: a teenager and his parents, all standing in a formal hall with a grand staircase behind them. Everyone in the portrait looks so serious that it takes me a moment to match the kid to the smiling guy in front of me.

I sit across from Vance as he pulls some files out from a cabinet and lays them out. Glimmer settles on the filing cabinet, watching us as Vance pulls out a pen. "Okay, standard nondisclosure forms. I'm sure you signed some of these for Mr. Stark."

I nod. Holly had me sign a one-page thing that basically said, 'Don't talk about cases, don't share secrets, don't talk to cops, don't break laws.' Compared to that, this is a heck of a stack. "Sure thing." I take a quick look at the papers. Near as I can tell, they're all the same rules, just laid out with a lot more legalese. I sign and pass them back. "Thanks for giving me a shot, Mr. Carson."

"Vance, please." Vance grins. "And you gave a hell of an interview." He takes the papers and puts them in a folder, and then reaches for another one. "Okay, from here on in, everything is confidential, understood?"

"Got it."

"Wonderful." He hands me the folder. "The client is Rupert Drainie. His father works for the mayor's office, and his mother is chair of the Everland Anti-Poverty Fund. Very highly placed in societal circles."

I open the folder and look at it. Rupert looks like the kind of guy I have to gently lead out of a bar from time to time — a bit reedy, but he carries himself like he can't imagine anything going wrong. He's with a few other classy types at a party, posing together with drinks. "Seems nice. What happened to him?"

"Gambling. A classic vice, but a rough one." Vance shakes his head. "Rupert has a bit of a problem, and he's run out his credit at the Paradise. So, he tried some shadier dens."

"Mob trouble?"

"He wasn't quite that dense, but in some ways it might be worse." Vance gestures to the second set of photos. "He took some jewelry from his mother's room to act as collateral until he could get some money together. Unfortunately, someone involved in the operation thought about the scandal if a child of two prominent figures was found to be gambling illegally, and acquired the jewelry from the pawnbroker that Drainie had left them with before he could get back."

"Oh, boy."

"Oh, boy, indeed. The owner of The Paradise isn't interested; he wasn't the one Rupert pawned the jewelry to, so it's off his turf, and not his problem. But Rupert is distraught. He's been asked to gather quite a lot of money if he wants the jewelry back, and he just doesn't have it."

"Okay. Yeah, that's a mess." I think about it for a moment. "Hang on. This is a blackmail case?"

"Yes. Why?"

"Do you get a lot of those?" It would be just my luck if Vance and Mr. Stark were working the same case from opposite ends.

"From time to time. Plenty of blackmailers in the city, after all."

"And you don't think it's too dangerous?"

"I laugh in the face of danger, my boy." Vance pats his chest. "There isn't a blackmailer born who can pull one over me. They're a cowardly bunch, generally. The sort of criminal without the guts for direct action, and usually not that bright, to boot. But I admit this one has been a bit trickier."

"Okay. And where did the mermaids come into it?"

"Hm? Oh. Yes. A dead end." Vance rubs the back of his neck. "Rupert was gambling at the Beached Whale, which has an area for mermaids to mingle with the rest of the clientele. One of them was in the game, and I thought they might have had an idea of who else was paying attention. There weren't that many people who saw the jewels, after all. But I don't know if I got the message across to them. They mostly made jokes about…"

I think about what I know about mermaids. "Family jewels?"

"Yes," Vance sighs. "But! I have another approach. I'm going to go and speak with the pawnbroker who originally purchased the jewels."

"You think that he'll say something?"

"I think that between the two of us, we can get what we need from Mr. Donner, yes."

"Mister Donner? Wait, did Silver Donny buy the jewels?" I can't help but look over to Glimmer, who is sharing my confused expression.

"You know him! Even better." Vance grins, and then his smile falters. "Is this a conflict of interest?"

"Naw, nothing like that. A lot of the musicians need to store their stuff at his place sometimes. You know how it is when the jobs are tight."

"Then why are you frowning?"

"Feels weird, is all. Donny selling something on that kinda turnaround."

"He's a pawnbroker, Todd," Vance says gently. "Selling things is what they do."

"It's what they do when people can't pay them back. This sounds like he sold it practically the same day."

"The lure of a big reward turns many heads," Vance says. "I've seen it all before. The blackmailer might have cut him in on it. He might even *be* the blackmailer." He stands and grabs his coat and hat from a hook on the wall. "But you raise a good avenue of thought. We can try working it into the interrogation. Maybe shame will make him hesitate. Come on, we'll take my car. We can park it a block away and disperse from there."

Vance's car is a sleek blue Roadster, and he hops into the driver's seat without opening the door, one hand keeping his fedora on. I get into the passenger side a bit more carefully, glad that it's not raining; if he had to put the hood up, I don't know if I'd fit. Glimmer follows us out, clearly determined to be quiet and observational like she promised; she slips into the space between the seats and settles back. As we start down the road, Vance asks me, "So, what gave you the detecting bug?"

"Huh?"

"You know! Why did you start working with Mr. Stark? Were you always interested in investigation, or did you bump into each other on a case?"

"Oh! Oh. Uh, actually, it was sort of Holly's fault. I started as a client. Kind of." I look out over the road, watching the passersby. "A friend of mine and Glimmer's got killed."

Vance is silent for a moment. "The stitcher case?"

"Yeah. Our friend busted it wide open, but she died for it." Glimmer climbs up the side of my shirt to give me a reassuring hug, and I reach up to hug her back. "When I first found out, I wished she'd trusted me with more of it to begin with, but she wanted to protect me. She was probably right, too. I bet I would have been dead pretty quick if I was in the know. Can't out-muscle shadows."

Vance shivers. "No," he says. "I suppose not."

"The funny thing is, it was actually Holly that brought me on board. She said she needed some help, but I think she might have been trying to keep me distracted. And it worked. She and I solved a little case while Mr. Stark was working the big one, and then I was around to help a little for the finale. And after that, they kept me on."

"They sound like good people."

"You must know them, too, right? I mean, there are only two detectives on the island, you've gotta cross paths."

Vance wobbles his hand, then moves to grab his hat as he takes a corner a bit too fast. For a moment I think we're going to lose control, and I grab the side of the door, but then his hands are back on the wheel and he's chatting like nothing happened. "The thing is, Mr. Stark and I mainly move in two different areas. He has clients with Second Star, with some of the lower-class workers, and with people in criminal troubles. My clients tend towards Hawthorne folk, political types, and high society." He focuses on the road for a moment, before adding, "I expect his cases are the more exciting ones."

"I think the exciting ones are the ones he hates," I say. "What about you? You always want to be a detective?"

"Oh, very much so. I grew up on Hammett and Heyer. *The Maltese Falcon* was the very first film I watched, and I daresay my parents weren't thrilled about it." Vance chuckles. "I don't suppose that I would have had the chance, if things had gone their way. Father was quite intent on my taking a place in the family business. But then the war came, and I was drafted."

"Did you go overseas?"

Vance shakes his head. "No, I spent the forties in the naval yard, helping move cargo from American boats to British ones to evade Atlantic piracy, and watching for u-boats. Important work, of course, but not very exciting. But I kept in shape, I practiced with the firearms, and most importantly, I saved my salary. When the war ended and I mustered out, I had enough of a nest egg to open my agency without needing my parents' support, and here I am!" Vance glances over at me. "Did you serve?"

"Just missed it," I say. "I got drafted, but by the time I got through basic training we'd taken back France. There were a few weeks it looked like I might get shipped over to help with the last push, but it never happened. My dad served, though. Naval officer. Died during the Italian campaigns."

Vance is quiet again. "My sympathies," he says eventually as he pulls over a block from Donny's.

"Thanks. What do you need me to do?"

"Right. Right! Head in the front door, try to get whatever you can out of Donner. Bullying, shaming, a bit of attempted bribery, whatever you need to do. If you can get something useful, so much the better. But meanwhile, I'll slip in the back way, get to his office, and check the ledger."

"Wait, you're just gonna break in?"

"No, I'm going on a mission of discovery."

Glimmer's eyes light up.

"Didn't I just sign a thing saying I wasn't gonna do anything illegal?"

"You did, you did. I didn't." Vance gives me a sparkling grin. "Besides, what's he going to do? Call the police and tell them that he caught someone looking at his records of illegal sales?"

"Uh, yeah. He will. Because the cops are on the take."

"Well, then, I suppose you'll just have to be very persuasive. Don't worry, if I get caught, I'll tell them you weren't involved."

"That's not why I'm—" But he's already hopped out of the car and is beelining towards the alley behind Donny's shop. "Uh, Glimmer? I know you're not technically on the job, but..."

Glimmer nods seriously and launches off my shoulder in the direction Vance went, so at least he'll have extra warning if something goes wrong. Swallowing the feeling that we're both going to get killed, I head to the front entrance.

'Silver Donner's' is a pawn shop right on the edge of the harbor, and for people like me it's *the* pawn shop. Even I can whistle his jingle, "Whatever you need, you can find it at Silver Donner's." Heard it on the radio a hundred times. And everyone knows that Donny's not just a salesman: he's a fence. He knows all the best muscle and all the best restaurants, and he pays his share to the mob, but he's not actually part of the organization. He's pretty much a local legend, and it feels real weird to be walking into his place like I'm the one with nothing to prove.

"Welcome to Silver Donner's! Oh, hey, I know you. The guy who hangs out with the musicians. Todd, right?" Donny gives me a grin and a wave. "What can I do you for? Looking for a nice suit for a show?"

"No, I, uh…" I walk up to the counter, and I take a moment to look at the rack of watches. "I'm looking for information."

Donny's smile drops off his face like I flicked a light switch. "You're not here with Stark, are you?"

"What? No. No! Why does everyone suddenly think I'm doing things with Mr. Stark?" I'm blinking too much.

"Because everyone knows he's on a case, and the last time he was on a case that took him around here he got my whole supply room busted up, and do you know that he never once offered to pay for it? Could have at least taken me out for some apology drinks, but not Mr. 'Bull-In-A-China-Shop' Stark." Donny frowns. "So, whaddaya want, and how are you paying?"

"Depends on the price?" I don't want to end up working jobs to pay for the job that I'm working. "I'm here about some jewelry."

If I thought Donny looked sour before, he looks downright grim now. "What jewelry?"

I think back to the picture Vance showed me. "Emerald ring, diamond necklace, a red one?"

"Get out of here," Donny says. "Whoever put you up to this, you're above your pay grade."

"What, just like that?"

"Yeah, just like that. You know how I keep this shop going? You know how I get your friends their good deals? It's because I don't get involved in the messy stuff. And buddy, I'm going to tell you this because I like your musician friends. This is the messy stuff." Donny turns away, waving his hand at me. "Now piss off."

"Seems like you're already involved."

Donny stops dead. He turns around slowly. "What did you say?"

I'm pretty sure this was a mistake, but there's nothing for it now, so I just lean on the counter, and look down at him. It's not hard. I'm at least a foot taller than he is, and as I get close it looks like he's starting to notice that. "I said, you're already involved. You sold pawned stuff early, Donny. You never do that. That's why people like my friends trust you with their stuff."

"Are you threatening me?" Donny looks up and meets my gaze.

"Someone is. I can't believe you'd do that otherwise."

"Thanks for the vote of confidence. If I don't tell you, what are you going to do? Mess up the place? Tell all your friends I'm no good? What leverage do you think you have?"

"I just want to understand, Donny."

"Well, good luck with that. I don't answer to you. You don't scare me. Get out of here before I call the cops."

I'm searching for something else to say when I hear a sound coming from the back. Donny frowns. "What was that?"

"What was what?"

He looks at me for a half-second, reaches under the counter, and then spins and starts marching back to the employees-only area with a revolver in his hand. I follow, desperately trying to sound angry. "Hey, hold on, we're not done talking!"

"You think I was born yesterday? You think I'm some two-bit punk? You think no one's ever tried to keep me talking so they could rob the place? Stark, I swear to God that if you are rooting around in my office, I am going to put so much lead in you you'll wish the Crocodile had got you first!" Donny kicks open the office door, and stops dead, looking around. I let out a quiet sigh of relief. No Vance, and no Glimmer.

Donny gives me a suspicious look, and does a quick loop around the room, checking the locks. "There was someone in here."

"Hey, I dunno, maybe. I just—"

"Yeah, you just want to understand." Donny stops at a safe tucked under a table against the wall and kneels down; keeping the gun half-pointed at me, he spins the dial and yanks it open, and I can see that his ledger book is there, next to a couple bundles of weird-colored cash. Donny looks down at it, and then shuts the safe door. "Employees only, kid."

"I told you Mr. Stark wasn't here."

"And I told you to get out of here, so I guess neither of us is a very good listener."

I sigh. "Okay, okay. I'm going. Sorry to bother you, Donny."

"Yeah, yeah." Now that the tension is fading, Donny looks more sad than angry. He sets the revolver down and shakes his head. "Sorry and a dime will buy you a coffee." He hesitates, starts to open his mouth, and then shuts it again, and I take the chance to get out before he follows through on his threat.

Vance is waiting back by the car, with Glimmer sitting smugly on the hood. "Did you get it?" I ask.

He shakes his head, looking glum. "Drawer was empty. Everything must have been in the safe. I was trying to figure it out when your friend just about yanked out my hair getting my attention. If it weren't for her, I'd probably have been caught."

Glimmer preens.

"She says you're welcome. Sorry I couldn't hold him longer."

"No, he's a tough customer. Did he have a gun?"

"Of course. He runs a pawn shop on the harbor."

Vance breathes out slowly. "Okay. So. That was not my finest plan. But now we're back at square one. I suppose I'll just have to start asking around after the other players."

There's something bothering me, and I think back over the scene as we pile back into the car. Revolver made sense. Donny was kind of jumpy, but from what I've heard, that's how he gets. "It wasn't cash."

"No, it was jewelry," Vance says absently, pulling the car into gear.

"Huh? No, I mean in his safe. I thought it was foreign cash, but it wasn't. Donny had a bunch of Hawthorne scrip locked up."

"Are you sure?"

"Yeah. All the loggers get scrip instead of bonuses. I've seen enough of the stuff around Holly's place." I frown. "Why would Donny have scrip? He doesn't work for Hawthorne."

"Trade?" Vance shakes his head. "No. It's against the law to trade scrip outside of Hawthorne property. They've almost lost the permits to use it a half-dozen times; making it strictly internal is the only thing that kept the mayor from cracking down. Second currency undermining Everland's independent businesses, and so on." He taps the steering wheel thoughtfully. "So, Donny has a bunch of scrip that he can't sell, sitting in a safe in his office. Are you thinking what I'm thinking?"

"I dunno. I'm thinking that it can't have been there too long," I say. "That safe is just for daily stuff. Sometimes he leaves rings and stuff there for a couple of weeks before they go on the floor, but that's about it. He wouldn't keep anything there he didn't think he'd need."

"Which means that someone, quite recently, gave Donny a lot of scrip under the expectation that he would be returning it to them."

"Donny doesn't take things he can't sell later, though."

"Unless he could use the scrip in another way. Say, to prove that someone was involved in a blackmail scheme?" Vance's eyes twinkle and he bumps my shoulder. "You've netted us our next lead, Todd! The blackmailer is someone with access to Hawthorne scrip, someone who could round up a bunch of it without anyone asking questions. They traded it to Donny. Probably promised him a cut of the profits in exchange for getting it back."

I mumble an agreement.

"Are you busy for the next few hours? We should drive up to Hawthorne and have a look around!"

"It's Sunday, Mr. Carson. Not many folks will be there."

"The perfect time to see what we can see." Vance laughs. "Come, Todd, the game is afoot!"

Glimmer laughs and claps her hands, and I sigh ruefully. "Sounds like I'm outvoted."

"Damn right you are. Bet I can make it in a half-hour."

"Do we need to?"

But Glimmer is shouting encouragement, and Vance guns the engine into high gear, taking us towards the main road out of town.

The next thirty-five minutes are just about the longest in my life, and by the time we're getting towards our goal I'm beginning to regret taking this job. Vance treats traffic signs as suggestions; we almost crash at least three times racing out of town. Once we're on what passes for a highway, he really opens it up; this time of day, the roads are empty, and there's nothing to slow us down except wanting to live. Glimmer doesn't seem to mind; she's laughing and whooping, and that just pushes Vance to keep showing off. I settle for gripping the door hard enough that I'm afraid the handle will come right off, and when we pull into the main lot for Hawthorne Logging, I stagger out of the car and try not to look as though my life flashed before my eyes a few dozen times.

Hawthorne Logging is one of the biggest businesses on the island, with more than a thousand employees, plus the cops and politicians they pay under the table. They're the only company allowed to cut down trees, mine Everland's special metals and rocks, and generally mess with resources anywhere there isn't a treaty stopping them — and when there's a treaty in the way, workers get slipped a bit of extra cash to mess up the survey lines. They can't fudge the survey lines too often, because Hawthorne has a bunch of Piccadilly employees with a lifetime of forest experience who'd take offense, but it's done often enough that no one is surprised when a 'mistake' happens.

This time, Glimmer elects to stay with the car and 'watch it for thieves.' She's not a fan of places like Hawthorne. Neither am I, really. But as we head up to the main desk, Vance tilts his hat and looks back with a grin. "Okay, Todd. Loom behind me and back me up. I've got a plan." Before I can ask what it is, Vance pushes through the glass doors and strides into the lobby. I put on a burst of speed and follow.

Vance is already at the reception desk, wearing his most winning smile. "Hello, there. Mr. Carson, this is Mr. Malcolm, we have a one o'clock appointment with James Matheson."

The secretary at the desk is taken aback. "What? Mr. Matheson doesn't work on Sundays."

"Special meeting. You know the one." Vance beams at the receptionist, and when she blinks back at him, he lets the smile fall gradually off his face. "You do know the one, right? Oh, dear. He didn't tell you."

"Tell me what?"

"Forget I said anything. Which way to his office?"

"It's just on the second floor, but I told you! He isn't in today!"

"Right, right, of course he isn't." Vance winks at her elaborately. "We'll just see ourselves in, then, and he won't see us. If you catch my drift."

The receptionist is entirely flustered at this point, and I screw up my face as menacing as it gets and stomp past her as well. "You didn't see us," I suggest. "Mr. Matheson would prefer it that way."

"Right. Okay. Of course."

As we walk down the hall, I lean in towards Vance. "Who's Mr. Matheson?"

"No idea. Saw his name on the timekeeping sheet. Let's get to accounting and find out who checked out a bunch of scrip this week before anyone cares to ask after us."

"Great. Which way is that?"

Vance hesitates, and then turns down a side hall and waves at a janitor. "Excuse me, which way to the accounting office? We've gotten a bit turned around."

"Back that way, left, down the hall to room one-o-six."

"Thank you, sir!" Vance waves a polite thank you. As we walk, he whispers, "Chances are the accounting office will be locked, but there might be someone in there. If there is, I'll pull the old forensic accountant trick and you glare at anyone who starts arguing too loud. If not, I bet I can snag a janitor to let us in." He grins. "Ah, here we are! And the door is open. Remember, I'll charm, you glare, and ... Oh. Hello."

The accounting office is occupied. And glaring is not likely to help us out much.

"Well, hello, Todd!" Michelle Arsenault gives me a very broad, very chilly smile. "Hkuri, did you invite Todd over today?"

Hkuri sniffs at me once, and then shakes her head. "No, it was not I. Cousin, did you invite any others to this meeting?"

"No." The second tiger with Michelle and Hkuri growls the word. She is quite a bit bigger than Hkuri. She looks like she could take my head off if she wanted to. Her fur is paler, light orange and grey, and her eyes glitter as she takes us in. "Are these humans more of your *friends*?"

She packs a lot of judgement in that last word, and Hkuri clearly chooses to ignore it. "I met one of them at my last performance. He is close to my band. Todd, yes. I do not know the other. Is this a band issue, Todd? Michelle does the managing of payment, but I think if Michelle were paying you as well, she would not be surprised to see you."

My mind is blank. Of all the things I thought I might see here, this was not it. "I'm with Mr. Carson."

Vance is looking faintly panicked, but plasters on a smile and holds out a hand. "Vance Carson. Pleasure to meet you, Ms...?"

"Arsenault. Michelle Arsenault, VP of Marketing. What are you doing here, Vance Carson?" Michelle frowns. "This room is off-limits to non-employees, and I don't think I recognize you."

"The receptionist let me through," Vance says without breaking a beat. "Following up on a minor regulatory issue. We can wait until your current work is done."

"Yes. You can." The second tiger bares her fangs at us.

"Amhara! Be kind," Hkuri says.

"Kind? Kind? A sunny day, and I am spending it in this dusty room ensuring that this human does not cheat you out of your proper rewards, and now even more humans are barging in during our negotiations." Amhara growls again. "None of you should be here. We came here today *because* there would be no more of you bothering us."

"Terribly sorry, of course. Like I said, it's no trouble at all." Vance says.

Michelle is looking at the both of us with narrowed eyes. "Do I know you from somewhere, Mr. Carson?"

"It's certainly possible, plenty of places on the island," Vance starts hesitantly.

"Oh my God, you're Grover's son. The detective."

"Detective?" Amhara's nose wrinkles, and I see claws start to slide out of her dinner-plate sized paws. "This is the pirate?"

"No, no, Vance is the other one," Michelle assures her quickly. "What the hell are you doing with Todd Malcolm?"

"He's assisting me on a case," Vance says. "Look, things seem to be getting a bit out of hand."

"Are you investigating us, *detective*?" Amhara pads towards us, her ears back and her fur standing on end. "Has someone hired you to look into my cousin, perhaps? Find out what makes a tiger leave her family and waste her time among humankind?"

Hkuri is in the background, crouching down. "Amhara, please do not cause a scene."

"I will cause whatever I wish to cause," Amhara growls. "Why are you here, now?"

"Sunday afternoon," Vance admits after a moment. "Thought no one would be here."

Amhara crouches back on her heels, and for a moment, I think she's about to pounce. And then she lets out a low, rumbling chuckle. "I see." She looks back to Michelle. "All you humans think alike, hm? We are here for the quiet, and so are they. How convenient." She looks back to us. "Are they allowed here?"

"No," Michelle says. "I rather think they should leave."

"Yes, they should," Amhara says, looking back to us. "And they should count themselves lucky that we met on your territory, and not on mine. Trespassing on tiger lands bears a more serious punishment."

"Got it. We'll go. Sorry to disturb you." Vance tips his hat and steps backwards from the room.

"I am sorry as well," Hkuri mutters from behind her cousin. Amhara's ears flick, but she otherwise pretends not to notice.

We beat a hasty retreat to the car, where Glimmer is waiting curiously.

"Damn it!" Vance says, slamming his hand down on the door. "Our luck is just rotten today. What were the chances we'd barge into the middle of a negotiation with a couple of tigers? Why were there even tigers there right now?"

"Michelle's covering Hkuri's singing career," I say.

"What does that have to do with Hawthorne money? Couldn't they have met in their own place?"

"Yeah, that's kind of weird," I agree. "Maybe Hkuri's contract is part of some bigger deal between Hawthorne and the tigers? Hawthorne's never made much headway with them before."

"I guess." Vance drums his fingers on the side of the car. "Well, we're torn, anyway. No chance of getting back inside with a higher-up knowing our names and faces. They'll have us on the list at the front door.

"Yeah. Damn."

"Well, hop in, and I'll drop you off at your place on the way back into town. I'll think about what the next avenue of investigation is, and let you know." He shakes his head. "Damn it, and Hawthorne seemed like such a good lead, too. What are the odds."

I nod glumly, and the three of us ride back into town in silence. When we reach my place, Vance reaches into his wallet and pulls out a few bills. "Here you go, Todd. Twelve dollars, as promised."

"I didn't work the full day," I protest.

"Then I'll grab an evening from you later in the week," Vance says with a grin. "Oh, and Glimmer." He folds another bill and passes it over to her. "I hope you'll be okay with ten; it's all I've got on me since I didn't know I was getting the extra help."

Glimmer blinks, and gestures to the bill, asking a question. I start to translate, and Vance holds up a hand. "Pretty sure I got that one. And you went into danger for me, and saved me from trouble with Donner. I'd say you made the team."

Glimmer takes the bill cautiously. She then grins, salutes, and flies up to sit on the stoop.

"You take care, both of you," Vance says. "I'll let you know when I have more work for you."

"Sounds good, Mr. Carson," I say. "Good luck."

"Thank you, Todd, but I make my own luck!" With that, Vance roars away from the curb, and I shake my head. Glimmer nudges me and says he's pretty wild.

"Yeah, he's a wild one. And I like him too. Come on, I'll get you some supper before we swing by Holly's to drop you off."

Glimmer gives me a thumbs-up, and we head into my apartment.

# Monday, August 20<sup>th</sup>

**Mondays are usually** a day off for musicians and bands; right after the weekend, there are not a lot of live shows. The gang has gotten into the habit of stopping in at Jessie's for brunch, and since I've got Vance's pay in my pocket, I figure I'll do what I told Emeka I would and tag along. As usual, I'm the last one to arrive, and there's already a cup of coffee waiting for me.

"Hey, Todd. You made the news! Congrats." Marta slides over to make room for me in the booth, leaving her newspaper for me to look at. Holly and Emeka are across from us, a pair of steaming coffees in front of them.

I look at the newspaper. It's from Saturday, when the arson was still front-page stuff. There's a photo of the kid who died, a heartfelt passage about how he snuck away from his family to go drinking because they didn't approve, and he thought he was an adult. It goes on to say that one of the rescuers at the scene assaulted a suspected arsonist and was taken into custody. They've got my name, which is just great, but there's no picture of me, and at least it doesn't say I am the suspected arsonist.

"Great. My reputation keeps growing." I pass the paper back to Marta, and quickly give my food order to a passing waitstaff.

"Cops still on your back?"

"Haven't heard from them since they let me go. Figure it depends on if that guy presses charges."

"He won't," Marta says confidently. "Either he's the arsonist, in which case he doesn't want to be in court stirring things up, or he was trying to sneak off unnoticed, in which case he doesn't want to be in court stirring things up. Trust me, you're in the clear."

"What makes you so sure?" Emeka asks.

"Do you know how often I've had to punch out a rich kid from the Hill who gets a bit handsy?" Marta laughs. "I don't keep count, man, and none of them want the story getting back to their parents. This is the same thing, but higher stakes."

"Good point." Holly leans back and takes a sip of coffee. "So, you're in a tiger band?"

"We're in a tiger band," Marta says with a grin.

"Why didn't you say so? I can't believe I missed it."

"It was a test, and you failed." Marta waves her hand. "S'what you get for being busy with your own cool stuff."

Holly puffs out her cheeks.

"Seriously, though," Marta says, "We were under strict instructions to keep it quiet. Michelle is a real taskmaster. It must have been wild knowing her back in the day, Emeka."

"She's changed," Emeka says. "But if I'm being honest, she hasn't changed that much. Hkuri's nice, though. Might have a real career ahead of her, even outside of the novelty factor."

"You should have brought her out today," Holly says. "I'd really like to meet her. There are so few tigers that like hanging out with people."

"Yeah, from what Hkuri's said, they're pretty solitary compared to us. She's one of the most social tigers she knows, and she still burns out on people after an hour or two." Marta smiles. "We did invite her today, but she wasn't up for it."

"I ran into her cousin yesterday," I say. "She sure seemed a lot angrier."

Emeka almost drops his fork. "Oh crap, you met Amhara? Are you okay?"

"I'm fine. She was a bit growly, but it's not like she threatened me or anything." I consider. "I mean, directly."

"I've only met her twice, and both times I got the feeling she'd as soon eat me as talk to me." Marta shivers. "Where did *you* run into her?"

"Up at Hawthorne. It's a long story."

"Oh, yeah, how's working with Vance going?" Holly asks.

"Fine, I guess. He's got his own style."

"Well, that sounds ominous."

"I can't really talk about the case we're working on. Sorry."

"But it's keeping food on the table?" Emeka asks.

"It's bringing food to this table, anyway. Between that and my other bouncing jobs, I should be okay." My other jobs all pretty much involve covering for people on the odd sick day, so they're not very steady, but they pay alright when I'm there.

"Good," Marta says. "Because I was going to say I knew people down at the docks, and that's bad work and you'd hate it."

"Look, Amhara is probably fine. But I'd stay away from her if I was you." Emeka pokes at his food. "Let Michelle handle her."

Marta raises an eyebrow. "Just how bad is she?"

Emeka shakes his head. "Amhara makes me nervous, and she is not happy about Hkuri wanting to sing with us. That's it. Let's change the subject."

My food arrives, and we settle into a conversation about the band's new musical style. Holly is still pouting about not getting to meet Hkuri, so she's less talkative than usual. Marta more than makes up for it with all her gossip about tiger culture. Seems that she and Hkuri have been hitting it off, even if she hasn't been making progress with Michelle. For his part, Emeka is a bit quieter than usual. When we're getting our things to go, I tap him on the shoulder. "You alright?"

"Hm? Yeah. Fine." Emeka gives me a tired smile. "Just got thrown by the two halves of my life bouncing into each other."

"Don't worry, I can handle myself. Not planning on starting any fights with tigers. I know my weight class."

"I'm not worried."

I give Emeka a look, and he chuckles ruefully. "Okay. I am worried. But you're right, you've been in some real scrapes. I think it just feels like a lot is happening all of a sudden. My new gig, the fire, your new gig, and now this."

"It really wasn't that bad. Amhara growled a bit, told us to go away, we went away."

"What were you even doing up there?" Holly asks, coming up between us and tossing an arm over each of our shoulders. It's a bit of a reach, and I end up half-carrying her.

"I told you, Holly, it's confidential."

"Maybe part of it isn't? Maybe I am a source." Holly waggles her eyebrows. "I'm a pretty good source."

"You might as well tell her what you can, she's not going to give in," Emeka says.

I lean in a bit. Holly's gossipy, but she can keep a secret if it's important, and she's right — she knows people. "We're looking for someone who got a lot of Hawthorne scrip together in the last few days."

Holly blinks. "Why?"

"I definitely can't tell you that. But someone took a bunch of it and traded it off-site."

"Oof, that's pretty illegal." Holly lets go of me, dropping back to the ground, and rubs her chin. "Hawthorne tracks scrip pretty closely. You can't just withdraw it from the store, it's cash, and you can't hold onto it that long, because it expires. You can go in and trade old scrip for new, but that gets tracked, too." Emeka is staring at her, and she shrugs. "About half the Piccadilly work for Hawthorne. You get to hear a *lot* of complaints about the scrip system. It's fake money set up so that they don't have to pay real bonuses."

I think about that. "Can you steal scrip from the back?"

"Nope. I mean, you could, if you were an accountant, but it would be worthless. You need to log it as being checked out, and for what? When it gets spent, you need to log who's spending it. If someone tried to spend stolen scrip they'd be caught pretty much instantly."

Emeka's frown is a lot bigger, now. "That's a hell of a system."

"Yeah, it's a real laugh riot." Holly shakes her head.

"Holly, could you get Vance and me up to chat with the loggers? This could actually be a lead."

Holly nods. "Let me make a couple calls. If Vance is available, you could probably go up this afternoon."

"You're the greatest, Holly!" I look over to Emeka and Marta. "Duty calls."

"Have fun." Marta scoops up her newspaper as she stands up. "A whole day out in the woods. Sounds a lot nicer than mucking around an old studio all day."

"Let me know when the next show is," Holly says.

"Damn right we will, and you had better show up," Marta shoots back.

I step outside while Holly makes her calls, my head spinning. Ten minutes ago, it seemed like the case was at a dead end, and now we had a lead. Was this how Mr. Stark felt all the time?

"Okay, you're set." Holly joins me at the door and flashes a thumbs-up. "Camp number two, just up on the west side. You're looking for Heron, he'll show you around. If Vance isn't available, call and let Heron know, it won't be a problem."

"Thanks, Holly."

"Hey, what are sources for?" Holly grins. "I'm going to bounce. Need to get back to the office and cover the phones. Say, what's Vance's secretary like?"

"He doesn't have one."

Holly stops, and turns to look at me. "Wait, seriously? Who answers the phones?"

"Vance."

"Who answers the phones when Vance is out investigating?"

"I don't think he takes more than one case at a time, so ... nobody?" I think about it. "Who handled the phones for Mr. Stark before you?"

"Oh, he went through secretaries at a pretty good clip. Someone would stick around for a few months, and then there'd be a shooting or a murder threat or mobsters would drop fractal scorpions through the window, and they'd quit. I think I'm the first one to stick around more than half a year." Holly shakes her head. "But I'm surprised Vance doesn't have one. He can afford it. You should ask him about it."

"Should I?"

"You are the least curious detective in the world, Todd Malcolm."

"I'm not a detective! I'm hired muscle."

"Sure, sure. Have fun muscling the logging camp." Holly winks and takes off.

I head to a payphone to give Vance a call. He picks up right away, and I explain the situation.

"Todd, that is amazing. Yes, I can clear my schedule for the afternoon!" Vance sounds over the moon. "Where are you at? I can swing by and pick you up."

I give Holly a thumbs-up, and answer. "Sure thing, Mr. Carson. I'm just on the corner by Jessie's. You know it?"

"The diner?"

"That's the place."

"Perfect. See you shortly."

Vance shows up a few minutes later. I get into the car gingerly, getting myself ready, and he predictably takes off at full speed. "So, you found a lead already! Maybe you should be the detective and I should be the assistant."

I chuckle politely. "Just got lucky. Holly knows some loggers, and they're willing to chat with us. Might be nothing."

"Every lead might be nothing, Todd. That's the nature of the game. But this sounds hopeful. If anyone would know who's gathering scrip, it's the people who are most often paid in it."

We roar up the highway towards the woods. An hour later, we're pulling into the makeshift lot of Camp #2, and the administrator sends someone to get Heron.

"You guys made some real speed getting up here. Must be important!" Heron is a big guy, just about as big as me, with long, thin scars on his arms and a tidy ponytail.

Vance gives him a firm handshake and a big smile. "Well, we certainly hope so, Mr. Heron. We're looking into scrip."

Heron grimaces at the mention of scrip. "Heard that. Might have something for you, depending. What's going on with it? Someone actually trying to stop it?"

"That's outside my power, I'm afraid. But there's a chance that it could be a bit of an embarrassment for Hawthorne if it gets out."

"Not too bad if the higher-ups get a bit embarrassed," Heron says. "Come on, let's go somewhere a bit quieter and I'll tell you all about it."

As we're walking, I notice that we've picked up a couple of followers. A pair of fairies are flitting through the air above us. "You get a lot of fairies out here?"

Heron glances up at the two, and then shrugs. "Sure. Woods are neutral territory. No Regulators up here causing trouble. We have to be careful when we're cutting, make sure we don't accidentally hit a nest. Sometimes we hire them to get animals out of the way, too. Always curious about newcomers."

"Hm. Maybe they spotted something," Vance suggests.

"If so, wouldn't matter. They don't bother remembering things that aren't important to them." Heron leads the way to one of the smaller cabins, and lets us in. "You hungry?"

"Already ate. But don't let us stop you."

"Wasn't planning to." Heron pulls out a battered lunch box and takes out a sandwich. "Holly's call got me thinking; usually, you can't get rid of scrip. Everyone knows it's not worth much, whatever Hawthorne wants to print on it. They may say a dollar is worth a dollar scrip, but the company store doesn't have much that's good, and what it does have costs twice what you'd pay at a shop in town. But last weekend, one of the office folk offered to buy my scrip off me at face value. Said she needed to balance an accounting error."

"That's weird," I say.

"Yeah."

"Did you do it?" Vance asks.

"Of course. Thing is, I checked with a few of the other guys. Two of 'em said that they got the same offer. Wondering if a lot of folks did."

"If you can't steal scrip from the office, buy it from the loggers." Vance rubs his chin. "Very interesting. Any idea how much she got together?"

"Nah. Too many people she might've talked to. But she got almost twenty bucks just off the three of us." Scrip is usually in pretty small amounts. The bundle that Donnie had might not have been more than fifty or a hundred dollars.

"Thanks, Heron," Vance says. "What's this worker's name? Maybe we should chat with her."

"Phyllis Graves. She's not in today, though. Works the weekend shift, Wednesday through Sunday."

"What's she like?"

"Don't know her that well, tell you the truth. Handles payments at the end of the day, doesn't spend a lot of time chatting with the boys.

"Thank you anyway. It's a definite lead."

"This isn't going to get us in trouble, is it?"

"Not from us," Vance assures him. "We won't tell a soul." He pulls out his wallet. "Can I get you anything for your time?"

"Don't worry about it." Heron waves the wallet down. "Friends of Holly are friends of mine."

We leave Heron and start back towards the car. I'm expecting Vance to be excited, but he's looking glum. "What's up?"

"Timeline. The client didn't go gambling until Monday."

"So, why was Graves already getting things together on the weekend?"

"Exactly. She couldn't have known Drainie would lose, or that he'd put up his jewelry as collateral. And if she had cash, why not just give that to Donner?"

I frown. "Maybe she knew someone at the bar. If Drainie was going day after day, she must have known he'd be short."

"And that he would lose? And that Donner would be around?"

"Donny's always around. If he's got a deal with the bar, he'd be the one to talk to."

Vance nods slowly. "Could be. Especially if Graves has connections."

Those two fairies are sitting on the hood of the car as we get back, and I pause to pull some of the sugared crackers I keep for Glimmer out of my pocket. "Hey, guys, any chance we could chat with you?"

One fairy takes off immediately, vanishing into the woods. The other one hops into the air and flies forward. She's about Glimmer's height, reedy, with curly blonde hair, wearing a tanned leather jacket and pants. She looks suspiciously at my cracker, and then up at me, and asks what I want.

"I'm Todd. What do you go by?"

She says I can call her Fletcher, and asks a second time what I want, even less politely.

"Seems like you keep an eye on this place. You see anyone around that shouldn't be here?"

She laughs derisively and snatches the cracker out of my hands, then points at the two of us.

"Okay, fair. Anyone else? Maybe someone trying to trade with the loggers?"

The fairy takes a bite of the cracker, and then tells me that fairies don't care about trading, and I should just go home. Spinning, she takes off, still laughing.

"What were you hoping for?" Vance asks.

"I dunno. Just thought that fairies see a lot and people don't pay them much attention. If someone was gathering scrip, maybe they'd be spotted."

Vance thinks about that for a moment, and then nods.

"So, what's the plan now? Wait until Wednesday and try to shake down Graves?"

"Too long a timeline. Drainie needs to do the drop-off tomorrow night. If we don't have something solid by then, I'll have to shift to helping him make the payment."

I stop and turn. "Tomorrow night? You didn't say anything!"

"Didn't want you to worry. But I have a plan. We'll look up Graves' address and go talk to her in person. Simplicity itself." Vance hops into the car. "Come on, daylight's burning."

I clamber in again and close my eyes as we take off down the road.

"Everything okay?"

I do not open my eyes. "I'm fine, Mr. Carson."

"I told you, Todd, you can call me Vance! What's wrong?"

"It's just a bit fast, is all. I don't drive much."

"Oh, come on, I can get a lot faster than this." There is a roar as the engine kicks in, and my eyes snap open to see trees whipping past us on either side. I swallow and try not to think about what impact at this speed would feel like. Vance grins over at me, but his smile fades as he takes in my expression. "Oh, hell, I'm sorry. Was just enjoying a chance to let loose."

I take a deep breath. "It's not a problem."

"No, it was rude." There is a brief pause, and when Vance speaks again, his voice is quieter. "Todd?"

"Yeah?"

"The brakes are out."

My eyes bug out. "What?!"

Vance is stamping his foot on the pedal. "They were working fine a few moments ago, and then something just gave!"

"Parking brake?"

"Not at this speed, we'd spin out!" Vance slams his foot on the pedal a few more times. "The road's pretty straight. I can cut the gas, glide us a bit."

"Uh, Vance?"

We're coming around the corner, going way too fast, and there's a fallen tree in the road up ahead. Vance stares at it, frozen. I reach over, grab the parking brake, and pull it halfway. Spinning out sounds bad, but not as bad as hitting a giant log at forty miles an hour.

The car starts to slow down, but it's not enough. I look frantically at the sides of the road, and yell, "Left!"

Vance snaps out of it. He follows my pointing finger, and spins the wheel; there's a small side path that looks pretty overgrown, but it's better than nothing. We slam through a couple of bushes, bounce over a hill, and into a small clearing. Vance pulls the emergency brake the rest of the way and puts the car into a spin, we tear up the ground, and then we roll into a tree with a quiet crunching sound.

For a few seconds, we both just sit there, breathing heavily. Vance asks, "Are you alright?"

"Dizzy," I say. "A little sick." I rub my forehead, and my hand comes away a bit bloody. "I think I got a couple of branches. It's not too bad. You?"

Vance checks himself. "I seem to be alright. Thank you for spotting the path. That's two I owe you."

"What the hell happened?"

"Something went wrong with the brakes," Vance said. "I shouldn't have been grandstanding."

I clamber out of the car. "So, what do we do?"

"Are you any good at mechanics?"

"Nah. You?"

"Nope." Vance forces his door open. "We'll have to walk back to the camp and get a mechanic down here. Damn, so much for being quick. Well, maybe we can put in a call and get someone to cover Graves' house until we get into town."

It takes us about half an hour to get back to the logging camp, and when we arrive, we're told that there's no direct phone line. We can radio Hawthorne and have them patch us through to the phone system, but if we do that everyone will know that Phyllis Graves is next on our list, and Vance isn't willing to do that.

We forgo the phone call and get a mechanic and a couple of loggers to come back to the clearing with us, prop the car up, and have a look at whether it can get running on the spot.

After a short inspection, the mechanic pulls herself out from underneath the car and shakes her head. "Going to have to tow it. Brake line is cut."

"Deliberately?" Vance asks.

The mechanic considers. "Can't see how. Looks more like a rock or something got up in there. Probably got caught on something on your way up, and then the fluid leaked out while you were sitting around. Happens from time to time, especially with these city cars."

Vance taps his chin. "Can we get a ride into town, then? Time is of the essence."

"We can get you onto the afternoon truck. There's room for a couple of passengers. Be another hour or so."

"It'll have to do." Vance pulls me aside. "I just hope Graves is still there when we get into town."

"You think someone did this on purpose?"

"Of course I do!" Vance waves a hand for emphasis. "We come up here, get a clear lead on the blackmailer, and someone cuts the brake line? It can't be a coincidence. Someone wants us delayed, or dead."

I frown. "No one was there when we were talking to Heron, though. They would have had to know what we were up to right away."

"Maybe Graves has an accomplice in the camp."

Vance is so excited at the idea of being in the thick of it all, I don't have the heart to say I'm pretty sure that the mechanic is right; we were roaring up a logging road at way past the speed limit, we probably hit a rock that skipped into the line, lost fluid slowly, and Vance didn't notice because he barely touches the brakes.

But Vance is clearly imagining breaking a big conspiracy, and he spends the whole time we're waiting for the truck back at camp speculating on who might have done it. He gets me to the point that I'm getting a bit suspicious myself.

I spot Heron and take him aside. "Hey, did you see anyone when we were talking?"

Heron's brow wrinkles. "No, I don't think so. Why?"

"Vance has this idea that the brakes were cut on purpose."

Heron snorts. "Course he does. Look, I know every logger here. Even if someone heard us talking about Graves, no one's going to do a murder over it. And frankly, it could have been a murder if you'd hit that tree."

"That tree wasn't in the road on the way up, though."

Heron shakes his head. "Lot of dead wood around here, especially on a windy day like this. We have a whole team that just goes ahead of the trucks to make sure the road is clear at the end of the day. No matter how clear it is, never stays that way." He smiles. "You just went through a lot. Reasonable to be looking for trouble. If it makes you feel any better, I'll go out with a couple of the boys and make sure that the tree wasn't cut. But trust me, it was just a bit of bad luck."

I thank Heron, and he goes off to arrange the check-in. When I get back to Vance he's bouncing on his toes.

"Ah, Todd! The truck has arrived, and we are ready to go. We'll be back in town before dinner. I just hope Graves hasn't made a run for it or disposed of the evidence."

"We don't actually know that she's our perp," I point out.

"It seems pretty open and shut. I'm confident that when we confront her, we'll learn everything." Vance grins. "We have this case in the bag, Todd!"

Vance keeps his enthusiasm up the whole trip back to town. He's tucked into the back seat; I offered, but I didn't fit, so I got the front passenger seat. Having someone else in the truck means that Vance can't really talk about the case, so instead, he peppers the driver with questions about his life, his job, and what the woods are like. He mostly gets one-word answers, but the driver's too polite to tell Vance to get bent.

We get dropped off at the lumber yard a little after six, and Vance goes over to the closest payphone and looks up Graves' address in the tattered directory. "Got her," he announces happily. "104-782 Spruce. Flag a taxi, and we can be there in ten minutes."

"Do we have a plan for when we get there?"

"Confront her with the evidence, threaten her, get the jewelry and any photos she took," Vance says.

I chew on that, and then ask, "And if she says, 'get out'? We can't call the cops on her if we want to keep things quiet."

"Well, we can ... hm." Vance muses for a moment. "I will threaten her with extralegal consequences. As much as we don't want to go to the police, neither does she, and the two of us cut quite imposing figures. And there are crimes we could implicate her in aside from the blackmail itself. Cutting the brakes, selling scrip to Donny. Quite a list is building up."

"Okay." This doesn't feel right, but he's the detective.

Vance flags a cab down and directs us to the address. It's one of the nicer apartment blocks north of the Hill. Brownstones again, but nicer than the one I live in or where Mr. Stark's office is. Most of the folks who live here work up at Hawthorne, down at Second Star, or directly for the city. It's not a good place to get into a fight, and it's not a place that I spend a lot of time.

Vance strolls along like he's right at home. As we step through the door, he tips his hat to the doorman and says, "Unit one-o-four, we're seeing Phyllis. She's in, isn't she?"

The doorman is a young guy, can't be more than twenty, and he nods before he thinks not to. "I need to call over—" he starts. Vance is already past him and walking down the hall. "I didn't get your name!" the doorman calls after him. He looks over to me.

"I'm with him," I say, and follow Vance before the kid can try to start something. My expression convinces him not to follow us, but I hear him pick up a phone as I storm down the hall. "Vance, he's calling ahead."

"No problem. We're not hiding." Vance raps sharply on the door. "Ms. Graves! The jig is up!"

I look at him. "These places have back windows."

"She's not going to run away now, Todd. What good would that do her?"

We hear the scrape of a window opening inside the apartment. I turn and sprint outside in time to see a lady drop into the azaleas. She takes off down the street, short a shoe.

"Ms. Graves, we just want to talk to you!" I shout after her. Some heads are turning as I break into a sprint of my own. I'm tired, but I've got good shoes and leg length, and she's not used to running. Instead of going for a jog, she pushes too hard, and slows down gasping ten seconds in.

I'm about to reach out and grab her when I notice the people staring. A guy starts towards us. "Hey, what do you think you're doing?" he shouts.

"Just talking," I say, holding my hands up.

"Damn right," Phyllis has been fumbling in her purse, and she comes out with a pistol. "Get the hell away from me."

"Woah, okay." I take a step back. The would-be rescuer does the same thing.

"Todd, did you catch her?" Vance is racing up behind me. He stops dead when he sees the gun. "Evening, ma'am."

Phyllis turns to point the gun at him, and then back at me. "You all stay away! Who are you?"

Vance very carefully reaches into his coat. "I'm not armed," he says, as the gun swings back towards him. "Vance Carson. I'm a private investigator."

Phyllis stares at him a moment, and then the gun sags. "Oh."

"It's not gonna be good if you shoot someone, Phyllis," I say. "You're in a heck of a lot of trouble already."

Phyllis stares at both of us, tears welling in her eyes, and lowers the gun. "It wasn't supposed to be like this."

Vance takes a few steps towards Phyllis. I take a step back towards the would-be rescuer. "Look," I say quietly, "it's nice that you're worried, but this is under control."

He nods and hurries off. Vance has taken the gun out of Phyllis's hand and is gently steering her back towards her building. "Come on," he's saying. "Let's just talk about it."

By the time we get back to the building, the doorman is standing there. "I've called the police!" he exclaims, pointing a finger at us shakily. "You'd better let her go and get out of here!"

Vance winces. "Do we need the police, Ms. Graves?" he asks.

"It doesn't matter," she says hollowly. "Let's just get it over with."

"Ms. Graves?" the doorman asks.

Phyllis breaks down crying. "I just needed the money so badly."

Vance's eyes are wide. "Ms. Graves..." he starts helplessly.

"It started small. I was just borrowing against my bonus, helping my family. But we didn't hit our targets this year, and the bonus was too small, and I couldn't get the money back in the account. The audit was coming up and I was going to lose my job."

I step over to the doorman. "Get her a glass of something, huh? Something strong."

He looks past me at Phyllis and Vance. "What the heck is going on?"

"Private investigators."

"Oh my god, is that Basil Stark?" The doorman's eyes go wide. "He looks younger than I imagined!"

I really hope Vance didn't hear that. "That's Vance Carson."

"Who?"

"Just get some damn brandy or something, would you?"

I go back to Vance and Phyllis. They're sitting on the bench in the lobby. I can hear a siren in the distance. "We don't have a lot of time. Ms. Graves, if the police arrive and find that jewelry, you and your mark are both in a lot of trouble."

She nods, still sobbing, and hands me a set of keys. "They're under the bed. I thought it would be easy for him to get the money. Another rich boy playing with his parents' estate, why not? No one was supposed to get hurt! But then I found out you were asking around, and I asked for help, and..."

"You had someone at the camp cut our brake line," Vance says.

"I didn't mean for them to go that far! I just asked them to slow you down!" Phyllis says. "They wanted to protect me."

"Who was it?"

She shakes her head.

While Vance tries to keep up the conversation, I head into her place. For someone who was embezzling money, it's pretty low rent. Not much furniture, not much art, a few books on the shelves, and a half-full closet. I check under the bed, and there's an old shoebox right where I'd expect. There's nothing inside but the jewels. I stash it all in my jacket and head back outside.

Outside, Vance hasn't made any more headway with Phyllis, but she's calmed down, now that the worst is past, and is dabbing away her tears. "I won't tell them about the gambling," she says, "if you don't go looking for my friend. You do, and I'll tell everyone. That's all you care about, right? His precious reputation?"

Vance nods reluctantly. "Alright, Ms. Graves. You have yourself a deal."

A patrol car is pulling up outside. Phyllis stands up, still shaky, and gives him a nod. "Well, then. I suppose we had better talk to the police."

"Maybe you can handle the embezzlement privately with Hawthorne? If there's no blackmail, there's no crime."

Phyllis shakes her head. "No. It's gone too far. I know what I did, even if I'm not going to tell anyone. If it ends here, I turn myself in, maybe it won't be so bad. Better the cops than—" She breaks off and gives us both a sad look. "You promise."

"We promise," Vance agrees. "The case ends here."

The police arrive, ready to deal with dangerous toughs, and are caught off-guard by a middle-aged lady marching up to them to turn herself in for embezzlement and unlawful possession of a firearm. They hold us for a solid hour while they call it in, take statements, and try to figure out just what the hell is going on.

I'm going through my story again, which is mainly just repeating variations on "that's confidential, talk to Vance," when a familiar figure steps through the door.

"Mister Malcolm," Agent Harper drawls, looking me up and down. "You don't do a very good job of staying out of trouble."

"I'm not the one under arrest here."

"Yet." Harper looks around. "Carrying on an investigation, are you? I thought I warned you."

"To stay out of the arson thing. I did. I'm doing this instead." I frown. "Why are you here?"

"Odd situations are sent in my direction. Especially when your name comes up." Harper takes a step forward. "Why are you meddling in Hawthorne's internal affairs?"

"Well, I lost my job because I got stuck cooling my heels in your cell, and Mr. Carson was hiring," I snap.

"Of course." Harper's lip curls, and he looks over at Vance Carson. "You have a knack for attaching yourself to private detectives, Mister Malcolm. I might suggest that you leave well enough alone."

"I might suggest that you—" I start, and then Vance is stepping up between us, putting a hand on my shoulder.

"You must be Agent Harper," he says smoothly, holding out a hand. "Vance Carson. My father mentioned that you were in town, and I was certainly hoping to meet you. Always wanted to meet a proper FBI agent."

Harper's sneer melts away like mist and is replaced by an ingratiating smile; he gives Vance a firm handshake. "Ah, yes, Mr. Carson. Your father mentioned you, as well.

Everland's finest detective, I understand. We owe you a debt of gratitude for capturing this dangerous criminal."

"Oh, I don't think Ms. Graves is particularly dangerous," Vance says. "Just a woman who made a few bad decisions."

"Well, you certainly have a good heart, given that I understand she pulled a gun on you."

Vance shrugs. "She didn't fire it."

Harper chuckles. "Quite true. Still, Hawthorne is a very important business when it comes to American interests. I suspect that when we find out how she was able to acquire access to the funds unnoticed, it will provide a lead in some other cases that I'm working on. I'm very glad that you were able to find her for us." He tips his hat to Vance. "If you're willing to sign a statement that you found Ms. Graves as part of a confidential investigation, and that your investigation is now complete, I can't imagine that we'll need to detain you any longer."

"Of course, Agent Harper. Anything to help."

Harper snaps his fingers, and an officer shows up with some paper and a pen. Vance scribbles down his statement and signs it with a flourish. "Is there anything else that my assistant and I can do?"

"No. No, I think we're done here." Harper gives me one last suspicious look, then turns his smile back to Vance. "Give my regards to your father, and congratulations on a successful case."

"Well, thank you, Agent Harper. If you need anything else, anything at all, just let me know."

Harper turns and walks out the door. I watch him with narrowed eyes, but it looks like he's actually telling the truth. The police leave us alone as they gather up Ms. Graves and go to check out her apartment.

"I do not like him," Vance says.

"Don't think he figured that out."

"It's not a good idea to let the authorities know you don't care for them," Vance says, collecting his hat and jacket. "But I'll tell you one thing: there's not a chance in hell that my father told him I was a detective, let alone a great one. He'd bite his own tongue off first."

"So, you think this is really over?"

"I suppose it is." Vance sighs heavily. "Poor Ms. Graves. Not the grand confrontation I was hoping for, I can tell you that, but with any luck, she'll get off easy, and I can report back to Drainie with the jewels." He chuckles. "I suppose we'll never know who cut the brakes, though."

"Seems like a bigger deal than the money," I point out.

"Maybe, but protective people make mistakes. They can't have known that I'm prone to aggressive driving, and a more cautious driver in those woods wouldn't have been in danger of more than a bump on the head, tree or no tree." Vance smiles. "Cheer up, Todd! We closed a case, and solidly. And this was a full day's work." He takes another twelve dollars out of his wallet.

"I still owe you a half-day," I point out.

"Closing bonus. Trust me, I'll make it back from Drainie." Vance presses the money into my hand. "You earned every dollar and more. Next case I'm on that could use another body, I will give you a call."

I take the money, and stuff it into my pocket. If Vance thinks I'm worth it, I'm not going to argue. But as I head off, I can't help but feel like a lot of this doesn't hang together. We still don't know how Ms. Graves knew Drainie was going to lose that night. We don't know who cut the brakes. And I'm pretty suspicious about Agent Harper showing up, just because it was a 'weird case.'

It's not too late, but I'm exhausted and I'm starving. I stop at a hot dog stand, grab a bite, and then head straight home. The whole time that I'm eating, the problem is rattling around my head. Is it a problem? Everything worked out exactly how Vance expected it to. Even the brake lines turned out to be cut, which means that either Ms. Graves called the camp while we were up there or someone at the camp called her, and we still have no idea who they were.

I feel like I've got something there, but I can't tell what that something is, and by the time I'm done showering my brain is mush and there's no point trying to push any more. It's only 8:30, but the sun's gone down and I'm done. I stagger into my room, pull on my pajamas in the dark, and fall face-first into my bed, only to find something papery between me and my pillow.

Frowning, I reach over and tug on my lamp cord, grabbing the thing I'd hit. It's a big manila envelope, sealed but unmarked. It's pretty crumpled up now that I've smashed my face into it, but there's no sign that there was anything next to it.

I sit up, eyes narrowed. I have a pretty good idea of what I'm going to see when I open it up, and I'm right. It looks like the case isn't over after all.

# Tuesday, August 21<sup>st</sup>

"**You assaulted an** upstanding member of society. We have the ability to make him press charges, or to make this problem go away. Do the right thing. Convince Basil Stark to stop prying into things that are none of his affair, or face the consequences. Do not tell anyone about this note." Mr. Stark looks down at the piece of paper in his hands "Well. They've certainly decided to escalate the situation, haven't they?"

We're all gathered around Holly's desk in Mr. Stark's office, with the offending piece of paper between us; it's still a bit crumpled from when I used it as a pillow. The note came with a few photos of me charging at that guy at the bar, taken from what looks like the opposite rooftop. It seems like kind of a waste of effort, since I already got pulled in for punching him and no one's really doubting it, but if the goal is to rattle me, then they're doing a great job. "What the heck is going on?" I ask Basil. "What are you looking into?"

"Blackmail," Mr. Stark says grimly. He grabs his tea and stares at it.

"You still haven't closed the blackmail case?" Holly asked.

"Oh, I closed it. But in the process, I found two more. The blackmail I was investigating was used to gain access to higher-profile targets to blackmail in turn."

Holly shakes her head. "That seems needlessly complicated."

"On the one hand, yes. On the other, it's doing wonders, so maybe we shouldn't make fun." Mr. Stark reaches into his pocket, pulls out a small hip flask, and pours a bit into his drink. Holly makes a face, which Basil ignores while he stirs the tea. "If you can't build a powerbase on loyalty, do it on fear. If this person can get enough people to owe them, they can parlay that into wealth, power, and control, and none of their victims dare to go to the police. It's insidious."

"So, it's not just about money?" I ask.

"No, it doesn't seem so. One of the people that I spoke to revealed that they committed one crime to gather the money they needed to pay off the initial blackmail, but they were found out, and forced to gather further blackmail material. There wasn't any proof it was the same blackmailer, but…"

"But that's a lot of blackmail." I think about Phyllis Graves.

"Exactly. Now, I need you to think back, Todd. Was your door locked when you came home last night?"

"Definitely. Would have noticed if it wasn't."

"The windows?"

"Closed and latched. I checked."

"So, whomever gained access to your apartment either had a key, was an accomplished lockpick who locked the door behind them as they left, or knows some kind of magic trick to get through walls. Which begs the question of why not slip the package through the mail slot."

"Trying to scare me?" I suggest. "I mean, if they can get in while I'm out, they can get in while I'm asleep."

Basil nods. "They've done similar tricks to others, and the whole operation seems needlessly dramatic, so that fits. None of the cases I've investigated involved photos or messages delivered through the mail. No one has ever seen the people taking photos, and while I caught one person expecting payment it was someone who was being blackmailed into receiving it. I'm not sure anyone is actually collecting money for the source."

"Okay. So, we don't know who's doing this, we don't know who's in their pocket, and we don't know what they really want. What do we do now?" I ask.

"*We* are not going to do anything. *I* am going to continue investigating, but I'm going to have to do it more carefully." Basil drums his fingers. "I'll have to go outside of my usual circle of informants, unfortunately. Too much risk that they're being watched. But I have other options."

Holly and I exchange glances. When Mr. Stark starts talking about other options, it usually means bad news. "Is that a good idea?" Holly asks tentatively.

"Not really, but it's the only one I've got." Mr. Stark drains his tea and stands, grabbing his coat off the rack.

"You want some muscle?"

"Absolutely not." Mr. Stark looks back at me. "Everything that I said about blackmailers before is doubly true now. At the best of times, blackmailers are dangerously unpredictable. This conspiracy seems to combine the worst aspects of that with the threat of organized crime, and that takes this to a whole new level."

"We fought shadow assassins last year," Holly says.

"If I'd known where that case was going when it started, I would have kept you out of that one, too. And this time, Todd, you are already a target. Stay here, stay quiet, and stay out of the line of fire. No more detective work for the time being. The last thing that we want is our mysterious organization deciding that you're ignoring their warnings and coming after them."

I frown. "Aw, come on."

"No!" Basil turns to point a finger at Holly. "That goes for you, too. We're not just dealing with a blackmailer; we're dealing with a whole group that moves like ghosts and may be willing to kill."

"Oh, hey, what if they *are* ghosts?" Holly asks. "Ghosts can walk through walls."

Basil frowns. "Ghosts don't organize, Holly. They just float around and moan until someone puts them to rest."

"Hear me out. What if we're dealing with some kind of necromancer? Like, what if some criminal knows how to compel ghosts to do tasks for them. Or what if someone found the technology to unstitch shadows again."

"It's not ghosts. It's not shadows. But if it makes you feel better, put a few salt lines down. It can't hurt." Basil looks over. "Glimmer, make sure these two stay out of trouble."

"Uncle Basil!"

"Covering all of my bases, Holly. Have a good day. I'll be back this evening."

Holly picks up Basil's empty teacup and looks about ready to throw it. Mr. Stark closes the door before she can, and we hear him moving down the hall.

"If you throw it now, you're just going to have to clean it up," I say

"I know!" Holly looks over to the window. "I bet I could nail him on his way out the front door."

"Probably. Are you going to?"

"No." Holly puts the cup back down.

"So, uh, how long has Mr. Stark been keeping a flask?" I ask.

"It was locked in our cabinet until yesterday," Holly says. "He pulled it out for something to do with the investigation. Didn't think he was going to hang on to it."

I nod. "Case must be going bad."

"Yeah." Holly sighs. "He's fully in 'I know what's best and I'm not sharing case details' mode. Today was the closest he's come to bouncing ideas off me." She looks up at me. "I'm getting worried, Todd, usually he picks up someone to talk to and work with, even if it's not me. I don't think he's doing that this time. He's taking it personally."

"It's a personal sort of thing," I say. "I mean, you know how he is. It's one thing if someone takes a chance and gets hurt. He doesn't like it, but it's how the game is played. But when someone gets caught in the middle, that's a whole other story, and it sounds like this is nothing *but* people getting caught in the middle."

"I think you're right. Which is why we have to get involved."

"Huh?"

Holly gives me a slow smile. "Look, Uncle Basil is going to get himself in trouble, right? Guaranteed. Which means we need to do some investigating of our own so that we're ready to get him out of it."

"That is a terrible idea. Back me up here, Glim."

Glimmer taps her chin thoughtfully, and then says something about being safest near Basil.

"That is not backing me up!" I look between the two of them. "Look, can you at least agree that we should not be following him to a meeting with mysterious informants?"

"Oh, yeah, obviously we're not doing that."

"Good."

"I'm not good enough at hiding, and no offense Todd, but you're even worse. Glimmer, you track Uncle Basil for now, and come get us if something goes wrong."

Glimmer laughs, salutes, and flits out the window before I can marshal an argument. "We are going to get in so much trouble," I mutter.

"Probably! But in the meantime, why don't we go grab a bite to eat?" Holly stands, patting me on the shoulder. "Cheer up, big guy. I have a plan."

"Yeah, that's what worries me."

We head down the street to a local bakery that Holly really likes. It's not until we turn the corner and I see the two people sitting under the umbrella that I realize I've been had. "Holly."

"Oh, look, it's Emeka and Marta! What a surprise!" Holly waves brightly, and starts walking a bit faster.

"You are really starting to take after your parents," I mutter to her. The first two months that I knew them, Plum and Panther Blossom spent all of their time trying to set me and Holly up, with occasional help from neighbors. They've figured out that we really aren't interested now, I think. At least, it's been a while since the last wistful off-hand comment, and the last time I was over Plum was asking me about which of my friends might be available.

Holly gives me a slightly hurt look. "I'm spending time with friends."

"I thought it was a surprise."

"It's a surprise for you. You need cheering up. Hey, folks. Three times in five days, that's some kind of record for us. How's the music going?"

"Holly, Todd, good to see you. Going well." Marta slides over on the bench to make room for Holly, leaving me to sit next to Emeka. He's got a little half-smile as he scoots over to let me sit down. I glance back to Marta as she asks, "How'd the case go?"

"Pretty much all wrapped up," I say. "Vance Carson is an energetic guy. Someone cut our brake lines."

"What!?" Holly overturns her water, and everyone at the surrounding tables turns to stare at us. She lowers her voice, leaning in. "Why the hell didn't you open with that? Does Uncle Basil know?"

I shake my head at Holly and shrug. I hadn't meant to keep it secret; I'd just forgotten.

"Are you okay?" Emeka asks.

"I mean, yeah. If I wasn't okay I would've said something when it happened."

"Tell. Me. Everything." Marta leans in, almost right up to my face.

"I can't tell you everything, it's a private case!"

"Well then tell me what you can tell me! Who cut your brake lines?"

"We don't actually know. But it was someone at the logging camp."

"What?" Holly frowns. "I mean, I realize that I don't know everyone up there, but that seems pretty extreme. How would they even do that? Wasn't your car in the main lot?"

"Yeah, I know. I figured it was just a rock that did it, but the person we were tracking down admitted that they had a friend at the camp who tried to slow us down. Only other thing that happened was a fallen tree across the road, and it wouldn't have slowed us more than a minute if it weren't for the brakes."

Holly grabs Marta's water and takes a sip. "Weird."

"Hey! Take a girl out to dinner first," Marta says. She looks around and steals Emeka's water while he's distracted by the story.

"Does Vance have a plan for dealing with this person?" he asks. "I mean, if I were willing to do something like that to protect someone, and that someone got caught anyway, I'd be pretty mad. I bet they are too."

"They probably are," I admit. "And we definitely pissed someone off, who may or may not be the same people, because they're trying to blackmail me into making Mr. Stark lay off his thing, too."

Marta whistles. "Malcolm, you do not do things by halves. I really thought our tiger band was going to be the biggest news of the week and you're in the middle of a full Basil Stark-style case! Possibly with Basil Stark!"

"So," Emeka asks, "are you laying off?"

I say "Maybe," at the exact same moment that Holly says "No!"

Holly turns to look at me. "We don't back down from bad guys."

"Yeah, but Mr. Stark specifically said to back down from these bad guys. I'm kind of thinking maybe I'm in over my head. We should leave it to the professionals."

"We are the professionals," Holly says.

"Holly, no offense, but you're kind of a professional in training," Marta points out. "You've only had one really serious case, and you almost died. Twice."

"But I didn't. Which is experience."

Emeka rubs his forehead. "This isn't a game, Holly. What have they got on Todd?"

"They claim they can get me put away for the assault," I say reluctantly.

Marta chokes on her water. "Hang on. That's jail time. Real jail time, I mean, not like when we get locked up for the night because we got rowdy at the bar."

"You don't even know who's behind it," Emeka says. "How do you investigate a thing like that without them pulling the trigger?"

"Simple. We're going to start by talking with Dolph Henries," Holly says.

"Who's that?"

"The guy Todd punched."

"Yeah. Wait, what?" I turn to look at Holly.

"The only person who can press charges against Todd is Henries. So, he's either involved, or he's being blackmailed. Which means that we need to go see him, figure out what he's up to, and convince him not to do anything, and then we can investigate all we want." Holly crosses her arms triumphantly. "I've thought this through."

"And if he's one of the bad guys?" Emeka asks.

"Then we need to prove he's the arsonist."

"Wow. That is a terrible idea," Marta says. "I mean, like, I have heard some bad ideas, but this one is something else. You sure about this?"

I swallow heavily. Everyone is looking at me — Holly hopeful, Emeka worried, and Marta excited and scared in equal parts. Truth is, I'm pretty scared myself. I take a moment to weigh my emotions and come to a decision. "I don't think Mr. Stark's going to make much progress with this guy. Maybe I can. But if Henries isn't cooperative, that's it. We're out."

Holly frowns, but nods. "Yeah. One person only."

Emeka nods. "Let me know if there's anything I can do to help."

"Don't worry about me," I say, reaching out to pat his hand. "I can handle myself."

"Yeah, that's what they all say," Emeka grumbles, but there's the edge of a smile on his lips.

I lean back. "I assume Holly has some crackerjack plan to get us in to see Henries, but I figure we've got some time before we gotta do it, right? Let's maybe not talk about danger and cases for a bit."

"That sounds like a great plan," Holly says. "How's the show going? Any big gigs lined up?"

"We're giving the pressure a few days to really build, but we've definitely got three shows planned for the weekend," Marta says. "I hear Michelle's phone is ringing off the hook. Everyone wants a piece of the Tiger Trio before the novelty wears off."

"Hkuri and the Steppers," Emeka reminds her.

"Yeah, about that. What's a stepper?" I ask.

"Humans," Holly says before Emeka can. "It's animal slang. I've heard some wolves use it."

"Yeah, exactly. Turning it on its head. To us, the big draw is that we've got a tiger for a lead singer, but to the tigers, the big draw is that a couple of humans are actually working with a tiger. Kind of a big deal," Emeka says. "Which is why we are not calling it the Tiger Trio."

Marta blows a raspberry at him, then considers. "Yeah, no, you're right. Sorry."

"You getting many gigs in tiger territory?" I ask.

"Zero and change," Emeka admits. "But Hkuri's hoping it'll build. And we've got a heck of a set lined up for the weekend shows."

"Well, walk us through it," Holly says. "I want all the details!"

We spend the next half-hour eating sandwiches and running through the Steppers' set. It's a pretty good one. Nothing too out there, mostly tunes that people will know. Apparently, Hkuri has a few originals, but Michelle wants to start with the familiar and not overwhelm people with too much at once. When lunch is done, and we're getting up to leave, Emeka grabs my hand and looks me in the eyes. "Just promise me you'll be careful, alright?"

My breath catches in my throat. "I promise. Geez, I've been in tougher scrapes than this. But thanks for worrying."

"Yeah." He lets go and steps back, and then nods. "Yeah."

As we head down the street, Holly nudges me. "Heartbreaker."

"Not now, Holly, please." I rub my forehead. "Okay, you want to meet a Second Star VIP. So, what's the plan?"

"I figure we tail him from his office and confront him on the street."

I choke. "That's not a plan, Holly, that's an arrest warrant with our names on it!"

"We're good at tailing people!"

"We're good at watching people. We don't actually tail people." I shake my head. "Back to the office. We're working out a new plan."

"You said you'd do it."

"That's because your plans are usually a heck of a lot better than that! What the hell, Holly?"

Holly swallows. "I'm worried, okay?"

"Huh?"

"Uncle Basil is freaking out, and you got arrested, and no one is telling me anything about what's going on! This guy could destroy you. You know that, right?" She rubs the back of her neck, breathing out slowly. "I just need to do something. Anything."

"Okay. That's cool. Why don't we make that 'anything' brainstorming, instead of causing trouble?"

"Yeah. Yeah, you're right. How are you so even-headed?"

I laugh. "I started this thing by punching a guy out because I thought he might be bad."

"So, practice?"

We're both laughing as we re-enter the office, which is when a coffee cup smashes against the wall next to my head. "Woah! Glimmer, what the heck?"

Glimmer launches across the room, spitting out words faster than I can follow them. She smacks me on the ear, then smacks Holly on the ear. "Ow!"

"We were just down the street!" Holly exclaims. "And we were only gone for, like, half an hour! I didn't even expect you to *be* at the meeting yet, let alone back!"

Glimmer yells that we didn't tell her to find us down the street, we told her to find us in the office, and we weren't here and she almost got killed and we would have been pretty sad if we had to go to a funeral and where would I even find a jacket.

"Wait, wait. You almost got killed?" I hold up a hand. "What happened?"

It takes a while to get all the details out of Glimmer, between her being freaked out and me being a little slow on the language, but the story as she tells it is like this:

Glimmer slipped out of her office window and followed Basil down the street, gliding from streetlamp to streetlamp to keep him in sight. He was alert, occasionally glancing behind him and tracking anyone who seemed to be following him, but he didn't look up enough to spot her. Humans almost never do, even ones who should know better.

She was expecting him to take a trip downtown, so it was a surprise when he stopped at a café a few blocks away and went right inside, nodding to the waiter at the door. Glimmer sat on the roof across the way and chewed her lip. This was a challenge; she was stealthy, but getting through the front door without being spotted was another level. She leaned back and studied the café's interior, looking for any route in, and spotted a large vent cover on the wall not far from where

Basil was sitting. Looking upwards from there, she spotted windows on the second floor, opened to take advantage of the summer breeze.

Glimmer flitted across the street quickly, ducked down by the windowsill, and peeked inside. It was someone's living room, but whoever it belonged to wasn't in. She ducked into and across the room, then shimmied out through their mail slot into the hall above the café, which was lined with grates in the floor up from which the smell of fresh-baked bread wafted. Glimmer grinned. It was almost as though no one even built these places to keep fairies out!

It only took a moment to find the right vent, pry the cover off, slip inside, and carefully replace the cover behind her. The vent was a bit narrow, but not narrow enough to stop her, and she easily climbed down to the downstairs cover and adjusted the grating just enough to be able to peek through and watch the humans scurrying around. With fresh air cradling her, Glimmer settled back to see what Basil was up to, and froze.

Basil was sitting at a table across from someone that Glimmer knew too well, the big-mustached figure of Commissioner Darling, who was hunched over a steaming cup of black coffee, looking even more menacing than usual. Glimmer strained to hear, blocking out the sounds of the rest of the café and focusing entirely on them.

"—hate that I am even talking to you," Darling was saying.

"Yes, I realize it. This is no different than the Questing Beast situation."

"A lot of people died in that situation, Stark." Darling held up a hand before Basil could respond. "I know, I know. A lot of people are going to die here. I still hate it."

"Well, then, we can hate it together. What did you learn?"

"The Rust Bucket wasn't a mob joint, so that rules out that motive. Too small to be on Schaefer's radar, and the lieutenants are too busy jockeying for position right now to care about the small fry."

"But that place was absolutely destroyed," Basil says.

"There, I might have something for you." Darling passes a small file folder across the table. "We found the remnants of several barrels of Pearl Diver in the basement. Under questioning, the owner, Halson, admitted to buying them for sale."

Basil swallowed. "Pearl Diver? Don't you need very special permits for that?"

"Yes, you do. And very specific storage spaces." Darling grimaced. "The damned stuff is two-twenty proof. God knows why anyone would want to make that damn mermaid brew. It's over one hundred percent alcohol, and I honestly don't know why anyone drinks it, aside from the novelty of having a mixed drink with the equivalent of eight shots in it. Been trying to get it banned for years."

Basil took a sip of his tea thoughtfully. "You need real shimmer-pearls to make that. The mermaids don't trade those easily, and they're even harder to steal."

"Unless you think a mermaid flopped onto land to set a fire, that doesn't mean much." Darling shook his head. "I think the fire was set to reduce the supply, help someone else move in. There's a new source selling Pearl Diver, and rumors say they aren't mob. We haven't tracked them down yet."

"Someone moving in on Schaefer's crown?"

"Possible. They're slippery, whoever they are. We've arrested a couple of distributors, but they have no idea who they're working for. Dead drops and written notes, dropped off at improbable times."

"Does this mystery outfit have a name?"

"Some people are starting to call them the ghost mob. Your blackmail story might line up with how they're operating." Darling took a long drink of his coffee. "The thing is, Harper's pretty much taken the investigation away from me. I'm trying to take it back, but it could be a while, and I don't know how many of my men he's already got on his payroll. This bastard is moving fast, Stark. He wants the whole island reporting to him."

"Oh, I just bet he does." Basil leaned forward to ask another question, but just then, Glimmer was distracted by a flicker of movement on the wall behind him. The vent directly across from hers had shifted, and there was a pair of eyes peering through it. For a moment, she stared at them in confusion, just as those eyes stared back at her, and then she gasped and started to climb, just as the fairy in the opposite vent did the same thing.

Glimmer burst out of the vent on the level above, ready to confront whatever fairy had the absolute gall to be spying on her friend. She raised her fists to fight, just as the other fairy burst out of their own vent. He was skinny, with birch-colored skin and a stitched-leather jacket and pants, and unlike Glimmer, he was armed. He had a sharp blade in his hand, and he looked her up and down with a sneer.

"We don't like spies," he said, taking to the air.

Glimmer launched herself into the air as well, flying backwards as the enemy fairy dove at her wings. She ducked under his wild slash, more confused than afraid. "I'm not a spy, I'm Glimmer Mop. Who are you?"

"Ash Cutter!" the other fairy crowed. "Slayer of crows, thief in the night, bane of the tall ones!" He grinned, diving at her again, and she took cover behind a potted plant as his knife sliced off one of its leaves.

"Too many names," she complained. "Take one, keep it."

"I take many names," Ash Cutter snapped. "I will take yours next!"

Glimmer considered her choices. This fairy was dangerous, and not much for chatting. She didn't have a weapon. It was time to go. She raced down the hallway, looking for another window, with Ash Cutter hot on her tail. She took off her hat and gave it a last look. It was a nice hat. But Holly would make her another one.

As Ash Cutter dove at her again, she spun and threw her hat directly into his face. Caught off-guard, he swung wildly at it, losing speed as he backed up and prepared for her attack. In that moment, she spun and dove at the window, grabbing its frame and pulling upward with all her might.

As the window inched upwards, Ash Cutter got the hat out of his face, stabbed it several times just to be safe, and spun in the air to try and find her. Spotting her at the window, he picked up speed, raising his blade as he raced for her. She slipped under the window, and slammed it down behind her, forcing him to pull up at the last moment. Then she raced away, dropping between buildings to avoid his pursuit. A few minutes later, she was diving through the window of the office, shouting a warning to Todd and Holly, and discovered that they weren't even there.

Which is the point in Glimmer's retelling at which she pauses and throws a marshmallow at my head.

"Okay, yes, you're right," I say, raising my hands defensively. "We didn't think you'd get attacked by another fairy." I pause. "Do fairies often attack each other?"

"Sometimes," Holly says. "I mean, it's not like every fairy is nice. But it's not usually like that, is it?"

Glimmer shrugs and points out that she doesn't spend that much time with other fairies, and definitely not with fairies vain enough to give themselves multiple stupid names. But she's heard about fairy wars happening in the woods, especially now that there's not as much space to spread out.

"Okay, got it. But why was another fairy spying on Mr. Stark?"

"Yeah, that is weird. Maybe revenge? When a fairy sets their mind to something, they do not stop until a new thing comes up."

Glimmer nods proudly.

"A new thing like killing Glimmer?" I ask.

Glimmer stops looking proud and starts looking worried.

Holly winces. "Yeah, you'd better stick with us for a while, Glimmer. I don't like the sound of this guy."

"Okay. So, how do we tell Basil that Glimmer was spying on him?"

"We do not," Holly says.

"Then how do we tell him another fairy is spying on him?" I point out. "He needs to know that."

"Huh." Holly frowns. "Glimmer, are you up for claiming you spotted the other fairy following Uncle Basil from our window, so you followed them both to the café?"

Glimmer and I share a look. "You think he'll buy that?" I ask.

"Anything's possible. The important thing is playing it cool." Holly leans back in her seat. "Anyway, I think I have an idea. You were asking how we'd tail Henries, right?"

"Yeah..."

"Glimmer can do it."

Glimmer beams.

"That seems kind of dangerous."

"No, it's perfect. She's great at tailing people, and no one ever looks up. She can find out where he goes when he leaves his office, and where we can talk to him alone. She might even get dirt on him." Holly is already pulling out her pencil. "Do they make cameras small enough for a fairy to carry? We could counter-blackmail him to stop him blackmailing you!"

"If he's doing something blackmail-worthy," I point out. "And I don't know of any cameras that weigh less than a pound and a half."

Glimmer snorts and points out that she can easily lift that much.

"There you go! She can follow him, we'll follow her at a distance, and she can grab gear from us! It's perfect."

It doesn't feel perfect, but Glimmer and Holly are both grinning like cats, so I figure I've already been outvoted. "Okay, but if there's any trouble, we get the heck out of there."

"Absolutely. Promise."

"Glimmer?"

Glimmer gives me a salute, and then asks if she can get a new hat first.

"Of course," Holly says. "We'll get started tomorrow."

We're in the middle of planning out how we're going to follow Glimmer when the phone rings. Holly grabs it. "Basil Stark Investigations! Oh, hi, Uncle Basil. Glimmer was looking for you." She listens for a moment. "I actually think this might be important. You've got a fairy tailing you."

I can hear Basil's cry of 'what' over the other end, and Holly quickly lays out what happened to Glimmer, minus the part where she was listening in. "So," she concludes, "keep an eye on the sky, and look out for tiny murderers. Oh, hey, have there been any tiny murders as part of your cases?

Well, I don't know, it's possible. Okay, fine. Sorry. No, no news. Did you learn anything about the arson?" She listens for a moment, and then nods. "Got it. I'll see you tomorrow."

"Well?" I ask, once she hangs up the phone.

"Get this. No new information."

"What about the exploding barrels, and the mermaids, and all of that?"

"Uncle Basil is not sharing. This is why we've got to do something, Todd. He's keeping us out of the loop. We need to bring him something good, so that he has to cut us in again."

I sigh. "I already said I was in, Holly."

"Yeah, but you were reluctant."

"I'm still reluctant." But she's right. It stings to have Mr. Stark think we're not up to handle this, and I don't like making him go into danger for me. "Okay. No more holding back. Let's get Henries, and get me off the hook."

# Friday, August 24ᵗʰ

**By Friday evening,** we have nothing to show for our last few days of sleuthing. Holly, Glimmer, and I had spent most of Wednesday, Thursday, and now Friday hanging around near the Second Star buildings, close enough to be ready if Glimmer got in trouble again, while she scouted out the place and started figuring out where Henries was going day to day. By the time Thursday rolled around, I was thoroughly bored of the whole thing, and Holly had resorted to spending all our time together working out complicated theories about what was going on and coming up with new excuses for why she needed her mother's car — but Glimmer was really into it; she happily spent hours every day watching Henries through his office window, following him while he did his shopping after work, and then going to his home and making sure that he'd fallen asleep.

The problem is that Henries isn't much of a socialite. He spends a lot of time in meetings with a lot of suits, grabs cheap noodles or sandwiches at lunch, and stays late at the office, all of which seems to be above-board and extremely boring. He doesn't meet up with any friends, he doesn't go out to the bars, and he definitely doesn't do anything suspicious.

Holly and I are hanging around a patio bar, a few blocks from Second Star. I'm starting to think that we're barking up the wrong tree, and that we need to either just go talk to him, or I need to give up on unpaid detective work and get back to looking for a bar that needs a bouncer when Glimmer rockets through the air, bounces off the table in front of us, and yells for us to follow her as she takes off again back the way she came. I've already got my wallet out, so I drop a couple of bills on the table and take off after her, with Holly just a couple of steps behind me.

We race down the street with Glimmer ahead of us. I bump into someone on their way home from work who turns to curse at me and then changes his mind in a hurry, but I get distracted long enough to lose track of Glimmer and I have to pause to try and figure out where she went. Holly grabs my shoulder, points me to a flicker of motion, and we keep going. A couple of blocks later, Glimmer drops out of the sky onto my shoulder, panting heavily.

"What the heck happened?" I ask.

Glimmer smiles smugly and tells us that she found one of the blackmailers. Holly and I look at each other in surprise.

"A blackmailer? Henries had a meeting?"

Glimmer's smile gets even broader, and she points up to the third floor of the building we're outside. Quickly, she explains that she saw someone slipping through Henries' office window to drop off a letter, and she tracked them back to here.

"Henries' office is on the fourth floor," Holly says. "How did someone get up to … oh my God, fairies."

Glimmer nods, still looking smug.

"Fairies are dropping off the blackmail letters. Of course, that's how they got one into my house! I can't believe we didn't think of that."

"Spying and delivering. Someone thought this through," Holly says thoughtfully. "What do you say, Todd? Do we want to confront a blackmailer?"

"Yeah. Yeah, I think we should. You got the room number, Glimmer?"

Glimmer nods, tilts her new hat down over her eyes, and cracks her knuckles. She's been wearing her detective getup all week, and she looks ready to throw down. "Hang back, okay? We don't want them to know that we've got fairy power on our side, too." I snap my fingers. "Actually, keep watch from outside the window in case their fairy makes a run for it."

She frowns at me, but nods, gives Holly the room number, and goes to sit on a lamppost and watch the building.

"Smart thinking," Holly says, as we start up the stairs. "Hey, maybe by the end of the night we'll have the whole situation sorted."

"Maybe." I think back over everything. "Say, you think that's how they're getting the pictures, too? Fairies can get into all sorts of places, and we know that there's at least one fairy following people around, that Ash Cutter guy."

"Huh. Yeah, you could do it. Fairies are really good at focusing on things as long as they care. You'd have to find a fairy who really liked spying on people, though. They're not going to care for a paycheck."

"Glimmer likes spying on people," I point out. "And she might not need a paycheck, but she was pretty thrilled when Vance gave her one."

"Yeah." Holly bites her lip. "I never really thought about it before. Guess I just figured fairies were too straightforward for this kind of thing."

"Yeah, me too. I bet a lot of people did. But straightforward doesn't mean dumb," I say. "Or nice. Maybe this guy can fill in some of the blanks. You want to be good cop?"

"I'm always good cop," Holly complains.

"That's because I'm really bad at it."

"Fine, fine. You be the muscle, I'll be the smile."

We knock on the door of the suite in question. The door opens a crack, and I give it my best kick right away. It's a cheap door with a cheap chain, which immediately pulls out of the wall. "Hi," I say. "Fairy inspectors. We hear you've got a problem."

The guy who was behind the door has collapsed back on the floor, and he scrambles backwards. Now that I can see him closely, he's sort of a wiry little guy, big teeth, too much hair and no good idea how to cut it. "Get outta here!" he shouts. "I'll call the cops!"

"And let them see what you're up to?" Holly asks, stepping out from behind me and looking around the room. "I don't think your boss will be too happy about any of that. Where's the fairy?"

"I don't know what you're talking about," the guy says shakily, getting up with one hand on the wall. "Who're you with?"

"Take a guess," I growl, stepping forward. "You think you can just pressure bigwigs at Second Star and no one gets called in? You think you're the first guy to think that he can use a fairy to make the drops, and no one knows how to follow them?"

"Look," Holly says, putting a calming hand on my shoulder to hold me back. "We don't want trouble. Trouble is bad for business. But you've created a liability that we need to resolve. Get the message?"

"Bigwigs? Huh? I just watch the place, I swear!" The guy is babbling at this point. "I don't even live here!"

I pause and look around. It does look kind of empty. There's a chair and a table, and a large cardboard box, but the place is basically deserted. "You were waiting for the fairy to come back from a drop," I say.

"Yeah. He'll show up, pick up a package or two and fly off with it, then come back for the next one. Does a bunch of them over the course of the night. I just help make sure the packages are in the right order and keep anyone from coming in, and I get fifteen bucks a night."

"Don't think you're getting that money, sorry," Holly says. "But hey, I'll give you five if you show me what's in the box."

The guy looks us over. "You believe me?"

"Let's say I'm open to believing you. Depending on what's in the box. I'll open it up, and you tell us how you got this job."

"Go ahead. I'm not getting the stuffing knocked out of me for fifteen bucks."

I head over to the boxes while the guy keeps talking.

"I get behind on my tab sometimes, bartender lines up side gigs for me to even out. Not strictly legal, you know? But nothing violent. This one's weird, but seems easy. Sort out some envelopes, keep some material, help some little fairy with the organization, then head home. If the fairy doesn't show, give someone a call and let them know. That's it."

"And you didn't wonder why a fairy was moving envelopes around?"

"Probably some kinda note-passing test. Like a mail system, but the feds don't run it, right? But I can't see it working for very long." Now that he's pretty sure that he's not going to get punched, the guy is cooling down. "I mean, fairies fly quick, but they can only carry a couple of envelopes at a time, and they can't manage packages for any real distance. Plus, what if they forget where they're going?" Holly frowns, and the guy raises his hands quickly. "Hey, nothing personal. I forget things sometimes, too. Planning to forget I ever saw any of you, for example."

"Smart," I say. "This fairy have a name?"

"Heck if I know. He's a little thing, really pale skin. Carries a knife, if that helps. Haven't seen many fairies go armed."

"Sounds like Ash Cutter, maybe." I open one of the envelopes, sort through it. It's a couple of photos of a couple walking close together, taken from a second-story window — or maybe a roof. The next envelope is a list of purchases. "Man, they've got everything in here. How many of these do you got?"

"It's usually just the one box each time I'm here. Maybe ten or twenty letters, different sizes." The guy shrugs. "I'm only here once or twice a week. Don't know if anyone else gets called in."

"That's a lot of blackmail," Holly says to me.

The guy blinks. "Blackmail?"

"Oh, yeah, you're helping operate a blackmail ring. Against politicians, and mobsters, and stuff. The sort of people who hire people who make these problems go away." Holly gives the guy a very cheerful smile. "Say, you didn't happen to look in any of these, did you?"

"No! No, I would never! I don't want any trouble, ma'am."

"Smart. Here's your five dollars. I'd suggest forgetting this whole situation. It's likely to be bad for your health." Holly hands the man a folded-up bill, and I loom behind her and glare at him. He gets the message, nods a few times, and races out the door.

Holly turns to look at me. "Congratulations, Todd, we've cracked the blackmail ring!"

"We've cracked *a* blackmail ring," I point out. I cross to the window, open it, and wave for Glimmer to come in and join us. "Glimmer, what do you think your range is, if you're flying back and forth from one place carrying envelopes?"

Glimmer thinks about it, and says she figures maybe ten blocks, and she's a pretty strong flyer. I nod glumly. "What I figured. So, if we've got this place being used for drops around the Second Star area, maybe the Hill. They can double the range if they're handing off to other fairies, cover half the east side, but there's gotta be more drops for ... well, for everywhere that things are happening."

Holly nods, biting her lip. "That's a lot of blackmail."

"We should get this stuff back to Mr. Stark," I say.

"Hang on. This is our chance to confront Henries. We know what's going on, now. He was blackmailed." Holly grabs me by the arm. "Take the box, though. We don't want it here when that fairy comes back."

Glimmer asks if we're going to wait and grab the spy. She looks ready for a good scrap.

"I don't think he'll fall for it," Holly says. "And we really don't want him spotting Todd here and pulling the trigger on that whole 'arrest' thing."

Glimmer frowns.

"Hey," Holly says. "If you were flying an operation like this, you'd check before going into the base each time, right?" When Glimmer nods reluctantly, Holly continues. "I'd bet our bad guy will, too. Plus, we don't have a cage or rope or anything. But we do have time to catch Henries on his way home, freshly spooked from whatever brand-new blackmail material that fairy dropped off. Let's move."

We head back to Henries' place to wait for him to get home. Like a lot of Second Star folks, especially the influential ones, Henries lives on the Hill, a little below the level where the real movers and shakers live in their fancy houses. His place is built out of local wood, plain-colored and fenced off, but we don't see any security guys hanging around and if he's got a housekeeper, she doesn't live on-site. The place is quiet and still, and we're able to sit down on the porch and wait for him to arrive.

As the big sedan pulls up the long driveway, Holly looks to me. "You want good cop or bad cop?"

"I think maybe it's gotta be good cop, good cop. Chances are he's gonna be pretty mad at me. We might need to talk quick."

"That makes sense. You want to take the lead?"

"Sure."

The car pulls up and stops, and Henries climbs out. He's halfway up the steps before he realizes that we're there, and he stops dead in his tracks, holding his briefcase out like a shield. In the light from his front porch, he looks skinnier than I remember from the bar. He's got the standard Second Star haircut, smooth and short, and his thin lips purse as he takes us in. "Get off my property," he says, voice quavering.

"Mr. Henries. We just want to talk," I say.

"We have nothing to talk about, you hooligan!"

"What about blackmail, Mr. Henries?" Holly holds up a manila envelope. We couldn't find one with his information in it, but hopefully he won't ask for a closer look. "Would you like to talk about that?"

Henries swallows. He looks at me, and then at Holly. "I don't understand."

"We're not blackmailers," I say before he can back any further away. "We just want to talk to you, to try and stop these guys." I look at his face. He's scared, but there's something else in the way he won't look me in the eyes. "People are getting hurt, Mr. Henries. You can help them."

Henries looks around, and then shudders. "Inside, quickly. If anyone finds out that I've been speaking with you..." He trails off uncomfortably and waves us to the door.

Looking around the inside of Dolph Henries' house, I can see why the police wouldn't finger him for arson. The place screams 'upstanding citizen': white carpets, leather furniture, a couple of paintings on the walls, a lot of bookshelves with histories and science texts on them, and nothing out of place. Henries leads us into the kitchen, pulls the blinds down, and moves to pull a bottle of wine out of the cupboard. "Would you like some?" he asks, almost like a reflex.

Holly smiles. "I'll take a small glass, thank you. Todd?"

"Water for me. I'm driving."

Henries nods and pours the drinks with a shaking hand. His own glass, he fills almost to the brim, and he drips a line of red across the kitchen tiles as he comes to sit down. "So," he says finally. "you figured it out."

"Everyone makes mistakes, Mr. Henries," Holly says gently.

"Other people's mistakes don't kill people," Henries says. He takes a long gulp of wine. "God, it wasn't supposed to be like this. None of it was."

I look him up and down. "You know they're trying to use you to get to me?"

He nods, and reaches into his briefcase, pulling out another one of those manila envelopes that I'm getting too used to. "I got another reminder this evening." He drops it on the table between us. "You might as well look at it, you know everything anyway."

I take the envelope and slide it open. It's got a typed note, just like the one I was sent. 'Delay the police for two more days. You will be instructed in what to tell them. We know that you are considering speaking with the press. Remember why this would be unwise.' Attached to the note is a photograph of a set of invoices for a bunch of stuff I don't really understand. I pass the envelope to Holly, and look back to Henries. "Did they want anything from you before the arson?"

"It was research, at first. They found out that I had been attending unsanctioned meetings. Discussions that the Old Man would be unhappy about." Henries rubs his forehead. "I'm in a good position at Second Star. I didn't want to lose it because the CEO found out I was rubbing shoulders with the wrong sort of people, and the research seemed harmless. Old studies, nothing that had proven valuable."

"Let me guess. It proved valuable," Holly said.

Henries nodded with a snort. "A week after I sent them copies of the old research, Second Star re-opened the project. Two weeks after that, we heard that Hawthorne was doing the same research, but was miles ahead of us. The Old Man was furious, convinced it was espionage. Which I suppose it was.

That's when they contacted me again. This time they didn't threaten me, not exactly. They told me they could make the problem go away, in exchange for another so-called favor."

"The arson."

"No one was supposed to get hurt!" Henries looked up at me desperately. "They said the owner was in on it. It needed to happen while he was tending bar, to keep him above suspicion, but he'd set up the basement. I just needed to light the fuse, slip away. Given my position, no one would believe I'd done it even if I were spotted in the area, which wouldn't be true of his other associates. They said that he needed the money. I would make his problem go away, and they would make my problem go away."

"But you didn't know about the barrels of Pearl Diver down there."

Henries breathes out slowly. "Is that what it was? I might have guessed." He nods. "I got too close. It blew up in my face, sent me sprawling. By the time I was on my feet, there was a crowd everywhere, and when I tried to slip away, you saw me. And then I found out about that poor boy."

"Why didn't you say something?" Holly asked. "You must have known you'd be blackmailed again."

"I can't."

"You're in too deep," I said. "They got you coming and going. They knew someone like you would never come clean, that's why they used you for the arson. Hell, maybe that was the real target, getting the rope around your neck tight enough that you'll never be able to escape."

Henries looks away from me. "I know. There's no way out, not anymore. They aren't even pretending that they won't contact me again. But if I turn myself in, I can't prove any of this. I would take the fall."

"You killed someone," I say. "You started a fire to save yourself. Maybe you should take the fall."

Henries doesn't answer. He just stares down at his wine like a bedraggled dog. I look at Holly, who shrugs helplessly. "Look, I can't make you come clean," I say. "But if you don't do something, this is only going to get worse. You know that, or you wouldn't be talking to us right now."

"I just don't know what to do," Henries says quietly.

"Yeah, you do. You just don't know if you can. Look, what was the research that they wanted? The stuff that set all of this off?"

"Fairy tracking."

"What?"

"I know, right? Ridiculous stuff, especially these days. But in the thirties, there was an idea of building devices that could identify the trails fairies leave behind and use that to find nests and colonies." Henries shakes his head. "It didn't go anywhere, originally. But now fairies are in the news again, and figuring out how many fairies even live on the island is becoming a bigger deal. Hawthorne claims they're developing it so that they can mark areas as unsafe for logging, but it's Hawthorne. They've never cared about the locals before."

"Damn," Holly says. "Every hidden fairy colony would be open to the Regulators. The research you took, I'm guessing Second Star's starting from scratch?"

"Yes, and with Hawthorne so far ahead they're giving up. The Old Man didn't really want to do it to begin with, but he was pressured."

"Well, that's one bit of good news." Everyone knows that George Ellery Hale, Second Star's founder and lead researcher, has a soft spot for fairies, but it's good to know he's standing by it. "Thanks for your time, Mr. Henries. I figure you're probably going to get that call about charging me for punching you, soon as these guys realize that I'm not staying out of it."

"I'll see what I can do to drag my heels. Maybe Second Star will want to get involved on the legal side. They can't fault me for that." Henries looks at me. "You probably hate me."

"I'm not sad about punching you the first time," I admit. "But I don't want to do it again, for what it's worth. We all gotta decide what we can and can't do."

"Thank you for the wine," Holly says, and we head out. Glimmer is waiting for us on the porch, and she lets us know that there was no sign of any eavesdroppers before dropping onto my shoulder and curling up sleepily. Poor thing's exhausted — she's had a heck of a week.

"Where to next?" I ask.

"Drop off this box at the office, see if Uncle Basil is in, and then back home. Mom'll probably insist on driving you to your place after. It's been a hell of a day. Can you believe that guy?"

"He's scared," I say, as we climb into the car. "In way over his head."

"Well, burying it in the sand isn't going to get him any higher."

"Huh?"

"You know what I mean." Holly stares out the window. Glimmer is lying down on the back seat, and the road is quiet. "He's going to be trapped forever if we don't solve this thing, and who knows how many other lives he'll ruin to stay afloat?"

"I hate this. Why can't there just be someone I can punch and feel good about it? Everyone we run into is another victim."

Glimmer mumbles sleepily that Ash Cutter isn't a victim and I can punch him if we see him again. I laugh.

"I promise you, Glimmer, if I see that guy, I will punch him into next week for you." Glimmer gives me a vague salute, and I look back to Holly. "Thanks for pushing me on this, Holly. If you hadn't, I'd probably be like Henries."

"Don't sell yourself short." Holly leans back in her seat, closing her eyes. "You're a fighter, Todd. One thing you won't do is stand by. But good job on not punching Henries a second time. Even if he deserved it."

"Thanks," I say again, turning my attention back to the road. I just can't help but wonder how many more people we're going to run into that might 'deserve it' before this is all done.

# Saturday, August 25<sup>th</sup>

**"Just once. Once.** I would like him to actually talk to people instead of running off following leads. We've cracked the case! He doesn't even know what he's looking for!" Holly is furious when we meet up back at the office in the morning: Mr. Stark had not been in his office last night, or at his house when Holly stopped by to check on him. Instead, there was just a note saying that he's following a lead, and that we should keep our heads down until he gets back.

"We warned him about being followed by fairies," I point out. "Maybe that'll be good enough."

The three of us are sitting in a circle around Holly's desk, looking through the envelopes that we stole and trying to identify who they were meant for. Mostly they fall into two categories: pictures of two people together, sometimes just arm in arm but sometimes explicit enough to make me blush; or pictures of people in the middle of stealing stuff. A few envelopes just have pictures of single objects — jewelry, handkerchiefs, and the like. The notes attached to them are also pretty much the same: Give us money, we forget what happened and make sure everyone else does, too. Don't give us money, your life is over.

There are only two so far that don't fit the mold. One to someone named Susan, telling her to lose a folder or else. The other one is to a "Mr. Ramone" and is telling him to be at a place at 8:00 p.m. Sunday and to drink with a specific person.

"How are they getting *this much blackmail?*" Holly asks.

"No one looks up," I say, looking through a couple more envelopes. "Have a fairy shadow someone for a while, you get something. Grab papers off someone's desk, watch them having meetings on the third floor. Then just use some of your people to get to other people." I drop the envelopes and sigh. "But it's not actually helpful."

"What do you mean?"

"I mean, great, we know how they're getting photos, and we have some of their victims. But none of their victims actually know them. That's the whole point. We busted up a little part of this thing, but we didn't actually get anywhere. I think we made the wrong call."

"I think you're right," Holly says, dropping the document she was looking at. "Uncle Basil would have tailed the fairy back to wherever they were coming from at the end of the night."

"So, what's the plan? We type all this stuff up for Mr. Stark, and hope that it's still useful when he gets back?"

"Maybe. Maybe we can go around and talk to a few of these people. Find out if there are any connections between them. If we can trace all of these back to a couple of sources, we might be able to figure out who's managed to hire fairies to do their dirty work for them."

"It's like chasing shadows," I mutter.

"No, that was our last case."

I laugh. "You got me there. Okay, so we keep sorting?"

The phone rings, and Holly holds up a finger for me to hold my thought while she picks it up. "Basil Stark Investigations," she says cheerfully. "How can we help? Oh! Well, yes, that is a bit unusual, but as it happens he's here with me right now. Of course." She puts a hand over the receiver. "It's for you."

"Huh?" I take the phone. "Uh, this is Todd."

"Todd, my boy! Glad that I caught you. Tried you at home but I didn't get an answer, and then I thought, well, maybe the folks at your other job have an idea."

"Oh, hi, Mr. Carson." Holly gapes at me, and I give her a shrug. "What do you need?"

Vance is ecstatic, almost laughing with each word. "We have a new case!"

"We do?"

"Phyllis Graves. You remember her, I presume?"

"Yeah, of course."

"Well, she would like to speak with me, and I'd like you to come along. There might be more to this case than we first guessed."

That seems pretty obvious, so I let it pass. "Okay. When does she want us?"

"In an hour. I'm leaving the house now. Can I pick you up?"

I press the receiver into my chest and look over to Holly. "Okay for me to run out? Might be connected."

"No problem. I'll get the files typed up and meet you later." She grins. "Oh, but take Glimmer along. Between the two of us, I'd rather have eyes in the sky on you."

"Sure thing." I pick up the phone again. "I'll be downstairs in five minutes, Mr. Carson."

"Splendid! I will see you momentarily." Vance hangs up, leaving me staring at the phone in confusion.

"Vance Carson is back in action?" Holly asks.

"Yeah, it looks like the blackmailer from our last case is the person hiring him for this one, which is something else." I look down at the packages. "Maybe Ms. Graves is the link that we need. If Mr. Stark doesn't come back, think we can share this with Mr. Carson?"

Holly makes a face. "I don't know, Todd. This is a pretty big thing, and Vance is nice and all, but he's not exactly a guy who goes after big cases."

"No, but he is a guy who knows all the rich folk in town, and can go talk to them without anyone setting their dogs on him."

"That only happened to Uncle Basil twice! Three times." Holly thinks about it. "I see your point. Okay, I'll get this stuff together. We don't know when Uncle Basil will be back, and it'll serve him right if we solve the case before he does. Let me know how your trip goes."

I nod and head downstairs, with Glimmer right behind me. By the time we get down, Vance is already pulling around the corner. "Got the car fixed up?" I ask as he pulls up.

"Turned out it was a pretty easy repair," he says. "I jumped the gun a bit, though; mechanic confirmed that the cut was too far into the car to be deliberate. Oh, hello, Miss Glimmer. Are you coming with us?"

"Yeah, about that. I think maybe you were right and I was wrong."

"How'd you mean?"

"Glimmer had a run-in with a nasty customer. Another fairy, but a stab-happy one. Working as part of a blackmail ring."

Vance is quiet for a moment as he steers us back into the flow of traffic. "Fairy criminals?"

"Any reason they couldn't be?"

"I suppose not. Never really thought about it before." Vance drums the wheel, staring ahead. "Weren't there a couple of fairies hanging around the camp?"

"That's what I was thinking," I nod. "Fletcher and that one that flew off. Wish you'd been there, Glimmer, you could have told us if one of them was the same guy."

Glimmer, crouched down pretty far so that the wind doesn't knock her out of the car, agrees that that would have been good. I continue. "Anyway, Glimmer's going to hang around and keep watch for us, make sure there isn't anyone doing the same for the other side."

"Clever. I like it." Vance nods. "If this is part of a grander scheme, especially one involving blackmailers, we'll want to be as careful as possible not to get poor Ms. Graves in any deeper."

Ms. Graves is being held at Kensington Point, the island's regional jail. Kensington Point is pretty new; it was built as a second military base during the war, with one wing for holding potential prisoners of war or saboteurs, and then we didn't really get many of those, so they started converting it to hold local prisoners, too. When the war ended, they started converting other wings into prison space, and now that's the only thing it's used for. There are four wings, two bigger ones for low-security inmates and two smaller ones for the high-security ones, with about two hundred and fifty people spread across them.

Ms. Graves is being held in the women's low-security wing. I'm a little surprised she's being held anywhere, and I say as much to Vance.

"Pressure from Hawthorne, I expect," he answers, parking the car. "I expect they're willing to argue that she's a flight risk, especially with the funds she's supposed to have taken, but we both know she spent that and doesn't have two nickels to rub together."

"Does she have two nickels to rub together for your fees?"

Vance smiles. "We'll figure something out."

I grin and nod. "Okay, Glimmer, I don't think they're letting you into the jail," I say to her. "But I bet you can track us from a safe distance. Don't spook any of the guards, follow us, and make sure that we're good."

Glimmer lets me know, pretty rudely, that I don't need to teach her how to sneak around and follow people, she's been doing it all her life. Vance cocks an eyebrow at us.

"Everything okay?"

Glimmer turns a sweet smile towards him, gives him a thumbs-up, lightly kicks me in the gut for doubting her, and takes off.

"She's a real firebrand, hey." Vance says.

"Hell of a good partner, though."

"Oh, I bet. Imagine the places you could get into. We should have had her break into the pawnbroker's and used me as the decoy."

I think about that for a moment. "Yeah, that might have worked, actually. I dunno if she can crack safes, though."

"Think she could learn?"

"I think we shouldn't be adding 'master thief' to her list of skills. Come on, the guards are looking at us."

Vance leads the way inside. After showing his credentials to the guards at the door and then again to the guard at the desk, they check us over for any contraband, and then we're led to a small room with a single table and two small chairs, overlooking the exercise yard. The guards leave us for a minute while they find an extra chair for me so I don't have to loom in the back like Frankenstein, and then we're left waiting another ten before the guard comes back with Phyllis, who is wearing a prison jumpsuit but no handcuffs. She looks a bit better than the last time I saw her — she's more tired, but her eyes don't look as haunted.

"You came," she says, and her whole face lightens up a little further.

"Of course, Ms. Graves. It would be my pleasure to help you." Vance looks at the guard. "Would you be able to give us some privacy?"

The guard frowns. "You family?"

"It's a confidential legal matter," Vance says.

The guard looks him up and down, and seems to decide that he's not dangerous. "Yeah, okay. Five minutes. I'll be right outside the door. Yell if you're in trouble." I'm not sure whether he's talking to Vance or to Phyllis, but Vance takes it as approval and gives the guard a thumbs-up.

Phyllis waits until the door clicks shut before letting out a slow breath. "Thank you," she says. "I don't know who might be reporting back to them."

"To be honest, I'm not sure that private detectives are actually promised privacy, so we should probably make it quick. I assume that this is related to your being blackmailed?"

Ms. Graves' eyes widen. "You knew I was being blackmailed?" she asks.

"I am a detective, Ms. Graves," Vance says with another reassuring smile. "Your associates, the fact that you went from embezzling money for your family to gathering scrip you couldn't spend, and your thankfulness for it to be done were all important clues. Combined with certain other client cases that I'm not at liberty to discuss, and it became clear that you were performing blackmail in order to deal with blackmail against you."

Tears well up in Ms. Graves' eyes. "I thought you wouldn't believe me," she admits, dabbing at them with her sleeve. "It all seemed so strange."

"Envelopes in mysterious places?" I suggest. Vance glances at me, one eyebrow raised, but lets me take over. I continue, "Maybe a phone call telling you to take the rap for the embezzlement, or else they'd nail you for that and the blackmail both."

She nods. "It was all my fault at first. The first money that I withdrew, it was to help my cousin. He was behind on his rent, just needed a bit of extra money. I thought I could help him pay, make up the difference out of my next couple paychecks, and get him to pay me back. That part that I told you was true. But it wasn't the bonus that wrecked everything. Someone spotted the difference before I could make it up. They sent me a message, demanding money or else. I didn't have money, but I had access to the accounts."

"So, you embezzled to pay blackmail threatening to expose you for embezzlement?" I ask. She looks down, and I wince. "Sorry. Just getting the facts straight."

"Yes," she finally says. "The strangest thing was the blackmailer insisted on being paid in Hawthorne scrip. It didn't make much sense, but I assumed they thought they could fence it somehow, and I wasn't going to argue."

"Huh," Vance says slowly. "So, what brought my client into the mix?"

"I don't know," Ms. Graves admitted. "I didn't blackmail him. I didn't know anything about it until I got a phone call that Saturday. She told me that if I confessed to the embezzlement and pretended to have been blackmailing someone named Drainie to a detective, my cousin's debts would be covered."

Vance is aghast. "What?"

"She told me that I was in trouble anyway, that the scrip would be tracked back and no one would believe I wasn't the blackmailer responsible. That I had a choice between helping my family or going to jail for nothing."

"And you got scared," I said slowly.

"I didn't know what to do. When you showed up, I ran away," Ms. Graves is crying now. "I don't know what I was thinking. It wasn't going to help. So, I gave up. I told you what she told me to, that it was my idea, that it was my friends at the logging camp, all of it. I just wanted it to be over. I needed it to be over."

Vance gives me a desperate look, and I reach across the table and take Ms. Graves' hand.

"But then you called us," I say slowly.

She looks up, nodding sadly. "Because it's not just me, is it?"

"It's not," I agree. "How'd you know?"

"I've had some time to think, waiting for my hearing," Ms. Graves says. "I realized that if you two followed the blackmail from this Drainie person to me, that meant that the scrip I was giving them was being used as part of some bigger blackmail thing, something that you got close enough to that they were willing to give up everything I was making for them and even pay me off just to get you off the trail. So, I called you. I don't know if they'll find out, but I just couldn't sit by."

"Ms. Graves," Vance says seriously, "that is extremely brave of you. And you might just have given us the break that we needed. The woman who called you, do you think you would know her voice if you heard it again?"

"I don't know. Maybe. It was low, like she was trying to cover it up. She had a trace of an accent, but I couldn't say from where."

Vance nods. "And when did she call you?"

"About two o' clock, I think. I don't know exactly."

"You don't need to know exactly." Vance looks at me and grins. "Ms. Graves, stay quiet for now, and thank you so much. Todd, come on! We've got a case to follow!"

"Uh, yeah. Thank you, Ms. Graves. You be careful now, okay?"

"Thank you, young man. You too. Please. I don't want anyone else to be hurt." Ms. Graves pats my hand once, and then lets me go. I stand and follow Vance, who's already halfway down the corridor.

As we collect our things, I say, "What gives?"

"It's simple, Todd. A phone call! While we were at the logging camp."

"Yeah, but we already knew that there were fairies at the camp…" I trail off. "Fairies wouldn't have access to the radio room, though."

"Exactly. And that radio only calls Hawthorne HQ, which we know because we couldn't use it without Hawthorne staff listening in. Which means that when we showed up, someone called Hawthorne to let them know what was going on. They might have lied about the content, but they can't hide who was on duty. If we check the radio logs, we'll know exactly where the next lead is!"

"Great. Who's paying us?"

Vance stops dead at the car. "Pardon?"

"I'm pretty sure you're not trying to get money from Ms. Graves, and I'll bet that Mr. Drainie isn't giving you a dime. So, who's the client?"

"Me, Todd. Someone set that poor woman up, and I intend to bring them to justice." Framed against the light, Vance actually looks pretty heroic, and I can't help but grin.

"That's pretty fine of you, Mr. Carson."

"Vance, Todd. Call me Vance."

"Okay, Vance. Oh, hey, Glimmer! How'd it go?"

Glimmer informs me that there was no aerial surveillance, and also that lady looked pretty nice and she hopes she's okay.

"You found the window?"

She gives me an offended look.

"Alright, everyone! We're heading up to Hawthorne. Glimmer, will you be joining us?"

Glimmer considers, and then nods and says something about seeing what happens next.

"Perfect. Then our next stop will be Hawthorne Logging!"

"How are we getting in?" I ask.

"I have a plan!" Vance guns the engine, and we tear away from the curb. I grab Glimmer to help her stay settled, and she leans into my arm.

Vance doesn't seem inclined to elaborate on his plan without prompting. We drive for six or seven minutes before I break and ask him what exactly he has planned.

"We go to the front desk, I charm the receptionist, and you sneak into the radio room and check the logs."

"Okay, that's a plan. Only I'm not great at sneaking, and also there's no way to sneak past the front desk, and also there's definitely going to be someone in the radio room. What am I supposed to do, beat them up?"

"Oh, no, that would be bad. Definitely don't do that." Vance frowns thoughtfully. "Let's consider our resources. We have a talented detective with some small amount of social cachet, a skilled investigator and brawler, and an extremely stealthy pint-sized spy. Ow!" The car almost veers into oncoming traffic, as Glimmer has kicked Vance in his knuckle just as he was changing gears. "A debonair and stealthy agent?" he hazards after a moment.

Glimmer smiles smugly and settles back into the crook of my arm.

"Right. I suppose we could just ask you to slip in through a window and let us in the back door," Vance says after a moment.

"And then one of us could distract the radio operator and the other one checks the logs?" I add.

"Perfect." Vance glances over at us. "Let's go and crack this case!"

The first hitch in our plan pops up before we're even at the parking lot. There's a barricade across the road, manned by two Regulator agents. They're both big, wearing black fatigues and helmets that cover most of their faces. One of them raises a hand to flag us down, and Glimmer shrinks into the seat as Vance pulls over. "Everything alright, officer?"

"I need to see your ID, sir," the Regulator says, holding out one hand. The other one is standing easily, but her hand is close to her rifle.

"Why?" Vance asks.

"This is an official checkpoint," the Regulator says. "Now. Your ID."

Vance frowns, but reaches into his pocket and fishes out his wallet. He pulls out a card and hands it to him. "My license."

"And them."

I grab my ID, and nudge Glimmer. She nods and passes me her papers, which we pass over to the Regulator, who gives my card a perfunctory look and Glimmer's papers a much closer pass. After assuring himself that it's not a forgery, he pulls out a notepad, writes down our names, and passes them back. "Thank you for your compliance, Mr. Carson. What business do you have at Hawthorne today?"

"Confidential, I'm afraid," Vance says with a smile. The Regulator does not smile back, and Vance's confidence wilts. "Following up on a private investigation. This is a public road, and we're going to a public business. What's going on?"

"We have been asked by Hawthorne to be on hand to deal with a potential incident," the Regulator says. "All non-essential personnel are being asked to turn back."

Vance and I share a look. The Regulators are Everland's very-own anti-magical enforcement agency. Day to day, most of them hunt down and arrest fairies who're dodging registration; capture and destroy rogue shadows that have slithered off their owners and are wreaking havoc; or show up places where people are trying to make magic artifacts and take them away — the artifacts and the people. When something really old and nasty shows up, like the Crocodile or the Drowned Ship, the Regulators deploy in force to deal with it. Supposedly, they've got a plan for everything, from the smallest wolf to the return of the Pan.

But the thing is, Hawthorne *hates* the Regulators. If anyone on the island is likely to fall into "having a magical thing they wanted to monetize taken away by the Regulators," it's Hawthorne. Every other month someone from Hawthorne has an op-ed in the paper or is down at the courthouse or takes out radio ads saying that the Regulators are in Second Star's pocket and accusing them of everything from uneven enforcement to actively giving things to Second Star that they're supposed to be destroying.

For the moment, Vance just nods to the Regulator. "Alright, then. Thank you for your time." He turns the car away and starts driving, much more slowly. As soon as we're out of earshot he says, "That doesn't seem right."

"It sure doesn't. Glimmer, think you can get high enough to get a look at what's going on? I don't see any helicopters."

Glimmer takes off, and Vance pulls the car over and parks us behind some bushes. She's back within a couple of minutes, and breathlessly says that there are tigers all over the parking lot.

"What?" I stare at her.

"How do we get in?" Vance asks.

"Why would we want to get in?"

Vance taps his temple. "There are no coincidences, Todd. If there are tigers at Hawthorne right now, just as we're planning to investigate, it's probably connected."

He thinks about it. "They've got a checkpoint on the main road, but they don't have a flying spy, and we're — what, ten minutes away on foot? Why don't we just slip into the area, find out what's going on? We'll never get a better distraction."

"I don't know if this is a good idea. Maybe we should just come back tomorrow, and read about it in the papers?"

"They won't put the good stuff in the papers. Come on, Todd! Where's your sense of adventure?"

"A little lower than my sense of getting eaten by a tiger?"

"Tigers don't eat people, that's just propaganda. Glimmer, what do you think? Can you get us through?"

Glimmer tells me it's child's play and launches back into the air. Vance climbs out of the car and starts after her, pausing just long enough to wave for me to join him.

I suddenly realize that I'm the responsible one here. The thought is maybe the scariest one I've had all day, and I run after Vance before he can go and get himself and Glimmer both killed.

It takes about twice as long as Vance thought for us to tromp through the woods to the Hawthorne lot. There are a few other Regulator groups around. Glimmer flies down to warn us before any of them are within sight, and we're able to change our routes to avoid them, but each time I just about have a heart attack, sure that every branch I'm breaking is going to lead to us into a really uncomfortable cell. Is this trespassing? They've got our names; they know that we know we're not supposed to be here.

Just as we're coming up on the edge of the woods, Glimmer comes down hard and fast. She's waving her arms, and I turn to see what she's so worried about just in time to see a big, fast something jumping at Vance. Instinct takes over, and I shove him in one direction and dive in the other. I almost make it; something hits my leg hard enough to bowl me over, and I feel a faint sting. I grab a fallen branch as I roll up, in time to find myself about four inches from a very large set of fangs.

"Skulkers, prowlers," the tiger growls, hackles up. "The Regulators send their spies to attack us!"

"Woah, no, we're not Regulators, promise!" I'm not putting down the branch, but I shift my grip so it's obviously not about to be swung at her. "We're just out for a walk."

"You lie! You believe us fools?" The tiger's ears twitch. "Your voice is familiar, human. I know you."

"Amhara!" The second growl comes from farther back, and another tiger pads into the clearing. This one is even larger than the first, and he growls low in his throat. "Are you attacking humans?"

Amhara snorts. "If I had attacked him, he would be lying dead on the ground. I swatted him."

"Amhara. Yeah, you're Hkuri's cousin, right?" I ask.

Amhara looks back at me, her head tilted, and her ears go even further back. "You are Todd. And the detective. You see, Fraal? They send spies to interfere with us."

"No, no no no. We're not with anyone. To be honest, we're dodging Regulators," Vance says. "It's a long story, but we were coming up to follow up on a case that I'm working, and, well, they've got the roads closed off for the moment."

"Of course they do," Fraal studies us closely. "You will come with us."

"Oh, I wouldn't want to—" Vance starts. Fraal growls, and Vance goes quiet.

"You will come with us," Fraal says again. "You are a 'detective,' you say. That is a human that looks for falsehoods done by other humans, yes?"

"Sometimes. Sometimes we look for things that have gone missing."

"Good. You will look for a falsehood for us." Fraal begins to pad away.

"You cannot be serious," Amhara snarls.

Fraal turns back to her, hackles raising. "You challenge me?"

Amhara looks like she's about to jump, and for a moment she and Fraal start to circle each other, eyes locked. Then she takes a step back and looks away. "Do as you will, and suffer the consequences," she snaps.

"Good." Fraal turns away and continues padding into the woods. Vance and I share a look and then follow. I don't like the idea of walking into the middle of whatever this is, but Amhara looks just about ready to explode, and I don't want to be the match that sets her off. My leg's hurting enough from that swat.

"So," Vance says after a moment, "you're interested in a detective?"

"We are. I do not know how this is done. I assume that there is some sort of payment involved."

"Traditionally, yes. Daily rates in exchange for reports."

"And then you sneak about and unearth information that is required?"

"I wouldn't quite phrase it..." Vance shrugs helplessly. "Yes, basically."

"Good. That is a good profession." Fraal glances back, sees our expression, and gives out a long, low snicker. "You are surprised? We are not bears, Mr. Vance. Most tigers are not comfortable pretending, but we know secrecy. We are not simple creatures."

"I'm sorry," Vance says. "You're right, of course."

"Good. Now, you will come with us, and I will explain."

Fraal leads us to the Hawthorne lot, where another dozen tigers are hanging around, in front of twice as many very nervous-looking Hawthorne security guards, plus five more Regulators. There's a truck parked by the front gates with another agent in it; things look pretty tense.

"The problem is simple," Fraal says. "Our borders have been challenged. Goods have been taken. We know that the thieves are from here, and we came to demand an investigation. Hawthorne tells us that it is impossible, and the thief must be a tiger."

"Bet that didn't go down well," I say.

"It did not. So, we came in larger numbers. Our treaties say that policing the humans is a human concern, as policing tigers is a tiger concern. We know that one tiger may be ignored. Many must be listened to." Fraal looks out over the situation, his ears back. "We came this morning. Hawthorne replied by calling for guns." He looks over the agents. "I am now wondering what a Hawthorne agent tastes of. This will not help, but it would be satisfying."

"Okay, right. I see where hiring a detective would come in handy." Vance steps forward, walking through the confused tigers towards the security guards. I'm caught off-guard for a moment, and Glimmer and I race after him just in time to catch up as he reaches the line of baffled guards. "Excuse me, Vance Carson, private detective. I need to speak with a Hawthorne representative. It's fairly urgent."

"What are you doing here?" one of the guards asks.

"Representing my clients, of course." Vance gives a pleasant smile. "Look, would you rather I have a quiet one-on-one with someone, or would you rather see what happens when the tigers get angry?"

"We can take a bunch of mangy—" one of the guards starts, before his partner shushes him. The guard in front of Vance looks from him to the tigers, and back to him.

"If you call it in, it's not your problem anymore," I suggest.

That pushes him, and he pulls out his walkie. "We have a representative from the tigers here to negotiate."

"Send them in," comes the voice after a moment. "We'll meet with them in the lobby."

Vance and I are quickly shown in, and I'm surprised to realize that I know two of the three people who are standing there — almost as surprised as they are to realize that they know us. "Vance Carson and Todd Malcolm," Michelle Arsenault says through gritted teeth. "How lovely to see you again. This is Mr. Hsi, our head of security, and Agent Harper, from—"

"We are acquainted," Agent Harper says, looking us up and down. "It seems that we just keep meeting in increasingly complex situations." He takes an extra moment to glower at me.

"Well, I'm told that there's a bit of a treaty dispute going on," Vance says.

"These beasts are interfering with the regular operations of a nationally-important business," Agent Harper says. "I do not much care for why. We have given them several opportunities to disperse, and they are distinctly unwilling to do so."

"Ms. Arsenault, I assume that you are here as the VP in charge of tiger contracts?" Vance asks.

Michelle nods stiffly. "The tigers seem to think that Hawthorne is violating their borders. Something to do with missing supplies. I've tried to explain that no one from Hawthorne goes anywhere *near* tiger territory, but they're demanding that we send teams to investigate their own thefts." She shakes her head. "As much as I would love to oblige, we don't have the time or the resources for that kind of investigation, especially not given the obvious answer: a tiger did it."

"On the other hand, if we end up with violence here, you know that the tigers will close their borders entirely. All of their borders." Vance looks between Michelle and Harper. "That's, what, a fifth of the terrain that you log? Never mind what happens if they start treating this like a war."

"That would be a mistake," Agent Harper says. "There are only a few hundred tigers on the island. They would be crushed in a direct conflict."

"Would they?" I ask. "They know the land, they don't have much stuff for you to take away, they weigh four hundred pounds, and every one of them knows how to fight. Five hundred commandos running solo ops through the woods sounds like a problem to me. Plus, if the other locals start thinking you're breaking treaties, things could get real rough."

Harper's eyes narrow at me. "Oh, and I suppose you're going to solve this."

I look over to Vance, who gives Harper his most beaming smile. "I am, actually! The tigers have asked me to investigate the thefts. I'll have permission to move through their territory, so I simply need permission to ask questions over here. If it does turn out that a tiger is involved, as you say, they'll cover payment. But if I find a human culprit is responsible, the municipal government shoulders the load." He turns his smile on Michelle. "Either way, Hawthorne won't have to pay a dime, and you won't have work shut down while I'm looking into things."

Michelle frowns, and looks at her companions. Mr. Hsi, who has been quiet up until now, says, "Ma'am, it's your call.

I would rather not get into a pitched battle with twelve tigers on our front steps, no matter how many feds and Regulators we might have backing us up. Even discounting the threat to my men, there's the optics. You know the news will have a field day with this."

"And I do know Mr. Carson," Agent Harper says after a moment. "I think we can trust him to act in the best interests of everyone involved."

"Fine. Yes." Michelle rubs her temple and turns away. "I'll let my people know to co-operate with you. Just get my parking lot back up and running, would you?"

"You won't regret this, ma'am," Vance says. He taps me on the shoulder. "Come on, Todd, let's tell them the good news."

Mr. Hsi follows us out the door and talks with Hawthorne security as we return to Fraal. Todd fills him in on the situation.

"This is ridiculous." Amhara has joined us again. "The only things that we know about these humans is that one of them claims to be a detective, and that they were attempting to sneak up on us. And that they failed!" The other tigers murmur a bit, thinking it over.

"We know that they are humans who work with a fairy," Fraal says. "They do not only consider human abilities. They were interested in our problems. And they have ensured that when we are proven right, the humans will pay for their investigation."

Amhara snorts. "They will pretend to investigate, and then say it was a tiger and leave. We should not trust them."

"Ma'am, I appreciate your concerns," I say, stepping forward. "But we will show you our work. We will give you our reports. If you need a human detective, Vance Carson is your guy."

Vance nods. "We'll need to be able to look over the territory that was invaded, of course, and I'll arrange to speak with Hawthorne. I can follow up on the investigation from there."

"Of course. The terrain is bordered by Gray Rock Ridge, near the Fallen Bluffs. Come to the borders of our territory tomorrow morning, and we will escort you the rest of the way. Bring no one but yourselves." Fraal dips his head respectfully, and seven of the other tigers do the same. The other four, including Amhara, glare at us.

"Thank you," Vance says. "I will see you tomorrow."

We turn, and start to walk back towards the car, taking the road this time. Behind us, the tigers are already returning to the woods. Vance keeps his firm walk for one quiet minute, and then lets out an explosive breath. "Oh my god, I thought we were going to be eaten back there."

"You were pretty chill about it."

"I was shaking! Thanks for standing up for me. Do you really think I'm their best option?"

I think about how Amhara almost attacked Vance back when she just *thought* he might be Mr. Stark. "Yeah, I'd say so. You don't think the Regulators are going to do anything about it?"

Vance mulls on that for a moment. "I would have expected them to, honestly."

"They protect humans from magic. They don't protect anyone from humans."

Vance makes a face. "Never really thought about it that way," he says. "But yeah, that makes sense. I guess we're lucky that we have trustworthy faces."

"I wonder," I say. "That Fraal guy seemed to have a pretty good handle on what was going on. I think maybe he was looking for a way to back down without losing his people even before we showed up."

"Maybe he already knew me. The other tiger did."

"That was Hkuri's cousin. We met her at Hawthorne, remember? She was dealing with accounting or something with Ms. Arsenault."

"Oh, that was the same tiger? That's interesting. For someone who dislikes humans so much, she sure spends a lot of time around them." Vance shrugs. "Well, the important thing is that we have the job, and if we're successful, this will be the start of some big things for us. Plus, it's a chance for us to gain access to Hawthorne and pursue our *other* investigation. Two for the price of one, you might say." Vance is grinning ear to ear.

"Heh, that is pretty good," I admit. "Good thing that you were with us, huh, Glimmer?" I turn to find a total lack of a flying companion next to us. "Glimmer?"

Vance turns. "Wait, where is she?"

"She didn't come inside with us, but I figured she was just out in the lot." I look around. "Glimmer?" I call out, more loudly.

"Okay, let's not worry yet. Back to the car, and we'll wait for her there," Vance says. "If she's not back in fifteen minutes, we go looking for her."

I nod reluctantly and return to the car with him. We don't have to wait long. Glimmer is back a few minutes later, looking very smug.

"Where were you?" I ask.

The story that Glimmer tells me, with a lot of pauses for me to translate for Vance and for follow-up questions, is this:

While everyone else was distracted by tigers and yelling, Glimmer was getting to work. The plan was to sneak into Hawthorne and find things out, and that's what she was going to do. Leaving us behind, she flew over to the nearest open window. It was even easier than she'd figured it would be — the window was in an office right next to the main hall, and whoever had been inside had come out to look at the tiger delegation, leaving their door wide open.

The question was, what to do next? This was supposed to be when Glimmer went to the back door to let us in, but if she knew humans, Vance was already distracted by the newer, shinier problem. The best thing to do was to get somewhere she could listen in on what people had to say about the tigers and everything that was going on. That would let her know whether Todd and Vance would need the door opened, or if she was doing the real work herself again.

Glimmer flew towards the lobby, staying low to the ground. She could hear my voice from just around the corner, which led her to where Vance and I were finishing our talk with the Hawthorne representatives. Looking around, she saw that the halls were lined with big, bushy plants in ceramic pots, perfect for hiding in. She ducked into one, keeping an eye out for any other spies, curled a few leaves around her for security. She watched Mr. Hsi escort Vance and me out and return alone a few minutes later to rejoin the others. "It's settled," he said. "Tigers are leaving."

"I cannot believe we have to deal with this, on top of everything else," Michelle muttered, turning and stalking down the corridor with the other two just behind her.

"Better them than us," Mr. Hsi suggested. "I'd like to keep all my security near our camps instead of sending them out chasing ghosts." He looked over at his companion. "We're dealing with enough as it is."

"Hm." Agent Harper glanced around, looking for eavesdroppers, and Glimmer sank farther back into her hiding place. "Perhaps this is a conversation we should have in the boardroom."

"Of course, Agent Harper." Michelle gestured. "This way, please."

Glimmer waited for them to walk through the door, and then flew over to look around. The bottom of the door was too tight to squeeze under, and even if she could have, they would have spotted her. There were no air ducts in the building, either. But when she looked up, she saw that this floor used the new dropped ceilings that were getting popular.

Glimmer flew up to the ceiling. With a grunt of effort, she shoved the tile up and crawled into the space above the ceiling. Settling the tile back down, she crawled along the pipes to the boardroom, and positioned herself just above one of the building's sprinklers to listen in more closely.

"—might convince the rest to mind their place," Agent Harper was saying. Glimmer tried to wriggle close enough to peer through the hole around the sprinkler, but she could only see the edge of the agent's shoes.

"I agree with Mr. Hsi. We could spin it in the news, but unless you have a few thousand soldiers ready to come in, shooting a tiger on Hawthorne property would be a disaster," Michelle argued. "Needing to send five-man squads with every logging team just in case of ambush would cut into our profits, and there's no telling what would happen if the other treaty-holders decided that it was time for a show of solidarity. We barely have relations with the bears at the best of times, and the wolves have made some serious inroads with the press lately. Not to mention that almost a third of our loggers are Piccadilly, and they're very sensitive about treaty violations. If they walked off the job, the other loggers might join them. Our operations would be shut down overnight."

"I could have two thousand soldiers here in two weeks. I just need to send the message. In fact, after today, I think I will." Harper turned his back on the others, and took a step away from them which brought him into Glimmer's field of view. He was scowling, but there was something else behind it, something that he was being careful not to let the other two see. Not for the first time, Glimmer wished that human emotions weren't so complicated. If he was a fairy, it would be easy to figure out, but he could be literally feeling anything right now. There was some disgust, she thought. Anger. Maybe fear? Was he afraid of Hawthorne going out of business?

"You don't think that Mr. Carson can defuse the situation?" Michelle asks.

"Of course not. The man's a fool. But he will buy us time for a proper response."

"With due respect, Agent Harper, it's one thing for the mayor to approve a dozen federal agents, and something else entirely to have a US military occupation," Mr. Hsi pointed out. "You'll never get approval. Besides which, you aren't here to help us with tiger issues. You're here to help us with our espionage problem."

"I am here," Agent Harper spat, spinning back to face them before Glimmer could finish getting a read on him, "to make sure that an important resource to the United States isn't compromised any further, for any reason. We've identified four blackmailed employees already, including one who managed to embezzle several thousand dollars from right under your nose and possibly attempted murder to cover her tracks."

"I really don't think that Ms. Graves tried to commit murder." Mr. Hsi said.

"I really don't care what you think, Mr. Hsi. If you were capable of doing your job, I wouldn't be here."

There was a very quiet moment before Mr. Hsi spoke again. "Well then," he said stiffly. "I suppose I'll go organize the security details and make sure the tigers didn't do any damage and leave you to keeping the world safe for democracy." As he stalked past, Glimmer didn't need to guess what he was feeling. Sometimes even humans got to the point where they only felt one thing, and Hsi was a boiler ready to explode.

The door slammed shut behind Hsi, and Michelle spoke. "That was a bit uncalled for, Agent Harper."

"Your head of security is an idiot," Harper said. "This was the perfect opportunity. We could have had the tiger situation wrapped up by the end of the month if he hadn't been afraid of a fight."

"What about the mermaids?" Michelle stepped into Glimmer's field of view, putting a hand gently on Harper's shoulder. She was still radiating anger, but as Glimmer watched it faded into a quiet certainty. "We know which way they would fall if you started a war today."

Harper snorted. "We can handle them."

"Can you? Do you remember what happened to the first American ship to take a mermaid back to the States? It never made it. Do you remember what happened to the second one? It never made it, either. Do you remember why there was never a third attempt?" She stepped past Harper, walking to the door. "We still don't know if the mermaids can stop shipping entirely. We do know that no Germans found this island for the entire war. Don't you think that's suspicious? Doesn't it make you wonder if your ships full of soldiers would ever make landfall?"

Harper looked after her, grinding his teeth. "What would you suggest? Bend the knee to monsters and beasts?"

"Mr. Hsi is right. You're here to keep things running smoothly. So, keep things running smoothly." Michelle walked out of the room, leaving Harper to clench his fists and take several deep breaths before following her.

Glimmer thought about what she'd heard. Harper was investigating the blackmail! And, she thought, trying to start some kind of war on the side. Soldiers all lined up to invade didn't sound good. Glimmer slipped back down the hall and waited to make sure there wasn't anyone coming before making her way back outside. Todd and Vance were going to want to hear this.

"Yeah," Vance says once Glimmer is done. "We were going to want to hear that."

"Harper wants a war?" I ask. "That's insane."

"Not that insane, unfortunately. There are people that think we gave up too much of the island to the non-human species when we first landed here. Not enough people to really do anything about it, but you hear it at every party."

"I don't."

Vance sighs. "Well, I hear it at every party. If Harper could convince people that the tigers started it ... maybe. I don't know. But I believe that he believes it, and he might even get the Americans to agree. He comes here looking for blackmail, finds angry tigers, and his only mission is to keep this island profitable? I don't like where that leads."

Glimmer asks whether we think the two cases are the same case.

"They could be," I say, before pausing to translate for a clearly confused Vance. "If there are more blackmail cases at Hawthorne, maybe someone got blackmailed into sneaking into tiger territory."

"All part of a grand scheme of some sort, no doubt. Yes, Miss Glimmer, I do believe that you're onto something! If we only had more pieces of information."

"We do," I say. I immediately regret it.

"We do?" Vance asks.

"I mean, Holly and I do. It's a long story, but the short version is we got some other blackmail notes. They're not all addressed."

"Todd, would you be able to do me a favor and bring those files to my office tomorrow? If there are other members of high society impacted, I might be able to identify them and figure out how far this goes."

"I'll check with Holly, but I figure we can probably do that. Every bit of help counts."

"Thank you, Todd." Vance smiles again. "You won't regret it."

# Sunday, August 26<sup>th</sup>

**Sunday morning, I'm** finishing up breakfast and getting ready to head over to Vance's office when there's a knock on the door. I head over and open it to find Emeka standing uncertainly in the hall. He's dressed for work, with short sleeves and a vest, and he smiles when he sees me. "Uh, hi. Mind if I come in?"

"Yeah! Sure." I look around as I step back. "Sorry about the mess. With all the case stuff, I haven't really been ... well, you can see." I grab a small stack of plates off the table and move them to the sink, then quickly brush crumbs off the counter. "You want anything to eat? Drink?"

"Orange juice would be great if you've got any left. Thanks." Emeka sits down and looks over at me. "Is this the case you're working on with Holly?"

"Maybe? Man, it's gotten busy."

"I figured. I haven't seen you since Tuesday."

I stop and think about that. "Aw, geez, you haven't. I've been so busy I didn't even think about it. How's the gigging going?"

"Taking off, man. Remember how we wanted to spend this week getting ready for the weekend? Well, every club in town wants to see the tiger and her chums. We've done five shows, now." Emeka settles back as I pass him a glass of juice. "Actually, that's kind of why I'm here."

"Oh, yeah?"

"So, last night's show was over at the Treehouse."

"You made it into the Treehouse? Holy cow, man, that place is serious business!"

"Yeah," Emeka says. "Not a big fan of the clientele, though."

"Oh, yeah." A lot of criminal types hang out there. Back in the day, they say it was where the Lost Boys lived when they were at war with the pirates and just about everyone else on the island. The place is still owned by one of the survivors, and he's turned it into a neutral ground for just about every power player in the city, whether for business deals or mob negotiations. Not really Emeka's sort of place. But they're loaded with cash, and all sorts of high rollers pay attention to who's on stage.

"Anyway, not the point. The point is that Hkuri told me you've been hired by the tigers' council to investigate sabotage?"

"Well, not really. Vance got hired, I'm just tagging along."

"Todd."

"Hey, it's okay. We were just in the right place at the right time."

"Really? That is not what it sounds like from my angle."

I sigh. "What does it sound like from your angle?"

"It sounds like the tigers were in a bad spot, and Fraal decided to use you as his scapegoats so that when you can't find anything he can blame you instead of going to war," Emeka says bluntly.

"Well, then, Fraal is in for a surprise when we solve the case, isn't he?"

"Are you trying to get killed?"

"Huh?"

Emeka waves his arm. "First the thing at the bar, and then you start actually investigating the people who are *trying to blackmail you,* and then the next thing I know you've given up on that to go and look into tigers!"

"We, uh, haven't actually given up on that. We caught a guy, found some more blackmail." Emeka stares at me, speechless. I scratch the back of my head. "I would've mentioned it sooner, Emeka, it's just been kind of a busy week."

"I can see that." Emeka picks up his juice, then sets it down again without taking a sip. "What the heck is going on, Todd? This isn't like you."

"What, just because I'm not Basil Stark, you don't think I can do it?"

"No, I just..." Emeka grinds his teeth. "That's not what I meant. I'm worried about you. You're a good guy, but lately, you've been throwing yourself face-first at every problem you see. What happens when you run into something that's too big to fight, huh? People die when they get involved with stuff like this."

"I've got Vance taking the lead."

"Vance is not a good detective! You know that! Everyone knows that!"

"Well, maybe he's better than people think!"

"Is he?" Emeka stares at me. "Can you look me in the eye and say that he's handling this sensibly?"

I think about the cut brakes, trying to break into Hawthorne, and slipping past the Regulators on a whim. "Okay, well, he's a bit eager, sure, but he's better than people think."

Emeka lets out a long breath. "Fine, I get it. Not my circus, not my monkey. I just ... please be careful, okay? When tigers play games, claws come out."

I grin lopsidedly. "Like I said last time, I've been in tougher scrapes than this."

Emeka stands up. "I'm sorry. I came at this all wrong. Seems like every time I see you lately, I'm just all doom and gloom. Look, have a good morning. I hope the case goes well."

I stand up too and follow him towards the door. "Hey, look, it's okay. I'm a tough, I get in trouble sometimes, but I know what I'm doing." I reach out and take his hand. "And yeah, it's a bit bigger, but it's not that different. Remember the Lock and Key? It's just like then."

Emeka turns around, and before I know quite what's going on, he's got his arms wrapped around me and his head buried in my chest. I hear a faint sob.

"What did I—"

"You were stabbed at the Lock and Key!"

"Uh..." I had actually forgotten that part.

It was about a year ago, when I was still pretty new to hanging out with the gang. We were out watching some of our friends play at one of the dives they liked to frequent when one of the regulars accused the guy he was with of sleeping around. It got heated, and the first guy pulled a knife.

I remember getting out of my chair in a hurry; the bouncer was halfway across the room, just starting to notice the trouble, and I was only a couple of tables over. I hit the guy as he went for a stab, and then he took a swing at me. The long and short of it was that he stabbed me, I punched him in the face and he went down, and then everyone was crowding around to see if I was okay.

"It didn't even need stitches," I say now, thinking back. "We just went into the back room and splashed some vodka on it. Plus, it got me one of my jobs." I'm not quite sure where to put my arms, but eventually I just get one around his shoulders and look down at the top of his head.

"And you probably saved that other guy from some serious scars," Emeka says, still slightly muffled. "And we stood around terrified, wondering if you were going to be okay."

"I'm pretty sure Marta said, and I quote, 'That was wild, can I see the wound, we should do this every night.' She was pretty into it."

"That is how Marta handles being scared, you big, dumb, angel." Emeka pushes me back and steps out of the hug. There are still tears in his eyes, but he's laughing. "For someone who's so good at noticing things, you can be really dense sometimes."

"Yeah. Yeah, I guess I can." I cough, still staring into his eyes. He hasn't stopped looking at me, kind of hopeful and scared and worried all at once, just like I'm feeling. "Holly says sometimes that I pretty much need to be hit across the face to get the message. Probably why I'm a fighter."

"Well, if you're going to be a fighter, I'm glad that you're a good one."

"The best around," I say. "But it's nice that someone's worried about me."

"A lot of people are worried about you."

"Then it's nice that you're one of them." The words just sort of slip out, and I can feel heat rising in my cheeks as I say them.

Emeka looks up at me again, and then he steps in again, going up on tip-toe. For a moment, he's right up at my face, and then our lips are pressed against each other. I freeze up for just a second, and then I melt into him, leaning down and into the kiss, feeling his warmth and the scent of orange. The second passes into two, and then he breaks away again.

"So," he says a bit breathlessly, "do you think you'll be back in time for dinner tonight?"

"I don't know," I admit. "It's a bit of a trek." Emeka nods, his smile slipping just a bit, and I quickly add, "What about Monday?"

"Rehearsals," he says with a laugh. "Tuesday?"

"Tuesday sounds good," I say. "Tuesday sounds great. Uh. Where?"

"Lock and Key?" Emeka asks.

I laugh. "I thought that was awful."

"It was also the first time that I ... never mind, it was just a thought."

"No. No, it's great. I love it. Six o'clock?"

"Perfect." Emeka nods. "See you there. Have a good investigation. And—"

"Be careful?"

"Sass." Emeka punches me lightly on the chest and heads out.

——— «»  ———

I can't stop grinning as I stroll down the street to Vance's office. Glimmer is already there, sitting on the railing. She raises an eyebrow suspiciously and asks how I'm doing. She's dressed for the forest, with a heavy jacket and boots replacing her detective getup from the day before.

"I'm good, Glimmer. Real good. Are we going up or is Vance coming out?"

"Coming out!" Vance says, as he closes the door behind him. He's got his full outfit on, complete with waistcoat, hat, and long coat, plus a large backpack at his side. He turns to Glimmer, nods to her, and manages a rough approximation of a fairy trill.

Glimmer stares at Vance for long enough that his smile fades. "I got it wrong, didn't I? I was trying to say good morning."

Glimmer shakes her head, and says that he did good, for a human; it was almost intelligible.

"Most people who learn fairy don't try to repeat it," I say. "Our throats aren't really built for it. It was a pretty solid try, though."

"Well, then," Vance says with a chuckle. "Let's be off."

"Can your car get us through the woods?" I ask as we pull away from the curb.

"Not much can. We're going to drive up to a local Hawthorne logging camp, then take a Jeep to the edge of where the logging trucks go. From there, we're moving on foot for about two hours to the edge of tiger territory. It's almost a four-hour trip, all told. Should arrive a little past noon. Did you bring snacks?"

I heft my own bag. "Thermos, trail mix, first aid kit."

"Wonderful. Then we're off!"

In the end, it takes us more than four hours to get up to the edge of tiger territory. Vance saves some time by speeding down the main highway and recklessly endangering us, and the pickup that's waiting for us makes decent time along the old logging paths, but once we're on foot it's a different story. Hawthorne reluctantly let one of the loggers be our guide, but Vance's coat keeps getting caught on bushes, and I'm not used to hiking. We end up taking more than two and a half hours on foot just to get to the large, brightly painted, orange post that marks the edge of tiger territory. "This is as far as I go," the guide lets us know. "You might have a pass, but I don't think I do. Have the tigers radio when you're on the way back, and I'll come out to get you again."

"Thank you for your help," Vance says, already turning to look at the woods.

"Hey, thank *you*. Last thing any of us out here want is the tigers mad. They're good neighbors and bad enemies." The guide waves and starts back. A few minutes later, a pair of tigers slip out from the other side.

"You're late," one of them says.

"But we expected that," says the other.

"I suppose that makes us lucky. I'm Vance, and this is Todd and Glimmer."

The tigers sniff at us, and then nod. "Jaar," says the first. "Riyu," says the second. "Fraal tells us you plan to find the thieves who took from us."

"We do. Maybe while we're heading over there, you can explain the situation. What exactly was taken, what was disturbed, and so on. I'll be looking, of course, but first-hand accounts are helpful."

Jaar just sniffs. He's smaller than most of the other tigers I've met, with dark stripes and glittering grey eyes. "The thefts came from one of our caches," he says. "They are near a series of bluffs that cross the north-east. The other side is wolf territory, but the wolves do not come over, generally. They have enough of their own."

"We store food there, mostly," Riyu adds. She's taller than her companion — not as tall as Amhara or Fraal, but a bit taller than Hkuri, and her whiskers are the longest I've seen. "We keep an eye on the area, but there is no security. If a tiger takes from the cache, we can scent it, so there's no need to lock the stores."

"No one's ever managed to cover their scent?" Vance asks.

"Once or twice. But even then, we knew who was in the area. There are not so many of us that we can vanish into a crowd," Riyu says with a snicker. "It has been many years since a tiger succeeded in a theft. And what would they gain? The meat there is for us all. And the gemstones are for trading with humans; if a tiger were to try, the others would hear that they had done so and know the thief."

Vance strokes his mustache thoughtfully. "But I would assume that you don't share the location of these caches with outsiders."

"No, of course not," Jaar says. "It has happened before, however, that human 'explorers' come into our territory without permission and stumble across them. They are concealed, but not impossible to find."

Vance pulls out a notepad and takes a few notes. "Alright. So, what's different this time? I assume that when someone found a cache in the past, you stopped them?

"Or followed them, and demanded recompense," Jaar agrees. "But this time, we could not trace them, and little was taken. It is not about the items, truly. It is the pride of the thing. Our borders must be inviolable. Humans are scavengers at heart. If they believe it is safe to invade, they will." He pauses, awkwardly. "That is—"

"No, I understand," Vance says. "Especially since most of the humans you deal with on a daily basis work for Hawthorne."

Riyu sighs. "It is true. They always look for advantage. Fraal and Amhara hold them off with threats and promises, but they come back."

I think back to the demonstration. "Fraal and Amhara are pretty much in charge right now, aren't they?"

"For such things as being in charge matters, yes. We are not pack creatures like humans or wolves, you know. Power is held by the one we are willing to listen to. It is not a formal process of voting or lineage."

"And I bet what happens in this investigation is going to change who listens to who, huh?"

Riyu and Jaar pause in their walking, ears twitching. "You catch on quickly," Jaar says quietly.

"And right now, one of you likes each of them, and each of them asked one of you to be here, which is why we have two guides and not one."

Riyu snickers. "Fraal was right to listen to these humans."

"Perhaps," Jaar says, tail flicking back and forth.

The rest of the walk is pretty quiet, and soon we're clambering through a veil of shrubs and down into a steep-sided ravine that our guides identify as the site. "We have found what we could already," Jaar says, "so you will not disturb anything in your searching."

"That's great," Vance says. "Thank you." He looks around the base of the ravine, and I step up to join him. The shrubs and bush that surround it keep it mostly invisible from the outside, but all the greenery inside has been cleared away, and the dirt where things could grow has been clawed up and removed. The result is a bunch of jagged rocks along the sides, leading down to a pebble-covered ground with a thin stream running through it. There aren't many ways in; most of the approaches would be too steep to climb. Vance steps in, looking up at the sky. "Surprised this place doesn't flood," he says.

"It does, sometimes. We keep the food higher up." Riyu inclines her head towards one side of the ravine, where some rocks have been pushed aside. "Each is secured in its own place, in case of wandering scavengers."

"Hm." Vance looks up. "Not sure I can make that climb. Todd?"

"Yeah, I can give it a try." I step across, almost slip on some wet rocks, and then start carefully shimmying up the side. Glimmer flies after me, looking worried. I don't know what she'd do if I fell, but it's nice to have her there. After a minute, I'm up to one of the spots Riyu pointed to. There's a small cave in the rock wall, large enough to shove a few pounds of meat into. "Not very big," I call down.

"They are of differing sizes. The one above you is larger."

I look up and see where a large rock has been wedged into place. There are claw marks around the base. "I don't think I could get anything out of that," I call back. "I see how a tiger could, but not a human, not without some serious climbing gear and a crowbar." I frown, thinking about it. "Are there any lower caches that weren't taken?"

"Oh, yes. There is quite a bit of meat here." Jaar hops up to the side and climbs up to meet me. It's scary-fast, and his claws easily tuck into places I wouldn't have thought anyone could. A few moments later, he's nudging one of the smaller rocks with a free paw, and I climb over to meet him.

"Wait, don't pull it out. I want to see if I can."

Jaar nods, pushes the rock back, and climbs above the cache as I carefully make my way to the rock in question. I'm able to wiggle it out without too much trouble, and I can see the leaf-wrapped bundle inside. "Okay, I can confirm that a human could get the smaller pieces out, but not the bigger ones." I replace the rock and climb back down.

"Thank you, Todd." Vance turns to the tigers. "How many pieces were taken?"

"Three caches of meat, and two of gemstones," Jaar said. "Each cache of meat was only about four pounds, by your numbers. They were choice cuts, but not impossible to find."

"Hm. Value of the gemstones? To humans, that is."

"Perhaps two hundred dollars."

"Not a bad haul for a smash and grab, but not exactly worth coming all the way out here for," Vance says thoughtfully. "Were those all of the gemstones being saved here?"

"Yes," Riyu confirms. "We only save a few in each site. They aren't very useful, except when we need something from outsiders."

"It sounds like someone stumbled onto this place and grabbed what they could carry," Vance says thoughtfully. "They might have been surprised. Does this ravine go anywhere?"

Jaar looks at him pityingly. "Of course it does. Otherwise the water would fill it."

"To a river, then? Or right to the bluffs?"

"It runs down to the Winding Way," Riyu says. "That river is broad, and divides tiger and wolf territory. From there, it flows down to the sea."

"We assume that the intruders came by boat, and that is why we could not scent them. Which is also why I do not see what you could find," Jaar says. "You cannot track over water."

"No, but we might be able to see where a boat was pulled ashore. Glimmer, can you scout from the air?"

Glimmer salutes and flies up. Riyu watches her go, and leans toward me. "Is she effective, your fairy?"

"She's not my fairy. But yeah, she's great."

"Hm. Tigers and fairies have little in common. I do not think I have ever seen one up close for so long." Riyu bares her fangs. "But then, they do not like to spend time near us, for fear of being eaten."

"Are they?"

"Not often. No more than anyone else." She pads down to the river, following Vance, and I swallow heavily and follow her.

"I don't see any boat marks on the shore. How long ago was this?" Vance asks.

"We found the theft two days ago. The cache was last checked six days before that," Jaar says. "It could have been any time between those points."

"Well, that's not helpful. A week is enough time for most tracks to fade." Vance strokes his mustache again. "It's pretty rocky here, though. I would have expected a boat being pushed ashore to leave some kind of a mark, but there's nothing."

Just then, Glimmer swoops down, waving something in one hand. She is grinning ear to ear, and we all crane in as she lands on Vance's arm and hands him something. He takes it, looks it over, and holds it up to the light. It's a glittering green rock, rough and unpolished. "This rather looks like an emerald."

"It is," Jaar says, sounding faintly surprised. "It could be one from the cache."

"Where was it?" I ask Glimmer.

She smirks and delivers some complicated directions. I turn to find everyone staring at me. "Basically, she found it in a hollow in a tree, along with ... wait, really?"

Glimmer nods.

"Along with three wrapped bundles of dried meat," I say. "Just the one gem, though."

Riyu's eyes narrow. "Are you suggesting that squirrels stole our supplies?"

Glimmer glares at her, and I shake my head. "No. She's suggesting fairies did. And ditched the meat because they were only after the gems. They probably spilled the gems while they were dumping everything else and missed one cleaning up."

"Fairies," comes a sarcastic snarl from above us. I look up to see Amhara perched on the edge of the ravine, staring down at me with her fangs slightly bared. "You expect us to believe that?"

"Why not?" Vance asks. "Fast, stealthy, hard to spot. Glimmer could get one of those smaller stones unwedged. She might even be better at it than most humans, since she wouldn't have to balance."

"And how would these fairies find one of our caches?" Amhara snaps. "They are hidden from above."

"The same way a human would, I'd think. Either they stumbled across it, or someone told them."

"And they happened to abandon a gemstone?"

"Fairies are less careful than humans, usually," Jaar says reluctantly. "It could be the case. The gemstones are kept in bundles, but they are not individually secured. One could easily slip out. Others as well, perhaps."

Amhara hops down, nostrils flaring. "How convenient that you have a fairy working with you, to think how a fairy criminal would."

"Hey, now," Vance says, stepping forward. "I realize that it's not the answer that you wanted to hear."

Amhara ignores him and turns to Glimmer and me. "It is the two of you. The pirate's helpers. Thieves consort with thieves."

Riyu looks over at me. "You work with the pirate?" she asks, her voice chillier than before. Jaar scrapes his claws across the rocky ground.

"Okay, first off, humans work with a lot of people," I say, raising my hands. "Secondly, Mr. Stark hasn't been a pirate since a long time before I met him. And third, right now I am working with the detective over there, not the one you're all afraid of."

That was probably a bad choice of words.

Amhara steps up to me, fixing me with her eyes. "We are not *afraid* of anyone," she growls, not breaking eye contact.

"What the heck is this about, anyway?" I snap. "You're so convinced that we're part of the problem you aren't even listening to what we found out! And don't try to say it's a tiger thing, because you're the only damned tiger who's doing it."

Amhara continues to stare at me, and this time I stare back. I feel my fists slowly clenching, and Amhara's claws start to come out. "Because you are poison," she hisses. "All of you. My cousin thinks to fit in with you, and she abases herself before human arrogance. Fraal thinks to manipulate you, and he makes promises in the face of human faithlessness. You swim in secrets, you bathe in hubris, and you think yourselves the superior species simply because there are so many of you." Her fangs are entirely bared. "Not one of you is fit even to eat."

I think about the times that I've seen Amhara and Hkuri together, the things that Hkuri and Emeka told me. "Do you really think Hkuri is abasing herself, or are you just mad that you aren't in control of her anymore?"

Amhara's hiss turns into a loud roar, and she pounces on me.

I did not have a plan for this, and the best that I can do is duck as low as I can and sock her in the jaw. She rears back in surprise, and instead of tearing my arm off entirely, her claws rip shallow gashes across the length of my arm. It's still enough force to send me sprawling. As she lands and turns to leap again, Glimmer lands on top of her head, ducks in tight and grabs her ear, twisting for all she's worth. Amhara roars even more loudly, and rolls across the rocks. Luckily, Glimmer is thrown free before she can be crushed into the dirt, and instead, she hits the wall of the ravine and flutters down. Vance rushes over to her, in time to keep her from hitting the ground.

Amhara is righting herself to pounce again when Riyu and Jaar step between us, tails lashing. "We do not attack guests," Riyu says defiantly.

For a moment I think Amhara's going to go for it and attack the lot of us. But she lets out a breath, hisses, and looks past Riyu and Jaar to me. "You know nothing of my family," she says.

"You're right," I say after a moment. "I was riled up. Shouldn't have said that."

"Good." Amhara takes a moment to groom her ear and then turns away. "Finish your investigation and leave. You are not worth a full challenge."

The others watch as she walks slowly away, until she's past the lip of the ravine again. Vance walks over to me, cradling Glimmer carefully in his hands. "What the hell just happened?" he asks.

"Amhara was following us," Riyu says. "She wanted to observe you. Are you broken?"

"Nah. Coat took most of it." The arm of my coat is shredded, and I pull it off to check the damage: four, long scratches where her claws tore through, but they're not bleeding too badly. "Good thing I brought a first aid kit, huh?"

"That was a brave challenge," Riyu says. "Foolish, but brave. And you landed a blow! When Amhara leaped, I thought that you would fall before we could intervene."

"Honestly, me too. She is fast."

"She is one of our best," Jaar agrees, sounding a bit wistful. "You are lucky that she was only challenging you. If she truly wished to kill, I think you would have been in more danger."

"There's a scary thought," I say. Seems like it's the right approach, because Jaar and Riyu both chuckle.

"Why did you challenge her?" Vance asks quietly, as he opens my bag and starts pulling out bandages and checking over my arm.

"I was mad, mostly," I admit. "I didn't figure she'd actually jump, I just knew that if I didn't do something, she'd make this all about how weak humans are and how we shouldn't finish looking around. If she'd convinced our guides that the investigation was tainted by pirates and pirate associates, we don't exactly have a higher authority to turn to."

"Well, you were very brave."

Glimmer says that I was very dumb, and that I'm lucky she was there to pull my fat out of the fire.

"Yeah, I was. How about you, Glim? You okay?"

She snorts and lets me know that it takes more than a rampaging tiger to stop her, and anyway, she had Vance to catch her.

Vance is looking at her right now. "That was a heck of a pull, firebrand," he tells her. "Remind me not to get you mad."

Glimmer blushes a bit and nods.

"Okay," Vance says, finishing binding my arm. "We've convinced Amhara to back off for a little while, and we've got a lead. I'm thinking we follow the river. Glimmer, you can observe from above, see if you spot any fairy tracks. If the bag was leaking or damaged, there might be other missing gemstones, and if we can reach the base of the bluffs, we might find traces of a boat." He looks at our faces. "I know, it's not much to go on, but it's what we've got."

We start down the river. This time of year, we've got a bit of space on the banks to follow along, and as we make our way towards the bluffs Glimmer finds another pair of gems. We've been at it for about an hour when the tigers, who had been hanging back to let us investigate, close the distance again. "We are approaching the edge of our territory," Riyu says. "You may continue, but we should not."

"We are not welcome on the coasts," Jaar agrees. "Either the merfolk or the wolves may think we are planning to enter their domains."

Vance nods. "Do you think they'll be upset with us?"

"Possibly," Riyu says.

Vance waits a moment, but there's nothing else forthcoming. "Should we ask ahead?"

"How?"

"Radio?"

Riyu gives Vance a look. "We have one radio. It is an hour away. Longer for you. Then the wolves would have to relay the message to their own kin out here. And mermaids do not have radios."

"Damn." Vance rubs his chin. "Okay. Mermaids have deals with humans, we're allowed on the coastlines here as long as we don't actually disturb the lakes. And if we don't *cross* the river, we're not in the wolf lands, and they're not as territorial as bears or tigers, no offense."

"Why would that be offensive?" Jaar asks. "Everyone knows that wolves and humans don't properly respect territory."

"Some humans think that being called territorial is bad," I explain.

Jaar snorts. "Of course they do. Well, your detective is correct. We will be here when you return. If you choose to leave by sea, please send someone back to inform us."

"Of course. Thank you for following us, and making sure that we weren't eaten," Vance says.

Jaar and Riyu nod and sit back to wait for us, and we head down towards the beach ahead.

It's a pretty nice beach, all in all, sandy and calm. The river is broad and slow at this point as it widens into a bay far ahead, and there are tall cliffs on either side leading up to the brushlands above.

Glimmer flies down and hands us two more gemstones, dripping wet and crusted with sand. They match the style of the ones that we are looking for. "It looks like the thieves brought the bag all the way down to the waterline," Vance says. "Which means they must have been meeting someone in a boat after all."

"Not much chance of getting tracks here. High tide would have washed them away," I point out.

"We might have one option," Vance says, looking out towards the water. He points to a rock out past the edge of the bay, where a mermaid is sunning herself. "The tigers mentioned that this beach is mermaid territory. Think a boat could get past them without anyone noticing?"

"Not a chance. And I bet they'd be pretty annoyed, too." I think about it. "On the other hand, remember what happened the last time you tried to ask some mermaids questions?"

"You saved me," Vance says. He waves an arm out towards the mermaid, who perks up upon spotting us and dives into the water. "I won't walk out into the lake this time, just to the water's edge."

"What are a couple of longlegs doing on tiger turf?" The mermaid surfaces a short distance out into the bay, then slips closer into the surf. She's got long black hair, a large grin, and her voice is low and musical. And familiar.

"We're looking into some things," Vance says. "I'm wondering if you can help us. Did a boat pull up here in the last week?"

"A boat?" The mermaid laughs. "Girls, he wants to know if other humans have been dumb enough to come here!"

A second head pops out of the water, closer to the shore than I would have thought someone could get without being noticed. "Humans who come here are eaten by tigers," she says. She looks a lot like the first mermaid, but with short, nut-brown hair and rippled bluish skin. Now I know I've seen them before. I start looking around. If I'm right, there's a third somewhere nearby.

"We could give you a gift if you've seen something," Vance suggests. "I have these lovely gemstones."

"We don't need more gemstones!" the first mermaid says. I notice that the tide seems to be coming in a bit faster.

"Uh, Vance?" I say quietly, stepping up to him. "I think we should…"

"More gemstones?" Vance asks.

The first mermaid blinks. The second mermaid laughs.

"They're the same mermaids!" I yell, grabbing him by the shoulder. "From the day we met!"

Which is when an impossible wave swells, crashes over us both, and starts pulling us out into the lake.

"Clever boy," the third mermaid says from right next to my ear. "Moira doesn't always think before she speaks." I have no idea how she got so close; the water shouldn't be deep enough, but there's a tail wrapped around my neck and a weight pushing me down. The current is still dragging us out, and the waves are pushing against the tide; even I know rivers don't naturally behave like this. I manage to get my head above water and see that the waves are crashing in time with the mermaids' swishing tails.

"Todd!" Vance is trying to stand up, but Moira is on top of him, leaping from the water like an orca and slamming into his chest. The waves leap after her, and swarm around Vance's face as he sputters for air.

"I'm glad you came!" she says brightly. "We missed playing with you before. You should come back home with us."

The second mermaid is approaching me, but she keeps having to dive back underwater as Glimmer dive-bombs her face. She swats at the air, looking faintly annoyed. "The fairies paid you!" I gasp, hands pushed against the riverbed to try to keep my face above the water.

"We're playing a different game right now!" the mermaid holding me down chirps. "It's not question time! It's drowning time! After you drown, we'll answer any questions you like."

My face goes under the water. I can't believe how strong she is, and the weight of the magicked current on my back is pushing my arms down further into the sand. As a way to die, this is definitely a dumb one.

I shove myself sideways, to try and get out from underneath her. As I do, there's a sound I can't make out, and the weight on me vanishes. I push myself out of the water and see a tiger bearing the mermaid down into the water.

"Selene!" Moira abandons Vance and swims towards the attacking tiger, and behind me the last mermaid does the same. I move towards the tiger, arms raised and ready to fight, and she turns her head to nod at me.

"Hkuri?"

"Hello, Todd. It is good to see you again." Hkuri has one paw firmly on Selene, pinning her underwater. "You will stop now," she says to the other mermaids. "There is blood, but there could be guts."

The two mermaids stop and look at each other. "It's not nice for tigers to interrupt a game," Moira says. "You're not supposed to be here."

"And you should not be drowning humans. Your people swore to stop that."

"This is different. These humans are not where they should be," Moira says. She starts to slip forward, and Hkuri presses her paw down a bit further on Selene's back.

"If you start violence," the third mermaid says, "we will play our games with tiger hides."

"Not if your people learn what you have been doing, I believe. Or if none of you live to tell them of this." Hkuri bares her fangs. "Leave."

The two mermaids not currently pinned look at each other, and Moira sighs. "Fine. I hope we see you again soon, detective. You are fun to play with."

They shimmy back into the deeper water, then turn and swim away. Hkuri looks to me. "Do you wish to question this one?"

"If she'll talk," I say. "We didn't do so good last time."

Hkuri lets up enough pressure for Selene's head to rise above the surface of the water. "You made my friends leave," she says grumpily.

"And you can join them," Vance says. "Just tell us why the fairies were giving you tiger gemstones."

"Oh, that." She looks bored. "We needed money for a poker game, and we weren't going to use our own treasures! We like those. They shine bright in the waves."

"A poker game with Rupert Drainie?" Vance asks.

"With humans," Selene says. "We were supposed to win. That isn't hard. Human card games are less fun than mermaid games, but they are fun. And humans aren't as good at them as they think." She gives me a broad, toothy smile. "It's fun to beat you at your games."

"Who were you working for?" Vance asks.

Selene shrugs. "The fairy came to us. Fletcher, she was called. She offered us fun and fortune. We didn't ask for more. Why would we? You're the ones who want everything to mean something. Fun is for fun."

"You didn't think that when Moira admitted to taking the gems."

"She lost that game," Selene admits. "We will tease her for it later. And then we lost our game against you, because you brought an extra player! But I told you I would answer questions after the drowning, and I drowned, so here we are."

"Who told the fairies where our gemstones were?" Hkuri asks.

Selene shrugs. "I didn't ask."

"Was she working with someone else?" Vance asks.

"I didn't ask."

"Why did you need to win the poker game?" I ask.

"I didn't ask."

"You don't ask very many questions, do you?"

"Only if I care about the answers," she says. "Do you want any other questions answered?

"Just one. That first day we met, when Vance tried to ask you questions and you attacked him."

"Played with him," Selene corrects me.

"Okay. Would you have drowned him if he'd lost?"

Selene thinks about it for a moment. "No. We don't drown humans near the city. We said that we wouldn't, and if we do, there would be no more human games. We can be patient."

"Well, that's encouraging." Vance shakes his head. "I suppose we'd better let her go."

"Are you sure?" Hkuri asks.

"There'd be a lot of trouble if a mermaid died here on the shore, right? Even if she started it. Anyway, she did answer our questions. Just because we don't like the answers doesn't make them false."

"Thank you!" Selene beams at Vance. "You understand the game."

Hkuri sighs and removes her paw from Selene. The mermaid quickly retreats into the deeper water. "If you want to play again, please come back," she calls, before vanishing under the waves.

"Mermaids," Hkuri growls. "It is all games to them."

"But we have a confession, and a tiger on hand to hear it," Vance says. "The fairies paid the three of them off to hook Rupert Drainie so that he could be blackmailed." He shakes his head. "It always comes back to the blackmail ring."

"Do you think they wanted the tigers to get mad?" I ask.

"Maybe. Maybe they were just covering their tracks. Whoever is behind this really hates having to show their hand. It's always 'get a person to do a job so that another person gets trapped and has to do a job to trap a third person' until the whole thing is so complicated there's no telling what started it." Vance rubs his chin. "Unrelatedly, I notice that the water is back down to ankle-deep. Did you know mermaids could control the water like that?"

"Does everyone not know that?" Hkuri asks.

"Hm." Vance gathers up his coat from around his knees and walks back to the shore. "We can report to Fraal that we know who took the gemstones and why, but I think he's going to want to know who the fairies are working for."

"They could be the bosses themselves," I suggest. "Fletcher was the name of that fairy I talked to at the camp, so she's probably the one that cut our brake lines."

"It was? Huh. But no, it doesn't fit. The mastermind is someone desperate to be behind the scenes, and like you said, Fletcher keeps showing up. Besides, all of this 'layers on layers' planning isn't how I'd expect a fairy criminal to behave. Too much to keep track of, too much chance of something going wrong. I'd guess she's working for someone else."

"You have found out much, then. It was worth the violence?"

"I feel like I've gotten beaten up more on this case than my whole career, but yeah." Vance chuckles. "Going to have a heck of a shiner in the morning. Come on, let's get back to our guides and report."

As we start back up the beach, I look over to Hkuri. "Sure was lucky, you being here. We could have been in real trouble otherwise."

"Yes, you are the lucky one," she agrees.

"Here, on a beach that tigers are supposed to leave alone, so much so that our guides wouldn't even come with us."

Hkuri coughs. "Yes, it was a fortunate occurrence."

I look over at her. "Okay. If you don't want to say, I'm not going to look a gift horse in the mouth."

Hkuri breathes out. "The truth, Todd Malcolm, is that I was asked to be here, and I was willing to do the favor." She gives me a sly smile. "You are cared for, you know."

"Emeka?"

Hkuri snickers. "I have not known him long, but he is good. And too worried about those he cares more deeply for. And perhaps he was right. As you said, you were in some danger when I arrived. I think you would have survived, but it is good to be sure."

I shake my head. "I'm going to have to do something real nice for that guy."

Hkuri snickers again. "Yes, you will." She pauses a moment. "I was concerned that I might have done wrong by telling you."

"Did Emeka ask you not to?"

"Not as such, but English is not my language of birth, and it bears much intricacy. It is easy to mistake intent when it is so similar, but so different, all at once. Among tigers, to say that another cannot protect themselves is a grave insult. It is one thing to ask if someone wishes for support. That can be given without shame. But if one says that they have the strength, and you doubt them, then you say that their strength is false."

"A lot of humans do the same thing." I grin. "But I'm always up to have a helping hand."

"Good. That makes you a wise human." Looking satisfied, Hkuri pads ahead. Glimmer comes and sits on my shoulder, looking exhausted.

"How are you holding up, Glimmer?"

She tells me that being a detective is more work than she'd thought and she might want a break from it.

"You and me both. Come on, we'll let Vance take the lead on the wrap-up and then eat everything we brought to snack on."

Glimmer says that sounds very nice, and we head back into tiger territory.

# Tuesday, August 28<sup>th</sup>

**Monday winds up** being pretty quiet. With everything we learned from the mermaids tying our cases together, we figure that our best bet is to find out who answered the radio at Hawthorne and called Phyllis Graves, and follow the trail from there. Fraal accepts that this might not be quick, but he's happy enough that it isn't a tiger, and that he was right about Hawthorne, to give us the time.

Of course, at this point breaking into Hawthorne is too big a risk, so Vance just asks them point-blank if we can have access to some things, which we will explain on site. He presents it as needing to exonerate Hawthorne, and I guess they buy it because we're told to come by on Tuesday and we'll be shown whatever we need.

"It's nice to have friends in high places," Holly says when I let her know. Glimmer and I had stopped by the office to see if Mr. Stark was back and found her manning the desk, so we've been catching her up while we play cards. "Think they'll let you find anything?"

"I hope so. It would be nice to actually figure something out." I lean back in my chair and toss a couple of hearts down. "I'd like to make it to dinner tonight without worrying about things."

"Dinner?" Holly's eyebrows rise suggestively.

"Yeah, it's, uh, you know … Emeka and I—"

"Oh my God, are you and Emeka finally, *finally*, going out? Like as a couple? *Together*?" Holly squeaks the last word. "Who asked who? Why did you not open with this? How have we spent the last twenty minutes yammering on about mermaids and blackmail when we could have been talking about this?"

"Because we would have been talking about this!"

"Exactly! This is big! When was the last time *you* went on a date?" Holly takes a card and drops a triple. "Gin, by the way."

"You know, for someone who doesn't date, you are really invested in other people's love lives." I have to think about her question for a minute, it had been a long time since I'd been on a proper date. "Two years? Maybe three."

"I can't help it! You're all just so cute when you're in love."

"I'm thrilled to be your latest story."

"Aw, come on. Where are you going? Oh, what are you wearing? You never got your suit cleaned, did you?"

"Couldn't afford it, at least not until I get my next pay from Vance. I have a green shirt that'll be fine."

"A green shirt." Holly is staring at me flatly. "Todd, would you like to borrow some money from me and get an outfit tailored for tonight?"

"Even if I did, and no, I don't have time. We've got a meeting at Hawthorne in about an hour and a half. Aren't you supposed to say that I'll look great just as myself?"

"No! I mean, yes, obviously you'll be great no matter what and after all the dancing around each other you two have done you could show up on fire and wearing a barrel and it would probably still be fine, but this is where you sweep him off his feet. Maybe literally, are you going to be dancing? Do you have dancing shoes?"

"Holly, we're just having dinner."

"And dancing?"

"This is why I didn't tell you earlier."

Holly sighs heavily. "I mean it, Todd. Dancing. Ask him after dinner, and he will say yes, and then you can show him what a great dancer you are."

"Just one problem: I'm not."

She waves her hand. "You'll do fine. Just lift him from time to time. And then tell me how it goes."

"Fine, fine. I'm gonna go check in with Vance about whether he found any of those people who were being blackmailed, and then go deal with the giant corporation that might be involved in the biggest blackmail scheme in Everland history, but I'll take a minute out to figure out how to dance."

"Good."

I grab my stuff and head for the door but pause with my hand on the handle. "You really think dancing?"

"Todd, I really, really think dancing."

"Well, you are the expert. I'll see."

Holly whoops with joy as I head out the door, and I can't help grinning.

———— «◇» ————

Vance is on the phone when I get to his office. "No, I understand that. But the tigers ... yes, I agree, but I think that Hawthorne could ... no, that is certainly ... I'm sorry. No. Of course. Give my regards to Father."

He hangs up and gives me a wave. "Todd. Todd, how are you doing?"

"I'm pretty good, Mr. Carson."

"You've got to call me Vance. I absolutely insist on it. You've been doing the 'Mr. Carson' thing since we met."

"Okay. Vance. I just figured since you're the boss and all."

"Well, it's the detective's way, isn't it?" Vance chuckles. "No Glimmer today?"

"She decided that since we've got a key to the door, she'd rather not hang around Hawthorne. They're kind of jerks to pretty much everyone, but especially everyone who's not human."

Vance nods, but he looks disappointed. "That makes sense. Yes. Well, we'll have to catch up with her another time."

"Everything okay on the home front?"

Vance winces. "Ah, well. I was just speaking with my mother about the progress of the case. She's worried about me, that's all."

I try not to look dubious, but I think he sees it. "She's concerned that if the papers start reporting that I'm doing free work for tigers, and against Hawthorne's interests to boot, it won't reflect well on the family. On me. But I think I explained the situation well enough."

"Look, I don't want to say anything wrong, but it kind of sounded like she did the explaining."

"That's just how a conversation with Mother goes. By the end, she was just making sure that I would treat the investigation with a proper sense of decorum, which is a huge improvement over how the call started."

"She wanted you to quit?"

"She wanted me to quit!" Vance chuckles and shakes his head. "She can be a bit forceful, but she is always worried about me. But when we crack this case, I think that she'll be very impressed. And we're coming on like Gangbusters! I took the advantage yesterday to check into some of the blackmail targets you passed along, and it is quite the list. Haven't had time to meet with any of them yet, of course. Hoping to do so soon. But I think that thing you said in the woods is spot-on. These targets are all either high society or connected with important local affairs. Second Star, City Hall, North Precinct — all people who have a lot to lose if their secrets get out. Even relatively minor skeletons can really wreck someone's career."

"So, they blackmailed people who weren't important to get access to the people who were, then moved on to blackmailing the important people. And in the end, you've got a whole lot of people who owe you a whole lot of favors."

"Exactly! And with the right touch, you convince them that doing those favors isn't just paying up, it's keeping them safe. It's elegant, in a nasty way." Vance shakes his head. "But the biggest thing is the emphasis on cutaways. The ringleader is obviously obsessed with staying secret."

"Well, someone's got to have met them."

"I agree. You would need a working inner circle to manage an operation of this size. I think that our best bet is still tracking them through whomever the fairies at the logging camp were reporting back to. That person knew enough to call Ms. Graves and was worried enough to risk revealing herself. Catch her, and we can follow her up the chain."

"So, back to plan A, then?"

"Back to plan A. Let's get to Hawthorne." Vance grins and pats me on the shoulder.

Vance is full of energy, and he spends the drive up speculating on what we're going to find, and how we could convince the culprit to snitch on their companions. I notice a bulge under his coat. "Are you carrying a gun?" I ask.

"Got the permit yesterday. We've been in more than a few scrapes recently, I thought it was high time that we went about armed. Do you shoot?"

"Nah. That sort of firepower pretty much means more trouble than it's worth in the circles I run in. You a good shot?"

"I have a decent score on the range."

"You been in a gunfight before?" I think about how every time we're in a brawl Vance is the last one to make a move, and usually the first to get jumped.

"Not as such..." he hedges. "But I know the basics. Besides, with any luck this will mean we don't need to be in a gunfight."

"I dunno about that. A fistfight is one thing, but if you draw a gun and the other guy has one too, he almost always ends up going for it, and the next thing you know someone's lying on the ground and someone else is arrested."

Vance's smile falters. "Well," he says a bit nervously, "I think I'll keep it on hand, if you don't mind."

"You're the boss."

When we arrive at Hawthorne and announce ourselves at the front desk, we aren't left waiting for long. I'm caught off-guard to see Michelle Arsenault is the one who comes down to meet us. She's dressed to the nines, as usual, and she looks about as enthusiastic as I feel to be here. "Mr. Carson, Mr. Malcolm, how lovely to see you."

Vance takes it on the level. "Ah, Ms. Arsenal, the pleasure is all mine."

"It's Arsenault." If I thought she looked annoyed before, now Michelle looks positively frigid. "But please, call me Michelle."

"Right, right. Of course. Michelle." Vance coughs. "I admit, I expected..."

"Mr. Hsi?" Michelle interrupts, not waiting to see how Vance will mangle that name. "He will stop by if needed, of course, but as the executive in charge of tiger relations, it's my desk that anything you stir up will land on. The Board decided that it would be best for me to clear my schedule and make sure that you get everything you need. Quickly."

"Well, we'll make sure not to take up too much of your valuable time."

Michelle starts walking down the corridor. "I assume that you have a goal here today? Or do you simply want a list of every person Hawthorne has working near tiger territory?"

"No, nothing so broad. Actually, we'd like to stop by the radio office and check the logs."

Michelle's stride falters, and she looks back at us. "Pardon?"

"The radio office. Communications? Wherever it is that the logging camps radio in to."

"What does that have to do with anything?"

"Confidential information, Ms. Arsenault," Vance says with a grin. "But don't worry, when we have a conclusion, you will be one of the first to hear it!"

Michelle frowns at both of us, and then turns and leads the way. "Our radio room is down this way. I couldn't tell you very much about how it operates, but I'm sure that someone on duty will be able to. It would help if you could give me an idea of what you're actually looking for. Since you're trying *not* to waste my time."

"We have some information about the thief that we want to double-check against some other information," Vance admits.

Michelle's eyes narrow. "How very vague of you. Well, I hope you find what you're looking for. Quickly."

The radio room is on the west side of the building, on the third floor, against an outer wall. There's a tiny window letting in a single ray of sunshine, and a small lamp, but the room is dark and crowded, with just enough space for a desk, filing cabinet, and a couple of extra chairs. The radio operator turns as we come in and waves. She's a petite lady with black hair and an infectious smile. "Good morning," she says. "How can I help you?"

"Suyin, this is Vance Carson and his associate," Michelle says. "They're detectives. They have some questions about the radio logs. Give them whatever they need, would you?"

Suyin nods. "Sure. Are you the guys working for the tigers?"

"I prefer to think of us as working for Hawthorne *and* the tigers, but yes," Vance says, stepping into the room. I squeeze in behind him; the two of us take up a lot of the floor space, and I end up pushing back into the corner to try and stay out of the way.

"Because everyone's been saying that we could have to cut back operations along the north side if we don't have things settled in the next few days. No one wants to get within claw's reach, especially people who remember the war." Suyin shudders. "We were lucky they were on our side back then, if you ask me. I can't imagine anyone wanting to make them mad."

"Yes, well." Michelle coughs, drawing Suyin's attention back. "As I said, we need to check the logs."

"Monday, the twentieth," Vance says "Were you on duty?"

Suyin thinks about it for a moment. "Yes, that was me." She looks nervously at Michelle. "Am I in some kind of trouble?"

"No, no, nothing like that," Vance assures her. He takes a step towards the radio equipment, looking it over. "You would have received a communique from Camp two, around lunch time. Might have been a strange voice on the other end."

"I don't remember anything like that. Let me check the logs. Do you have an exact time?" Suyin turns and starts rummaging through the papers.

"Not really, no. Somewhere between twelve and three, I would expect."

"Well, that's not going to narrow it down. Might have come in on my lunch break." Suyin is busy looking through the papers. "But I'd be surprised. I mostly eat at my desk, and I don't think I was out of here for more than ... oh, no, here it is. I'd forgotten all about that."

"Forgotten about what?" Vance asks.

"There was a coded signal. They get sent in sometimes by surveyors or scouts. It's like a morse code, but you need the right codebook to decode it, and it comes with instructions to re-route the message to a particular department. Didn't recognize the code, but I sent it on."

"Do you know who picked it up?" Michelle asks.

"Let me cross-check." Suyin pulls out another book, checking through the lines. "It was marked for delivery to accounting, care of James Hope."

"Hm," Michelle mutters.

"You know him?" Vance asks.

"In passing, yes."

"Well, then, we'll need to speak with him."

"Good luck," Michelle says. "He doesn't work here anymore."

Vance and I exchange suspicious looks. "Why not?" Vance asks.

"Because he was Phyllis Graves' manager. The fact that he missed her embezzlement was considered disqualifying for further employment. He was let go on Friday."

"Damn it," Vance mutters. "Can you get us his home address?"

"Of course. Wait here, and I'll be right back with it." Michelle turns on her heel, leaving the two of us in the radio room with Suyin.

"So," I say awkwardly. "It's been kind of a weird week at Hawthorne, huh?"

"Honestly, it's been a weird month. Not that we don't get weirdness around here from time to time, but ever since the FBI started paying attention to us..." Suyin trails off guiltily.

Vance leans in. "Ever since the FBI started paying attention to you?" he asks.

"I probably shouldn't have mentioned that."

"I assume you mean Agent Harper's investigations. Don't worry, we've been apprised of the situation."

"Oh! You have. Well, then." Suyin lets out a breath. "I'm glad, because Ms. Arsenault said that if anyone breathed a *word* of it, we'd be in a world of unemployed. We're supposed to keep it quiet."

"When did you first become aware of his investigation?" Vance asks.

"Maybe three weeks ago, give or take. I think he was around before then, but the senior brass managed to keep a lid on it. Espionage isn't as big a deal at Hawthorne as it would be at Second Star, but it's still a pretty big deal." She sighs. "That's why I don't know any of the codes anymore. The radio operators used to have all the code books, but the codes got changed so that we couldn't share confidential reports coming from the camps."

I look over at Vance, and back to Suyin. "Would an accounting shift lead know survey codes?"

"I don't know, maybe. I don't know who knows which codes."

"They might not have used an official Hawthorne code," Vance points out. "Or they could have blackmailed someone who *did* know the codes into sharing them."

"Yeah. Just a bit weird."

Michelle comes back about then, holding a slip of paper. "I have a home address, the last known one on file. And here's a phone number. Hopefully that helps with your investigations?"

"I hope so, too. Don't let him know that we're coming. If he is up to something shady, I don't want that information to leave this room." Vance tips his hat and walks out of the room.

"So, what's the plan?" I ask as we return to his car.

"Drive over as quickly as possible before someone at Hawthorne calls to warn him we're coming," Vance says.

"You figure they will?"

"I figure if this blackmail thing is so widespread that they had time to call in the feds, there's no telling who's involved. Anyone that Ms. Arsenault spoke to getting that address could have an idea about what it represents."

"One other thing," I say.

"Oh?"

"Ms. Graves said it was a woman's voice on the other end of the phone. Which means not Mr. Hope."

Vance nods glumly. "Like I said," he says. "Anyone could call him."

Hope's address isn't as fancy as I would have expected for a Hawthorne manager, even one who was lower down the ladder. It's another brownstone apartment, a lot like the one that Ms. Graves lived in, but there's no one down at the front desk when we show up. "Looks like we've got a clear walk," Vance says, making for the stairs. "Let's make the most of it."

We climb up to the third floor, and head down to the number on the address we were given, 304. Vance raps sharply on the door, and we wait a minute. When no one answers, he glances both ways and then kneels by the lock, pulling a pair of wires out of his coat pocket.

"You pick locks?" I ask.

"I've been practicing," Vance mutters, working at the lock. "You know, most indoor locks aren't actually very difficult if you just know how to work with them..."

"Is this a good idea? If the cops catch us breaking into someone's house, I don't think they'll take 'we're on a mission from the tigers' as an excuse."

"I realize the concern, but we're dealing with a dangerous situation here," Vance says. "We can't just wait around until Mr. Hope gets back, not with the level of opposition we're up against."

"It doesn't feel right," I say.

"Todd, sometimes you have to do things that aren't entirely right in order to save the day."

I don't know what to say to this, so I just stand there for a few minutes, feeling pretty exposed, while Vance messes around with the lock, sometimes pausing to curse or mutter to himself. Finally, I hear the lock flipping into place, and Vance grins up at me. "Got it!"

"Great, let's get this over with."

Vance's smile slips at my expression, and he gets back to his feet, tucking the lockpicks into his pocket. "We're not going to do any damage, Todd," he says, opening the door. "And it's not as though this is the first place we've gained access to under less than legitimate means."

"It's someone's house, though," I say. "Donny's was a store and Hawthorne is a big business; I don't care so much about that. But this is a guy's house, and we don't have any proof that he's part of this. It just doesn't feel the same."

"We'll have a quick look around and be gone with no one the wiser," Vance says soothingly. "And if Mr. Hope comes home, we'll talk with him then."

I close the door behind us, and nod. "Let's just get this over with. What are we looking for, exactly?"

"Mysterious envelopes, journals, something that might shine a light on Mr. Hope's part in all of this," Vance says from the kitchen. "Looks like he hasn't been home recently."

I glance into the bedroom. There are clothes spread out on the bed — not like the place has been tossed, but like someone was sorting through them. "I think maybe he left."

"There's still food in the fridge. Quite fresh," Vance calls back.

"Then maybe he left in a hurry." I go into the bathroom and take a quick look around. "Toothbrush is gone, and I think some clothes? Hard to say for sure. No suitcase in the closet, either."

"Of course. He's making a run for it." Vance pops out of the kitchen, holding a pad of paper triumphantly. He's got a pencil in one hand. "There was an imprint on the pad. Mr. Hope writes with quite the heavy hand."

I look at the pad. "Pier seventeen, eleven p.m., Tuesday."

Vance meets my eyes. "He's getting a boat off the island, under cover of night. Jotted down the time and day, tore it off, packed a suitcase to hide in a hotel until it was time to go."

"So, now what? Do we call the cops?"

"We don't have any proof that Mr. Hope has done something illegal, aside from trying to slip town. And there won't be any proof of that if they arrive." Vance shakes his head. "No, we'll show up early, stake out a position, and then we confront him. I think we'll be able to get some information out of him."

"I have a dinner tonight."

Vance blinks. "Pardon?"

"Dinner. I have one. Tonight." I rub the back of my head. "At six."

"Will you be done by ten?"

"I mean, I guess I could be."

"This is our one shot, Todd. We've got to take it."

I sigh. "Sure thing, Vance."

"Wonderful. Bring Glimmer, if she's available. We can get some aerial surveillance."

Vance leads the way out the door, and I follow. This whole thing feels like it's spinning out of control, and I wish that Mr. Stark were around to talk to.

———— «» ————

Tuesdays at the Lock and Key aren't packed, but there's already a decent number of folks sitting at tables by the time I arrive — mainly dockworkers and folks from the factories, fresh off their shifts and ready to grab some food and a beer before they head home for the night. There's a dance floor, but it's still covered in tables and the band hasn't set up yet, just an old record player belting out some jazz from the twenties.

Emeka's at the curb when I get there, lounging against the wall chatting with a couple of guys when he spots me. He turns to look at me, and one of the guys nudges him and says something that draws an embarrassed smile out of him.

All the ways this evening could go wrong start to float in my mind. I shove them out of my thoughts, put on a smile to match his, and walk up as casually as I can. "Hi," I say.

"Catch you later, guys," Emeka says to the others, who give some quick goodbyes and head off. He turns to look me over. "Looking good, Todd."

"Well, you're looking great." I'm not kidding. Somehow, Emeka's managed to look casual and perfect all at the same time. He's wearing a plain white shirt with the top button undone, and a pair of jeans that are shaping his legs in a way that jeans really shouldn't be able to. I glance down at my one good shirt, which is kind of straining a bit at the buttons. They don't make them in my size, at least not on my salary.

Emeka hooks an arm into mine. "Well, then, we're a pair of good-looking fellows. Let's go and get some grub."

I don't think heads actually turn as we walk through the door, but I feel like it. Emeka leads us to a table near a window, and flags over a waiter for a couple of beers. "You working tonight?" he asks.

"Not until ten," I say. "I can handle a few beers."

"Four hours, huh. I was kind of hoping to have you to myself tonight," Emeka says lightly.

"Me too," I admit. "But something came up. Long story."

"Four hours long?"

"I'd rather talk about you. Seems like all we do lately is talk about my problems."

"I like talking about your problems. Makes me feel like my life is under control." Emeka's eyes sparkle as he looks into mine. "Tell you what. No trouble talk tonight. We just talk about nice things, and go back to problems tomorrow."

"I think I can handle that."

"Great. Then why don't we start with the movies. Seen anything good lately?"

Over a couple of plates of lasagna, we settle into a chat about recent movies, or at least as recent as anything gets around here. We end up chatting about Westerns, comparing *Shane* to *High Noon* and discussing cowboy works, and then the conversation moves to the war in Korea for a bit, and from there to World War II. "You know, you've never mentioned whether you served." I say at one point.

Emeka nods. "You're right." I wait, and he chuckles. "Sorry. I don't talk about it much. Yes, I served for a couple of years. Didn't see any real combat, but I was assigned to helping with reconstruction in France. Lots of supply work for the people on the front lines." Emeka thinks about it. "Never went home again."

"Wait, really?"

He nods. "Those two years there I spent in the army showed me a different world. The people weren't great, but they were better. And when I was discharged, I realized I didn't want to go back to the States, to have to deal with all the crap day after day. I was talking to someone else on the base, and they'd just finished a shipping tour, visited Everland a couple of times. Couldn't stop talking about what a wild and free place it was. I figured I needed to see it for myself."

"You have family back in the States?"

Emeka shakes his head. "That falls under the 'no troubles on the first date' rule."

"How about dancing on the first date?" I blurt out before I can let myself get scared again.

"Dancing on the first date, I will definitely do." Emeka looks over to where the tables are being cleared. "May I have the first dance?"

"You stole the words right out of my mouth."

We finish our food as the band sets up, and I down my beer in one swig. Now that the moment is here, I'm pretty sure it's a mistake, but I don't know how to take it back.

Emeka stands up, sees my face, and grins. "Need me to lead?"

"Usually."

He laughs and grabs my hand. "Come on, bruiser."

We head over to the dance floor. There are only a few people here already, all of them about half my size and dressed to kill. The music starts up quick, and Emeka pulls on my arms to set the pace, some fancy swing tune that makes me sure I'm going to mess up. I stumble, almost bump into the person behind me, and then do a half-spin that ends with me out of sync with him. I hear someone at a table laugh, and feel heat rise in my cheeks.

Emeka locks eyes with me, takes both of my hands, and pulls me in close. As he slowly steps backward, bringing me with him, he steps in and gets on his tiptoes for a moment.

"I've seen you fight," he whispers in my ear. "You're a lot more graceful than this." He steps down and back, and I follow him, leaning in to keep the motion going.

"I fight like an out-of-control truck," I counter. "It's why I get punched so much."

"You really don't. React to my moves. Sidestep, flow. Think like when someone you don't want to hurt is causing trouble, and you're just wearing them down, matching them. Follow my eyes, ignore everyone staring." He gives me a light tap on the arm.

I take a deep breath and fall into step with him. I start focusing on his physical movements and let myself react to them. It gets easier, but I think it probably still looks a bit strange — he steps in and I back up, he flows left and I stomp right, and when he comes in for a tight press I have to remember to match him instead of going for a shove. But after a couple of minutes, it starts to feel natural.

When the song stops, Emeka breaks over to one side and leans against the bar to watch the next set of dancers take the floor. Most of the workers are on their way out by now and the late crowd is filing in, and the hall is getting younger and fancier by the minute. "Sorry about that," I say, gesturing to the bartender for a couple of beers. "I don't dance much."

"You did fine," Emeka assures me, giving me a quick peck on the cheek. "Didn't even step on my toes."

"You expected me to?"

"Maybe a little. I know you don't dance much." He grins as I hand him his beer. "You're a great follower."

"Tell me about it." I smile crookedly. "Pretty much my life."

Emeka's face falls. "I wish you wouldn't do that."

"Do what?"

"Get so down on yourself. Learn to take a compliment, Todd. You're a really amazing guy, and sometimes I think the only person that doesn't realize that is you."

"Coming from you, that means a lot."

"Really? Why me?"

"Now who isn't taking a compliment?"

"Okay, okay. I'll trust your opinion of me if you trust mine of you." Emeka leans in against my arm. "Thanks for asking me out tonight. It's nice to just forget things and have a good time."

"Is everything okay?"

"Sure, yeah. There's just a lot going on. For both of us."

"There really is, huh?" I lean back against him, looking over the dance floor. "Thanks for carving out some time for me."

"Right back at you." Emeka takes my hand. "Do you have time for another dance?"

"I'm all yours," I say, pulling him back to the dance floor.

———— «» ————

I show up at the docks at about 10 p.m., to find Glimmer already there with a familiar looking friend. "What are you doing here, Holly?"

"You think I would miss a stakeout?" Holly asks.

"You think that Mr. Stark would be okay with you being here with a competitor?"

"I think I don't actually care. If he wants to vanish for a week, he can deal with things when he gets back. Consider me an interested volunteer. How was dinner?"

I frown at her. "Are you just here right now to pump me for information about the date?"

"No, that's a side benefit. How was dinner?"

I chuckle. "It was nice. We danced."

"And...?"

"And I didn't step on his feet, so I'm calling it a win. You want to focus on the job?"

"Can't, your boss isn't here yet."

As if on cue, Vance walks up from the street. "Evening, Todd. Glimmer. And ... is this your backup?" He gives Holly a quick look-over, trying not to sound dubious, but I can see her bristle just a little.

"This is Holly. She gave us the in at the logging camp. She's a solid pair of eyes for a stake-out, and if things go wonky, she can get herself out without needing a helping hand."

"Holly Blossom?" Vance's dubious expression vanishes instantly, replaced by a beaming grin.

"You know me?" Holly asks, surprised.

"Of course I know you! Well, know of you. You're Basil Stark's partner. Plus, you've pushed a couple of clients my way this year, and they mentioned you." He holds out a hand. "Always meant to stop by and give my regards, professional to professional, but time kept slipping away from me. Glad to have you onboard."

Holly beams and shakes Vance's hand firmly. "Glad to be here. Just in a volunteer capacity, of course, but I'm sure you've heard that we might be working a case that overlaps with yours. It seemed like a good time to help each other out."

Vance nods. "You got me those clues earlier, I'm happy to help out however I can. Here's what I'm thinking. We know that Mr. Hope is due to be at pier seventeen in about an hour. We don't want to be so close that the folks on the boat spot us, but we do want to make sure that Mr. Hope doesn't slip past, so I suggest we take up positions around the thoroughfare near the pier. Glimmer, you're our eyes in the sky. Holly, you can cover the west side, and I'll take east, leaving Todd to watch the boat itself. What do you think?"

"What do we do if a watchman comes by?" Holly asks. "Being here early is good, but it means there's almost certainly going to be a patrol or two, and while it's not actually illegal to be here, if we don't have a good reason, they're going to tell us to scram."

"Good point." Vance thinks about that for a moment. "Glimmer, can you let us know when the watchmen are coming? We can slip away, and then double-back when they leave and get back in position. It's not perfect, but it should give us the time we need."

Holly nods. "Sounds like a plan. Here's hoping that we don't have to wait too long."

The next half-hour is pretty quiet. A watchman comes by around 10:15, but Glimmer gives us plenty of notice and he doesn't seem too interested in poking around. The boat down at the end of pier 17 is dark and looks like one of the smaller cargo ships; if they're planning to slip away, they've probably already bribed the security staff not to come down this way. This happens more often than the Port Authority would like to admit; there are too many powerful people with a lot invested in being able to leave port quietly for the staff to be clean, and the best you can hope for in a head of security is that they're only corrupt enough to look the other way. Anyone who tries to clean things up ends up getting framed or pressured into early retirement.

It's about 10:45 when Glimmer dives out of the sky into my face and hisses some kind of alarm too quickly for me to follow. "Woah, Glim, slow down a moment," I say.

Someone is walking down the pier towards us, coming from the main harbor. They're bundled up, wearing a heavy coat and low hat, but they could be our target. "Is that the guy?" I ask Glimmer.

She slaps me, and repeats what she was saying, louder and more slowly.

"Ash Cutter?" I swallow. "He's following Hope?"

Glimmer shakes her head, and points back towards the boat.

"There are people already here?"

She nods.

"Oh, hell." It all falls together. The helpful address at Hope's house, the packed suitcase, even the watchmen not coming this far down. "Tell Holly, I'll get Vance."

Glimmer nods and zips away, and I break cover just in time to see that Vance is doing the same thing, already starting towards the guy coming towards us. Vance's coat billows out behind him, and I have to admit he cuts a pretty ominous figure under the buzzing streetlamp that's the only light we've got.

"Mr. Hope," Vance starts, raising his voice.

"Get down!" I yell, as the guy in the coat pulls a gun.

Vance freezes, staring at the gunman across from him. Another guy comes around the corner, cocking a pistol. I can hear the sound of stomping boots coming from the boat behind us, but I don't have time for that. As the first guy opens fire, I tackle Vance, knocking us both behind the crates Vance was using as a hiding place. A pair of bullets crack into the crates, but whatever's inside is heavy enough to block them. Lucky us.

"Get your gun!" I yell at Vance, risking a look past the crates. It's just the two guys on the far side, but it looks like three more are climbing off the boat, and we won't have any cover when they get to us.

Vance nods shakily and starts fumbling for his holster. I look at the guys coming off the boat and around the corner; I grab a rock, and hurl it as hard as I can at them. It skips off the wall next to the guy in the lead, but all three of them move for cover anyway, so I've bought us a moment. And then I look back to see that Vance has his gun out and he's popped out of cover to take a shot, but while we were under cover the goon coming towards us moved and Vance is way out of position.

The gunman grins and raises his pistol. Vance is shifting his aim, realizing that he's pointing the wrong way, but he's not going to make it. And then there's a blur of motion as

Glimmer dives out of the night, slams into the gunman's pistol just as it goes off, and the goon screams as he shoots himself in the foot. She leaps back into the sky as someone takes a potshot at her, missing by a mile.

The second gunshot jolts Vance back into motion, and he fires three shots in the general direction of the second goon, who ducks behind a crate of his own instead of keeping up the chase against Glimmer. "What do we do?" Vance yells.

"We need cover! Quick!" I glance over my shoulder, just in time to see the last of the three men from the boat grab the guy in front of him and flip him into the harbor. "Wait, hang on!" I put a hand on Vance's shoulder as he moves to run.

The goon who ducked for cover when I threw that rock realizes that something's going on behind him and he turns around in time to get a cane jabbed into his throat; as he goes down his former companion kicks his gun out of his hand and then delivers a couple of quick punches to the chest. I grin as I recognize the style. "It's Mr. Stark!"

Vance looks back, a smile breaking out as Mr. Stark kicks his opponent's gun off the dock, then dives towards us as the last two still-armed gunmen realize that he's not on their side.

"Todd," Mr. Stark says severely, pressing against the crates between us, "we are going to have to have a word about the meaning of staying low and not getting involved."

"Okay, things got a little bit out of hand, but we didn't know where you were…"

"I was infiltrating a blackmail ring, Todd. That takes rather a few days. Is that Vance Carson?"

"Hello, Mr. Stark, it's a pleasure—" Vance breaks off and ducks for cover as a gunshot ricochets off the lamppost behind us.

"Charmed," Mr. Stark says blandly, before turning back to me. "If I had realized that *you* were the people my target was trying to get rid of, I might have done things differently. Was that Glimmer?"

"Yeah, she's pretty slick."

"It was incredibly dangerous! She's not a fighter!" Basil's eyes narrow. "And I assume Holly is nearby. Where?"

"Should we really be doing this now?"

"Yes," Mr. Stark says flatly.

"I dunno, she was over by the west side."

"Then that's where we're going. Carson, your gun."

Vance hands it over mutely, and Mr. Stark pops up from the crates, fires twice in rapid succession, and drops back down. I hear someone curse. "Winged him," Mr. Stark says. "You two run for the west side. I'll cover you."

I nod, and grab Vance by the shoulder. "Come on!" As we break cover, racing up towards the west side, Mr. Stark fires a couple more shots in the direction of the gunmen, pinning them down.

"You're not getting paid enough for this," Basil yells at the goons as he takes another shot. "Why not give it up and go home?"

Vance and I reach the old car Holly was using for cover, and duck behind it. No sign of her. Vance looks around wildly. "What do we do?"

"Wait a moment. Mr. Stark will follow us."

At that we all hear sirens. Close. A pair of floodlights opens from the water, one shining on Mr. Stark and the other on the two gunmen. A voice booms over the loudspeaker. "Weapons down! Everyone on the ground, now!"

"Okay, new plan. Run!"

Vance looks at me. "What?"

I grab him again, and he's too shocked and confused to stop. "You don't know that voice?" I ask. "It's Harper! We gotta go, now!"

"What about Stark?"

"He'll get free, don't worry! Glimmer?"

Glimmer ducks out of the sky and lets me know that there are policemen closing in on the docks from all sides, but she's found an alley that they're not watching.

"Good one. Let's move!"

As we race down the narrow gap between two warehouses that Glimmer spotted, I see about thirty cops descending on the area behind us. The boat with the floodlights is closing in, and while I can't quite make out the tall, thin figure standing on the front, I'm pretty sure that I know who it is. Agent Harper got exactly what he wanted out of this.

Glimmer leads us around the corner and across a couple more buildings, to where Holly is waiting by Vance's car. "There are police everywhere," she hisses. "What happened?"

"It was a trap," I say. "Maybe two traps, I'm not sure. But we gotta get out of here. Glimmer, see if you can find Mr. Stark."

"Uncle Basil is here?" Holly asks.

"Saved our skins, yeah. But you know him. If we stick around we'd just slow him down. Glimmer has got it. But Glimmer, stay high! Harper will definitely shoot you if he has the chance."

Glimmer nods and lets me know that she's been shot at enough for one day; she'll meet us at Jessie's. I climb into the back seat and Vance takes the wheel. "Drive slow," I say. "Real slow. If anyone shows up, we just got here."

Holly makes a show of looking at the still-shivering Vance, then back at me, and grasping the edges of her seat to keep herself steady. Vance starts the car up, and we begin to drive

We get lucky. We parked pretty far away because Vance was worried about the car getting spotted, so we're outside the police cordon and we make it all the way to Jessie's without getting stopped. The waiter takes one look at us and brings out a bottle of whiskey and three slices of pie; I pour Vance a healthy shot. "You okay?"

"I think I'm getting full up on excitement," Vance admits.

Holly grimaces. "You and me both. What the hell happened?"

"Hope wasn't there. Five gunmen showed up instead, but one of them was Mr. Stark in disguise. If he hadn't been, I don't think Vance and I would've made it out."

"We almost didn't as it was," Vance says. "Glimmer saved my life. Again."There's a rap on the door, and the waiter frowns and walks over. As he opens it, Glimmer zips in. The waiter raises his hands and starts to say something, but Vance throws a few bills on the table, shoots the waiter a look that dares him to press the issue, and motions Glimmer over. "Dinner is on me," he says. "Whatever anyone wants."

"What did you see?" Holly asks.

Glimmer explains that she saw the police taking a body off the boat, and Agent Harper called it 'Hope,' so it was probably the guy we're looking for. Then she says that Basil got grabbed.

"What?" Holly gasps. "How?"

Glimmer's face is dark. She says that a fairy was tracking him and told the police where he got out of the water.

I sit back in my chair. "The fairies are working with Harper?"

"Harper's the bad guy," Vance says, tapping the table. "It makes sense. He shows up, things get bad. He wants to control the island, here's a way to do it. He wants a war with tigers, someone steals from them."

"I thought it started before he got here, though," Holly points out.

"He probably has co-conspirators," Vance says. "Is Mr. Stark alright?"

Glimmer shrugs, and says that he probably is, he gets arrested often enough. There were a lot of police around.

Holly rubs her forehead. "Okay. We'll have to go and see him tomorrow."

Vance nods. "I'll go through my files, figure things out. Harper may be government, but he's not *local* government. There are a lot of people who don't want more American control over Everland, and I might be able to figure something out."

"Meet back at your office tomorrow evening?" I suggest.

Vance nods. "That sounds perfect."

We order our food and settle down to eat. Glimmer asks if Vance is alright.

"I'm fine. Didn't take a scratch," Vance assures her before I can finish translating. He looks at Holly and I as we blink in surprise. "What?"

"I thought you didn't speak fairy."

Vance shrugs again. "I'm getting better, I think. Practice makes perfect."

Glimmer nods and grabs a French fry from Vance's plate. She says that Vance is a quick learner.

"Sorry about your gun," I say.

"It's fine. I hope Mr. Stark doesn't get in trouble for having it." Vance stares off into space for a moment. "I don't think it was a good choice to bring it, after all. I should probably stick to my strengths."

"Hey, I bet you haven't been in a lot of gunfights," I point out. "You did fine."

"Thanks for the vote of confidence," Vance says. He shakes his head. "Do you think Harper had Hope killed to cover his tracks?"

"Might have been to trap us," I say. "I think there were two traps, and I don't know who was doing what. Someone sent gunmen to kill us, but someone else sent Harper to arrest us. Maybe they figured we'd be able to kill the gunmen?"

"Or they were covering all their bases," Holly says. "Harper didn't move in until Uncle Basil showed up. Maybe they were trying to trap him, not us."

"We were bait," Vance says quietly.

"Damn," I say. "That makes sense."

"Now what do we do?" Holly asks.

"We act like we weren't there," Vance says after a moment. "It probably won't fool anyone, but the cops didn't spot us. You work with Mr. Stark, so you can try to see him as soon as you 'find out' he was arrested. I'll work the other angle, try to get in touch with more blackmailed people and see what I can uncover."

I reach out and pat him on the shoulder. "It's gonna work out fine, Vance."

"I hope so, Todd," Vance says. "We don't have a lot of people to fall back on."

# Wednesday, August 29<sup>th</sup>

**The good news** is, we don't have to pretend we haven't heard the news for long. The shootout made the news, and I wake up to a headline in the *Everland Times* reading: "CITY'S LAST PIRATE: A MURDERER?" According to the story, federal agents raided a suspected smuggling operation and found Mr. Hope dead and Basil Stark on the scene with a smoking gun. The reporter speculates that Hope was Stark's informant at Hawthorne, helping him do something very vague but definitely terrible; then, when he got scared and tried to back out, Stark killed him. It also helpfully says that police are looking for information about any associates that Stark might have.

I head down to Mr. Stark's office to check in, which turns out to be a mistake. A reporter jumps at my face as I get up to the door. "Excuse me! Do you work in this building? Are you familiar with Stark Investigations?"

"I'm a janitor," I growl, pushing past him. I can see a second reporter behind him, scenting a story, and I slam the door in their faces before anyone recognizes me from my own mugshots in the paper. Then I turn around and see a *third* reporter in the hallway upstairs, knocking on the office door and yelling questions.

In for a penny, in for a pound. I storm up the stairs and yell, "Alright, clear out, show's over!"

The reporter turns to snap at me, and then adjusts as he has to look up a heck of a lot further than he expected. "You can't intimidate the news," he says.

"This is a place of business. There's no story here. Clear out." I growl the words, and the guy takes a step back.

"C'mon, man," he says, holding up his hands. "You work here? I need a lead. *The Times* scooped us. There's someone in the office, and they're not opening the door. If you could just get me a lead."

"I'll get you a lead down the stairs if you don't stop bothering folks around here." I take a deep breath. "Look, you want a lead? How many times has Basil Stark gotten arrested, and how many times has he been convicted? I'd go sniffing around Hawthorne if I was you."

The reporter sighs. "That's the best you're giving me? Fine, fine." He presses a card into my hand. "If you change your mind, let me know."

I wait until he's down the stairs and out the door before I knock on the office door. Holly lets me in after a minute. "You should have come up the fire escape," she says, leading me into the main office. Glimmer is crouched by the window, watching the reporters outside balefully.

"Yeah, probably. How's it going in here?"

"Everland only has three newspapers, six radio shows, and a lifestyle magazine, but somehow a hundred people want a scoop. The phone's ringing every time I put it down." She shakes her head. "Glimmer wanted to drop things on them, and it's all I could do to convince her not to."

"Maybe she should. It would definitely change the story," I say. Holly glares at me, and I raise my hands defensively. "Or not."

"Well, we've got permission to visit Uncle Basil in jail, but not for very long, and we need to be there by eleven. Think we can shake these guys?"

"I think they'll be watching the stairwell," I say. Then I smile slowly. "Hey, Glimmer, you still want to throw things?"

Glimmer grins and hefts a mug.

"No, that's my favorite one!" Holly says quickly. She goes into the kitchen and comes out with three more mugs. "Throw these ones, they're ugly and Uncle Basil won't get rid of them. And don't actually hit anybody, please. We don't need you arrested, too."

Glimmer salutes and promises to be a distraction big enough for us to get away.

"Just keep safe, huh? We'll meet back at … let's say my place," I say. "Don't think anyone knows to check there."

Holly and I climb out onto the fire escape and start carefully making our way down. From the other side of the building, we hear a cacophony of fairy swear words and the sound of a mug smashing into the street, along with the surprised shouts of the news folk. I peek around the corner in time to see Glimmer take off, with two reporters in hot pursuit. "Right, coast is clear."

"Great. Mom's car is over here, let's go."

"She's still letting us have it?" I ask, surprised. I really thought we'd have run that well dry by now.

"She said she wouldn't feel safe with me on the bus right now. She wanted me to stay home, but," Holly shrugs, hopping into the old blue sedan, "we both knew that wasn't going to happen."

We make it to the prison before the press even realizes that we've left the office, and we're able to park without any trouble. Things are going pretty smoothly until we get inside and find the Commissioner waiting for us.

"Holly Blossom and Todd Malcolm." Commissioner Darling's a scary guy when he wants to be. Even though I've got a few inches on him, I feel like he's the one looming over me, his eyebrows furrowed and his words clipped. "I heard you were coming."

"Morning, Commissioner," Holly says brightly. "Are you here to let Uncle Basil go?"

"Hardly. He's in real trouble this time."

"Unlike all the other times?"

"All the other times didn't involve American federal agents," Darling says. "And as usual, Stark is being a tight-lipped fool. He won't give me anything. Not why he was there, and not who he's working this case for. I don't suppose you'll be more cooperative."

"I don't know anything about it," Holly says. "I'm just here to check up on him for the family."

"Really."

Holly nods.

"Do you know why I became a police officer, Miss Blossom?"

"A desperate need for control stemming from a childhood without any?" Holly suggests.

I didn't think Darling could look dourer. I was wrong. "Because I don't like seeing people get away with things. I don't like it when people think that they're smarter than everyone around them, and I don't plan to stand by and watch them ruin my city."

Holly bristles. "We know you were talking with Uncle Basil," she says quietly. "Maybe you should have done more. Were there local police on the operation, or just the feds?"

"A few. No one I trust." Darling leans in. "I'm being shut out. And as much as I dislike your uncle, I find myself in an unpleasantly familiar situation, so yes, I was talking with him, and yet here I am with no leads. What is Harper up to?"

Holly and I share a look, and then we look back at Commissioner Darling. I don't like the idea of him getting hold of a bunch of blackmail and arresting a lot of people. On the other hand, we're in the soup. "We don't have any proof of anything," I say.

"You have theories."

"The sort of theories that get people in trouble. You can't just accuse a federal agent of running a blackmail ring," Holly says.

Darling's eyebrows rise. "No. No, that could cause trouble. That's the case?"

"That's a case. I think we're stuck in three or four by now," I admit.

"Hrm. And you're here to report to Stark on it?"

I shrug. "Things are just a total mess."

"They are." Darling frowns at us. "You realize that I *also* can't accuse a federal agent of running a blackmail ring. Not without some extremely solid evidence."

"If we had any extremely solid evidence, Uncle Basil wouldn't be the one in jail," Holly says tiredly.

Darling nods grimly. "You'd better go in and see him, then. Maybe you can convince him to cooperate." He turns away. "I have to go and make a call to let Agent Harper know that someone is visiting, but the nearest phone isn't working. Might take me some time to find a secure line."

Holly grins. "Thanks, Commish."

"Don't thank me. Please. And if you do find something actionable, let the law take care of it. Don't be vigilantes."

Darling stalks away, grumbling under his breath.

"He really hates it when he has to let us do stuff for him," Holly chuckles.

"Then why does he?"

She shrugs. "The man spends all his time trying to fix corruption in the most corrupt organization in the city, which he is theoretically in charge of, after spending his entire childhood fighting pirates before moving to London and studying law. I don't know why he does anything. Come on, let's see if Uncle Basil has anything useful for us."

Basil Stark looks a little bit the worse for wear, but he gives the two of us a nod as we're brought into the meeting room. He's wearing a grey jumpsuit and has a few big bruises on one side of his face, and he's been handcuffed to the table.

The guard looks us over. "I'll be right outside. Knock on the door when you're done. No funny business."

We nod to him and sit down across from Mr. Stark. "How are you doing, Uncle Basil?" Holly asks.

Mr. Stark grimaces, twisting his hands and slipping out of the cuffs. "Simply kicking myself, mostly. Such a blatant trap and I fell directly into it. I should have realized that the enemy was willing to have Hope killed to get at us."

"Uh, should you...?" I look down at the handcuffs.

Mr. Stark shrugs. "I'll put them back on before you leave. Won't take a moment. Honestly, it's a bit insulting of the guards to think these would hold me." He looks around. "The jail, on the other hand, is quite capable of doing so. I don't expect to be here more than a few weeks, but it all depends on how much evidence Harper can draft up. If he fakes enough material, it might actually go to trial, and from there, who knows."

"How'd they catch you?"

Mr. Stark sighs. "Harper stationed officers at the banks of the river. Knew I'd swim for it, and somehow they figured out exactly where I was coming ashore."

"Harper had a fairy doing aerial surveillance," Holly explains. "Glimmer spotted them while we were making our getaway. They must have signaled your position to the officers."

"Fascinating. Well, that's what I get for not looking up. I'm glad you escaped."

"We've got some leads," Holly says, leaning in. "The bulk of it is the fairies. They're not just spying; they're delivering messages and making payoffs."

"Damn." Mr. Stark taps his chin thoughtfully. "That simultaneously fits and makes everything more complicated, and it strongly suggests that Harper is highly placed in the conspiracy."

"Which doesn't make a lot of sense, because as near as we can tell, he wants to start a war, get troops on the island, and take over everyone's turf," Holly says. "Why would anyone local work with him?"

"Not by choice, largely. The first blackmail cases that I was investigating were centered on Second Star. An employee there was being blackmailed by anonymous sources into acting as an intermediary, setting up blackmail of his fellow employees. He would gather money or information and leave it in inaccessible places. The fairies must have picked it up from there."

"Matches everything else they were doing. How'd you get from there to the docks?" I ask.

"Once I connected the blackmail at Second Star to the blackmail targeting you, I did some digging. I created a false persona, used a few of my less traditional mob connections to give him a minor reputation, and I started trying to get hired for the sorts of jobs that this 'ghost mob' was hiring for, hoping I could work my way up the chain of command. I didn't have much luck at first, until I was put in contact with a woman by the name of Michelle Arsenault. Has that name come up for you as well?"

"Yeah," I say. "I've met her a bunch. She's supposed to be helping Harper figure out who's doing the blackmailing." I mull it over. "Except that if Harper's doing the blackmailing, and she's working with him..."

"Yes. I think she's supplying him with connections to local criminals, and possibly to blackmail targets. I don't know if she's a partner or a pawn. I doubt she's in charge, or she wouldn't be moving openly."

"And Harper and the fairies don't like each other, so there needs to be someone else involved," I say.

Mr. Stark looks surprised. "An excellent point, Todd. Thank you. I have one more lead I was planning to follow up on, but it might be a trap as well. Arsenault hired me alongside the other four gunmen to ambush Vance Carson at the docks. I wasn't able to get in touch with any of you to warn you, so I went along and turned the tables when the ambushers appeared. Of course, she neglected to tell any of us that Hope's body would be there, or that the police were on the way. But she did say that if things went south, we were to report to a particular place at four thirty this afternoon in order to plan out our next steps."

"And most of the gunmen got away," Holly says.

"Exactly. I'd go so far as to say that Harper wasn't even trying to round them up, which suggests that he didn't feel the need to silence them."

"Huh. Are they meeting with Harper?" I ask.

"I've no idea, but I expect someone will be there, either to coordinate or to remove them. I have the location in my drawer at the office."

"You want us to investigate?" Holly asks.

"Not particularly, but I'm out of action and you two are my most trustworthy surveillance." Mr. Stark shakes his head. "I think I've been out of step for this entire case. Holly, Todd, I'm going to have to rely on you. Entirely."

"Right. We'll go over and see what's up, and then we can come back and— "

"No. I mean entirely. Darling's men are the ones watching me for now, but there's no telling when Harper will take over that as well. I expect he'll do it as soon as he hears that you visited and he doesn't have a record of what we spoke about. You won't be able to come back safely."

"Then how do we solve this?"

"Check my notes. Check your notes. We've found Harper out; we're most of the way there." Mr. Stark smiles. "I trust you." He coughs and leans back in his seat. "Now get moving.

You need to be there in time to see whoever shows up, and to listen in if possible. Be careful; it's possible that Harper will have the place staked out."

"Yes, Uncle Basil," Holly says. "We'll be as quiet as mice."

As we head out the doors, Holly leans in toward me. "We've got a few hours until this stakeout. I'm going to check out the area, see if anyone has noticed anything."

"I've got to talk to Emeka," I say. "Michelle's the one who set him up with Hkuri's band, and she's running things. If she's part of Harper's plan to mess things up with the tigers, she could be setting the Steppers up for a fall."

"Oh, heck, I didn't even think of that." Holly bites her lip. "Okay. Drop me off at the office, I'll take Glimmer with me. Meet you at three-thirty?"

"Sounds perfect."

———— 《》 ————

I call Emeka from a payphone, but there's no answer at his place. I take a deep breath, and remind myself that he's probably fine, and then try the bar that Hkuri and the Steppers are scheduled to play tonight. To my relief, the guy on the phone says that the band is in the back rehearsing. He offers to go and get them for me, but I tell him it's okay and that I'll be there in fifteen minutes.

When I show up at the place and knock on the service entrance, Marta lets me in. "Todd, you look terrible," she says.

"Thanks."

"No, really. Is everything okay?"

"Is Emeka here?" I ask.

"Sure. We're all here." Marta looks me up and down. "What the hell is going on?"

"Case went bad," I say. "I need to talk to Emeka. Actually, I need to talk to all of you."

"Why? Are you about to hop a freighter out of town?" Marta starts to chuckle, but one look at my face has her back to serious. "When you say 'bad,' you really mean it, huh? Come on, we're just doing some lighting checks. There's time for a chat."

Marta leads me into the main room. Emeka and Hkuri are on stage at their positions, while the bar's technician noodles around with the lighting. "Hey, take five, Johnny," Marta says. "We've got a little situation. Won't be long."

The technician groans, but gets up, shuts down the lights, and heads out front to take a smoke. Emeka hops off the stage and walks over. "Hey, what's up?"

"Hopefully nothing. Maybe a really big something. I don't really know how to tell you this, guys, but you might be in danger."

"In danger?" Hkuri pads up and looks at me. "You are thinking there is a threat?"

"Yeah. Yeah, pretty much. Remember Agent Harper? Tall, skinny, federal agent?"

"No." Hkuri says.

"Really? You didn't ... huh, I guess you weren't there that day. Oh, boy, this is going to take a lot."

"Sit down, have a drink, tell us what's going on." Marta pushes a chair up and starts passing out bottles of beer from the band's minifridge. I take a sip to cool my nerves and then jump right in. As quickly as I can, I fill everyone in on Agent Harper, the fairies, the blackmail, and last night's disaster.

"That is bad," Hkuri says as I wrap up, "but it does not sound as though it concerns us directly."

"Harper really wants to crack down on the island. He was up at Hawthorne the other day, trying to turn that standoff with Fraal and Amhara into a fight."

Hkuri's tongue runs over her teeth. "I begin to see how it may concern us. You think he will target us?"

"Yeah." I look over at Emeka, and wince. "And on top of all that, Harper's liaison at Hawthorne is Michelle Arsenault."

Marta breathes in sharply. "That's not great."

"It gets worse. Before he got arrested, Mr. Stark had evidence that she's been giving Harper connections to crooks and stuff. She's probably the one getting blackmail material together, too. I dunno if she's doing it by choice or because he's got something on her, but either way, the fact that she just set up a band with humans and tigers in it is more than a little worrying." I look over at Emeka. "Emeka, I'm sorry, but I think she's using you."

Emeka's face has gone slack. "Oh, no," he says quietly.

"Emeka?"

Emeka pushes his chair back and starts to pace. "The Rust Bucket. Michelle's the one who suggested the place. Wanted me to go down there with you."

My jaw drops. "What?"

"She wanted me to give a letter to the bartender! It wasn't anything to do with the arson! I mean, I didn't think it was anything to do with it..." Emeka is still pacing.

"Emeka, hey, it's okay—" Marta starts.

"No, it isn't! I knew she was up to something, or she wouldn't have pressured me into the band, but then Hkuri was cool, and I let myself think maybe I'd lucked out. And then she kept asking questions about you, but that made sense, you'd showed up at Hawthorne..." Emeka collapses back into his chair, his head in his hands. "I was so stupid!"

"But you didn't tell her anything," I say.

Emeka doesn't look up.

"What?" I ask quietly.

"We didn't meet up on the ship over to Everland," Emeka says, just as quiet. "We met back in France, after the war. When I decided to come here, I couldn't get a visa. Embassy wouldn't even see me. Michelle, she pulled some strings. I thought it was just influence, at first. When things started to go wrong in our relationship, she told me the truth. She'd gotten forged documents. Threatened to turn them over to the police. I walked out on her, and she never did."

"And then?"

"She mentioned them again when she asked me to be in the band. Said I owed her." Emeka is still staring down into his hands. "It wasn't blackmail, not exactly. But then all that stuff with The Rust Bucket happened, and she kept asking how things were going."

My head is spinning. The room is too hot. I push the chair back. "The whole time, and you didn't say anything. I thought that you..." I turn quickly. "I gotta go."

"Todd, wait." Emeka's voice is faint.

Marta and Hkuri are frozen in place. Emeka's halfway out of his seat, like he's not sure if he should follow through or sit back down. I don't give him the chance. "Just watch your backs," I say, feeling my voice crack. "Only reason I came by."

And then, before I can scream and break something, or scream and break down, I'm out the door and into the street. Could go either way, and either way I don't want them to be around for it.

———— ‹›› ————

The meeting spot Mr. Stark found out about is down on the east side, near the bluffs. The buildings around here are about as old as anything gets in Everland, built twenty years ago when everyone thought this place was going to be a shining beacon of industry. Row houses for factory workers got built in a hurry, and then the factories almost all closed, and the row houses weren't too close to anywhere else, so they're all full of whoever can't afford to live anywhere else, usually paying by the week. The bright side is that the locals don't ask many questions. It's so on-point as a secret meeting place that I almost don't believe it's real.

I hop a bus and meet up with Holly and Glimmer a few blocks away. Holly takes one look at my expression and pulls me in. "Is everything okay?"

"Fine. It's a long story. I'll tell you later, okay?"

"Yeah. Whenever you're ready. Come on, we've scoped out the area and it's clear."

Trying not to look too suspicious, we walk the rest of the way to the building. Glimmer lets us in the side door, and we find the room Mr. Stark had marked out. The wallpaper is peeling and the furniture looks like it might collapse if I try to sit on it. I look around dubiously. "You see anything?"

"Nothing jumps out," Holly admits, "but I trust Uncle Basil. Either someone is going to show up, or there'll be something here." She goes over to the side table and pulls a drawer open. "No tell-tale envelopes," she says.

"No tell-tale anything," I agree. "Maybe it's an in-person meeting after all." I look around the room. There's an old, slotted closet door, and I give it a rattle. "Locked."

"Let me look. Uncle Basil's been teaching me some things, and I can't imagine they're paying much for a closet lock." Holly pulls out a couple of pins and kneels by the door. A minute later, the door clicks open. "Piece of cake." She peers through. "I think there's room for the three of us in here."

We pile into the closet; Holly grabs a large shirt from its hanger and stuffs it under the base of the door just to be safe, and we settle in to wait. The heat is intense, and I'm starting to drift off when the door to the room opens with a bang. The guy who staggers in is limping heavily, and he pulls off his hat and looks around. "Goddamn bastard," he mutters, "can't even make a meeting on time." He collapses into a chair, which groans under his weight, and we spend the next two minutes waiting to see who his contact is.

"You're on time. At least you can do one thing right." Harper steps into the room and closes the door gently behind him. He turns to look the other guy over, and frowns. "Only you?"

"Yeah, well, the guys aren't doing so hot. Gordy got shot, so he's at a doctor we trust. Ken almost drowned, got picked up by harbor patrol. And Carl's got cracked ribs and a broken nose."

I shift to get a better look at Harper's face through the slats of the closet. He seems coldly furious. "Ms. Arsenault told me you would be adequate for the job."

"Well then, maybe Ms. Arsenault shouldn't have hired Basil goddamn Stark to be our fifth guy!"

Harper blinks. "Excuse me?"

"'Jimmy?' The guy who was supposed to be cutting off the west route. Goddamn Stark in disguise. That's why Ken took a bath, and Gordy got the crap knocked out of him."

"Huh. I had assumed he'd outflanked you. I will have to have a word with Ms. Arsenault about that particular lapse in security."

"Yeah, well. Carson's still kicking, and so's that gorilla of his. You want us to take him out once everyone's patched up?"

"No. Of course not. We've already got Stark in custody; it makes no difference if we can only get him for Mr. Hope's murder, rather than for Hope and Carson both. Perhaps it would have been a bonus for Ms. Arsenault to get Carson and that idiot he goes around with out of the picture, but what matters is that Stark arrived as intended."

"You were trying to frame Stark?" The gunman's eyes bug. "You knew he'd be there?"

Harper sneers. "You think we spent all those resources on *Carson*? I didn't expect Stark to arrive until *after* you clowns did your job and left, but I suppose that's what I get for trusting Arsenault's connections." He shakes his head. "Just get out."

"We got some medical expenses…" the goon starts.

Harper cuts him off. "You're fortunate that you don't have funeral expenses, given how badly you screwed this operation up. Get out of here and be thankful for small mercies."

There's a moment during which the goon sizes Harper up, and then he decides that discretion is the better part of valor and bails. Harper waits for the door to close and the sound of footsteps to recede down the hall and then says, "I suppose you heard all of that. You might as well get in here."

Holly and I look at each other, eyes wide. Holly gestures to the door questioningly, and I shake my head. If Harper really knows we're in here, he'll come over, and maybe I can get him with the door.

Instead, it's the window that opens, and a small fairy climbs through. He's got a sword in one hand and an envelope in the other. Glimmer hops to my ear and whispers, "Ash Cutter."

Ash Cutter speaks fast, and I'm having trouble following along, but I'm pretty sure that he says Harper should have killed the guy.

"I don't know why you bother with that gibberish," Harper snaps. "Just hand over the information."

Ash Cutter's jaw clenches, and he mutters that maybe he'll decide that Harper needs to be taken care of, too. He holds out the envelope he's holding gracelessly, staring murder at Harper.

"Knock it off," Harper says. "We can't kill everyone who disappoints us. Ruffians like that are very hard to blackmail because they've already committed too many crimes. And Ms. Arsenault only has so many contacts left in the community. Much as I might like to haul one in as an example, it will only cause trouble in the long run." He opens the envelope, looks over its contents, and turns towards the door with a smile. "The lost material is in Carson's offices? Wonderful. Ms. Arsenault has men stationed there. Go and tell them to burn the building down. Leave nothing behind."

Ash Cutter snaps that he's not an errand boy, he's a ringleader.

Harper looks over his shoulder. "Why are you still here?"

Ash Cutter's hand falls to his sword, and he looks at Harper for five very still seconds before he turns and flies out the window.

"Fairies," Harper mutters. "We'll need to put them back on leashes at the end of all this." He strides out of the room, and closes the door behind him just as carefully as when he came in.

Glimmer spits and says that she'd like to see how Harper looks with a leash on him.

"Yeah, sounds nice. But right now we have to move." Holly bites her lips. "Harper's going after Vance. We need to warn him."

"There's a payphone down the street," I say. "Should be working. I'll phone Vance, and you bring your mom's car around."

I head up to the worn, wooden phone booth on the corner and stick a nickel in the payphone. Glimmer sits on my shoulder to listen in. The line rings and rings. "I don't think he's picking up," I say.

Glimmer asks if that means Vance isn't there, which I can only answer with a worried shrug. She gives me a stricken look and says that he's not up for fighting arsonists.

"Yeah. We better get there fast."

We're interrupted by the sound of a police siren. Peeking my head out of the phone booth, I see Holly pulling over at the corner, as a pair of officers step out of their cars. Agent Harper is there too, holding a cigarette and giving her one of his thin smiles. "Oh, hell," I whisper.

We watch for a moment, as Harper and Holly speak. From this far away, we can't hear what they're saying, but the gist of it is pretty straightforward, especially since it ends with one of the officers walking up with a pair of handcuffs, and the other one pulling Holly's car keys out of her hands. As they force her into the police car, Glimmer and I exchange horrified looks.

"We can't do anything," I say before Glimmer can rush off to punch Harper in the eye. "There's three of them, they're armed, and they'd love an excuse to bring us in. We've got to get to Vance's office."

Glimmer points out that we don't have a car anymore.

"That's why you're in the lead, Glim. Get down to the office, and if Vance is there, warn him. If he's not, get the blackmail stuff out. Whatever it takes. I'm going to call the fire department, and then I'll be right behind you."

Glimmer gives me a nod, and takes off. As the police pull away, I pick up the phone and dial the emergency line. "Fire department?" I say. "I see smoke. I think there's an office on fire." I give Vance's address, and then ensure the coast is clear; it's only a few minutes by car, but it's a longer jog.

I reach Vance's office building about fifteen minutes later, building up to a dead sprint for the last block. The street is deserted, but as I grab the office door and throw it open, there's a noise from the other side. I dance back as a length of pipe swings through the air where my head was.

A guy steps out of the hallway, looking me up and down. He's big, broad, wearing a sooty shirt, and he's got the pipe dangling loosely in one hand. "Hey, it's Todd Malcolm. Here just in time." He gives me a nasty smile. "Thought you weren't going to make it."

I narrow my eyes. "Out of the way."

"No chance, tough guy. You're a bonus hundred dollars." The guy darts forward, swinging the club. I duck in close, hitting his arm before he can finish the swing, and slam my other fist into his belly. He doubles over, coughing, and I shake my head, grabbing the pipe out of his hand. "Where do they get you guys?"

"You're ... dead..." the man wheezes between gasps. I leave him trying to catch his breath and run inside.

The hallway looks clear, but I can smell smoke. I take the stairs two at a time up to Vance's office and try the door. It's locked. "Vance!" I holler, pounding on it. "Open up!"

Just as I think I'm going to have to smash it, the lock clicks and I hear the bolt slide back. I throw it open to find two more surprises: Glimmer hovering in the air across from me, and a dazed-looking goon lying slumped across a table, clutching at his head and groaning.

"The hell?" I ask.

Glimmer tells me that she caught the guy working Vance over. He's in the other room and he's not moving and she doesn't know how to wake him up and this guy kept getting up so she hit him with Vance's phone but now he's getting up again.

I hold up a hand and turn to the goon. "Where's the fire?" I growl.

The guy looks up at me, panicked. "Downstairs!" he says. "The whole place is going to blow any minute. That guy wasn't supposed to be here; I was just looking for the evidence. I didn't mean to hit him!"

"Get. Out." I run into Vance's office. He's slumped across his desk, bleeding from a head wound. "Come on, man, be okay." I reach down to heft him up, and the fire downstairs chooses that moment to hit whatever accelerant they were using. I hear a faint 'whumpf' and then the whole world goes white.

I don't think I'm out for more than a moment. I'm lying on the floor, and everything feels hot. Glimmer is over me, shaking me by the collar, and yelling at me to get up. There's blood running down her face. I sit up shakily, ignoring the pain radiating through my body. There's smoke everywhere, and fire licking at the floorboards. I don't think the explosion actually reached us, but it sure sped things up. I don't have time to figure out where Vance stashed anything. "Glimmer, get out! Make sure those goons aren't waiting at the door. I've got Vance."

She nods, still looking worried. Quickly, she grabs the receiver of Vance's phone and pulls the cord out, then flies out the office window holding it like a bat.

I heft Vance over my shoulder. He's a lanky guy, and I'm able to get a grip on him and stagger into the front room. As I pull open the office door more smoke pours over the two of us, and I cough and wave it away as I try to gauge how bad the fire is. Starting it on the first floor was a good idea; it's spread up the walls and the stairs don't look safe. I take a step forward, ready to try anyway, and the heat forces me back halfway down the hall.

Swearing under my breath, I double back and go for the fire escape. The window is jammed, and I fiddle with it for a moment before I realize that it's not a mistake. Someone shoved a piece of metal through the outside frame, keeping it from pulling up. I stare at it for a moment, and then a small face appears opposite me. Ash Cutter gives me a nasty smile, waves, and then flies up to the roof opposite to watch us die.

Nothing for it. We're going to have to try the main hall after all. Vance is stirring on my back, which is a good sign, but he's also coughing. I can barely breathe myself; I can't imagine how he's doing. I stop, pull off his coat, and wrap it around us both. It looks ridiculous, but it's better than nothing. Then, taking a deep breath, I charge into the hallway and make for the stairs.

The boards under my feet give way, and I stumble as a section of the floor collapses into the deli below. I recover, step around a fallen beam, and start down the stairs. About halfway down, a stair cracks underneath me, and I duck and try to shield Vance as I slam into the ground. We're close, but we're not close enough. I grab Vance. "Come on, man. We've gotta move." I try to get up, stumble, and collapse again. I'm tired. Maybe I need to wait a moment, catch my breath, and then pick him up again. Only it's too hard to catch my breath with all the smoke.

A hand grabs me. "We've got two people here!" someone shouts. I look up at my new favorite person — a firefighter in full gear.

"He's hurt," I manage to groan.

"Buddy, you're not looking too good yourself," the firefighter says. "Can you stand?"

There's water spraying around us. The heat isn't as bad, but the smoke is still making me dizzy. I nod anyway and give it a try. With the firefighter's help, I'm able to get out the door, and stagger to the street. I look over my shoulder, and there's another firefighter helping Vance.

The street is a mess of activity. There are firefighters hosing the building down, two cop cars parked half a block down, and dozens of people coming out to see what's going on. As I'm led over to the curb, I look around for Glimmer and spot her hovering anxiously over to one side. She zips over to me. "You okay, Glim?" I ask her.

The firefighter looks at me. "This your fairy?"

"She's her own fairy, but she came with me," I say.

He nods. "She was here when we arrived. Pointed us in the right direction. You're lucky that fire got called in so fast."

"Yeah," I say. "Who made the call?"

The firefighter shrugs. "I don't take the dispatch. How's your head?"

"I'll be fine. Thanks."

"Stay here. Cops will want to talk to you."

As soon as he's gone, I scan the skyline. "Ash Cutter was here," I say.

Glimmer nods. She says that she spotted him, but he vanished when the firefighters showed up.

"Got a talent for that," I mutter, before sitting and waiting for my latest police interview.

The cops make me go over my story about three times before they seem satisfied. I don't tell them about Harper or Ash Cutter. I don't want him to know that we were spying on Harper, and the story will get back to him one way or another. Instead, I just say that I was coming to see Vance because I work for him, saw the fire, and went in after him. I give a rough description of the two guys that I saw inside, and let the officers know that they probably ran off.

"Two arsons in as many weeks. You have a way of getting around," one of them says to me.

"Might be the two are connected," I say. "Mr. Carson was looking into some things, and I was helping him out."

The cop considers me. "You expect me to believe you're a detective?"

"Nah. I'm just the help. Mr. Carson is the brains of the operation." I look over to the private detective in question. Vance is sitting on the curb, his coat flopped over him like a blanket, staring up at what's left of his office. The firefighters are still hosing it down; I can see a lick of flame from time to time, but they've got it under control, and it looks like the building's not coming down. "Mind if I go and check on him?"

"Yeah, go ahead. If we need you, we know where to find you," the first officer says.

I walk over to Vance and sit down next to him. "You should head to the hospital, Vance."

For a second, I don't think he heard me, but then he shakes his head. "I need to talk to the officers. I'll be okay. You and Glimmer saw to that."

I don't know what to say, so I don't say anything. After a few seconds, he starts talking again. "You can go home, Todd. I'm afraid I don't think I'll be able to cover your paycheck for this week."

"What about you?"

"What about me?" He gives me a hollow-eyed look. "I'm done. It's over."

"You don't mean that."

Vance pushes himself to his feet. I reach out to help him and he swats my hand away. "I sure as hell do. I'm going to explain the situation to the police, and then I'm going to let someone else take care of it. Probably it'll be Basil Stark, or someone else capable."

"But you're Vance Carson!" I say helplessly. "You never give up, right?"

"A hero never gives up. I'm not a hero. I'm a joke." Vance won't look me in the eye. "Everland's *other* detective. The guy they call when it's not important enough for the police, not sensitive enough for the real detective. The one you hire to show that you're making an effort, not the one you hire to get the job done. I thought that if I kept pretending that I mattered, maybe someday I would." He stands up and looks over his shoulder at me. The tears on his cheeks catch the fading light from the fires.

I take a step forward, start to reach out, but I don't know what to do with my hand. I let it fall back. "You found something. They wouldn't have tried to kill you if you didn't."

"You found something. I just flashed my card and claimed the credit. You handled the questions. Glimmer did the sneaking, saved my life a couple of times. Your friend Holly got us our leads. This whole time, what have I done? I've crashed a car, almost gotten myself killed three times, and jumped to a lot of conclusions. I didn't help. I slowed you down." Vance's voice is shaking as he turns back and starts walking towards the police. "I was a buzzing insect, and they swatted me. Go home, Todd. I never had anything to give you."

If Holly were here, she'd say something to inspire him. If Mr. Stark were here, he'd say something that would snap him out of it.

I'm not them. Vance Carson walks away, and I can't do a damned thing about it but stand and watch him go.

# Thursday, August 30<sup>th</sup>

**I've had some** rough mornings, but this one puts them all to shame.

The light is too bright. My head feels like someone is driving a train through it. Every part of my body hurts, to the point that I can't tell what's a bruise, what's a burn, and what's just strain from lying face-down on the couch.

Also, I am lying face-down on the couch, which is never a good sign.

Something shakes my shoulder, and I groan and reach up to swat it away. "No…" I mutter.

"I've heard I have this effect on people, but you're really taking it a long way."

I turn my head as much as I'm able and open my eyes. Emeka is next to me, kneeling down, with a hand on my shoulder. I groan again and turn back to bury my head in the pillow. "Go 'way."

"Make me."

"Wha?"

"If you can get up from that couch and push me out the door, I will leave. I won't even fight you."

I try to push myself up, and instantly slide halfway off the couch. Emeka catches me and pushes me back onto it. "Want to try again?"

I groan again. "Why are you here?" I ask weakly.

"Glimmer dragged me all the way over. She seemed really worried."

"No, I mean why did you come?"

"Because I care about you." Emeka sits back and sighs. "Look, if you want me to leave, I'll go. I don't want to, though, and frankly, you look like you need some help."

"I was an asshole."

"Glad you noticed." Emeka runs a hand through his hair. "But I had been lying to you."

"It wasn't that. I … look, it's like you said. I get down on myself. And when you said all of that, well, I kind of figured maybe that's why—" I break off and bury my head in the cushion.

There is a short pause, and then I feel Emeka's fingers running through my hair. "You thought I kissed you because Michelle asked me to keep an eye on you."

"It sounds stupid when you say it like that," I mumble into the pillow.

"You don't say. Come on, big guy. We're getting you into the shower. How much did you drink last night?"

I gesture vaguely to the table. The truth is, I don't remember. I came home last night and finished off all the beer in my fridge and all the gin in my cupboard, and things get pretty hazy after that. I remember thinking I should go out and get some more, but I don't think I actually did.

With a lot of help from Emeka, I get to my feet and we totter towards the bathroom. "I saw in the paper that Vance Carson's office burned down, but no one was badly hurt. Is that where all this happened?"

"Pretty much. All the evidence that we gathered got burned up," I say. "Vance gave up the case. Mr. Stark and Holly both got arrested. We lost everything."

"You lost this shirt, too," Emeka says. "I don't think these burns are washing out."

"It's not funny."

"Best time to laugh." Emeka pushes me into the bathroom before closing the door between us. "Get clean, and then we can talk about everything that went wrong."

I struggle for a moment, and then let out a quiet yelp.

"What was that?"

"I can't get my shirt off," I admit reluctantly.

There's a pause from the other side of the door. "Do you want help?"

"No. But I might need it."

Emeka opens the door and steps into my tiny bathroom. He takes a step closer and looks my bruised torso up and down. "You really got yourself banged up, huh?"

"I mean, I've gotten myself banged up five times in a week. The fire at the bar, the car crash, the mermaid fight, the gunfight, and then the fire at Vance's."

"What gunfight?

"Oh, crap, I didn't tell you about the gunfight." I look down at him, trying not to wince as he carefully works my arm out my sleeve. "I wasn't shooting anyone, if you're worried."

"Not what I was worried about."

"I didn't get shot either."

"Better." I yelp again as Emeka gets my arm free, and he winces. "Sorry."

"I've had worse."

"Have you?"

"Maybe not, I don't know. Everything hurts a lot, but I'm hung over. Maybe it's not so bad."

Emeka looks up at me with a flat expression, and then pokes me in the chest.

"Ow!" I tense and hunch over, and he catches me and helps me stand back up.

"It's so bad," he says. "Why aren't you in the hospital?"

"Got drunk instead."

I yelp again as he reaches up and wiggles the shirt over my head. Emeka sighs heavily. "I would be angrier, but I also spent last night getting drunk so I guess I don't have a leg to stand on."

"You're holding up well, then."

"It's all an act; I'm a mess." He takes a step back. "Okay, shirt's off. You look ... well, you look pretty terrible, honestly."

I look down. My whole chest is covered in bruises, but other than a few scratches I don't see any blood. "Could be worse. Thank you." I reach out to take his arm, and then grunt in pain as my shoulder lets me know that is not a good idea right now.

"Right. Shower. Cold, for the swelling. We'll talk after." Emeka steps in and cups my cheek in one hand. "I'm glad that you're safe," he whispers, before letting go quickly and darting out the door.

A long, cold shower leaves me shivering but feeling a bit more human and a couple of aspirins do even more. I'm able to change into a new shirt and pair of pants without having to call for help, which is good because I'd probably blush myself to death if I had to ask Emeka to help with my pants. Last night's clothes are pretty much wrecked, and I leave them on the floor as I walk into the living room. Emeka's got some buttered toast and the last of my orange juice waiting for me, and he guides me to sit down before sitting across from me. "How's your head?"

"Better." I dig into the toast ravenously. "Thank you." I look up to find him watching me shyly, and I take a breath. "I guess you want to talk about yesterday."

"I didn't mean to lie to you," Emeka says. "And if I'd thought I was sharing anything bad ... I just figured that Michelle was worried about her stupid career."

"I don't think I even told you anything that she could use against us," I admit. "I'm sorry I thought you were using me."

"Tell you what: if you'll give me a second chance for keeping secrets, I'll give you one for walking out." Emeka takes my hand.

"That seems fair." I nod slowly. "Except I don't know what happens next. Have you heard from Holly?"

"No, I just heard from Marta that Holly got arrested for obstruction of justice. Nothing in the news about it, though. It's all being kept quiet."

I try to breathe. "Where's Glimmer?"

"Flew off," Emeka says. "She made some kissing faces and gestured at the shower first." He grins. "I like her."

"Yeah, me too." I shake my head. "But that doesn't help us. Vance is out. He was broken. I've never seen him so down. And we're out of evidence, and out of leads. I don't know what to do, Emeka. Harper's probably gotten to Mr. Stark's office by now, and he can plant whatever evidence he wants. I don't have Mr. Stark, I don't have Holly. It's just me and Glimmer."

"And me," Emeka says, putting his hand on top of mine. "If you'll have me."

"If you want to jump on the train right before it goes off the cliff, be my guest. What do we do now?"

Emeka takes a deep breath. "We've got one lead."

I raise my eyebrows, and then it clicks. "Michelle."

"We don't have proof, but I have details from before. I could ruin her career."

"And end up in jail."

"So, all we have to do is convince her that I'd go ahead with it," he says. "I have a meeting with her in an hour. She probably wants to know where you are. If we ambush her there, we might be able to get something out of her."

"Would you do something like that for me?" I ask.

"I think I've been running long enough," Emeka says. "It's time to fight back."

I reach over and put my hand on his. "I'll be there with you."

"Thank you," Emeka says. He smiles. "Let's finish our breakfast before I throw up."

Glimmer arrives about ten minutes later, knocking at my window. I let her in, and she fumes as she drops onto the kitchen table and crosses her arms. "No luck with Vance?" I ask her.

Glimmer informs me that Vance is a big dumb idiot who doesn't deserve to come with us anyway, and if she let herself get down just because someone burned down her home, she would never have become the amazing detective that she is today, and that we should just forget about him and get moving.

"That bad, huh?"

She nods and says that he wouldn't even let her into his house, and when she snuck in the back window, he wouldn't let her into his room, not even after she threw a plate at his door. Then she flops back against the table and closes her eyes, saying that she's been up all night, and she's happy to come with us but she'd actually rather sleep.

"That might be a good idea," I say. "You can keep an eye on this place in case someone tries to burn it down, too."

Glimmer cracks one eye open suspiciously to see if I'm trying to sideline her, but whatever she sees in my face seems to convince her that I'm not just being a jerk, so she nods, flies over to the sofa, and collapses on a cushion. I gesture to Emeka, and the two of us slip out of the apartment.

"Okay, where are you meeting Michelle, and do you want me in with you right away, or hiding around the corner, or...?" I ask as we head down the stairs.

"Right away. It's a quiet restaurant, maybe a twenty-minute walk from here." He notes my slow pace, "or bit longer. We can show up a few minutes late. Should be easy enough." Emeka smiles, but his hands are shaking. I reach my arm around his shoulders.

"You've got this."

"Yeah, I'm a real trooper. Come on, let's do this before I completely lose my nerve."

The place that Michelle has chosen for the meet-up suits her to a tee. It's a little restaurant just north of the Hill, with private booths and dim lighting. Emeka and I aren't quite dressed for it, but we don't get more than a slightly raised eyebrow from the maître d' as we arrive and ask to be shown to Michelle's booth.

Michelle already has a martini in front of her. She looks up, smiling brightly at Emeka, and then she sees me and her face freezes. "What is this?" she hisses.

"It's time to talk, Michelle," Emeka says, sliding into the booth next to her as I take the seat across from the two of them. "No more games."

"This is a private meeting," Michelle snaps at me.

"Todd will be acting as my agent for these negotiations," Emeka says.

Michelle's eyes narrow, and then she forces herself back to a casual expression. "Why, Emeka, I didn't think that we needed to have an agent present for this. It's really not that big of a deal."

"We know that you're working with Agent Harper," I say before she can get any further. "We know that you supplied the men who he sent to Vance Carson's office. He's fine, by the way, but your goons did a number on him."

"I don't know what you're talking about," Michelle says. "Emeka, whatever's going on, you can tell your friend—"

"He knows about The Rust Bucket," Emeka says.

Michelle stops dead. She looks at me, and back to Emeka. "What did you tell him?" she asks softly.

"People are dying," Emeka snaps. "I told him that you've been blackmailing me, and that you forge immigration documents for business connections. And in about five minutes we'll be telling Commissioner Darling."

"I haven't done that sort of work in years," Michelle says after a moment. "I don't have those connections anymore."

"Funny, that's not what your bruiser told Agent Harper yesterday," I say. "You know that one of your boys was Basil Stark?"

The last of Michelle's composure falls away. "If I go down, you go down," she snaps at Emeka. "You know that."

Emeka looks at her for a long moment, and then nods. "Then I guess we go down together." He shakes his head. "The hell of it is, I really thought that you might have changed. When you looked me up, talked about Hkuri. You just wanted someone you could keep under your thumb, huh?"

"Me? You're the one who changed. You could have been great, but you just got scared. I wanted you to succeed. I want you and the Steppers to be a good band. This wasn't about—" Michelle breaks off and stares down at her drink. "Forget it. What the hell do you care, anyway. You abandoned me when I needed you. Well, I don't need you anymore."

Emeka stares at Michelle, and then shakes his head. "You actually believe that, don't you? Everything that happened, and your takeaway is that I ran away." Emeka sighs. "And nothing's changed. You still want to protect yourself and you still don't care who gets hurt to get there."

Michelle glares at him, then leans back and crosses her arms. "I assume you didn't agree to come here to talk about the good old days," she says. "If you were going to go to the police, you would have arrived with officers to arrest me. If you wanted revenge, you wouldn't be discussing the police. So, what do you want?"

"We want the ringleader," I say. "We want Harper."

Michelle laughs bitterly. "You have no idea how much danger you're putting me in."

"You tried to burn my friend alive," I say bluntly, leaning forward. "I don't really care how much danger I'm putting you in."

Michelle looks me in the eyes, then swallows and looks away. "Carson wasn't supposed to be there."

"And Mr. Hope? Was he one of your people, or just another sacrifice?"

"Hope wasn't supposed to die!" she says. Then she hesitates, and her hands clench into fists. "I didn't know he was going to die," she says more softly.

"Then give us something concrete!" Emeka snaps.

"Fine. Harper's involved, but this predates him." Michelle doesn't uncross her arms, but she also won't meet my eyes anymore. "The first I knew about it was when I got one of those damned envelopes. I've been working off the books for Hawthorne. Helping with some extra cargo."

"You've been smuggling things off-island," I say.

Michelle sighs, and nods. "I used the same ambassadorial connections that used to get me visas. Curiosities, antiquities, starstone, and the occasional magical plant. Some drugs, through Schaefer's gangs. Nothing too big, nothing too dangerous, but it secured Hawthorne some of our most valuable contracts."

I rub my forehead. "You were smuggling in exchange for promotions?"

"Don't give me that look. You don't get ahead in this business by playing nice. Do you have any idea how much money Hawthorne brings into this community?"

"I actually do, yeah, because I know a lot of the people you don't pay." I shake my head. "You know what, forget it. So, you got blackmailed."

"They wanted information about Hawthorne, dangerous secrets, and it smelled to high heaven. I strung them along, and then went to our private investigators to uncover what was going on. We found several other people who had been approached in the same way. And then the FBI arrived."

"Harper?"

"Not at first. It was another agent. He claimed that Hawthorne was being tested for vulnerabilities. All part of securing critical infrastructure against the Communist menace." Michelle scoffs. "The next thing I knew, Harper showed up and took over the investigation. He started pulling on the same strings the blackmailers had been. He spun a hell of a line, but he had enough dirt on me that it didn't matter. He said we needed Hawthorne to be protected, that there were too many people vulnerable to pressure, but we could solve that by being the ones pressuring them. We could use this to reassert control over the island."

"Reassert?" Emeka asks.

Michelle nods. "You've noticed, haven't you? The laws here aren't exactly what's approved of back in the United States, never mind the U.K., Second Star and Hawthorne are following their own playbook. Criminal elements control most of the shipping, and the mayor is in the pocket of whoever paid him most recently." She shakes her head. "Everland has always been in a governmental grey zone, but it's getting more independent by the day, and everyone knows it. Harper was supposed to fix that."

"Is it a real government operation, or is he rogue?"

"I don't know. I'd guess that if he succeeds it'll be official, and if he fails he'll have always been rogue."

"Was he the one who wanted us at The Rust Bucket?" I ask.

Michelle nods. "The package was nothing, a few trinkets that I could pretend Hawthorne wanted smuggled. Harper was convinced that if you were in the area, he could pin the arson on you, and use that to blackmail Stark into backing down. An idiotic plan, but I wasn't about to disagree with him. When that didn't work, and you got closer, he kept changing the plan. First it was to make Graves the villain, so you would leave. Then it was to frame Hope, get him out of town, and have some people chase you off if you tried to follow. And then someone changed *those* orders, and Hope was killed to frame Stark."

"Who changed the orders? Who's in charge?"

"I don't know. All I know is that things are getting worse by the day. Those fairies are everywhere." Michelle looks at us. "If you really want answers, that's who you talk to. They're the only ones who know everyone."

"How are we supposed to do that?" I ask. "We haven't been able to track any of them down."

"I could tell you, but I'd need some guarantees in return." Michelle taps her fingers. "My name stays out of the news, and my connections stay away from the law. In return, I'll give you a location you can deal with the fairies, and I won't let Harper know that you're on to him. And I'll give you one last piece of information that I think you'll find valuable."

I look over to Emeka. He shrugs. "Your call."

I hate the idea of Michelle getting away with everything, but without her lead we're pretty much stuck. "Fine," I growl eventually. "But only if you're out. No more arson, no more violence. If you do anything else, and I mean anything, we will know."

"Charming," Michelle says, stirring her martini. She takes a sip. "I have a meeting point that you haven't found out yet, and the one who comes there is highly placed. Ash Cutter, he calls himself. A violent little fellow, but effective — and talkative. Seems to be the leader of the fairies city-side. If you can catch him, he'll be able to tell you whatever you need."

"Why didn't you push him, then?" Emeka asks.

"Because I don't want to know who's in charge. That sounds like a very dangerous secret to be keeping, and I think he would kill to keep it that way." Michelle sighs and finishes her drink. "But I know where Ash is going to be tonight. I'm supposed to report to him privately, tonight at ten-thirty in a room at the Hotel Lily. We've got a gig there tomorrow, so I have a reason to be there, but he won't be expecting anyone else. You might be able to ambush him there. And honestly, I think that will be your only chance."

"Why is that?" I ask.

"Because of the second piece of information. Harper's put a case against you, Mr. Malcolm. He's using information from his raid on Stark's office to pin the arson at Vance Carson's office on you. I was going to convince Emeka to get you to a public place where you could be brought in."

"Son of a…" Emeka takes a deep breath. "You don't care at all, do you?"

"Welcome to the real world, Eme. We do what we have to to survive."

Emeka stands up from the table. "I always hated it when you called me that." He looks over at me. "Come on, Todd."

I stand up, and pause to look down at her as Emeka walks out. "We've got a deal right now, Ms. Arsenault. Don't break it."

"Don't you worry about me, Todd. I know when the wheels are coming off. This entire operation was a bad idea from start to finish, and if you're able to shut it down, so much the better. I'll just let Agent Harper know that Emeka was quite upset and didn't want to meet with me." She shakes her head. "Poor boy. He really could have made something of himself."

"He did," I say, turning and walking away.

I find Emeka outside, leaning against the wall of the restaurant and breathing heavily. "You did great," I say.

"I don't feel great," he answers. "I feel like throwing up."

"Yeah, that'll happen." I put an arm around his shoulder and pull him in. "But you were cool as ice in there."

"I just ... I knew that she was bad, but I thought that she would care more." Emeka returns my hug. "Was she always like that, and I just didn't see it? She used to look out for me. I thought that she was someone I could trust. Someone I could love. I always thought..." He breaks off. "Forget it, it's stupid."

"You always thought you did something wrong?" I say softly.

Emeka looks up at me. "Yeah. That I pushed her away when I should have helped her. That I gave up on her too early."

"Nah. You did the right thing." I pull him in tight. "It's good to offer a hand, but people need to want to be helped." I take a deep breath. "But speaking of offering a hand, I want to go and try Vance again."

"Yeah?"

"We don't have a lot of folks on our side. What do you say?"

"Screw it, I'm in." Emeka slips out of the embrace, wiping his eyes quickly. "I'd like to meet this guy."

"Let's get Glimmer and head over, then. I think she'll want to be here for this, and I don't want her there if Harper stops by looking for me."

We stop by my apartment, keeping an eye out for cops, but it looks like we're still ahead of Harper. I head upstairs to get Glimmer while Emeka stays at the door to keep watch. She's happy to see me and lets me know that she had a good nap, then got bored as heck, and we should tell her where we're going next time so that she can follow us.

I fill Glimmer in on the situation, and she agrees to come with us and see Vance, but she tells me that it's not going to help because he's a big baby who doesn't help his friends.

"Everyone gets down sometimes, Glim," I say.

She tells me that we helped him out a whole bunch, and even saved his life, and he won't help us out now so she doesn't see why she has to be the nice one. Then she suggests that maybe we should try to set his house on fire, since he seems to like giving in to people who threaten him so much.

"Yeah, let's not, okay?"

Glimmer grumbles a bit more but agrees to give him one more chance. She follows me out of the apartment, just in time for us to see Emeka race up the stairs two at a time. "Back way! Back way!" he says urgently, pushing us back into my apartment. "Police just pulled up out front."

"Damn it, I thought we had time. Should have just called you, Glim." I head to my kitchen and open the fire escape, judging whether I'm in any shape to climb it. "Alright, are you up for some scouting? Harper might have fairies keeping an eye out for us again."

Glimmer zips out the window as quick as a bullet. She comes back after a moment and says we're clear but that there are officers moving towards the alley so we had better move fast.

"Right. Down the ladder!"

I let Emeka take the lead and we shinny down the fire escape in record time. I hit the ground harder than I'd like, and Glimmer leads us out one end of the alley and around the corner just as a couple of quiet patrol cars pull up. I lower my head and try to look like just another guy out for a walk, and Glimmer slips back up into the air to look around. She comes back and lets me know that the cops are heading into my place and staking out the alley, but no one's following us. Not even any fairies. She looks a bit disappointed.

"No fairies," I relay to Emeka. "Must not think I'm worth the risk. Middle of the day, most of these cops probably aren't in on the con. Is Harper here?"

Glimmer shakes her head.

"There it is. Must not be anyone here that would listen to a fairy even if they were around."

Whatever the reason, it gives us the edge in getting away. We catch a trolley around the edge of the Hill and stop at Vance's home. It's a rowhouse, part of a series of well-kept but identical facades that stretch down the street. Emeka looks it over as Glimmer leads us up to it. "Not quite what I expected," he admits.

"What did you expect?"

"Fancier. Carson's rich, isn't he?"

"He has rich family," I say. "I don't know how much his agency actually brings in, but I think most of his investments go to the business." I walk up to the front porch, and firmly press the buzzer. "Hope he's in."

Glimmer says there's no way he left yet, but she still doesn't think he'll answer.

I press the buzzer a second time. "I think he'll answer."

"Why?" Emeka asks.

"Because that buzzer sounds annoying," I say, pressing it for the third time.

There is a click from the lock, and I turn to give Emeka a triumphant look as the door swings open, revealing … Glimmer. She gives me a smirk and waves us in.

"I'm wondering if maybe I shouldn't have told you it was okay to do this," I say to her, closing the door behind us and looking around the front hall. It's tasteful, but sparse. There's a nice carpet on the floor, and I carefully wipe my shoes before continuing onto it. A hall table and a small painting of a lake complete the setup.

Glimmer points out that she was doing this before I even knew about it and she doesn't need my permission, and then tells me that Vance's room is upstairs and down the hall.

"Mr. Carson?" I call as I head up the stairs. "Vance? It's me, Todd."

"Go 'way," comes the muffled voice from down the hall.

I walk over to his hall door, which is surrounded by shards of broken crockery. It looks like Glimmer might have been understating the situation when she said she threw one plate. "Are you alright?" I call through the door.

There is a short pause, and then the door opens a crack. Vance is on the other side, hair mussed, eyes bleary, wearing a navy-blue pajama set. "How are you inside my house?" he asks after a moment.

"Glimmer let us in."

"Gimmer has a bad sense of boundaries," he snaps. "Why are you inside my house?"

"Because Emeka kicked me out of my funk, so it's time for me to kick you out of yours. How long have you been in your room?"

"I don't know. What time is it?"

"Just after three," Emeka supplies.

"Fifteen hours," Vance says. "In bed. Where I plan to return."

"Look, man. I know things are bad. We lost a round. But we can't just give up."

"Todd, I told you. You don't need me. You don't want me. I'm just going to slow you down."

Emeka looks over at me. "Suddenly, I see why you two get along so well."

I give him a sour look. "Not helping."

"Who are you?" Vance asks.

"This is Emeka. He got me our next lead, and we've got the thread that could turn this whole thing around."

"Great. Give it to Stark. He's the detective."

"He's in jail," I point out.

"Then solve it with Holly and Glimmer."

"Holly is also in jail."

Vance gives me a long look. "So, you're here because you have literally no other options."

"No! I'm here because you are better at this than you think you are. Who got us the job with the tigers, Vance? Not me. Who figured out to track down the mermaids the first time around, when I wasn't even working with you? Who kept Harper off our backs long enough for us to figure out he was a bad guy? Also you."

Glimmer points out that also Vance is the only one of us who owns a car, and thus very important for the rest of these big dumb-dumbs to be able to keep up with her.

"Not helping, Glimmer," I mutter to her.

"Whatever she said, she's probably right," Vance mutters.

Glimmer throws up her hands and flies away downstairs. Vance looks after her, and then shakes his head. "I do appreciate you coming out here, Todd. But nothing has changed. We're still in the same position we were in yesterday, and I still don't have anything to offer."

"Can you come downstairs and at least hear us out?"

Vance opens his mouth to respond, and then Glimmer is flying back up the stairs, looking panicked. She urgently tells me that there is a police car pulling up outside.

"Okay," I say. "That's not great."

"What?" Vance asks.

The doorbell rings.

"I'm probably kind of wanted by the cops right now," I say.

"For what?"

"Harper's claiming that I burned down your office."

Vance stares at me, and something changes in his face. "He is."

"He's probably here to get you to sign something."

"Is he." Vance takes a deep breath and closes the door to his room. The doorbell rings a second time. Vance opens his bedroom door again, but now he is wearing a light smoking jacket and proper pants. "You two hide up here. I'll go down and chase him off." He gives me a tired smile. "I may not be much of a detective, but I'm a pretty good obstacle. And Todd?" He takes my hand, shakes it firmly, and presses something into my palm. "Just in case."

Emeka shakes his head as Vance vanishes down the stairs. "And I thought you were feeling down," he says.

"Yeah," I say worriedly, looking down at the car key Vance gave me. "Come on, I passed a study here earlier. We can listen in, and it makes sense for the door to be closed."

We slip into Vance's study and close the door most of the way, so that we can still listen to what's going on downstairs. Emeka goes over to the closet and opens it halfway, just in case, and Glimmer hides behind a leafy potted plant. I glance around as we settle in; it reminds me of Vance's office. Same type of desk, same wall color, a few small trophies and certificates hanging up.

Emeka joins me by the door and we crouch down. From our angle, we can look out over the stairs at the front door without being seen in return. I end up pressing up against him, head leaning on his shoulder so that I can get a look too, and he shifts slightly to look up at me. "We should surveil more often," he whispers.

Glimmer shushes him as Vance reaches the front door and opens it. "Agent Harper," he says. "I'm surprised to see you in person. Following up on last night?"

"Yes, indeed," Harper says. He takes a half-step forward, just into my field of view, then hesitates as Vance doesn't step aside to let him past. "May I come in?" he asks belatedly.

"Sorry," Vance says. "I've been told to rest, so this will have to be short." He doesn't step back.

Harper looks back at what I assume are some of his men, and then squares his shoulders and recovers his composure. "Right, then," he says. "I will keep it brief. Mr. Carson, have you been in contact with Todd Malcolm today?"

"Haven't seen him since he saved my life," Vance says evenly. "He was pretty hurt, too. I expect he's at home resting up, just like me. Why?"

Harper coughs. "I'm sorry to be the one to have to tell you, but evidence has come to light that Mr. Malcolm may have had a hand in the fire at your office."

"No," Vance says.

"We need to locate him, so that ... I'm sorry, what?"

"I said no."

"I don't understand," Harper says slowly. "No to what, precisely?"

"No to Todd being involved in the fire, unless you count saving my life as involvement. No to your evidence. No to whatever case you think I'm going to help you construct, and no to you, Agent Harper. Now get off my property."

Harper stiffens, and he takes another half-step forward, putting him entirely too close to Vance. "I would suggest that you watch your tone, Mr. Carson. Your position affords you some respect, but obstructing a federal investigation is a serious offense."

"I will do whatever I want with my tone," Vance snaps back. "You seem to have forgotten, but I have not, that Everland is not fully under your jurisdiction. We accept American oversight here, but we are not an American territory. Your investigation is taking place on the sufferance of local government. So, I'll thank you to stop muscling in here, accusing Todd Malcolm of ludicrous and impossible crimes just because you're too incompetent to figure out what's actually going on." Vance crosses his arms. "No wonder people need private detectives, with you as a representative of the law."

Harper is staring at Vance with the expression of a man who has just been mauled by a duckling. He opens his mouth a few times, starts to say something, and then stops. He looks over his shoulder to the people behind him, but I don't think he gets much support because when he looks back his expression is shifting from shocked to furious. "I'm very sorry that you feel that way, Mr. Carson. I can't imagine the scandal that will come to light when the press reports that you're protecting a dangerous fugitive."

"Pardon?"

"Well, as you say, I will need official permission to search your home. Which means that I will have to make a very public report to the local police about your intransigence, which I can guarantee will come up in the press." He shakes his head. "It will be hard on your father, with all of his business connections back in the United States. But you're absolutely right, we must do things properly." He smiles thinly. "Unless you'd care to step down and let us leave a couple of officers here. Informally."

Vance is still for a moment. He rubs his chin, starts to turn away, and then clenches his fist and clocks Harper across the mouth as hard as he can. As the agent collapses backwards, Vance steps forward and roars, "You think you can blackmail me? After everything that you've done?"

Emeka and I share shocked looks. Glimmer laughs and claps her hands, then quickly covers her mouth and ducks back down. She inches her way to the window, peeking her head up to watch the brawl unfurling outside.

"What do we do now?" Emeka hisses.

I'm halfway to my feet. What I want to do is run downstairs and wade into the fight alongside Vance. But then I glance down at the key in my hand and take a deep breath. "We run," I say.

Glimmer turns to stare at me and asks what the heck I mean.

"Vance bought us an opening. As soon as he's down, Harper is coming in guns blazing. We run for the garage and we get out of here while everyone's still trying to book him." I grab Emeka's hand. "Come on!"

We race down the stairs and past the hall, where I get a quick glimpse of Vance in a fistfight with four officers. Three more people are racing from the squad cars parked on the side of the street. No one yells after us, and a few moments later we're out the kitchen door and running for Vance's car, which is a bit sooty from last night but still in good shape. Emeka dives into the passenger seat as I hop into the driver's side and jam the key into the ignition.

Emeka looks at me as the car roars to life. "Are you okay to drive?"

"Yeah," I say, shifting the car into gear and slamming my foot on the gas. The car roars down the alleyway, and the first pothole sends a wave of pain through my chest. "I'll be fine," I say with a wince.

We take a hard turn on the street, and I get a glimpse of the fight in the front yard as we pass by. Harper is slumped against a wall, breathing heavily, his glasses knocked askew. There are a pair of cops beating on Vance, but he's holding his own and four more people are rushing from their cars to converge on him. He gives me a grin and a wink as we pass, and the people surrounding him all start to turn, faces screwed up in confusion or shock.

And then we're around the corner, and we've got enough of a head start that there's no one chasing us. I keep my foot on the pedal and take another tight left, merging into traffic as we head west. "Do you think he's going to be okay?" Emeka asks.

"I think it depends on if we can solve this thing," I admit. "If we can pin Harper to the mat, he's not going to be able to go to court and explain that he got into a fight with a rich businessman's son because he was busy covering his tracks."

Glimmer tells me that we'd better get our proof, then. Vance was pretty dashing in the yard like that. And it was nice to see the big agent get punched.

"Sure showed him," I agree. "Okay. Let's catch ourselves an enemy agent and get to the bottom of this." I check my mirrors, and sigh. "We've got a good ten hours until Michelle was going to meet with Ash Cutter. Where do we spend it?"

"Stop by a hardware store, get some gear to fight a fairy with, and then we go to the hotel room Michelle booked," Emeka says. "Safest place, and if Ash Cutter shows up early we'll be ready."

"Do you think she'll tell Harper we're there?"

"And let him know how much she told us?" Emeka laughs. "Spite only takes you so far. She does not want us caught there."

"Then we've got the best place to hide out until the meeting." I grin.

We stop by the hardware store and buy a couple of fairy-nets for Glimmer to throw, I grab a pair of wrenches for Emeka and I to use as clubs. Emeka spends a moment looking at the first-aid kits, then sheepishly selects some bandages. We then park Vance's car about three blocks from Hotel Lily, since the police have probably put out the word to look for it by now. Glimmer hides in my pocket as we approach the hotel, and I look myself over. "We don't look too fancy," I say. "Think they'll recognize you?"

"Yeah, we were by earlier in the week. Got to know some of the staff."

"Do you think Harper's looking for you by name?" I point out.

"I think the people at this hotel are very discreet, and they don't like cops much. If Harper gets to the point of calling around to every hotel in the city to see if we've been by, they'll say they aren't sure."

"Okay, then. Let's do this."

I straighten my shoulders and let Emeka take the lead as he strolls into the lobby, nodding pleasantly to the door guard. He walks up to the front desk and leans on it lightly, sharing a bright smile with the woman behind the counter. "Afternoon, Linda. How's it going?"

"Oh, hello, Mr. Ross! I wasn't expecting you today."

"I just have a few things to check in on. Nothing major, just feeling out the concert space. Mind if we go by?"

"Go ahead. I don't think anyone is in there right now, so you should have some time." Linda looks past Emeka at me. "And this is…?"

"He'll be lending a hand with the lighting," Emeka says breezily. "Needs to check sight lines."

"Of course. Go right ahead."

"Thanks." Emeka strolls past her towards the back. Once we're a good distance away, he leans over to me. "There's a service elevator in the back past the green room. We can take it up to the third floor and slip into the hotel room from there. Chances are, anyone who notices we're not checking the space out will just think we left by the back."

"You're good at this stuff."

"Maybe if music doesn't pan out, I should go into the detective business."

"I'd work for you," I say. "But I'd rather hear you play."

"Flatterer."

The back area is just like Emeka said — totally empty. Getting to Michelle's room unnoticed is a piece of cake. When we get inside, though, we have a bit of a surprise.

"Is that a cushion?" I ask. "Where's the bed?" The room is almost totally empty. The only furniture is a floor lamp, a small icebox under the counter, and a giant spongy cushion laid across the middle of the room with a few blankets on top of it.

"Oh my God, she booked it for Hkuri," Emeka says. "I cannot believe she wouldn't mention that." He rubs his forehead.

"Huh," I say. "Makes sense, I guess. Damn, I was kind of hoping to nap for a bit."

"You still could," Emeka says.

Glimmer slips out of my coat and flies directly to the cushion, where she flops down into a corner and announces that we can do whatever we want, but she's going to nap some more, and not to lie down on top of her.

I chuckle and nod. "Have a good rest. Emeka, if I lie down on that thing, I am not going to be able to get back up. I'm way too stiff."

"I've got you covered." Emeka pushes the cushion against the wall, prompting a mumbled complaint from Glimmer, and then props it up so that there's a folded section. "Sit down, and lean against this."

"That looks wonderful," I walk over and collapse into the nest Emeka made. I don't expect that I'll get much rest, but a few hours of quiet sounds nice.

The next thing I know, Emeka is shaking me gently. "Alright, Prince Charming," he says, "it's time to slay a dragon."

"Wha … don't I still have to take a shift?"

"You slept through it. And you snore. It's already ten o'clock." He hands me a steaming mug as I sit up, groaning. "I left Glimmer on watch for a few minutes and snuck downstairs for some coffee."

Glimmer is crouched on the side table, sipping from a thimble-sized cup of her own. She gives me a thumbs up and tells me that this one is a keeper.

"You didn't wake me up?" I take the coffee. Coffee sounds very good right about now.

"I'm going to be honest, I tried. You muttered something about setting an alarm and then rolled over." Emeka shrugs. "I gave up."

"Fair enough." I try the coffee.

"How is it?"

"Terrible, but it has sugar and cream so I'm pretty happy with it." I finish my coffee before carefully standing up, wincing as my muscles protest. "Everyone ready? Ash Cutter will be expecting a light to be on and Michelle to be here, but he might show up early, so we've got to set up now. We'll need to be away from the window until he comes in, and then jump on him. Glimmer, you've got your nets?"

Glimmer finishes her coffee and pats the two nets folded up beside her.

"Great. Be careful, you might need to get in close. I've got this thing." I reach down and pick up my wrench, feeling a bit ridiculous. "Emeka, you're on window duty. It's his best chance of slipping out. And watch out. He's got a knife."

"Yeah, I'm a little worried about that." Emeka takes his wrench and goes to crouch by the window. "Do we have a plan if he just goes right for your throat?"

"I mean, hopefully I hit him really hard and then he doesn't cut my throat."

"That's more of a goal than a plan."

"Then no, we don't have a plan. This is kind of a last-ditch effort situation."

"Okay, then. Let's do this."

We settle in to wait, Glimmer laying low in the bedding, me and Emeka on either side of the window. I'm feeling the tension like lightning, and I keep thinking I've seen something and start to move, only to realize it's a leaf, or some car headlights passing by outside, and then I settle back in and try not to look too embarrassed. Emeka catches my expression and winks at me. "You're going to be fine," he says.

"Or I'll have my throat cut."

"Yeah, I shouldn't have brought that up, huh?"

"Probably not. Should I be wearing a choker or something?"

"You'd look nice in one, but we really don't have time to go shopping."

I chuckle, shaking my head. "Alright, enough flattery. That window could open at any moment."

It would be pretty ironic if the window opened when I say that, but it doesn't. The door opens instead, and Hkuri freezes halfway across the threshold as she sees us lying in wait. "What...?" she starts.

Emeka's jaw drops. "Hkuri?" he asks. "You're not supposed to be here until tomorrow!"

"A letter was left for me," Hkuri says. "I was needed for rehearsals immediately in the morning. I am always happier

to travel in the early night than the dawn, so I came now."
Her muzzle twitches. "But what are you being here for?"

"We're ambushing a fairy," I say.

Hkuri pads into the room, and nudges the door shut
behind her. "Ambushing a fairy."

"It's a long story."

"I have all night."

"We don't," Emeka says. "There's a fairy that's about
to come through that window, and he's expecting to meet
Michelle here. If he spots you, he won't come in, and we
won't be able to catch him. And then Todd is going to go to
jail, and probably so will I."

Hkuri's nose wrinkles. "This does sound like a long
story," she agrees. "This fairy, it is one of the ones that was
causing trouble for us before?"

"Yeah," I say. "We're tracking down the ringleader.
They're blackmailing Michelle."

"Hm. Then I will join you." Hkuri pads over to us and
lies down under the window. Her tail lashes by Emeka's feet,
and she looks up at me. I feel a shiver down my spine at her
expression. "I do not like it when my friends are blackmailed."

I don't know what to say to that, so I crouch some more.
Hkuri settles in as though finding her bandmate and his
pal lying in ambush is the most normal thing in the world.
Maybe it is for her. Either way, we don't have to wait too
much longer, but for the second time in the night, we don't
have the entrance we're expecting.

There's a quiet tap on the window, and Emeka moves
to open it. We had figured that Ash Cutter would slip in
stealthily, giving us a chance to grab him. That's not what
happens. What happens is that he comes through the window
like a bullet, carrying a long-handled axe with a curved bone
blade, and five more fairies come in right behind him.

"Holy hell!" Emeka jumps up and grabs the window
frame to pull it down only to let go and dive backwards as
two of the fairies come at him with axes of their own. They're
clearly confused and their swings don't have the force to do
serious damage, and they take to the ceiling to survey the
area.

Hkuri rises like a shark surfacing, and her claws flash as the third fairy is caught off-guard. She yelps as he manages to swing his axe up and into the delicate webbing between her toes; but she's already moving fast and her claws are out, she tears apart one of his wings and sends him crashing back out the window to spiral to the ground below.

I ignore my groaning muscles and take a swing at the fourth fairy, who is too busy trying to avoid Hkuri to notice that I'm right there, catching her in the face with my wrench and knocking her into the wall. She crashes unconscious to the floor. The last fairy lunges around my wrench while I'm still recovering from the swing and catches me in the hand; I drop the wrench with a curse and take a step away, reaching for anything to defend myself with. All I get is the clock sitting on the dresser, which I hold up like a shield, stepping in to try and keep him from being able to get a good swing in at me. He backs up, looking for an opening.

Ash Cutter spins in mid-air, looking somewhere between furious and desperate. He looks at his accomplice on the ground and then out the window to the other fallen one, and then focuses on Hkuri, his eyes as wide as saucers. He says that she's not supposed to be here, brandishes his knife, and yells that if she doesn't get out, he'll stab her in the eye.

"How is your fairy-speech?" Hkuri asks me.

"I can follow along, basically," I say. I look at Ash Cutter. "Okay, I think maybe everyone here is a little worked up, and — hey! No stabbing! Yeah, I'm looking at you!" I glare at the second fairy, who tried to take advantage of everyone's confusion to swoop in at Emeka, and he guilty retreats to the center of the room to cover Ash Cutter's flank. "Listen up, pal, Hkuri's not going anywhere. She's with us."

Ash Cutter's eyes narrow, and he tells me that as far as he's concerned, she's a rug. He brandishes his knives and asks me to guess whether I can punch him faster than he can kill me.

"Here's what I think," I say. "I think if you all come at me, Hkuri can pick at least one of you off on the approach. I think those axes are nasty-looking, but I'm a big guy and I can probably grab and crush another one. I think the two

who are left can't take Emeka and a tiger working together."
I crack my knuckles. "So, do we want to do that dance? How
many of you want to die to get a shot at me?"

Ash Cutter looks around. He tells me that Hkuri looks
hurt, I've only got a clock, and my buddy isn't a fighter.
He thinks that he can take all three of us. The three fairies
surrounding him look a bit more nervous. One of them is
still eyeing Emeka, but the other two are focused on the tiger
in the room.

I take a step towards Hkuri. "Or, we could just cool down,
and no one else gets their wings torn off." I look around. "It's
not just Hkuri you didn't expect to be here, right? You don't
have the numbers for a straight fight against two humans
who were waiting for you. I'm guessing you were planning
to jump Michelle before she knew she was in trouble." I half-
kneel, picking up the axe that the fairy I knocked out lost. It's
long, slightly curved, and nasty-looking. "This look familiar
to anyone?"

"It looks like a claw," Hkuri says.

"Yeah. 'Cause it is one. Or was, I guess." It looks pretty
silly in my hand, but it's definitely a long tiger claw, polished
and attached to a hilt. With enough of a dive behind them, a
fairy could do some serious damage with this. "Hey, Hkuri,
any reason that someone would want to fake a tiger attack
against your manager in your room?"

Ash Cutter's lip curls, and his wings flutter as he inches
closer. The fairies behind him are all focused on me, which
is good, because they don't see Glimmer coming up out of the
rug with her net at the ready. Before anyone can react, she's
thrown the net over the rear-most fairy. The enemy fairy falls
to the ground, axe landing tangled next to him, and Glimmer
cackles and waves her second net triumphantly as Ash
Cutter and his allies turn and realize they're surrounded.

This is obviously too much for Ash Cutter, who makes
for the window at top speed. His buddies panic, one of them
going after Glimmer in a rage while the one who managed
to cut my hand makes the decision to try again. I duck back,
and swing the clock I'm still holding with my left hand,
fending the little monster off. He darts in and out, leaving

scratches on my arms, but he can't get the speed for a serious hit. A moment later, he howls in pain as Glimmer appears behind him and slashes him in the arm with one of their own axes. He drops his weapon and flutters to the ground, whimpering softly.

I turn, ready for the next attack, but the fight is over. Ash Cutter is gone, but he's left his entire retinue behind. Hkuri has swatted the last fairy out of the air, and he's lying dazed on the ground next to the one I smacked with my wrench, the one in the net, and the still-whimpering one that Glimmer got for me. I go over to the window and look outside, to see the fairy that Hkuri got earlier is a small, still figure on the ground below, already starting to dissolve into glittering dust.

Emeka comes up beside me. "Are you okay?"

"I don't know," I say, looking down at the little form. She was trying to kill us, but still.

"Sorry. I tried to get the window closed."

"Not your fault." I turn away from the window. We have bigger problems right now. "Glimmer, you good?"

Glimmer gives me two thumbs up, and then sets about cutting up her spare net to make rope for our captives.

"Hkuri?"

Hkuri is licking her injured paw. "I am not good," she says. "Why would fairies wish to hurt Michelle? Why would they wish to blame me? It makes no sense."

Emeka sighs, collapsing back against the wall. "Someone must have figured out that Michelle wasn't a safe bet anymore. You might have just been convenient." He looks around at our captives. "What do we do about these guys? Ash Cutter got away, which means he's probably going to let his partner know that he mucked it up. We probably don't have that long before the police are on their way."

I drum my fingers on my knee and feel my palm sting in response. I'd almost forgotten my own injury. I smear the blood on my pant leg and take a look at the gash. It could have been a lot worse; I probably won't need stitches. "Right. We can't leave the fairies here. If Harper doesn't grab them, the Regulators will, and either way we won't hear any evidence from them. We've got to bundle them up and bounce."

"Bounce to where?" Emeka points out. He heaves himself off the floor and digs out the bandages he bought earlier. "We're out of hideouts."

For a moment I freeze, both at the question and at Emeka's touch as he begins to wrap my hand in gauze, and then I smile. "Mr. Stark's house."

Emeka stares at me. "They'll be looking for us there."

"It's Piccadilly land. No federal cops. Harper said so when he warned me off from going there. We can stay long enough to regroup." I look over the team. "If you're willing to go there, Hkuri."

"It has been long since our nations fought," Hkuri tells me. "If they will not be upset, I will go."

"I hope they won't. I mean, we'll be pretty quiet, probably no one will even notice."

Everyone gives me suspicious looks, but no one has any better ideas, so we all end up piling into Vance's car and heading up to Piccadilly Cross, driving slowly and carefully. Hkuri takes up the whole back seat, crouching low to avoid too much notice and growling under her breath about the tight fit. The fairies are stuffed in the trunk, tied up and with their wounds bandaged, and if they're grumbling, they're doing it quietly enough that I can't hear them. Glimmer goes up to scout again and comes down three times to divert us around cop cars, but other than that our drive is a quiet one.

My hopes that we can slip up to Piccadilly Cross unnoticed are dashed as we come up to Boundary Road. Back when the first treaties were signed, the road was pretty far outside of town, but these days there are houses almost right up to the treaty line. There's a fence that runs along the road on one side, with a few cross-streets that go into the Cross; usually, you can just drive up.

Tonight, though, there are a couple of people standing by the fence, and they've got rifles. One of them shines a flashlight and waves us over. I recognize him as Fox, a friend of Holly's that I've hung out with a few times. "Todd?" he asks. "That's some car."

"Belongs to a friend," I say. "What the heck is going on?"

"Holly Blossom and Basil Stark have been arrested," Fox's friend says. She looks us over, and her already-grim expression gets darker. "Do you have a tiger with you?"

"This is Hkuri. She's in a band with Emeka." I cough. "Oh, and this is Emeka. He's good people."

"So, you're vouching for him, and he's vouching for her? Who's vouching for you?"

"Hey, Calla, take it easy. Todd works with Holly and Basil." Fox puts out a hand, pushing her rifle gently away from us, and then turns back. "Everyone's pretty worked up, Todd. We saw the news, and it's garbage. We all know Basil's not a blackmailer." He snorts. "And Holly?"

"What'd they grab her for, anyway?" I ask.

"Aiding and abetting," Fox says. "Which she might, but not for the crimes they're trying to pin on her."

"Well, can't argue with that. I might have a warrant out on me, too."

"For what?"

"Burning down Vance Carson's office."

"Damn," Calla says, looking me up and down. "What did Carson do to you?"

"I didn't do it!" I protest. "Hell, I think Vance is under arrest now, too."

"Okay, now I've heard everything. What could the feds possibly try to hang on that rich pretty boy?"

"Punching out a federal officer."

"What?"

"And I guess giving me his car? He did that after he found out I was a fugitive, so it's probably aiding and abetting, too."

"Vance Carson punched out a fed. Vance Carson." Calla stares at me.

I shrug. "He's got hidden depths."

"I'll say. Good for him." Calla considers. "Okay. If Fox vouches for you, you can go through. If the feds come by, we never saw you. Don't stay too long, though. We don't want a war."

"If it comes down to it, we'll leave," I say. "We just need somewhere to lay low while we figure some things out."

Fox nods and waves us through. As we drive the last few blocks to Mr. Stark's house, Emeka shakes his head. "Things are getting bad," he says. "How long has it been since the Piccadilly needed to post guards?"

"Harper's getting what he wants," I say, pulling up to Mr. Stark's drive. "A war. This whole thing is the perfect excuse for him. Hell, if Michelle had turned up dead tomorrow from a tiger attack it probably would have set everything off."

The street is quiet, and Mr. Stark's little house seems ominously still. "I'd better call her," Emeka says as we pile out of the car. "When Ash Cutter gets back to his boss, he'll probably want to try again." Glimmer flies ahead to let us in, and Hkuri stretches and works out the kinks from the long drive.

"Yeah, give her a call. Maybe she'll have some new information for us now that she's in the crosshairs." I pull our captives out from the trunk. They're all wrapped up in a blanket, which helps when they repeatedly try to kick me on the way into the house. I set them down in the living room and wait for everyone else to join me before pulling the blanket away from their faces. "Okay, listen up. I don't do a lot of interrogations, but I'm hoping we can all talk this out."

"I could interrogate them," Hkuri says, yawning widely as she looks down at our three captives. "I am hungry."

"We're not eating anyone," I say. "You shouldn't eat people."

"Are fairies people?"

Glimmer flies over and smacks Hkuri on the ear. The tiger looks up at her, eyes narrowed, and then reluctantly nods. "I will not eat anyone," she mutters.

One of the fairies mumbles something about dying instead of betraying the cause, and I sigh. "No one is dying, either. At least, no one else. The fight got pretty nasty back at the hotel, and I'm sorry about your friend, but you were trying to kill us, too."

The fairy who I hit asks what I want.

"It's simple. You can tell us what you know about this situation, or we can drop you off with the Regulators."

All four fairies stiffen. I shrug. "I don't like the Regulators, either. But we're way past handling this in-house. Ash Cutter ran out on you. Whoever you're working for, are they really worth your loyalty?"

The death-before-betrayal fairy just glares daggers at me. The one Glimmer stabbed is crouched in on himself whimpering softly, and the one Hkuri smacked still seems kind of out of it. The last one looks at her fellows, and then tells me that we have to promise to let them go after.

"You're Fletcher, right? We met at the logging camp."

She nods reluctantly.

"We promise to let you go tomorrow night," I say. "We're kind of running low on hideouts, and I don't trust that you won't go running right back to Ash Cutter."

Fletcher tells me that she can't, because she doesn't even know where Ash Cutter is. Usually, he's in charge of the city operations, and she handles the forest. Everyone got pulled in for this operation.

"Okay. Pulled in by who?"

She tells me Ash Cutter.

"Damn it," I mutter. "And who hired Ash Cutter?"

They all look at each other dubiously, and then shrug. Fletcher says that Ash Cutter is in charge, because he's the one that goes out and does things, and he's a city fairy so he knows all the crooks and dangerous types. He's helping them all to get revenge on the loggers and protect their woods.

"Should have seen that coming," Emeka says.

"Uh, Glimmer, a little help?"

Glimmer smiles sweetly and flies over to sit on my right shoulder. She asks the fairies who Ash Cutter's researcher is, the person that gives him the names of people to mess with.

The fairies nod thoughtfully. Fletcher says that no one knows. Ash Cutter doesn't want anyone to steal his fun, so he won't cut any of the others in on that. He's the only one who gets to know the full story.

Glimmer suggests that this is very mean of him, when everyone could have been having their own fun. What kind of person doesn't share?

The previously-loyal fairy nods and says that they've been saying that for a while. The one that's scared snaps that maybe they should have said something before any more tigers got involved, and then maybe he wouldn't have gotten stabbed.

"More tigers?" I ask, before the two can start fighting in earnest.

The injured fairy explains that all of them live near tiger territory. It's how they met Ash Cutter; Cutter used to sneak across the border to steal gemstones. But tigers are super-scary and being given gemstones to deal with humans was easier.

"Oh my God," I say slowly.

Emeka raises an eyebrow. "Todd?"

"Wow, we've been looking at this all wrong. This isn't about criminal gangs." I feel myself grinning as I jump up. Everyone is staring at me, and I don't even care. "See, the whole thing about this case is that it's big. Big problems, big, complicated plans. And when you think about the whole thing, it's just too much to untangle." I pause and scratch the back of my head. "But I've never been good at thinking big. I usually just think little, and when you think little, it's actually pretty easy."

"Oh my God," Emeka says, "you're doing a detective speech."

"Am I? Sorry."

"No, keep going, it's really sexy."

I cough, and feel my face grow warm. "I lost my train of thought."

Glimmer tells me to think little.

"Right. Think little. Think direct." I shake my head, grinning. "When this whole thing started, it started at Hawthorne. Messing up their people, getting in the way. Who hates Hawthorne?"

"Everyone?" Emeka suggests.

"Okay, yes. But who hates Hawthorne, knows mermaids, and has a supply of gemstones ready to hand?"

Hkuri's eyes narrow. "The tigers do. Are you saying that my people are behind this?"

"Not your people, Hkuri. Just one person. How many tigers do you know that really, really, don't like humans? Who might be pretty happy with relations with Hawthorne collapsing after the first tiger to work in human society in the last few years gets accused of murder, especially if they can make a profit off it and end up in control of a lot of humans? Who knows exactly what your schedule is, and what Michelle's schedule is, and who keeps popping up when we're on the case?"

"Amhara," Hkuri breathes out slowly.

"But the fairies were working with Agent Harper!" Emeka protests.

"With. Not for. Ash Cutter didn't have any real respect for him." I look over to Fletcher. "The tall jerky cop who thinks he runs everything. I'm guessing you didn't take orders from him."

Fletcher agrees that they were working with that guy, but only because Ash Cutter said it would let them cause more trouble later.

"Harper wasn't here to start with," I point out. "He showed up later. He started poking around at Hawthorne, and then ... damn, I'm out of ideas. Hkuri, did you ever see him around?"

She shakes her head. "I only know of him what was spoken at the conclaves. That he was a human from overseas, who wanted to start a war that would ruin us both. We were told to walk softly around his people."

"Succinct," Emeka says. "Does Harper actually know who's in charge?"

"Good question," I say.

"And if Amhara is our blackmailer, how do we stop her?"

"Also a good question."

"If Amhara is in charge of this, and you have set her plans back, she will stop at nothing to kill you," Hkuri says. "You are in very great danger."

"And you?"

"I am probably also in very great danger." Hkuri ponders. "But also, you have no proof at all. Everything that you have said sounds right, but it is just guesses and possibilities. How do you prove it?"

"A lot of good questions," I admit, slumping down in a chair. "See, I feel like usually I'd say the tiger thing, and then

Mr. Stark would say something like, 'Todd, that's it!' and then he'd lay out all the last bits and turn that into a plan that saves the day. I'm not really a planning-type guy."

Glimmer comes over and pats me on the back. She says that she always likes my plans.

"My plans are usually just punching someone who looks guilty and then really, really hoping that I punched the right person," I say.

Glimmer nods and says that's what she likes about them. They're straightforward.

"Yeah, well, unless you want to walk into the woods and punch Amhara on the snout, I don't think that's a line that we want to follow," Emeka says. "What's our next option?"

Glimmer says that we could take our new captives and try to trade them back to Ash Cutter in exchange for his testimony.

"Ash Cutter doesn't care about these guys, though," I say. "If he did, he wouldn't have run out on them."

"Maybe we can be convincing Harper that Amhara is the one he should be chasing?" Hkuri suggests.

"Harper's not going to buy that he was tricked by a tiger," I say. "If we could just get the cops to focus on the right people, it would be great, but we'd need them to believe us." I look up slowly. "Hang on. I think I've got a plan."

"I'm all ears," Emeka says.

"Alright," I say, leaning forward. "Here's what we're going to do…"

# Friday, August 31st

**Agent Harper's office** isn't as nice as I'd expected it to be. For one thing, he's not working out of any actual precinct buildings, which admittedly makes sneaking in a heck of a lot easier. Instead, he's grabbed an office down at City Hall, which I think belonged to someone else recently because the wall has a couple of pale squares where there were pictures hanging up before it turned into a completely bland room with one desk, one filing cabinet, exactly three chairs, and a small potted plant by the door.

Harper is the sort of guy who shows up to work at 8:30 on the dot, which is a bit of a shame because I've been sitting in his chair since 8:10 waiting for him and I'm starting to get sore. He looks like he didn't sleep well, and he's got a beauty of a black eye on the left, but otherwise, he's as put-together as ever. When he opens the door and sees me, his eyes go very wide, and he starts to open his mouth to yell. I wave a file folder vaguely in his direction before he can. "I wouldn't, Agent Harper. This is a private conversation."

His eyes narrow, and he looks at the folder. I can see him running the numbers, and he seems to decide that he can always shoot me later. He steps towards me. "You're in my chair."

"I figure I'm in some accountant's chair, which you borrowed," I say. "Found a certificate in the drawer. You should lock those better."

"You've got twenty seconds to explain why I shouldn't fill this room with cops," Harper snaps.

"That was quick. Glimmer thought we'd get through three rounds of random insults before you threatened to call the cops. Guess I'm just that good." I shrug. "You're not going to call the cops because if you do, you'll be the first one they arrest."

Harper frowns at me. "That's quite the claim."

"We know about your fairy operatives," I say. "You've been using them to track people, gather information."

"Hmph. And if this were true, I don't see what it has to do with anything." Harper walks up to the desk and leans on its edge, looking me in the eyes. "You're threatening me with using unregistered creatures as information sources?"

"Unregistered blackmailers, yeah. The ones you're supposed to be hunting down."

I didn't think Harper could look sourer, but he manages it. "Please. Things like that don't have the brain capacity for blackmail. They barely have the ability to follow someone for five minutes."

"That argument would probably fly with most cops. The problem is, Michelle keeps receipts."

"What?"

"Michelle wasn't interesting in talking to us. But then your silent partner sent Ash Cutter to kill her, and now she's pissed, and quite chatty." I let out a long breath. "Probably even angrier than you were when you showed up at the hotel and didn't find the body you were looking for."

Harper's face is cool, but I see his right eye twitch just a little bit. "Am I to assume that this 'Ash Cutter' is one of my informants?"

I stand up and shake my head. "Okay, fine. I thought we could talk this out, just cause I'm a patriotic sort of guy, but I guess not. It's fine, we've got a meeting with *The Courier* next. You know *The Times* keeps scooping them on this case, right? Well, they're about to get a pretty big score."

Harper takes a step back and reaches into his coat, pulling a gun. "You're not going anywhere."

I sigh. "Okay, you were right."

"What?"

Before Harper can get the gun trained on me, Glimmer has shot out from the potted plant and slammed her full force into his hand. The gun goes flying from his hand and skids across the floor, and I step on it as Harper curses and grabs his hand. "I really thought that he'd want to find out more before he tried to arrest me," I say to Glimmer.

Glimmer shrugs and says that he didn't seem like a very curious person to her and she was surprised that he waited as long as he did.

"Should we try this again, or are you going to start yelling for people?" I ask Harper.

"You think you're so smart," he sneers, still clutching his injured hand.

"I really don't. Ask anyone."

"Why are you here, Malcolm? You waltz into my office, claim to have evidence connecting me to the blackmail ring that I'm investigating, and then threaten to turn that evidence over to the papers. So, if you've really got such a thing, why wasn't that the morning edition?"

"Because I want a meeting with Amhara."

"And what makes you think I can arrange that?"

"You've got all the connections, don't you? With Hawthorne, with the government, with the fairies. I'd ask Michelle, but she very reasonably doesn't want to be anywhere nearby anymore. So, here we are."

I can see the wheels turning as Harper looks for a way out. "I don't believe that you have anything," he says. "I think this is just a pathetic attempt at a shakedown. Hiding a fairy in the plant wasn't bad, but the rest? If you had evidence, you'd have shown up with it. You're just trying to drive a wedge between me and my informants."

"You're saying you really don't know that your people are Amhara's people."

"I'm saying I don't believe you. Amhara is nothing but a tiger rabble-rouser, and I have that situation well in hand."

"If that were true, there'd be troops here already." I shake my head. "You want a war. You think it will give you an excuse to station a permanent garrison, pressure the local government to roll back laws that don't benefit the US. But you can't actually start the war yourself, because Amhara won't let you. She doesn't want a war, just a lot of people off-balance."

Harper scoffs. "Conjecture and whimsy."

"I'm getting to the good part. If you had proof she was involved, you could move in. Take her out and discredit her material. After that, who knows?"

"Fine. Bring your proof here and we'll talk."

"I know I said that I don't think I'm smart, but I'm not *that* dumb. We'll get the evidence, and then meet at a neutral location. No other cops. I'll call you with the address."

Harper gives me a long look. "Deal," he bites out.

"Thank you, Agent Harper. I'm still gonna take your gun, just to be safe." I bend over and scoop up the gun, keeping one eye on Harper while I drop it in my coat pocket. "I'll be in touch."

Glimmer flies over and perches on my shoulder. I stroll out the door, take a deep breath, and break into a jog as we move for the closest door. My bruised chest starts burning almost immediately and I have to slow back down. Glimmer pats me on the ear and says that we're fine, he's not going to call anyone.

"Yeah, well, if someone else spots us the whole thing kind of goes up in smoke. Come on." I push through the door and out to the street, where Emeka is waiting. We've loaned Vance's car to Fox in exchange for his old truck. It doesn't move quickly, but no one's looking for it. Fox promised us he wasn't going to drive into town with Vance's car, and no one in the woods was likely to cause trouble.

"Everything go well?" Emeka asks, as I climb in and we take off.

"We'll have to see if we pick up a flying tail any time soon. Glimmer, keep an eye out? I don't want to get too far away and lose them."

"You're really gambling a lot on Harper sharing this meeting with Amhara," Emeka points out.

"It's like I said, he pretty much has to. If Michelle had actually made recordings of her conversations with Harper, it could sink him."

While Michelle had been shocked to learn that Amhara had tried to kill her, it turned out that she'd only actually kept files on the people she was personally involved with. I'd tried to get her to take part in my operation, but she was adamant that she wasn't putting herself out as tiger bait, and I couldn't really blame her. I didn't want to be tiger bait, either. But here I was.

"Anyway," I continue, pushing that thought away, "there's no way that Amhara will let Harper go to a source of documents that could take the operation away from her, and no matter what he thinks, she's in charge of the fairies."

Glimmer nods and says that it's amazing that none of Ash Cutter's people have punched the big jerk in the face yet, let alone that they're letting him give any orders. They must be really scared of Amhara. She casually follows up by telling me that we've got our tail. Ash Cutter again, moving from building to building and almost staying out of sight, but not staying out of sight enough to avoid being spotted.

"Not everyone is as good a spy as you," I point out. Glimmer beams.

"So, we've got the follower. What next?"

"Next, I drop you off."

Emeka gives me a sour look. "Change of plan. I want to help."

"Emeka, you're great. You are a great musician, and I literally could not have gotten this far without you. Having said that..." I trail off. "You can't throw a punch, man. I don't want you to get hurt."

"Why? Because you get hurt enough for the both of us?"

"Yeah, basically. We've had one date, and I'd like us both to be alive to have another one."

Emeka glowers. "You're not allowed to be cute while I'm being mad at you."

"Besides, if this goes wrong, we need someone still alive who knows what's going on. Heck, your part of the plan might save my life."

Emeka breathes out slowly, and nods. "Yeah, yeah. You win. Again."

"I know, it's hard to be me. Look, I've got Glimmer and Hkuri backing me up. I'm gonna be fine." I pull up in front of the public library. "And honestly, I figure there's a good chance you're going to have to spend the next few hours dodging the cops. It's not like I'm shoving you in a safe room."

Emeka gets out of the car, and circles around to my side to lean in through the window. "Don't worry about me," he says. "I've dodged cops before." His lips brush lightly over mine, and then he steps back and smiles at Glimmer. "Watch out for the big guy, huh? He doesn't know when to quit."

Glimmer salutes and promises to keep me safe.

"See you soon," I say.

"You'd better," Emeka says.

As we drive north, Glimmer pats me on the shoulder and says that Emeka is going to be fine. I nod. "Truth be told, Glim, I'm more worried about me. Do you think this is a dumb plan?"

She shakes her head, and says that it's my kind of plan, and that's why it's going to work.

I wish I could just nod and accept it, but I don't know if I'm going to pull this off. It's a bit of a long shot, and I'm in bad shape. The only reason my hand doesn't hurt more is that all my chest pain keeps drawing my attention away from it, and my head is still faintly threatening to run off from the rest of my body and make for the hills. If there's a part of me that hasn't been bludgeoned, clawed, or crushed in the last week, I don't know what it is, and I need to be sharp for this next part.

I'm starting to see why Mr. Stark always ends up drinking near the end of a case. It's probably just as well that there isn't any booze in the truck, because as nice as it would be, it wouldn't be a good idea.

We keep a steady pace as we drive north, making sure that Ash Cutter doesn't lose us. Pretty soon we're on old logging trails, and I have to slow down to make sure the truck can get over fallen branches and head-sized rocks; it's just as well that we don't have Vance's Roadster, because I don't know if it could handle the trip. Once we're in the trees it's harder to tell if we're still being followed, but Glimmer keeps an eye out and gives me a thumbs-up every once in a while. Midway through the woods, she lets me know that she's pretty sure she spotted Ash Cutter again.

"Thank God," I say. If he'd lost us, this whole plan would have been for nothing. "Ready for a fight?"

Glimmer grins and hefts her commandeered tiger-claw axe.

The spot that we picked for our decoy is actually an old Hawthorne cache site. Back when this part of the woods was being logged more heavily, it was where spare batteries, a radio, and some dried jerky and fruit could be locked up for loggers to use in an emergency. But the area is in a growing phase, and no one has used the place for a couple of years. It's perfect for hiding compromising material, and hopefully, it'll have everything that we need.

I park the truck on the edge of the clearing, and Glimmer heads into the treeline as I walk over to the cache. It's a wooden box set several feet off the ground, secured with a heavy padlock and covered in grey paint to protect it from the weather. I've got a key that Hkuri left with me before she started north. I let out another sigh of relief as the key turns in the lock, and I'm able to get it open. There are four large manila envelopes inside, taking up most of the box, and I pull them out and shuffle through them for a minute, opening them one at a time and looking over the material inside.

"I will be taking those," comes a growl from the edge of the clearing. I look up sharply as Amhara melts out of the woods, taking up a position next to the truck and looking me over. Ash Cutter flits out of the tree beside her and lands lightly on a tree stump, on his hip, like a jacked-up embroidery needle, is a shiny new sword.

"Amhara," I say with a nod. "Was wondering if you'd show up. Guessing that Harper's tail reported to you."

"Harper himself reported to me," Amhara says with a low chuckle. "You were a fool to trust him. He is a duplicitous monkey."

"Hey, no arguments here. I hate the guy." I take a step back, leaving the cache between me and her. "Maybe we can bond over it, huh?"

Ash Cutter says maybe he and Amhara will bond over my organs.

"Okay, so that's where we're at."

"That is, indeed, where we are at," Amhara bites the last word off as she looks me up and down. "I warned Harper that you were a threat, but no. He was so certain that the pirate was the one orchestrating our troubles, and that it would be simple to remove you once Stark was dealt with." She hisses softly. "You act the fool, but you are just like all the rest, scheming and treacherous."

"You know, I don't think that someone who is literally running a blackmail ring gets to talk about scheming like it's a bad thing."

"It is such a human thing, though." Amhara begins to pad softly to the left, circling around the edge of the clearing. I move to keep the cache between us, even though I know it's not going to last long. "All of you, so many secrets. So many lies. So many things to be ashamed of. It makes you so easy to dominate."

"Right, like you wouldn't pay up if someone threatened to reveal this operation to your enemies."

"No. I would kill them. And then I would kill anyone they had told, and then my secrets would be safe again." Amhara chuckles. "It is your silly human shame that makes this so easy, Todd, not the secrets. May I call you Todd?"

"I feel like we're about to be real close, so sure."

"Thank you. In return, I will admit that for a human, you are not so bad. You pay attention to what is happening, not only to your own thoughts. You persist. I do not know exactly what ploy you were planning with Harper, but I think you were not simply hoping to give him those materials."

"Nah. If I handed these to Harper, I'd be in jail five minutes later. It was you I wanted to meet." I chuckle. "Emeka's going to laugh, but I wanted to figure out how it all went down. I feel like you'd like to know where you went wrong, too."

"I would." Amhara bares her teeth, in what might be an attempt to fake a smile. "You have been an irritant that I would not like to have repeat. I am willing to indulge your curiosity, if you will indulge mine."

Ash Cutter groans loudly and starts ostentatiously sharpening his sword and ignoring our conversation.

"Very neighborly of you," I say, trying to ignore him.

Amhara doesn't even seem to notice. "What first drew your attention to me?"

"Letting Harper have the fairies. There was no way they were working with him by choice. Ash Cutter was openly talking about killing him when we overheard their last chat."

Ash Cutter nods without looking up.

"So, the question became: who got Ash Cutter to play nice with Harper, and how? You can't blackmail a fairy. The person giving him orders had to be someone who could offer him what he wanted, and who wasn't someone he'd hate. That narrowed it down a lot." I shrug.

"Perhaps that was a mistake," Amhara says. "But it was necessary."

"Yeah, I get it. You blackmailed Harper, but you weren't going to let him run around unsupervised. You're too smart for that."

Amhara snorts softly and looks over to Ash Cutter. He pretends not to notice. "Astute," she says. "You are correct. I approached Ash Cutter originally. He relished the chance to gain revenge on Hawthorne for its crimes against his people, and in return for offering him direction and targets, I gained control over a great many humans."

"Including Michelle. And that was your real mistake, trying to kill her. I'm guessing that your goal was to clear up loose ends."

Amhara nods. "She knew too much of our operations, and she was becoming squeamish as events escalated. I could push Harper into leaving once I was done with him, but she needed to be removed. But why was that a mistake? Because of her records?"

"No. Because not that many people knew Hkuri's schedule. Not many people knew which hotel room she'd be staying at. If anyone else had wanted to kill Michelle at that hotel, they wouldn't have known to frame your cousin. But you did. You were managing her. Granted, you also messed up your timing. Hkuri arrived before Ash Cutter and his crew."

"Hm. That is good to know." Amhara chuckles. "You only found me out because you and your detective happened to see me with them. But I am impressed that you remembered."

"I'm not a clever guy," I say. "I just pay attention."

"Do you?"

"Yeah. For example, I notice that every time we do a loop, you're a couple feet closer. Pretty soon I figure you're going to pounce on me, eat me, destroy these files, and let Harper know that the problem is solved. Am I getting warm?"

"Very," Amhara says. She tenses, and her claws flex. "If I thought you were the fool you pretend to be, I would have pounced already. But I think you knew that I would come here."

"You couldn't let Harper slip out of your control," I agree. "You might be suspicious, but you'd show up."

"Very true. And I do not think you believe you can punch me to death."

"Nah."

"And I have spotted your own fairy hiding in the trees just over there."

I let out a small breath that I didn't know I was holding. "Oh, yeah?" I say, as casually as possible, while letting my hands fall to my coat.

"You have a gun, but I do not think you are skilled with it, or you would have pulled it. I must assume that you have trapped the clearing. But the strange thing is, I cannot seem to find the trap."

"Like what, a snare? I told you, I'm not a clever guy. I didn't think I could set up anything like that without you spotting it." I hold up the envelopes. "You want your blackmail material? Take it."

I toss the envelopes into the middle of the clearing. Amhara looks them over, still suspicious, but Ash Cutter swoops down and grabs them triumphantly, abandoning his sword on the stump he'd been sitting on in his excitement. A moment later, as he sees the one I had half-opened, his expression turns confused, and he turns and shows it to Amhara, telling her that it's just a bunch of newspaper articles.

Amhara lets out her breath slowly. "Oh, I see. The clearing is not the trap. The files are not here."

"They're not, no. I figure if I have them on me, you can just bite me clean in two and take them off my corpse. It was nice of Hkuri to run ahead and set up this fake cache for us, though."

Amhara pounces, leaping over the box between us in a single fluid motion. She is a lot faster than I expected, and while I manage to roll to one side, I come up to find a heck of a lot of claws a heck of a lot closer than I'd have preferred. Amhara has reared up on her hind legs and is face to face with me, one paw raised, claws out.

"Where are my files?!" she roars.

"Somewhere safe, I'm guessing."

"You think you can blackmail me? Me! I will tear your heart out, and then I will track down your little friend and tear their location from her!"

"Woah, easy, easy." I back up, hands raised, and Amhara thumps her front feet back to the ground and keeps pace with me, her tail twitching and her ears back flat against her head. "I'm guessing they're safe because they're wherever you left them. Michelle's files didn't implicate you. They were just copies of the things she passed to Ash Cutter, in case she needed samples herself." Even though my heart is pounding like a drum, I manage to give Amhara a smile. "I just needed to get you here."

"You think that you can kill me after all?" Amhara tenses for another pounce. I figure as soon as I stop saying things she cares about, I'm a dead man.

"That's probably what Mr. Stark would have done," I say. "Lure you here, put together a whole tricky plan, get you angry and then attack when you're distracted. I'm not very good at that sort of thing. I just called the authorities."

"The—" Amhara is so taken aback that she sits on her haunches and bats her front paws at the air like a housecat, then she throws back her head and roars with laughter. "I own the authorities, you stupid ape! Do you have any idea how many sordid secrets they wish to keep secret? The police, the Regulators, none of them will move against me with the things I know."

"Oh, no, not a chance. But that doesn't matter anyway. You aren't answerable to human law."

"Of course not." Amhara stiffens, and she finally pauses to sniff the air. She looks to the right as tigers begin to emerge from the clearing's edge, with Fraal in the lead, and Hkuri hanging back just behind him. "Oh," she says softly. "Oh, I see."

"You're a tiger, and you're bound by your own laws. And it turns out blackmailing and murdering humans is a crime here, too. I just needed you somewhere where you'd be comfortable admitting all of it."

"Well." For a moment, Amhara actually smiles. "You won fairly, human. I hope that comforts you in your next life."

And she pounces again, this time with her claws fully out and her fangs bared. I scramble for my gun, but Amhara was right. I'm no gunman. I fall to the ground and pull the trigger; the force of the bullet is just enough to turn what was sure to be a disemboweling strike into a headbutt. I feel something twist in my left arm, and a spike of pain. For a moment, Amhara is above me, ready to bite my head off, and then she howls and falls to the side as a needle-thin blade punches into her eye.

I roll away, vision blurred, and I see that the tigers have joined the fray. Fraal and Amhara are snarling and slashing, with more tigers pouring in behind. Hkuri is hanging back, looking worried.

Glimmer lands next to me and drops Ash Cutter's sword. She asks me if I'm alive.

"I think so. Good job," I mumble. "Might be in shock. Did we think of calling a doctor? I bet Mr. Stark would have had a doctor on hand." And then I make the best decision that I've made in days, which is to pass out.

# Tuesday, September 4<sup>th</sup>

**"Thank you for** coming to see us today, Agent Harper."

Michelle is smiling broadly as she sits at the front of the boardroom table. She's the only one smiling right now. We've gathered at Hawthorne's main offices, and Michelle made sure that the best boardroom was available; large, cushioned platforms for Fraal and Hkuri to lounge on, smaller perches for Glimmer and Fletcher, and the fanciest leather chairs I've ever sat in for Michelle, Commissioner Darling, and myself. I'm glad for it; I'm still in a lot of pain, and I can lean my cast on the armrest instead of having to keep it in a sling. My poor shot had managed to turn away Amhara's teeth and claws, but the weight of her had twisted my left arm to the literal breaking point.

Harper did not get a fancy leather chair; Michelle got him one of the spares from down the hall. He glowers at the lot of us, but especially at me. "What's the meaning of this?" he growls at Darling. "This man is a wanted criminal, and you are sitting in a room with him."

"Mr. Malcolm is currently operating under diplomatic immunity," Commissioner Darling explains. For the first time since I've known him, he doesn't look sour. I think I might even see the edge of a smile, even if it's well-hidden under his mustache. "Depending on the results of this meeting, I expect that the Everland Police Department will not be filing any charges against him."

"He's wanted by the United States of America," Harper growls.

"Well, that's why we're here," Darling says. "The mayor has concluded his conversation with the tiger and fairy delegates, and is leaving this legal matter to me." He glances over at me. "I think he'd rather not be involved."

"I don't blame him," I say. "I'd rather not be involved."

"Will someone explain to me what is going on?" Harper snaps.

"Mr. Malcolm has solved the case of our stolen goods," Fraal says, his voice rumbling with amusement. "And it seems that we owe you an apology. It was not, in fact, a human who was responsible. The thieves have been punished according to our laws, and will not be troubling anyone further."

"Lovely. And?"

"And along the way, we discovered that the thieves had rather more information than we had suspected."

It hadn't been easy to figure out where Amhara had hidden her cache, especially after she and Ash Cutter had both chosen to go down fighting. But it turned out that there were only so many places that a collection of documents could be hidden in tiger territory, and with the help of Fletcher, who was very interested in proving that she could be trusted and should not be eaten, we'd managed to uncover a lot of files. Right now, Fraal was pushing one such file across the table towards Harper. "You may wish to review it."

Harper scoffs as he picks up the folder. A moment later, his face goes still, and he looks up. "This is a fake, of course," he says.

"Of course. After all, transcripts of a federal agent plotting a war against a sovereign nation without the permission of his government would be ridiculous," Fraal says. "Surely, Amhara simply found someone with a similar voice to yours. And of course, you never spoke to her of this."

"Of course." Harper says slowly, looking around at the rest of us. "My job is merely to ensure that the peace is kept."

"And if this material is forged, surely the other materials that Amhara was collecting were forged as well. I believe that if you consider the situation, you will realize that your materials implicating Basil Stark and Todd Malcolm in this blackmail ring were likely among them.

Harper taps the table. "I see," he says.

"In fact," Darling adds, "I think it would be best if everyone you arrested over this affair were released. With the formal apologies of the United States of America."

Harper lets out a brief bark of laughter. "So, that's how it's going to be," he says.

"That is indeed how it is going to be," Fraal says, dropping his pleasant attitude. "And only because these worthies have convinced me that if your bones are found picked clean, it will not matter to your government what your crimes were. In the absence of judgement, I will at least have your departure from our island, and your crimes atoned for."

Harper's jaw drops, and he turns to Darling. "Are you going to let that creature speak to me like this?"

Darling gives him a slow, menacing smile. "Agent Harper, I am sorely tempted to truss you up and deliver you to the border myself, and legally, if the tigers demanded it, I would be obliged to. If the worst thing that happens to you today is this conversation, you had better count yourself lucky."

Harper looks around the room. Glimmer is openly making throat-cutting gestures, and even Hkuri is giving him a flat stare with her teeth very slightly out. He coughs and looks back to Fraal. "So," he says. "I recant my investigation, announce that it's formally closed, and return to the United States. In return, this ... forged material ... is destroyed?"

"No," Fraal says. "It will remain with us, just in case you should choose to return here in the future. But it will not be released, either to your government or to the local press."

"My government won't accept that a gaggle of cats solved this problem, especially with no criminals to bring to justice."

"Well, I suppose it will be up to you to convince them."

"You're talking about my taking a career-ending position."

"As career-ending as what will happen if your name and Amhara's are released to the public together?" Darling asks.

"Darling. The rest of these incompetents are beyond help, but you can't think that this is the correct path. We must uphold law and order—"

"The way I see it," Darling says, "that's exactly what I'm doing. Now, do we have a deal?"

Harper breathes out slowly. He looks at each of us with hate-filled eyes, and then he shakes his head. "The case is closed," he says reluctantly. "I'll go and file the paperwork immediately."

"Thank you, Agent Harper. You may depart. We have a few other matters to discuss."

Harper grinds his teeth and stands from the table. As he steps towards the door, he turns to me. "This is all your fault," he snarls.

"Thanks. But actually, it's kind of all yours," I say. "If you hadn't gone and arrested me to prove a point, I wouldn't have lost my job, and if I hadn't lost my job I wouldn't have gone to work with Vance and gotten involved in the case in the first place." I shrug. "So, I guess you did solve the case, sort of."

"This isn't over, Malcolm. My closing this case won't stop the department. This island will be brought under control."

"They can come, and we'll deal with them." I give him a polite wave with my good hand. "Have a nice trip back home."

Harper sputters for a moment, and then turns and stalks out of the room. Glimmer laughs and congratulates me on keeping my cool.

"Well," Michelle says, "we'll want to keep an eye on him, but I think we've resolved the situation. Thank you for coming, Commissioner. I think your presence added the legitimacy that we needed."

"If I hadn't, he would have just barged into my office and demanded I arrest everyone." Commissioner Darling stands. "Besides, I owe you some thanks as well. The material you turned over to me will be very helpful when it comes to police reform."

Fraal inclines his head. "While we do not think it would be overly helpful for human-tiger relations if we were to damage the reputations of Everland's elite, those files in particular seemed appropriate for your discretion. We were disturbed to learn that Amhara had succeeded in suborning nineteen police officers, and we trust that you will handle the situation."

I look over to the Commissioner. "You're taking finding out about a bunch of corrupt cops pretty well."

For the first time that I've known him, Darling smiles without a hint of anger or threat. "There have been six attempts on my life in my time as police commissioner, Mr.

Malcolm, and that doesn't count what I dealt with climbing the ranks. With those files, I've got nineteen fewer problems and a chance to finally start changing things around here. I'm looking forward to the fight."

He tips his hat to the tigers and strolls out the door.

I look over to Michelle and the tigers. "Do you all need me for anything else?"

It's Fraal who answers. "We will be finishing our negotiations with Hawthorne regarding the proper use of the bordering lands. I do not think that we need you present."

Michelle smiles at me, looking just a bit pained. "Yes," she says, "I think that you've done plenty. Go get some rest."

Hkuri coughs.

"And thank you for saving my life," Michelle adds.

"No problem. Thanks for all your help with the case. Glimmer?"

Glimmer flies over and lands on my shoulder, taking care to avoid my sling, and we make our way outside. As we head down the hall, Glimmer complains that it doesn't seem right that Michelle gets out of this with a promotion after everything that she did. Now that she's entirely in charge of negotiations with the tigers and the fairies of the northern woods, she's going to be an even bigger name than before.

"Yeah, but she's got tigers keeping an eye on her, now. They know what she did. Makes negotiations a bit more even-handed." I reach over and pat Glimmer on the shoulder with one finger. "I'd like it if Harper and Michelle were arrested, too, but we have to take the wins we can, Glim. Amhara's out of the picture, and the stuff that she gathered is going to help keep Hawthorne from running roughshod over the area. Heck, the fact that they're negotiating with fairies at all is going to be kind of a huge deal. The Regulators are going to flip their lids."

Glimmer chuckles at that thought, and then nods. She says that we might not have gotten rid of them entirely, but at least we don't have to worry about them anymore.

Before we can say any more, the door to the meeting room nudges open and Hkuri slips out quietly, leaving the sound of spirited negotiations. She pauses when she sees me, then pads down the hall to join us. "Todd. I was thinking you would have left already."

"I was just about to. Do you need a ride anywhere?"

She shakes her head. "I will be going back home for a time. It has been a lot, these past two weeks."

"Yeah, I know the feeling. How are you holding up?"

"Holding … ah. Emotionally, you mean." Hkuri thinks about it. "I grieve, of course. Amhara was my cousin, and in her way, she looked out for me. But also, she tried to put another friend's death on my shoulders, and while the tigers might not have believed it, it would have led to many bad things." She looks away, and then blinks slowly. "I will miss her, but I do not regret our choices."

I nod slowly. "Well, I'm still sorry that we had to do it."

Hkuri chuckles. "Thank you, Todd Malcolm. And you, Glimmer Mop. Know that you are both welcome to visit whenever you wish, either on stage, or at my home."

"Wow. That's a heck of an honor."

"You stopped a war. I think it is about appropriate." Hkuri snickers. "Although I think that you would have visitation at our shows no matter what I said, yes?"

Glimmer grins and gives Hkuri a thumbs-up.

"Okay, okay, you two. Listen, we need to get some food and then go and pick up everyone who got locked up. Hkuri, I'll see you around, right?"

"Of course. Best of luck to you, and good healing." Hkuri steps forward and nuzzles her head against my chest.

I'm not sure what the appropriate response is, so I settle for a light one-handed hug, which seems to be okay. She rumbles softly, and then we head our separate ways.

I'm still in Vance's car — Fox cleaned it until it shone while I was in the hospital, and delivered it to me the minute I got out, declaring that it was a crime to let such a beautiful car get so filthy — and I drive pretty carefully down to the jail, swinging by a friendly diner to grab lunch for Glimmer and me, plus takeout for everyone that we're picking up. As it turns out, we don't need to rush. Even driving one-handed and taking traffic carefully, we end up at Kensington Point a good two hours before anyone shows up.

Holly is the first one out, and she rushes in for a big hug as soon as she sees me, only letting me go when she notices me wince in pain. "Todd, you did it!" she laughs. "I told you that you could handle a big case." She's wearing the same clothes as the last time I saw her, and looks exhausted, but otherwise she's in good shape.

"Everyone else did most of the work," I say. "I just called the right people."

"And figured out the right culprit, and got attacked by a tiger, from what I heard."

"From who?"

"Emeka stopped by yesterday to let me know that things were going well. He told me everything."

"He might have exaggerated a bit," I protest.

Glimmer says that Emeka definitely didn't, she was there and it was pretty awesome.

"We may have to start worrying about Everland's third detective," Holly says, nudging me in the ribs.

"Ow."

"Oh! Sorry!" She quickly steps back. "How are you doing?"

"I mean, I'm on a lot of painkillers right now, but considering I wrestled a dangerous, angry predator I think I'm doing pretty good. Did you know that Glimmer saved my life?"

Glimmer says that she saves a lot of lives, so I'm not to go about feeling special.

"You really did, huh? Holly, you want to worry about Everland's third detective, I'd point her way."

"I've been thinking about that." Basil Stark strolls up to us as the door opens, as though he was part of the conversation the whole time. He's got his coat on already, hands in his pockets, and he nods to each of us in passing. "I may have been underusing your talents, Glimmer. I'm quite sorry."

Glimmer flies over and pats him on the head, telling him that she forgives him because he's very old and forgetful.

Mr. Stark gives her a suspicious look, then turns to me. "And Todd! You ignored my direct orders and got more involved in all of this than anything … and you were right. I should have brought the lot of you in sooner."

"Oh my God, Basil Stark is admitting that he's wrong. Does anyone have a camera?" Holly looks over at the prison guards. "We might need a signed witness statement!"

"Is everyone mocking me today?" Mr. Stark asks plaintively. "I was imprisoned unjustly, you know."

"You wouldn't have been if you'd stopped into the office and found out what was going on," Holly points out. "We could have solved the case days earlier."

"Maybe, maybe not. The biggest clue was that the fairies were working with Harper, and we didn't get that until the night Mr. Stark got arrested," I point out.

Holly narrows her eyes at me. "And whose side are you on?"

"I'm on everyone's side. Kind of my thing."

"Well said, Todd. But yes, Holly, I will try to be more forthcoming next time."

Vance strolls up from the claims counter. Somehow, even though he's been in jail for four days, he looks much better than the last time I saw him; he managed to get a clean shave, and he's wearing a fresh suit. He catches my look, and blushes faintly. "Mother had some clothes dropped off for my release. She said I would feel much better if I were properly dressed. You should have heard her, Todd. You'd think the greatest injustice in the world was that I wasn't already out on bail."

"So, your parents weren't mad that you punched an FBI agent?"

Vance laughs. "They were not thrilled about the publicity, but Father said Harper was a devious little worm anyway, and Mother was too angry that they were blaming the guy who saved her baby's life to be mad at me for getting in the position in the first place. I think I dodged a bullet." He nods to Basil and Holly. "Mr. Stark, Ms. Blossom. Glad to see that you're doing well."

"Vance Carson." Mr. Stark holds out his hand. "I heard about everything you did. Good man. Wish I could have been there when you showed Harper up. It sounded absolutely glorious."

Vance stares at Mr. Stark's hand for a moment, and then he grins widely and shakes it. "Well, thank you, Mr. Stark! Coming from you, that means a lot."

"Not at all, Vance. May I call you Vance? You did good work out there, on every front. Will you be joining us for lunch?"

Vance swallows. "Really?"

"Of course. We always have a good meal after we close a case, and this one wouldn't have been closed without your hard work."

"I'd be delighted!" Vance says.

"Good," I say, "because otherwise we were going to have to ask you for a ride and it would have been awkward. Also, I got you a sandwich and fries so someone else would have had to eat them."

"Well, alright then! Can't turn down a free sandwich. Where are we heading?"

"Let's just go to my office," Mr. Stark suggests. "It's closer, and once we wrap up, I can put some things away."

As we're turning to go, Glimmer flies over and tells Vance that she's sorry for getting mad, and she really liked how he did all that punching. Then she kisses him on the cheek and flies off after Basil.

Vance looks over at me, blushing bright red. "I didn't catch most of that," he admits.

"She's impressed," I say. "We all are. You did really great, Vance."

"Thank you, Todd." Vance looks after Glimmer. "She's a hell of a lady, isn't she?"

"Yeah. Maybe you should focus on learning more fairy," I suggest.

"Maybe I should," Vance agrees absently, still staring after her.

We pile into Vance's car, and Mr. Stark spends the first two minutes of the drive down grilling me about what happened in tiger territory and the rest gripping the door handle and trying not to look terrified. I give the gist of everything that went down, as much as I'm able to through the wind whipping around us.

The press is all up at Hawthorne by now, waiting to see what the company and the tiger government are sorting out, and they've all apparently missed that Mr. Stark is out of jail;

so, it's quiet when we pull up in front of Stark's office, with only one person present. Emeka is sitting on the front steps of the building, and he stands up and waves as we pull up.

"How the heck did you know when we were showing up?" I ask, climbing out of the back seat.

"Holly called from the jail."

"Guilty as charged." Holly thinks about that. "Is it weird to say that right now?"

"I'd rather you didn't," Mr. Stark says. "I'm not sure we've been introduced."

"Oh, this is Emeka Ross, Mr. Stark. He's ... well, he was real helpful, and..."

"Ah, yes, Mr. Ross. Holly has told me all about you. Are you joining us?"

"Thought I might."

"Splendid. We'll see you inside, then. Vance, you'll have to tell me about the situation with the mermaids. I'm given to understand that's what started all of this."

Everyone heads inside, leaving Emeka and I alone on the steps. Emeka takes my bandaged arm gently. "Is it bad?"

"It's not great," I admit. "Doctors said it'll heal, basically, but there's muscle damage and stuff. We're gonna have to wait and see how much I can do with it."

"Well, hell."

"Could be worse. She was aiming for my throat."

"You mean I might not have gotten to hear your singing voice?"

"You do not want to hear that. You thought getting attacked by a tiger was bad, you just gotta listen to me belt out Sinatra for a bit."

Emeka laughs and leans against me. "So, for our first date we went dancing, and for our second we got into a fight with fairy assassins. What've you got planned for date number three?"

"Hey, I picked the first two dates, it's your turn next." I grin, and then bite my lip. "I mean, assuming there's a next and all."

"I'm thinking something a lot less exciting," Emeka says. "Movie, maybe?"

"A comedy?"

"Now, that sounds nice." Emeka smiles and takes my good hand. "You did amazing, Todd."

"I guess I must have, everyone keeps saying so." His eyes start to narrow, and I raise my hand in surrender. "Okay, okay! I did good."

"Saved the day, I'd say."

"Coming from you, I'll take it." I squeeze his hand lightly. "Couldn't have done it without you, you know. I'd have been sulking in my apartment when Harper came to arrest me."

"Well, you listened. A lot of guys would have pushed me out the door."

"Anyone dumb enough to push you out the door doesn't deserve you."

Emeka hops up a step, and turns to look me in the eyes. He leans in close. "And don't you forget it," he whispers, then presses his lips against mine. I lean into his embrace, and for a moment the world melts away and I'm lost in his touch.

And then I try to reach out with my left hand to hug him back, forgetting that I'm in a cast, overbalance, and just about fall on top of him. Emeka uses his free arm to steady us both. "Woah, hey, hey!" he says.

"Just made me weak in the knees."

"Yeah, I bet. Come on. Let's get inside and have something to eat. We've got plenty of time for the rest later."

"Sure thing." Hands held, we head inside to join the celebrations. It's like Emeka said. We've got plenty of time to figure out the details; the important thing is, we got through this together.

# Acknowledgements

This is a novel that I wasn't sure would ever get written, and I'm delighted that you've decided to read it. The first *Everland Mystery* novel, *Shadow Stitcher*, had the misfortune of being released only a few months ahead of a global pandemic, and the process of marketing and promoting it was simultaneously a welcome distraction and an exhausting process; working online, talking to potential reviewers remotely, and generally trying to invent a new process to reach people who had never heard of me. With all of that, finding the time to write the sequel was a grueling process, but one that I think worked out very well.

To my beloved spouse, Gabriel, thank you for the support and suggestions, and for putting up with me while we were trapped in a two-bedroom apartment for months slowly developing cabin fever. My writing is better with you in my life, and I can honestly say that without your suggestions this book would not have developed how it did.

To my family, thank you for your editing and reading advice as I worked through various drafts, ranging from plot to grammatical suggestions. You've been supporting me as long as I've been at this wild ride, and it means the world to me.

To my publisher, Brian, thank you for your relentless faith in my abilities. You took a chance on a new book, and now it has grown into something bigger. I literally wouldn't be here without your trust in my work.

To my editor, Kathryn, thank you for your keen eye and pointing out when I've used the word 'shrug' eighty-seven times and I should really try something different. This is a far better book than it would have been without you pushing me to improve scenes and delve into the characters.

And of course, to everyone reading this. Thank you for taking a chance on an Everland investigation, and I hope that you'll follow along to whatever comes next!

## *If you enjoyed this read*

Please leave a review on Amazon, Facebook, Good Reads or Instagram.

It takes less than five minutes and it really does make a difference.

If you're not sure how to leave a review on Amazon:

1. Go to amazon.com.

2. Type in Pawns and Phantoms by Misha Handman and when you see it, click on it.

3. Scroll down to Customer Reviews. Nearby you'll see a box labeled Write a Review. Click it.

4. Now, if you've never written a review before on Amazon, they might ask you to create a name for yourself.

5. Reviews can be as simple as, "Loved the book! Can't wait for the Next!" (Please don't give the story away.)

And that's it!

Brian Hades, publisher

# About the Author

**Born on Vancouver** Island, Canada, Misha Handman spent his early life immersed in the arts, with one parent a teacher and the other a manager of theatre and opera. Moving across the country to Ottawa, and then Toronto, he began writing at a young age – first writing comics and designing card games for his closest friends and then, buoyed by their approval, gradually expanding out to submissions to magazines and short story collections, and graduating from the University of Toronto with a classic English degree.

Misha has always believed in the transformative power of fiction, and the importance of entertainment to our health and well-being. He is also interested in our shared fictional history, working in game design to develop collaborative games and story-driven experiences and exploring the new worlds that we are sharing. His fascination with these things led to the development of his first novel, Shadow Stitcher, as an exploration of the English classic "Peter Pan."

When not writing, Misha spends his time in Victoria, Canada, working as a professional fundraiser for charities – a job he describes as "helping people to help people." He continues to work on game design on the side, and is always excited to see the myriad ways that people approach story construction and creation, both as a voracious reader of genre fiction and a dedicated player of games.

# Need something new to read?

If you liked Pawns and Phantoms, you should also consider these other EDGE-Lite titles...

# The Rosetta Mind
## (Book Two of the Rosetta Series)
### by Claire McCague

Estlin Hume was living off-grid on 12 acres outside of Twin Butte,

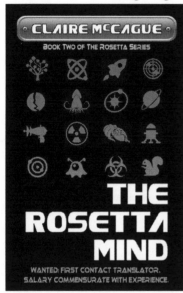

Alberta when he got snagged into being translator for first contact. Home again, he wakes to find himself surrounded by aliens, affectionate squirrels, government representatives, and military personnel. That's nothing new. But he hadn't planned on hosting one thousand three hundred and sixty-one cuttlefish in a massive saltwater tank suspended above his house!

Stuck at the center of the alien contact crisis, Estlin is challenged by ill-advised directives from government officials, trenchant military interference, and random acts of violence from unknown nefarious agents—all of whom are determined to find out for themselves what the aliens really want. No matter the cost! No matter the outcome!

### *About Claire McCague*

Claire McCague is a Canadian writer, scientist, musician, and science fiction fan. She works on sustainable energy systems, plays with words, and owns an excessive number of musical instruments. She's performed with dance bands for decades. As a theatre director and playwright, she's had productions on stages and in fields from the Fraser Common Farm in BC to the Manhattan Theatre Source.

# Wolf is a Four-letter Word
## (Book 2 of the Eternal Spring, Invisible Forest series)
## by Carrie Newberry

What do you do when the nightmare is real? That's the question facing Kellan Faolanni.

Following the betrayal of her sister in the previous book, Kellan must set aside her own emotions and thwart an enemy who has the upper hand at every turn. Kellan, a member of the Sankhain, is a shapeshifter, half-wolf, half-human. Kellan's superiors task her to investigate a man killed by what appears to be a wolf pack. Meanwhile, Kellan's human friend, Darcy reveals that he's being stalked. Kellan learns that the killer and Darcy's stalker are one and the same: a faery named Aza. But Aza is a high-ranking member of the Shadow Court, and to kill him would start a war with the fey, a war that Kellan's superiors want to avoid at all costs. Kellan must find a way to eliminate the threat and save her friend. Her solution could cost her everything, including a new relationship with another Sankha, Tony, as well as her sanity.

### *About Carrie Newberry*

Carrie Newberry studied creative writing at both the University of Wisconsin-Madison and UW-Eau Claire. But when she realized they would no longer let her take writing workshops for credit, she left academia and started work full time at a dog grooming shop. She lives in Madison with a dog who sings along with the radio, a cat who talks in her sleep, and an enormous collection of books. Also the author of Pick Your Teeth With My Bones, the first book in the Eternal Spring, Invisible Forest series, Carrie is hard at work writing Kellan's next adventure.

**For more EDGE titles and information about upcoming speculative fiction please visit us at:**

www.edgewebsite.com

Don't forget to sign-up for our Special Offers